THEY HAVE NC

By Shaun Lewis

Elegy in a Country Churchyard
By G K Chesterton

And they that rule in England
In stately conclave met
Alas, alas for England
They have no graves as yet

© Shaun Lewis 2021

Shaun Lewis has asserted his rights under the Copyright, Design and Patents Act, 1988, to be identified as the author of this work.

OTHER BOOKS BY SHAUN LEWIS

The *For Those in Peril* series comprising:

The Custom of the Trade

Now the Darkness Gathers

The Wings of the Wind

Where the Baltic Ice is Thin

DEDICATIONS

To Lieutenant Commander John Bridge, GC, GM and Bar, RNVR, whose courage and selfless duty motivated me to write this story

To all those Rendering Mines Safe (RMS) and Mine Clearance Diving (MCD) officers and men, past and present, who have risked their lives to keep civilians safe by rendering safe unexploded ordnance

To Lieutenant Commander 'Morty' Drummond, Royal Navy, father of my good friend and one of the founding members of the Mine Clearance Diving branch

FOREWORD

The power of the naval mine as a defensive and offensive weapon was first recognised by both the Royal and Imperial German Navies during World War I. As that war progressed, contact mines emerged as a cheap and highly effect weapon that posed a real and most deadly threat to Allied shipping. Some 20 years later as Nazi Germany prepared for hostilities and the eventual outbreak of World War II, the *Kriegsmarine* and *Luftwaffe* unveiled a more deadly, hidden menace, the influence sea mine. This new version of the sea mine would lay in wait on the seabed ready to detect the invisible magnetic signature created by steel hulled ships, whether they were warships or merchant vessels. When detonated, the catastrophic effects of the resultant underwater explosion would break keels and breach hulls. The physical impact of a detonation was also accompanied by a psychological and quite reasonable reaction to avoid the vicinity until it was positively cleared of the threat. The magnetic influence mine thus became a key anti access, area denial weapon that threatened to close the sea lanes surrounding the British Isles, blockade every major port and completely isolate Britain. Prime Minister Churchill recognised the danger and charged the Admiralty with the task of finding a solution, and quickly. The Royal Navy created the Render Mines Safe Units that feature in '*They Have No Graves as Yet*'.

With Churchill's keen interest, the Ministry's backing and the Admiralty's demand of early and effective action, the Render Mines Safe Units were under intense and consistent pressure to perform. With little or no intelligence to work from, they took every opportunity to discover all they could from the deadly black cylindrical magnetic mines when they were found intact. They conducted their practical theory on live, large explosive devices, recording successful investigations and developing new techniques. They knew that they would probably die, but went willingly to do their duty. They were not the dogs of war, fired up by the heat of battle. They were not facing the enemy, but were certainly facing death. They successfully rendered a threat safe by not making the same mistake or following an unsuccessful technique that had led to previous casualties and fatalities amongst their small band of brothers. Incredibly brave men would volunteer to go first, try something out and if they survived, tell others to do what they did and avoid their mistakes if they didn't make it through the render safe procedure. Early progress and successes were quickly challenged by the enemy who would drop mines with booby traps aimed specifically at killing the Render Mines Safe Officers and Men. What was actually playing was a deadly long-distance duel between the German scientists trying to catch out the Render Mines Safe Units who in turn were trying to investigate, exploit and render safe the latest version of the mines they found.

The Render Mines Safe Units (RMSUs) were the forerunners of the Clearance Diving Branch of today's Royal Navy. More than 80 years after the early WWII years depicted in this excellent novel, today's version of the RMSUs are still called out regularly to render safe threats that have sat waiting on the seabed for an opportune moment to spoil your day. These extraordinary men face each threat as those in Shaun Lewis's story did all those years ago: stoically, calmly, and professionally, totally focussed, trusting in their training, often alone with the mine, and keenly aware of every movement and action in trying to ensure the threat is extinguished.

Shaun Lewis captures the very essence of the incredible men who took on the deadly threat posed by the magnetic sea mine and explains in detail the challenges they faced throughout WWII in this hugely entertaining novel.

Paddy McAlpine CBE
Rear Admiral (Retired)

Paddy McAlpine joined the Royal Navy in 1982 with the specific goal of becoming a Minewarfare and Clearance Diving Officer. He achieved his aim and was Mentioned in Dispatches after clearing mines off Kuwait during the First Gulf War in 1991.

GLOSSARY

Abwehr	German Military Intelligence
ADC	*Aide-de-camp* (personal staff officer)
Braw	Scottish for fine, good or pleasing
DSC	Distinguished Service Cross
DSM	Distinguished Service Medal
DSO	Distinguished Service Order
Froschfesser	Frog eaters, a German derogatory term for the French
Gag	Any form of tool used to prevent further movement of a fuzing system
Gaine	A unit combining a detonator and primer to initiate a two-stage explosion of the main charge
General der Flieger	Lieutenant General, equivalent to an Air Marshal in the RAF
Generalleutnant	Major General, equivalent to an Air Vice Marshal in the RAF
Generalmajor	Brigadier, equivalent to an Air Commodore in the RAF
Keeper ring	A ring holding in place the detonator or primer of a bomb/mine
Korvettenkapitän	Lieutenant Commander
Laoch	Gaelic for hero or champion
Lar	Scouse for friend or mate
Oberkommando der Wermacht or **OKW**	German High Command of the Armed Forces
Oberst	Colonel, equivalent to a Group Captain in the RAF
Oberstleutnant	Lieutenant Colonel, equivalent to a Wing Commander in the RAF

O-I-C   Officer-in-Charge
PDQ   Pretty Damned Quick
RMSO   Rendering Mines Safe Officer
Seekriegsleitung or *Skl*   German Naval War Command
Seeluftstreitkräfter   Maritime Aviation Forces of the *Luftwaffe*

Sturzkampfgeschwader   Dive bomber wing

PART ONE

**The Beginning
May 1939 – August 1940**

PROLOGUE
May 1939

Ernst Scholtz made his way to the upper floor of the restaurant overlooking the *Unter den Linden*. He was ten minutes early for his rendezvous. Not through nerves, although he was nervous about meeting his former boss again, but because of a habit ingrained in him through his service in the *Kriegsmarine*. The restaurant was smarter than one he would have chosen and he was conscious of the none-too-discreet stares of the waiters at his twenty-year-old, threadbare suit and scuffed shoes. He had spent an hour working on his shoes, but they were still an embarrassment. Perhaps he should have come in uniform, but a meeting between a mere *Korvettenkapitän* and a *Generalmajor* of the *Luftwaffe* might have excited too much attention and subsequent comment. Ernst was conscious of the clandestine nature of this meeting.

To his surprise, notwithstanding his early arrival, his host was already seated at a table by an open window. On seeing his guest, General Schott immediately rose and came forward to meet him.

'My dear Ernst. It's so good to see you again.' Schott clapped Ernst on the back and guided him to a chair. 'Sit down. Sit down. I've had us seated here to benefit from some cool air. Isn't it a wonderful evening?' Schott gestured to the blue sky above Berlin and the rows of lime trees lining the boulevard below; their broad, bright-green leaves shimmering in the evening sunshine and light breeze.

Ernst took his seat and surveyed the general opposite him. Both men were thin, but Schott had filled out a little since their last meeting and, unlike Ernst, he still had a good head of hair, despite being a few years older. Like Ernst, he wore a double-breasted suit, but although clearly off the peg from the way it hung on Schott's narrow shoulders, it was newer and of a better quality than Ernst's own. That was a sign of the difference in pay of a major general and a lieutenant commander, Ernst thought. Looking round the sumptuous velvet upholstery and gilded carvings around the restaurant, he was glad that Schott was paying for the dinner tonight. He hoped the information he was carrying would be worth the price. In any case, it was probably the *Luftwaffe* that would be picking up the tab and not Schott himself. Göring's blue-eyed boys had more latitude than officers of the *Kriegsmarine*.

'So, Ernst. How long is it now? Two years since we last met?'

'Nearly three, General. It was December '36 I parted as your assistant to join the Naval Staff.' Ernst lowered his eyes. 'I shall always be grateful to you for giving me the chance to don the uniform of the Fatherland again.'

'Nonsense, Ernst. You have a brilliant mind and it was going to waste in… What was it you were doing before 1935? I forget.'

'I was a salesman… selling cheap radios, General,' Ernst replied quietly.

'That's right. Now I remember. Hardly fit employment for someone with a doctorate in electrical engineering. From Berlin's Technical Academy, wasn't it?'

'Yes, General, but the job was all I could find. I had already been unemployed two years.' Ernst still couldn't meet his former superior in the eye.

'Yes, but… Ach, Germany is in a better place since the *Führer* came to power… and then you joined the Party. Mark my words, Ernst. You deserve your success. When our armed forces go to war, we won't just need their might and courage, but brains, Ernst, brains. We must harness the minds of you and all our clever scientists, too.'

'You're referring to Case White, General?' Ernst's skin tingled at this information and he finally felt comfortable enough to look Schott in the eye again. He marvelled at the thought. So, Germany really is going to invade Poland. He had heard rumours of the plans, but no indication that they might be executed.

'Precisely. As you know, the *Führer* hasn't yet signed off the plans for the invasion, but he has said that we cannot expect it to come about without resistance. The Poles are not like the Czechs.'

'I realise that, General. You forget that I and my family come from Danzig.'

'Quite right, Ernst. I had forgotten. And talking of family, I saw that your younger brother has been promoted to *Oberstleutnant* and given a command of a *Sturzkampfgeschwader* of Junkers 87 *Stukas*.'

'Indeed, General. He has been well rewarded for his service in Spain. It's a pity that his older brother is of no more use than polishing his arse on the seat of a desk in the *Seekriegsleitung*.' Ernst spoke with remorse.

'Ach, Ernst. You're too modest. Your position on the Naval Staff is an important one. Now it is you that forget, dear Ernst. Battles can be won by good staff work as well as by courage on the battlefield. How's the arm?'

Ernst was rubbing his lower left arm. It was his habit when agitated. In fact, he had lost this part of his arm in 1919 and had been fitted with a prosthetic hand.

'It still hurts – in more ways than one. I know it's not there, but it still hurts.' Ernst looked wistfully into the distance.

'I understand,' Schott said gently and he, too, looked wistful for a moment before coming to again. 'Come, let's order some wine. I think on a warm evening such as this we could do with a dry *pinot gris*. The left bank of the Rhine might still be *temporarily* occupied by the *Froschfesser* of Alsace, but we put down some great vines when it was part of the Fatherland.'

Schott snapped his fingers for a waiter and whilst he discussed the wine, Ernst reflected on the humiliation he had endured in 1919 that had led him to lose his left hand. At the end of the war, he had been in command of a mine layer, based at Wilhelmshaven, at the age of just twenty-eight. Germany's agreement of the Armistice, the unconditional surrender of Germany, had led to the *diktat* of the Treaty of Versailles which had stabbed Germany in the back. Even so, the British hadn't lifted their blockade and his family in Danzig, comprising his parents, sister and brother, had continued to starve. Ernst and his ship's company had co-operated fully with the Royal Navy in identifying the locations and types of mines in their defensive minefields. A squadron of minesweepers had even helped the British to sweep these minefields, but that hadn't been enough for the damned British. They had sought to crush the national spirit of the Germans. When one of the German mines had been washed ashore after its mooring cable had been cut, a high-handed Royal Navy commander had insisted that Ernst defuze the mine personally whilst Ernst's men looked on. Ernst had not minded being asked to defuze the mine – he was an expert in mine warfare, after all. What had stung was the way the Royal Navy had lined up his men to watch him wade through the mudflats to the mine - to show his sailors that the British were the masters now. It was as he was holding aloft the detonator as a gesture of defiance that it had exploded prematurely. With only one arm and the size of the German Navy limited to 15,000, he was inevitably kicked out afterwards. He had applied for hundreds of jobs, but even with his doctorate, who had wanted a cripple with little experience other than naval service when there were so many other men out there chasing the same job? And then his parents and sister had died from starvation. The pain of the memory burned deeply inside him.

'Ernst. You were in a far-away place.' Schott brought Ernst back to the present. 'I've ordered for us both – soup and *Wiener Schnitzel*. I hope you approve.'

The waiter returned with the wine. Its dry taste matched Ernst's mood and he found it pleasant, but he was no expert on wine. Bringing up a younger brother had taught him the habit of thrift and he had learned to content himself with just the occasional beer. However, he did enjoy a cigarette and taking out his case, offered one to Schott. Schott lit both cigarettes with his stainless-steel lighter before resuming the conversation.

'So, whilst we wait on our food, why don't you tell me why you suggested we meet? You said you had some information for me and I surmised from your note that you didn't want your colleagues on the Naval Staff to know.'

'Yes, General. I am anxious not to face a charge of disloyalty, but as you well know, my loyalty to you and the *Führer* is beyond question.' Ernst reached into his inside pocket and retrieved a long, thin, well-filled envelope. 'Take great care of that I beg, General.'

Schott placed the envelope in his own inside pocket without examining it. 'Best you tell me of its contents, hey Ernst.' Schott sipped his wine approvingly.

'As you would expect, General, as a specialist in mine warfare, I work closely with *Konteradmiral* Müller of the *Sperrwaffe*. His division has developed a brand-new type of mine that I'm convinced would come as a complete surprise to the enemy - for which they have no counter measures. It is an influence mine, so can explode without any form of contact.'

'Yes, I know of such mines. I presume it is the magnetically-fired M1 unit.' Schott swirled the wine before burying his nose in his glass and breathing its bouquet deeply. 'Very good,' he muttered to himself with satisfaction before turning his attention back to Ernst. 'The British had something similar in the last war. Our version is of the needle type that responds to a change in strength of the vertical component of the earth's magnetic field to make an electrical connection to the firing mechanism. Tell me something new.'

'What is new, General, is that we have perfected it and it's now very good, indeed. It has a sensitivity that's not subject to spurious firing in normal magnetic storms and can be laid in depths up to thirty metres.'

'I'm pleased to hear it, Ernst, if you're sure of it. But you have still to explain why it should interest the *Luftwaffe*? We looked at this together in 1936.'

'Because, General, the *SkI* only plans to use the mine in a limited fashion. Their plan is to open any campaign in a small way only… and then to increase the numbers if early results justify it. I am convinced that the results will be justified, but that we should be more ambitious.' Ernst became more emphatic in his speech and Schott had to warn him to keep down his voice.

'I'm sorry, General. Quite right. I was getting carried away. However, earlier, you mentioned Case White. We all know that if we are to invade Poland, the British may feel obliged to intervene.

Unlike Russia, Britain is a maritime nation and completely dependent on sea traffic for her imports. Our U-boats are well equipped to lay mines close inshore and in river estuaries, but we don't have enough units to mount an intensive campaign. But we do have plenty of aircraft. Only the *Luftwaffe* has the ability to saturate Britain's inner waterways.'

'It is an intriguing thought, Ernst.'

'General, I am convinced that to defeat the British, we don't need to sink her merchant ships the way our U-boats did in the last war. All we need to do is to prevent them entering harbour. Blockade Britain the way it's navy has successfully operated blockades in their wars with France… and us in 1914. Just imagine the fear and chaos an intensive mining campaign could effect. The British are too dependent on their empire for food.'

Schott waved to Ernst to pause speaking for a moment and finally took a long draught of the wine. He considered Ernst's plan in silence for a short while before wiping his lips with his napkin and leaning across the table and speaking quietly, but excitedly.

'If I understand you correctly, Ernst, you are saying that with the *Luftwaffe*'s help, we could effectively knock the British out of any war very quickly with these mines. But that the *Kriegsmarine* want to take a softly-softly approach. Is that so?'

'Precisely, General.'

Schott played with his wine glass again. 'I can see how that might work, but what about counter measures? After all, it was the British who invented this mine. You must give them some credit… and you know it's a cardinal principle of the High Command that no mine may be deployed until a suitable sweep has been developed. Surely the same would apply to the British?'

Ernst paused before replying. 'You would think that, General, but according to our intelligence assessments, the British have taken no steps to develop influence mines and, thus, no steps to counter them. That is why I argue for a larger-scale attack in the early stages of any war with them. We would take them by surprise. Moreover, even were the British to deploy some form of sweep to clear a newly-laid field, the *Luftwaffe* is well positioned to refresh the minefield very rapidly and easily.'

'I see. I can see the logic of your reasoning. And all this is laid out in the envelope you have given me, Ernst?' Ernst nodded eagerly. 'Very well. I think you have earned your dinner, Ernst. I see the waiter approaching with our food. But first, let us drink a toast. *Heil Hitler.*'

*****

Stephen Cunningham buttoned up his freshly-laundered white laboratory coat as if it was a protective suit of armour and girded himself to push open the double swing doors into the physics laboratory. He could hear the hubbub of the fifteen-year-old girls the other side of the doors. His coat buttoned-up, he silently paraphrased a prayer he had heard at the last meeting of his local Quaker house. *Grant me peace, oh God. Not the peace of slumber, but of quiet confidence in the triumph over Form Four C.* He entered the lab and the girls immediately fell silent and stood to welcome him.

'G-g-good m-m-morning, g-girls,' he said. The girls responded with the same greeting, but three in the far-left corner repeated his stutter. One of them was Kathy Sykes, his *bête-noire*.

'S-s-sit d-down, ladies. This m-morning, w-we will d-discuss the p-principles of electro-m-magnetic f-force – EMF.' Stephen approached the blackboard to write the title of the lesson, but could not find any chalk nor the blackboard duster. As he searched the inside of his desk, he noticed a smirk among the girls near Kathy Sykes. One of them raised a hand and spoke.

'P-p-please, s-s-sir. W-w-what w-w-will w-w-we b-b-be d-d-discussing t-t-today?' Other members of the form tittered. Stephen's heart sank. The summer holidays might only be two weeks away, but they couldn't come quickly enough for him.

*****

Thomas 'Monty' Montcalm bought a copy of the newspaper from the street vendor on the Strand. It was a lovely July afternoon and only a four-minute walk from the Admiralty Court back to his chambers on King's Bench Walk, so he stopped at a seat by the Temple Church to catch up with the latest news. His previously buoyant mood following the winning of his case was dampened by the news of the recent Nazi rallies in Danzig and the hope of the district leaders that the city might be *liberated* by Hitler. It was not very encouraging and Monty feared that this time Britain *would* be going to war. He planned on taking his yacht *Firefly* out over the weekend, but wondered if he ought to lay her up in Gosport afterwards. As a member of the Royal Naval Volunteer Reserve, he would be one of the first to be called up were Britain to go to war with Germany, successful barrister or otherwise.

*****

In the last week of August, Ernst and his superior officer were surprised by the summons for Ernst to appear immediately at the headquarters of the *Luftwaffe* on *Leipziger Strasse* to meet General Schott in his office. Even though Ernst had previously worked in the building, he was still impressed by its grandeur and size compared with that in which he and the Naval Staff worked. Today, however, he was much more impressed by the bustle in the foyers and corridors of the Ministry of Aviation building. The Naval Staff were busy working on Plan Z to achieve parity with the Royal Navy's surface fleet within five years, but in comparison with the sense of urgency on display of the *Luftwaffe* Staff, the *Kriegsmarine* was working almost sedately. The atmosphere in the building was electric and Ernst caught the mood with a tingle of excitement.

Schott received him cordially and invited him to sit and take a cup of coffee.

'Ernst, I suspect you are surprised to find yourself back in the *Reichsluftfahrtministerium*. Get used to it as it will soon become a home from home.' Ernst checked lifting his coffee cup to his mouth in anticipation of the answer to the puzzle just posed.

Schott left him in suspense for a moment before continuing. 'Now the *Führer* has concluded his pact with Russia, we go into Poland this week. With that in mind, the High Command has given thought to the possible British reaction. I put your ideas on mining the estuaries to the Chief of the General Staff and Koller in turn has passed them on to Göring himself.' Schott smiled and continued quietly, almost in embarrassment. 'I confess I made out that I had come up with the plan myself or else it would have been ignored. You don't mind that, Ernst, do you?' Ernst just shook his head. He was flabbergasted that his ideas had been taken so seriously.

'The fact is, dear Ernst, the fat *Reichschmarshall* liked the idea and has given instructions for the *Seeluftstreitkräfter* to resume practising aerial minelaying. But, naturally, the *Luftwaffe* is not as expert on mine warfare as the *Kriegsmarine* and we have no history of developing them. Accordingly, you are to be transferred to the *Luftwaffe* with immediate effect.'

Ernst was still so surprised by the general's words that he had yet to take a sip of his black coffee, but he eventually found the words to speak. 'General, I'm most gratified to hear my ideas taken to such a high level and, of course, it doesn't matter who gets the credit for them. It is credit enough for me that they might be implemented. But what am I to do in this building that I couldn't do from an office in the *Seekriegsleitung*?'

'Firstly, you won't be based in this building, Ernst. I'm having you posted to Travemünde. You'll feel at home there, back on the Baltic coast. And, you're to be promoted to *Oberstleutnant* and take command of our trials unit. We need a new type of air-launched mine, ideally one that can be dropped without a parachute and whose mechanism would still not be damaged on impact with the water.'

'But what's wrong with the parachute method, General? And where is the *Luftwaffe* to find the skilled engineers to develop such a mine? They all work for the navy.'

'Ach, the innocence of the mariner.' Schott opened his arms wide and looked to the heavens. 'The wind's the problem with a parachute. It means that it can drift off course and not land in the exact spot intended. As for the engineers, we've approached AEG to design something. They're sworn to strict secrecy… as are you. This isn't news for the ears of even the *Kriegsmarine*. So, Ernst, you will be responsible for working with AEG and any other firms you deem it necessary, to develop and test a new form of mine. So, what do you say, Ernst? Are we to have two *Luftwaffe* colonels in the Scholtz family?'

Ernst was stunned by the idea, but his attention focused on the offer of promotion. No longer would he be an elderly lieutenant commander subordinate to his younger brother. What did it matter if he turned his back on the navy? He had come up with the strategy for Germany to neuter the all-powerful Royal Navy and it was going to be implemented.

'Come on, Ernst. The cat got your tongue? What do you say?'

Ernst's face broke into a rare and beaming smile. 'Very well, General. I accept and, as we did just a few months ago, I propose a toast. *Heil Hitler.*' Ernst finally raised his cup to his lips to discover that the coffee was now cold.

CHAPTER ONE
September 1939

The coxswain of the Aldeburgh lifeboat was tending his vegetable garden when he heard the explosion to the east. As his garden lay on the coast of the Suffolk village, that meant the explosion had to have occurred at sea. He immediately looked out across the shingle beach to sea and it didn't need his many years of experience as a fisherman to spot the scene of the explosion. It was obvious to all the villagers whose hitherto peaceful Sunday afternoon had been disturbed just a week after war with Germany had been declared. Out in the channel between the Napes and Sizewell Bank, the gentle sea was disturbed by a ship sinking rapidly in a cloud of smoke and steam. The coxswain immediately threw down his fork and rushed to the lifeboat station. As he ran, he saw several others of his crew rushing in the same direction. The sound of the explosion had already been enough of an alarm to summon his crew, but from the corner of his eye, he could see the two maroon flares rising into the sky from the coastguard station before exploding with a loud bang.

By the time the coxswain arrived at the lifeboat station, the *Abdy Beauclerk* was almost ready for launch. As usual, several of the villagers had quickly gathered to help with the launch and the head launcher had already issued all his brass tickets. These could later be redeemed for a share in any small reward that might be issued. The coxswain had just enough time to don his oilskins and kapok lifejacket before the slip chain was released and the lifeboat hurtled down the slipway, gathering speed as it did so. It was two hours after low water and the launch helpers had set up rollers on the beach beneath the slipway to help the boat cover the shingle into the sea, causing a rumble before the boat smashed into a large wave coming onshore. Without orders, the mechanic engaged the engine and the *Abdy Beauclerk* was on her way to rescue the seamen of the stricken cargo ship.

The coxswain assumed the ship must have been torpedoed by a German U-boat as this much-used channel had only just been swept for mines. His friend in the local Coastguard had told him that the Royal Navy had cause to be concerned with a mine threat. Only a week before the outbreak of war, a mysterious German ship had been sighted manoeuvring near the Napes, but had disappeared before she could be contacted. According to this friend, the Admiralty had been suspicious that Jerry had either been carrying out a reconnaissance for an offensive minefield in these parts or even dropping mines before war had been declared.

    He approached the damaged ship from the north and through his binoculars read her name from the transom. She was the *SS Magdeburg*, but by the time his boat was within five cables of the ship, she had sunk, her back broken, and settled on the bottom in seventy feet of water, her two masts still showing in a ghostly fashion. He ordered the mizzen sail to be hoisted as he approached the rescue site – he found the sail useful to steady the lifeboat against sudden vague winds. Before she had gone down, the *Magdeburg* had had time to launch her lifeboats, but even so, there were still dozens of men in the water, many of them lascars. The lifeboat's coxswain reflected that after all the months of tension, from the perspective of these men at least, the war could no longer be termed 'the Bore War'.

*****

Six days later, this time in the evening, the coxswain and the *Abdy Beauclerk* were again called out to a ship damaged by an explosion off the Napes. She was a passenger ship, the *SS City of Paris*, and, to the lifeboat crew's relief, all the crew and passengers had managed to take to her lifeboats. Once the crew and passengers were safely ashore, the coxswain discussed the incident with the master.

    'I'd say you were lucky then, sir, only to have one person killed. You sure it were a mine?'

    'Definitely. I was mined in the last war and saw the effects of shock on a human body 'tween decks. Moreover, a torpedo would have caused more water ingress.'

'Mebbe, but I was in the last war, too - in armed trawlers - and saw many a ship damaged by mines. They usually had their bows blown orff and if you look yonder, you'll see your ship looks pretty intact to me.'

The master looked back to his ship and yelped with surprise. 'Good gracious. She's still floating… just a little low in the water. I don't understand it. There was a massive explosion and we all felt the ship lift. The engines stopped running and the Chief reported flooding in the engine room, but…'

'What say you if I give you and one of your boats a tow back out there and you check her over a bit then, sir?' The master quickly agreed.

The journey back to the *City of Paris* proved challenging in the darkness, but was achieved without incident. An hour later, the master informed the lifeboatmen that his men had restored propulsion and would be capable of taking the ship on to Tilbury under her own steam. Her heavy machinery was badly damaged and her deck plates buckled from some form of violent explosion under the water, but surprisingly the hull was intact. That was odd, the coxswain thought as he returned ashore.

*****

'Lieutenant Montcalm,' the short, fair-haired officer announced to the hall porter of the wardroom of HMS *Victory*, the accommodation barracks for Portsmouth dockyard. 'That's spelt M-O-N-T-C-A-L-M. You have a cabin for me.' Monty was well aware from experience that people assumed his name was spelt as it was pronounced, Mon-com.

It was late evening and that morning Monty had said farewell to the members of his chambers before taking the train to Portsmouth. He was now, at last, exchanging his career as a successful London barrister for one in the Royal Navy.

'Ah yes, sir. I have it here. Lieutenant the Honourable Thomas Montcalm… joining the admiral's staff. Is that right, sir?'

Monty nodded. His appointment was a sore point with him. A keen yachtsman, several years earlier he had joined the 'wavy navy', so called on account of the wavy gold stripes worn on the sleeves of its officers. When war had been declared two months before, he had assumed he would be sent to sea and not kicking around an admiral's staff ashore. It was all very frustrating.

'Here's your key, sir… and there's an urgent message for you. I was told to give it to you as soon as you'd arrived, sir. There you are.'

Monty took the sealed envelope and key from the hall porter. 'Do you mind if I read it here?' He gestured to one of the tall, enclosed, leather armchairs seated by the foyer fire. The hall porter nodded and gestured him to take the seat. He offered him a cup of tea from his Thermos bottle, but Monty declined.

The message was from the Admiralty and customarily brief. *'Report to NA 2SL forthwith.'* Enclosed with the message was a railway warrant for a single ticket back to London. Typical, Monty thought. I've just travelled all the way down from London and now I'm wanted back there. It sounds like something from that nursery rhyme about the Duke of York. At least, I assume I have to go to London. He returned to the hall porter's desk.

'Would you happen to know two things? Firstly, who is "NA 2SL" and when's the next train to London?'

'Oh dear. It's like that is it, sir? You're already too late to catch a train up to London, sir. You'll have to catch one in the mornin'. As for your other question, sir, that'll be the Naval Assistant to the Second Sea Lord. I assume he'll be in Admiralty Building up at Whitehall, sir. He's responsible for personnel, sir,' the hall porter added helpfully. 'Shall I put you down for a shake at 06.00, sir?'

'Er, yes, thanks. This warrant's only for a single so, like as not, I'll not be coming back. So just book me in for one night only.'

Monty turned in, but lay awake pondering his fate. What could the mystery summons entail? Please don't let it entail a staff appointment at the Admiralty. Working on the admiral's staff in Portsmouth was bad enough, but at least it was near the sea and he had *Firefly* at nearby Gosport. He might just as well have carried on his practice as a barrister in London…

He gave way to sleep.

*****

Having eventually found his way to the office of the NA to the Second Sea Lord, Monty was surprised then to be taken by a commander to the office of Rear Admiral Wake-Walker, Rear Admiral Minelayers. When Monty entered the room, the admiral was standing by a huge map of the British Isles, covering an entire wall of his large office.

'You're late, Montcalm. I was expecting you yesterday.' The admiral spoke tersely. He was six-feet-two-inches tall, eight inches taller than Monty, and Monty thought him intimidating.

'I'm sorry, sir. I only received the message late last night and it was too late to get a train back to London. Sorry, sir.'

'Oh, you'd already left for Portsmouth, had you?' Like Monty, the admiral's hair was fair, but his eyes were a more vivid blue than Monty's. These eyes fixed Monty with a piercing gaze before Wake-Walker smiled and suddenly became less intimidating. 'I'm sorry you've had the run around. Had we got onto you more quickly, we might have saved you a wasted trip. I gather you're some kind of lawyer.'

Monty's heart had risen on seeing the admiral's smile, but it sunk again at the last words. If he had been summoned because of his legal background, that didn't bode well for a sea appointment. 'Yes, sir. I'm a barrister. I tend to take on salvage cases.' Monty wasn't sure why he'd added the last bit.

'Salvage hey? Know anything about mines?'

'I presume you mean sea mines, sir? No, nothing at all, sir. Sorry.'

'A pity, but it can't be helped. The fact is you're a lawyer and that'll do. Come and look at this chart. For some time, Hitler's been threatening us with some form of secret weapon and it now looks like he's using it. You see here?' Wake-Walker gestured to several points along the coast on the map. 'Each of these harbours and navigable rivers have been blocked by some sort of unconventional mine. All our efforts to sweep the areas have come to nothing. We think it might be magnetic – what the Americans call an *inflooence* mine - but we've failed to recover one to confirm that or otherwise.

'The whole of the east coast is impassable. We've had to close the Thames, Tees, Tyne and Humber - all because vessels moving in those waters tend to blow up. We're not just losing six ships a day, but in the southern approaches to the Thames we've 185 ships held offshore - vulnerable to submarine attack - and another 70 sitting in London's Docks unable to move. It's a situation that can't be allowed to go on.' The admiral sat down at his desk and gestured for Monty to take a chair opposite.

'Quite frankly, Montcalm, if we can't check this new attack, Britain will lose the war within six weeks!'

CHAPTER 2

After his meeting with Wake-Walker, Monty was introduced to the admiral's chief of staff, Captain Boyd. He learned that Boyd had once commanded the Torpedo School at HMS *Vernon* in Portsmouth and was one of the Royal Navy's experts on underwater weapons.

'I suppose you're wondering why you're here, Montcalm?'

'Indeed, sir. Am I to be trained in bomb disposal, sir?'

Boyd laughed. 'Hardly, old boy. I can't imagine a lawyer rendering a mine safe – and that's what we call it by the way. RMS, not bomb disposal. Of course, we dispose of bombs, too, but only on our patch. The Royal Engineers take care of the bombs. No, it's your legal mind we want. The admiral's setting up a new department called the Department of Torpedoes and Mines Investigation – DTMI for short - and he wants you to be a part of it. We're getting much contradictory information on these mystery explosions from the masters and crews of the ships damaged or sunk and the admiral wants somebody to analyse and sift the evidence bloody quickly. I suggested it might be the job for a lawyer, so here you are.'

Monty's stomach sank at the news. So, he was to be a staff officer, after all. At least the task sounded more interesting than dealing with punishment returns and courts martial down in Portsmouth. He was intrigued and shocked by the admiral's assessment that Britain could lose the war within six weeks. He cast aside his disappointment and gave thought to the job in hand.

'How do we know these explosions have been caused by mines, sir, and not torpedoes?'

'That's for you to find out, Montcalm, but trust me. I'm long enough in the tooth to recognise some new form of mine at work here... But don't let that influence your analysis,' Boyd added. 'Some are even claiming that their ships were sunk by a weapon that sits on the bottom and then hunts for the ship. Somebody heard a mechanical whirring before the explosion. It could be true, of course, but I suspect that may have been an electric torpedo.

'And don't expect to be cossetted the way you lawyers normally are. We don't have the time for luxuries and that includes accommodation. From now on, we work day and night until we've got this mystery cracked. I've arranged a camp bed for you here at the Admiralty.'

Monty ignored the jibe about his profession. 'Sir, my knowledge of mines is limited. When I think of mines, I think of globes floating in the water with horns. The admiral mentioned something called *influence* mines. Could you explain?'

'Certainly. It seems a good place to start, but first I need to mention that we're attending a high-level conference at 14.00 sharp, so let's discuss this over lunch.'

A short while later, over a sandwich and mug of tea, Boyd explained the basics of mines. 'Those mines you mentioned are a form of contact mine. The mine is stuffed with explosive and moored on the sea bed to await its prey.'

'You mean it doesn't just float about, sir?'

'Of course, it doesn't.' Boyd seemed affronted by the suggestion. 'Who knows what damage it might then do, including to one's own side? No, it has to be placed carefully, either to defend channels from enemy interference, much as we did to protect the Channel crossings during the last show, or offensively to stop the enemy leaving his ports. Again, we did that successfully in the last war when we closed off to submarines the exit from the northern part of the North Sea with a barrage of mines from the east coast of Scotland to the coast of Norway. But to keep the mines in place, they need a sinker, a heavy block on the sea bed. and then a long mooring line. There are ways to regulate the depth according to the tide, but I haven't time to go into that now. The point is that we want the mine to float at a depth far enough beneath the surface for it not to be spotted, but shallow enough for it to come into contact with a passing ship. Does that make sense?'

'Yes, sir.' Monty was beginning to find the subject of mine warfare quite interesting. He had previously had no idea of the extent of British minelaying during the last war. His favourite uncle had been a submarine commanding officer during the Great War and had given the impression that it was the Germans that had laid great barrages of mines.

'Good,' Boyd responded. 'Now those horns you mentioned were invented by a Doctor Herz last century, but even today they work damned well. The lead horns contain a phial of glass which, when broken on contact with the hull of a ship, releases a chemical solution onto carbon and zinc plates in the base of the horn unit. This forms a battery cell and generates an electrical pulse to fire the detonator. Is this all too confusing for a lawyer?'

'Not at all, sir,' Monty bristled. 'Several of my cases involved disputes over salvage and I had to acquire a detailed technical knowledge of ships.'

'Ah. Is that so? That accounts for why you were recommended for the job.'

'Excuse me, sir, but just who did recommend me for this post?'

'Your uncle, Admiral Montcalm. He mentioned you to Admiral Little, the Second Sea Lord, and you know the rest. The Navy still operates on patronage, even in these times. But I don't mean that unkindly,' Boyd quickly added as Monty coloured.

'I see, sir. So, what about these influence or magnetic mines?'

'They're going to be bloody bitches to deal with if that's what we're up against. We should know as we invented them before the end of the last war, but never bothered to develop them further. What's your knowledge of physics?'

'Er, not great, sir. I took classics and humanities at school.'

'Sounds like it was a public school, then?'

'Oh, yes, sir. Eton.'

'I see,' Boyd said non-committedly, but Monty couldn't tell what he meant by the remark. Boyd began a short lecture on physics.

'You need to understand that all ships are magnetic. They pick it up from the earth's field wherever they're built. In the northern hemisphere they have what we call a *red* polarity and in the southern hemisphere, a blue. Then everything ferrous we put into ships, such as engines, electrical wiring… even the anchor and cables… it all makes a ship one hell of a magnet. As it approaches a magnetic mine, the unit detects the change in the magnetic field around it, a little needle flickers and… hey presto! It makes a circuit and fires the mine. No contact with the ship is necessary and the beauty of it is that instead of blowing off the bows or blasting a bloody great hole in the hull, it explodes underneath the ship and breaks its back. That's why the ships are going down so fast.'

'So, you're fairly sure that these new mines are magnetic, sir?'

'Er, good point, Montcalm. You *are* a lawyer. I'm getting ahead of myself, but yes, my gut instinct and all my years of experience tell me we're dealing with magnetic mines. Then again, it could be something else. These new mines seem to have been laid in comparatively shallow water… we think by aircraft flying low at night when the moon's nearly full… and resting on the bottom – not moored like the contact mine. They might be initiated by pressure. As a ship steams along, her hull displaces water, creating a pressure wave downwards. In relatively shallow water, that could be enough to set off a mine, but the pressure's less noticeable in deeper water. Moreover, the pressure's greater with a fast-moving, larger ship so one of the first things I want you to do is to check the records and see if there's any correlation. Understood?'

'Yes, sir. Can I get you another tea?' Monty gathered together the two mugs and plates and stood up.

Boyd checked his watch before answering. 'No thanks. We can't be late for this meeting, but I've just time to tell you about our other suspect - the acoustic mine. Water conducts sound beautifully. Sound travels through it five times as fast as through air. That's how our submarines detect targets… through the noise of the ship's engines. The sound would be enough to trigger a mine. Obviously, the noisier the ship – a coaster with old-fashioned, thumping diesel engines for example – the further away it could set off a mine. That's something else I want you to investigate. What type of ships are being sunk by these mines?'

'And presumably, sir, it would be worth examining reports of any ships having experience of explosions nearby for some unaccountable reason. After all, a fast MTB or destroyer might create just as much noise as a slow merchantman.'

'Now you're getting the hang of it, Montcalm. I like the way your mind is working. It makes me glad I persuaded the admiral we needed a lawyer on the team. There aren't many professions more devious to my mind, excepting bloody politicians, of course, and that's what we need in this business. Now come. We have that meeting to attend.'

*****

Monty felt very self-conscious amidst the assembly of gold braid at the afternoon's conference. After him, the most junior officers present were all commanders and wing commanders, but the majority of officers seemed to be admirals, air marshals and the occasional general. At the centre, completely dominating proceedings, Monty recognised the portly figure dressed in a dark suit and spotted bow tie, the First Lord of the Admiralty, Winston Churchill.

Churchill questioned Wake-Walker on the steps being taken to free up the logjam of shipping that threatened to lose Britain the war.

'We suspect the enemy is using a new type of magnetic mine, sir, and probably air-launched. Our mine watchers have reported several sightings of low-flying aircraft dropping some form of object by parachute.'

'And what counter measures are you deploying, admiral?' Churchill took a deep puff on his cigar. 'The magnetic mine is, after all, a British invention.'

'We've tried grappling and trawling for the mines on the seabed, sir, using non-magnetic materials. Sadly, on our first attempt, we made the mistake of using steel-hulled trawlers and lost five men and a trawler in the attempt. As a result, we've converted two Scottish wooden-hulled trawlers to tow a number of bar magnets suspended between them. The two trawlers managed to explode something in the Bristol Channel, but we can't be sure this wasn't just a chance explosion of some other mine and it seems to have been our solitary success in sweeping.'

'So then? What other steps is your department taking, admiral? Remember, time is of the essence.'

'Our team at *Vernon* is working flat out on the problem, sir, trying to devise a more effective magnetic sweep. I've, also, set up a new department to investigate and analyse all information held on the recent mining incidents. Captain Boyd – you already know – is heading it with the assistance of technical experts and a lawyer.'

'A lawyer?' Churchill choked mid puff of his enormous cigar and had to brush away much ash from his waistcoat and the lapels of his jacket. 'Let me see this lawyer.'

The admiral turned to Monty, who was doing his best to hide at the back of the conference room, and gestured for him to stand. 'This is Lieutenant Montcalm, sir, lately a barrister.'

Monty wanted the earth to swallow him up as the First Lord peered at him intently through his glasses.

'Montcalm. Montcalm. Sounds French. Was there not a Montcalm who fought against us in America?'

'There was, sir. But a distant relative.'

'Well, I suppose the French are on our side now. Tell me. Are you a good lawyer?'

Monty was taken aback by the question. Something told him that to reply with false modesty would not be the correct response. 'I believe so, sir. Leastways, I made a successful living at the Bar.' Monty felt himself squirming like a worm on a hook as all eyes of the conference room were on him. Suddenly, it felt like a court room again and that gave him confidence.

'You don't look very fat,' Churchill replied.

Again, Monty was nonplussed by the remark and unsure how to answer. 'I'm sorry, sir. I don't take your meaning.'

Churchill seemed to have anticipated the reaction and smiled. He poked his cigar in Monty's direction. 'Good lawyers are usually fat. It has been said of lawyers that one lawyer in a town will starve, but two lawyers in a town will grow fat. What do you say to that?'

'One could hardly accuse Sir Donald Somervell of obesity, sir... and he's the Attorney General,' Monty replied quickly. His remark caused much laughter amongst the audience.

'Harrumph,' Churchill snorted and the laughter stopped immediately. 'You have a quick wit. I like that. But just remember, young man, that your job is to seek the truth and truth can only be known based on the examination of the facts. And if you fail to find this truth - and quickly - we'll all be eating Frankfurters and *sauerkraut* for Christmas lunch.' Churchill turned to the senior officers at his sides and added, 'Gentlemen, let's just hope this young man doesn't end up suing us all for losing the war.'

CHAPTER 3
November 1939

'There's nothing else for it, Boyd. That's fifteen ships in the past four days lost off the east coast. We just have to clear a channel for our shipping. If we don't, we might as well start learning to goose step. Hitler's going to win the war at this rate.' Admiral Wake-Walker was not in a mood to be crossed.

'But the risk to life, sir. I wouldn't want to be in *Wivern*'s captain's shoes.'

'This is war, Boyd. It's what we signed up for when we took the King's shilling. Casualties have to be accepted and what's a few seamen's lives and the loss of a destroyer compared with the possibility of complete defeat. Anyway, I've already sent the signal to C-in-C Nore, so there's no point in arguing.'

Monty had never before heard an officer argue with an admiral. Boyd didn't approve of the plan for the destroyer, HMS *Wivern* to conduct four high-speed runs in a line joining the wrecks of two Royal Navy warships and two neutral merchant ships recently blown up by mines with the loss of several lives. The expectation was that the destroyer's speed would enable her to pass ahead of any mines in her path before they exploded. As a precaution, the captain had been ordered to keep only a minimum of men below decks, in the engine room or boiler room, and two trawlers were being kept available to rescue survivors should the probable happen.

Embarrassed to hear the disagreement between two senior officers, Monty was glad to interrupt the meeting with the news from the fresh signal he held high.

'Excuse me, sirs. I'm sorry to interrupt, but we've just had word of mines being dropped by parachute over the Humber and the Thames and Stour estuaries. One of them's been spotted on the mud flats at Shoeburyness. I think this is our chance, sir!'

Both senior officers rushed over to the map on the wall of Wake-Walker's office.

'Where's Shoeburyness?' the admiral asked.

'Just here, sir.' Boyd pointed to a spot off Southend. 'And we're in luck. There's a team of Royal Engineers at Shoebury Fort. They can help with lifting gear if necessary. I think Montcalm's right, sir. This is our chance. Monty, what's the tide state at Shoeburyness?'

'It's high water now, sir.'

'Excellent. In six hours' time the tide will have ebbed so far the mine will be miles inland. I'll send Ouvry and Lewis on their way then, sir?'

Lieutenant Commanders Ouvry and Lewis were two Rendering Mines Safe Officers, RMSOs, who had been waiting at the Admiralty for just such a discovery.

'No, wait. I think you're right. This is the moment we've been waiting for. Send the *Vernon* party on their way, but I first want Ouvry to come with me to brief Churchill before he and Lewis leave.' The admiral turned to Monty. 'You'd better be in on the brief, too, Montcalm. And I want you down at Shoeburyness as well, to write up the proceedings. Go fetch Ouvry and you, Boyd, had better warn the First Lord we're coming.'

*****

Despite it being after midnight, Churchill was still at his desk working when he was interrupted by the small group of naval officers from Wake-Walker's team. As well as his habitual cigar burning in the ashtray, a bottle of cognac rested on Churchill's desk. The admiral quickly briefed him on the situation. Monty noted that although the First Lord had at first seemed very tired, the news had suddenly energised him. At the end of the briefing, he addressed Ouvry directly.

'Commander, you and your type are the bravest of brave men, but you must be fully aware of what is at stake. The whole course of the war might turn on your success or failure tonight, but your orders are quite simple. The mine must be recovered at all costs! I salute you.' Churchill raised his glass of cognac before shaking Ouvry warmly by the hand.

'To be clear, sir,' Wake-Walker responded in an emphatic tone, despite Churchill returning to his papers. 'You are saying that these men are expendable?'

Churchill looked up, removed his glasses and massaged the top of his nose before replacing them. He then replied wearily. 'Yes, Admiral. Sadly, I am. The future of the country is at stake.'

*****

Monty, Ouvry and Lewis were driven down to Southend in a fast and powerful Humber. The admiral had ordered Ouvry to get some sleep in the back of the car, but Monty, in the front passenger seat, could hear him chatting quietly with Lewis. The Royal Marine driver drove the big car with assurance and paid little attention to the speed limits, even jumping red lights, but the streets were deserted. Outside the city, the driver kept his foot to the floor of the car for most of the journey and Monty had to avoid looking at the hedges of the Kent countryside rushing past to avoid feeling sick. Instead, he looked across the empty fields. There was an almost full moon to light up the wintry landscape, but everything was in monochrome. It felt quite eerie.

He tried making small talk with the driver, but he was a taciturn man and soon after giving up to leave the driver to concentrate on the road, Monty fell asleep. Just after 03.00, a change in the motion of the car woke him. They had arrived at Southend in record time. From there they were escorted to Shoeburyness by two police motorcyclists where they were met by a Commander Maton. The bright-white silk scarf at his throat seemed vivid in the moonlight.

'Everything's arranged for you chaps. We've ropes, stakes and thigh boots for you. Hope they're the right size. It's pretty muddy out there. And by the way... the Royal Engineers on scene have found a second object similar to the first three hundred yards nearer the low water mark.'

'I suppose that's good news, Roger,' Ouvry said to Lewis. 'It gives us a double chance of success. I'll take the first job and should I fail, you can avoid my mistake on the second.' Ouvry pulled out his pipe and lit it before selecting a pair of boots.

John Ouvry was a dark-haired officer in his early forties. Monty knew that he had served in the last war and been present at the Battle of Jutland. He had ended the war as the youngest mining officer in the fleet.

Ouvry turned to Maton. 'Thank you, sir. We'll take it from here. There's no point too many of us taking a risk. We don't know the state of that thing.' He pointed in the direction of the distant sea. The beach was shrouded in fog. 'We'll just need a guide.'

'That'll be me, sir.' A young gunner private stepped forward. 'I'm the one that spotted it come down, sir.'

'Fine. Right, sir. We could do with a couple of photographers, too, but it'll just be the four of us for now… at least until the team from *Vernon* arrive. That's me, you, you and you.' Ouvry pointed at Lewis, Monty and the private. He removed his watch and added, 'It's already 04.00. There's not going to be enough light to deal with the bugger on this tide and I need the *Vernon* team, so we'll tackle the job on the afternoon tide, but for now let's have a look at the beasts.

'First things first, though. Empty your pockets of anything metal. If that thing is magnetic, we're taking no chances. And that includes your buttons, too.'

It was a black night as well as wet because of the pools of water left behind by the ebbing tide. The near-full moon Monty had noted on the way down had disappeared. The sky was now black on account of the low mist. The private waded on ahead holding aloft a small Aldis lamp to light the way. Monty found it hard going to walk through the soft sand and mud, sometimes sinking down to his knees. It was odd, too. Apart from the sloshing of their boots through the puddles and the occasional murmur from Lewis or Ouvry, silence prevailed. Gone were the usual sounds of seagulls and the waves crashing on the shoreline. The beach was flat and featureless and the mist offered no horizon. The effect was disorientating, but even so, within a few minutes the soldier stopped and cried out, 'There it is, sirs. Right ahead.'

Monty looked back to the shoreline, but could see nothing. He estimated that they had walked about half a mile and were now, perhaps, five hundred yards below the high-water mark. Out to sea, he could make out the fleeting light of a buoy, probably marking the channel of the Deeps or one of the many sandbanks in the estuary and twinkling behind its curtain of mist. As a keen yachtsman, he had always found these navigation marks useful at night, but it suddenly dawned on him that an enemy minelaying submarine would find them just as useful. He made a mental note to discuss it with Captain Boyd on his return.

Ouvry ordered the soldier to stay put, but for him and Lewis to advance carefully by the light of their torches. Monty's heart began to pound. This was his first mine – if that's what it was. As he stepped forward, the monster appeared from the darkness ahead. It was black, sinister and shiny. Part of it was embedded in the mud. A pool of water had formed round its buried end and the remainder stood several feet proud like a toppling grave stone. Monty shuddered at the thought that this might well mark their graves, but that was stupid. Were this monster to go off, there would be no graves. There wouldn't be enough of them left to bury. The thought brought to mind a poem he had learned at school. It had been written by Chesterton railing against the government and war. He, like *'they that fought for England,'* would not *'have their graves afar'*. His reverie was interrupted by a movement by Ouvry.

Ouvry pointed out the tubular horns poking up from the sand, attached to the object's rounded, embedded end and he gestured for silence. The mine might be fitted with an acoustic vibrator capable of responding to a human voice and setting off a booby trap within. Monty withdrew his notebook and started to draw the shape of the mine and note its dimensions. That was why he was here. Should these two brave men before him fail, then somebody had to take back all the evidence available. He wrote that it was about seven feet in length, cylindrical, about two feet in diameter and looked to be made of some form of aluminium alloy.

Lewis drew Ouvry's attention to the tail of the mine. It was hollow and open with a massive, phosphor-bronze spring protruding.

This must have been where the parachute had once been attached. Monty did his best to draw it in the light of his torch tucked between his neck and his shoulder. He noted two prominent fittings on top of the mine. One reflected Ouvry's torchlight dully and was probably made of brass. It looked like a hydrostatic valve. The other he didn't recognise. It seemed to be made of shiny aluminium and secured with a screwed ring sealed with tallow. Ouvry motioned to Lewis to take an impression on a sheet of paper. Lewis passed it to Monty for safe keeping afterwards. Monty noted that a four-pin spanner was going to be needed to unlock that ring, but knew that none of the *Vernon* team would have such a tool. It needed to be non-magnetic, too.

Ouvry and Lewis stepped back from the monster. Ouvry removed his black-covered cap and wiped his brow. Beads of sweat glistened from his forehead. 'Monty, you and the private head back up the beach. Send down the sappers with something to tie this bugger down for when the tide returns. And ask Commander Maton to send a couple of photographers down. I want a good series of flashlight photos from every angle possible. Then we'll go hunting for the second mine. It's odd that we should go for ages without seeing a single mine and then two turn up at once.'

'Not really, sir. Intel reports that the aircraft for dropping mines are fitted with a cradle to house two mines. It means they're always dropped in pairs,' Monty replied.

'Really?' Ouvry looked at Monty quizzically. 'I never knew that.'

Monty bit his lip at the thought he might have come across as a smart aleck.

*****

Over an hour later, the naval officers found the second mine, having first found its dark-green parachute buried in the sand. Monty couldn't help thinking that a fair few of the local ladies might be glad of the silk, but it was a ghastly colour. Instead, with Ouvry's permission, he cut himself a length of the silk-like parachute cords.

They would make excellent dressing gown cords and he could think of many a young lady that might be grateful for some. Unfortunately, it was nearly 06.00 and the flood tide was coming in too quickly for the men to do more than note the location of the mine itself. It was already just about covered by water and it was too late to tie it down. They had no choice but to leave it until the afternoon.

On their return to the shoreline, Ouvry and Lewis were visibly pleased to welcome the *Vernon* mine recovery party, led by Chief Petty Officer Charles Baldwin and Able Seaman Archie Vearncombe. Ouvry brought them up to speed with their investigations of the last couple of hours before turning to Maton.

'Sir, I wonder if you could ask the engineers to make us up two four-pronged spanners in brass. Monty's got the dimensions. We'll need them by noon.'

'No problem at all, John. I'll get some brass rods of all sizes made up, too, in case they might prove useful. Now, gentlemen. It's been a long night. Come along to my house for some breakfast and rest. Whilst you sleep, I'll have those photos developed, too.'

*****

Ouvry was delighted by the spanners the Royal Engineers had manufactured so quickly. The flashlight photographs had come out well and were left in Maton's possession whilst the mine disposal party approached the first mine. Ouvry explained his plan to Monty.

'I'm going to tackle the first mine with Chief Baldwin as I've spent more time thinking about tackling these sorts of mines. Lieutenant Commander Lewis and Lofty Vearncombe will take the second mine. I've already briefed Lieutenant Commander Lewis on my plan and I'll signal every move I make. That way, if I miscalculate, he'll know where I was up to and avoid my mistake when he comes to the second mine. If you stay with him in this dugout, you'll have plenty of opportunity to observe what goes on... Just one more thing.' Ouvry removed his watch again. 'If I don't come back, give this to Lorna, my wife. It's a good one and I'd like one of the boys to have it.'

Without a further word, Ouvry shook hands with Lewis and trudged quickly out to his mine with Baldwin alongside. Monty's skin crawled at Ouvry's last words. The man had a wife and family and yet he was calmly walking out to undergo a task that almost inevitably would bring about his death. It brought to mind Churchill's words in the early hours that day. The stakes couldn't be greater and Ouvry was expendable. Monty's admiration for him couldn't have been higher.

He tucked away the watch safely and settled on his front with his binoculars and notebook ready to record the afternoon's proceedings. He was glad of the sandbags as protection from the cold winter wind whistling around the shelter the engineers had carefully dug by hand about 250 yards from the mine. They had helpfully dug another and smaller hole in the mud about 150 yards from the mine as a refuge in case Ouvry and Baldwin had to make a run for it. Monty thought Ouvry and Baldwin resembled two pioneers entering unknown territory. There was something cold about their courage. They weren't fired up by the heat of battle. They knew they would probably die, but yet they went willingly to do their duty. For them there would be no Victoria Crosses to reward their courage as they were not facing the enemy. Yet again he remembered the responsibility these men held for the course of the war.

Lewis, too, was lying prone, observing the men in the distance through binoculars. 'How are they planning to tackle the job, sir?' Monty asked.

Lewis replied without taking his eyes off the scene before him. 'You need to understand that there's three hazards with a mine. There's the main charge itself, but it can't explode on its own. If it did, we'd not be storing munitions or dropping them from the minelayers, so we use a two-stage method of initiation. We insert a detonator into a primer. We call the primer the *gaine* and ours tend to be a cylindrical tube containing picric acid. With the primer fitted, the mine's still safe to handle with reasonable care, but the problem comes when it becomes connected by electrical leads to the detonator. That's called arming the mine. Our job as RMS officers is to remove the gaine and any detonators. That then makes it safe for the mine recovery team to take it back to *Vernon* for the main charge to be removed. John and I think that aluminium fitting is a detonator, so that's the first thing he plans on removing. To do that, he needs to unscrew the ring locking it in place - funnily enough called a *locking* ring - and that's where our army-special spanner comes in. Hang on a minute. The chief's signalling.'

Monty noted the time as 13.48 and that he was barely breathing with the suspense. He looked at his surroundings. The mist had lifted and he could see clearly the pier at Southend. Nobody moved there, but he could see life going on as normal on the cliffs above. But for the deadly weapons part-buried in this beach, it would be hard to imagine there was a war on. He and the *Vernon* team seemed to be part of a different world and quite alone.

'Something's wrong!' Lewis exclaimed, bringing Monty's full attention back to the beach. 'The chief's coming back!'

CHAPTER 4

Baldwin appeared at the dugout, his thigh-length waders completely spattered with mud. 'No panic, sir,' he said before Lewis could question him. 'We could do with a hand, that's all. The Boss is fairly sure it's a magnetic variant. He's seen some form of magnetic needle device in the innards. We've removed one detonator, but can't get the primer out. But that ain't our problem right now. We need to have a go at the underside of the mine and with just the two of us, there's no shifting the bugger.'

'Fine, Chief. Lofty and I'll give you a hand. Grab some ropes.' Lewis and Vearncombe joined Baldwin and began to hurry towards Ouvry.

'I'll give you a hand, too, sir.' Monty clambered out of the dugout, but Lewis stopped him.

'No, Monty. You're the observing officer. Your job is to stay here, observe and record the proceedings, and report back to the Admiralty.'

'But I'd like to help, sir. I could leave my notes safely here,' Monty protested.

Lewis returned to the dugout and spoke quietly out of earshot of the two ratings. 'No, Monty. That's not how it works. We each have our jobs to do. I'm no keener to put my life at risk disposing of mines than the next man. I'm no hero, but I've been trained to do it and it's my job. So, I get on with it. Your job is to observe. So, be a good chap and leave us to go about our business.'

Feeling slightly humiliated, Monty returned to his position in the dugout and noted the time as 14.05 along with a summary of Baldwin's update. However, just five minutes later, he was summoned across to the mine by a wave from Lewis. He ran as fast as his boots would allow him across to the group of four mine experts.

'Yes, sir. What's up?' he asked breathlessly of Lewis, but it was Ouvry that replied.

'We still can't shift it and need another pair of hands. We could ask the army, but the tide'll be in within a couple of hours. In any case, the honour of the Service is at stake. It's our mine.'

Monty placed his shoulder up against the black cylinder and pushed with all his might when called to do so. His extra muscle seemed to tilt the balance and the mine rolled over about another third, exposing the bottom fittings of the mine, partly covered by the damp mixture of mud and sand.

'That'll do, thanks,' said Lewis. 'Now cut along to the dugout. We're going to stay to help and there'd be hell to pay if this brute went up with the observing officer, too. We'd probably all get court martialled,' he chuckled, but added in a more serious tone, 'More to the point, it would all have been a waste of time.'

Reluctantly, but without protest, Monty retreated to safety. It was 14.26.

Thirty minutes later and Ouvry signalled that it was all over and called for the recovery crane and truck. Monty approached the mine again and observed no end of gadgets strewn on the sand. Despite the keen wind, sweat was pouring off all the *Vernon* men, but they all shared a sense of elation. Together, they had cracked their first German magnetic mine. Now it was up to the scientists to work out how it worked and might be defeated.

Ouvry picked up an aluminium fitting lying discarded on the beach and looked at it intently before looking out at the advancing tide. 'Roger, it's too late to deal with that other mine. We're losing the light and the tide's coming in fast. In any case, we're both bushed. I suggest you and Monty hot-foot it back to London. I'll stay here overnight and pay a visit to Woolwich Arsenal in the morning. I want to discuss this little toy with the boffins.'

'That's fine by me, John,' Lewis replied, tossing the arming clock in the air nonchalantly, but failing to catch it again. As it hit the sand, it began to start ticking. Without hesitation, the *Vernon* men scattered at high speed, leaving Monty confused. 'Run, you bloody fool. For Christ's sake run, Monty,' Lewis called. 'Booby trap!'

Monty needed no further explanation and ran towards the dugout as if his life depended on it. Fortunately, it didn't as he hadn't covered the 250 yards before the other men stopped running. They seemed to know that if the bomb was to have gone off, it would have done so by now. Ouvry removed his cap and threw it on the sand laughing loudly. 'It was only the spindle, chaps,' he called out between fits of laughter. Monty didn't know what Ouvry meant, but it was enough for him to join in the joyous laughter of the whole party.

*****

Within a few days, the scientists and naval experts had stripped down the first mine to discover its secrets and the second mine had been defuzed by Lieutenant John Glenny from HMS *Vernon*. Admiral Wake-Walker called an immediate conference of all the preeminent scientists in the field of magnetism and mine warfare.

'Gentlemen, we have four short weeks in which to solve two problems. The first and most important, is how to protect our merchant ships from this weapon. It's vital that we give them the immunity to ply their trade. The second, is to come up with a design for an effective sweep. I'm open to all ideas.'

For over two hours, the scientists argued amongst themselves. The admiral wasn't happy with their answer that it would take at least a year and even then, it might not work. As the meeting broke up, he turned to Boyd in exasperation.

'I'm not asking them to completely demagnetise a ship. Just cut its magnetic signature. Do you think a naval team might succeed where the scientists fail?

'Possibly, sir, and I've an idea,' Boyd replied and turned to Monty. 'Monty, ring *Vernon* and ask them to wind an electric coil round a ship and see what it does.'

Monty immediately spoke to a Lieutenant Commander Ryan at HMS *Vernon* who replied, 'Don't worry, Montcalm. Tell the admiral that the idea's already occurred to us and we're working on it now.'

*****

The prostitute whimpered in the corner of her room, lying still naked on the floor beside the bed. Ernst buckled the belt of his trousers and reached for his tunic. He knew he shouldn't have hurt the girl. She was quite pretty and hadn't been the cause of his anger. He'd slip her a few extra marks. Hush money wouldn't be necessary. No slut was going to dare to complain about a *Luftwaffe* colonel, even in the naval town of Lübeck. But he did feel bad about the way he'd treated her. He finished dressing and withdrew some notes from his wallet. He showed them to the girl. She flinched and retreated further into the corner, moving into a sitting position, not bothering to hide her nakedness.

'I'm sorry. Look, I've paid more than double the normal rate. Skip your next client and clean yourself up.'

The girl didn't take the money, but glared sullenly at Ernst. He paused and then put the cash carefully on the make-shift dressing table before donning his cap. As he checked the cap's alignment in the mirror, he noted the loose change on the dressing table with his keys. He pocketed the keys, but piled the coins on the pile of notes he had just left. With a further tinge of remorse, he added another five marks to the pile of cash before leaving the room and heading out of the brothel. It had been worth it and he could afford it, after all.

He hadn't poked a woman since the early thirties when his marriage had broken up. That's when he'd joined the Nazi Party. He'd been at rock bottom, but his fortunes had reversed with the rise of the glorious *Führer*. First, his Party connections had brought him to the attention of General Schott, his reinstatement into the navy and promotion to lieutenant commander. Now, like little Max, he was a colonel in the air force and could afford the occasional screw with a whore. He recognised that his deformity, age and baldness were unlikely to attract a woman without the aid of some cash.

Outside, on the street, he found his *Kübelwagen*, another benefit of his new position, and began the journey back to his quarters in Travemünde. To his right, his cat, Gisela, woke and immediately transferred herself from the passenger seat to his lap. He wasn't supposed to have a pet in his quarters, but the rules were honoured more in the breach than the observance and some of the other officers had small dogs. It was a case of ensuring that none of the pets became a nuisance and drew attention to themselves. Absent-mindedly, he stroked Gisela's head and ears and drew pleasure from her purring in response. He liked cats. They weren't pack animals and could fend for themselves.

Ernst reflected on his anger. Why did he feel it? He was no longer in straightened circumstances. The war was going well and he could take much credit for that. As he had predicted, the combined efforts of the air force and navy had crippled British maritime trade and he hoped it was only a matter of weeks before Chamberlain sued for peace. Even so, whilst Germany had started the war with 22,000 mines in stock, only 200 were of the magnetic variety and they were now in short supply. If the war wasn't over by the end of the year, Ernst would have to find a way to increase production. But the High Command was very happy with the mining campaign. Schott had even hinted that Ernst might be up for a decoration. A Knight's Cross would be good. Wouldn't that make his brother Max jealous? Yet he still harboured a molten anger. He didn't know why and he couldn't stop it.

*****

The week before Christmas, Monty was in Falmouth. A mystery surrounded the sinking of the tanker *Caroni River* as it had been blown up in a channel regularly swept for mines. It was Monty's job to solve the mystery. He had met with Captain Hodson, the captain in charge of minesweeping, and interviewed the survivors of the tanker. There had been no reports of any aircraft in the area and nor had any parachutes been sighted. Monty suspected that the mine had been laid by a submarine, despite the shallowness of Falmouth Bay. He and Hodson planned to board a minesweeping trawler for a short night-cruise to view the area as it might have appeared to a U-boat captain.

Monty returned to the morning's newspaper whilst he waited for Hodson. He read again the account of the King's visit to Portsmouth and HMS *Vernon*. Once more he felt a twinge of jealousy at the news that the King had conferred the DSO on Ouvry and Lewis for their courageously successful efforts to defuze the magnetic mine at Shoeburyness. Baldwin and Vearncombe had been awarded the DSM for their parts in the evolution. The second mine had been defuzed by Lieutenant John Glenny and the King had conferred on him the DSC. These were the first medals of the war! It seemed to Monty that the only person involved with the operations not to have been decorated was himself. He felt a little hard done by. After all, he had helped with the first one and there *had* been a risk attached. Then again, he had to admit that he hadn't been involved with the nerve-shattering procedures to open the mine and remove its contents. Even so, somebody might have invited him to the shindig at *Vernon*. He would have liked to have met the King and Mother would have been so interested to hear all about it. Instead, he was deep in snow in the bitterly cold West Country.

*****

Ernst had hoped the weather in Berlin might be better than that on the Baltic coast on this extremely cold January morning. The whole of the continent seemed to be iced up by this freakish winter blast and his sea trials had had to be temporarily abandoned. The temperature in Berlin was only about a degree warmer. As he sat outside General Schott's office, he wondered why he had been summoned to Berlin so peremptorily. From within Schott's office he could hear raised voices, so loud he could make out fragments of the conversation.

'Fat heads… I haven't finished yet…' Ernst recognised the bull-like voice of Schott. As the conversation progressed - or more accurately, exchange of words, as the dialogue didn't sound very conversational - he could hear the other person's voice becoming louder.

'I resent that, General. Of course, my men can navigate, but...'

'Bollocks. Any idiot could tell from just a quick glance of the chart that those waters dry out at low water,' Schott retorted. 'Your men are just incompetent.'

Ernst tried hard not to listen to the angry words next door and picked up the newspaper to divert his attention, but caught the words, *'give us a weapon that doesn't need a parachute'* before, since the dialogue quietened, tempers seemed to have calmed. Soon afterwards, a full colonel emerged from the general's office, his face flushed. Ernst recognised him as the *Kommodore* of a bomber wing. The wing included the Heinkel 111s being used for dropping mines on Britain's coast. The colonel turned towards Ernst and their eyes met. The colonel's eyes immediately changed from one signalling recognition to one of hatred. Without a word, he stormed out of the office. Ernst's stomach sank. Clearly something was awry and he was next to see the general.

A few minutes later and the telephone on the desk of Schott's ADC rang. The lieutenant ushered Ernst into the general's lair. Schott was seated at his desk surveying a chart of the south-east coast of England. On seeing Ernst, he let it roll itself up and gestured for Ernst to sit down. The action calmed Ernst's nervousness. Were he to be dressed down, the general would have had him stand at attention, much as he imagined Schott had done for the *Oberst* just now. The general, however, seemed flustered.

'In a few minutes, Ernst, I and the Chief of the General Staff are going to meet with Göring to have our arses roasted thanks to the incompetence of a Heinkel crew. Were I to have my way, they'd all be in the glasshouse peeling potatoes. Idiots.'

'Forgive me, General. What's happened?'

'An incompetent navigator - or a jittery pilot, I don't care which - have cost us the chance to win the war with England by the end of the month. That's what's happened.' Schott rummaged amongst the papers on his desk and pulled out a couple of sheets of paper. 'Here. Read it for yourself.'

One of the sheets of paper was a photograph of a British newspaper clipping showing a British admiral presenting a medal to a Royal Navy lieutenant commander. As Ernst knew little English, it was fortunate that on another sheet of paper was a translation of the newspaper article. With the transcript was a note of explanation from the *Abwehr*. It was the King of England himself that was presenting the medal, to a man called Ouvry. According to the newspaper article, the medal was awarded for Ouvry's 'great courage and skill in securing and stripping live enemy mines'. The note from the *Abwehr* source explained that Ouvry had been one of several men decorated for rendering safe two magnetic mines near Southend.

The penny dropped and the blood drained from Ernst's face. 'God in Heaven,' he said quietly.

'Precisely,' Schott replied as he took back the clipping. 'The cat's out of the bag. Our secret weapon is no longer secret. It's only a matter of time before the English develop counter measures. Indeed, they may have done so already. Intelligence suggests that the ports are open again and fewer ships are being lost to mines. And all because some callow youth of a pilot had the wind up from a bit of anti-aircraft fire and thought it expedient to rush home for his breakfast and medals.'

Both men sat in silence for a few minutes. Ernst wondered how this development would affect his future and what might have been. His mind whirled. Was there a modification that would render his precious mines less vulnerable to counter measures? He would ask the question of the scientists and engineers. The silence was interrupted by the general's ADC reminding him that General Koller was ready to proceed to the *Reichsmarschall*'s office. Ernst stood up to leave.

'No. Wait here, Ernst. I shall want to discuss this further after my meeting with Göring.' Schott buckled on his belt and left the room saying, 'As the English playwright Shakespeare wrote, Ernst, *"Once more unto the breach, dear friends, once more."*'

*****

Monty was called into Rear Admiral Wake-Walker's office and was surprised to see a tall, thin captain in his mid-fifties seated at the table in the office, to the right of the admiral's desk. The captain stared at Monty with curiosity from his cold, blue-grey eyes before returning to the papers before him without a word of greeting or introduction.

'Ah, Montcalm. Thank you for coming. I hear from Captain Hodson that you did a good job down at Falmouth. He liked the way you looked at the problem through a U-boat commander's eyes. You were right. In all, he and his team have detonated eight magnetic mines, in a diagonal lay as you suggested, and the bay's now clear. Mind you, each mine has cost us a skid at three-grand apiece so we need to find a better sweep method, but *Vernon* and the boffins think they've come up with something. Take a pew.'

Monty took his seat with surprise that he still hadn't been introduced to the captain now sitting behind him.

'You ever thought of volunteering for submarines, Montcalm?' the admiral asked.

What? Monty thought. Those smelly things. Not on your nelly. 'Er, no, sir. Not my line, I'm afraid. I rather hoped for a destroyer appointment.' Monty thought it logical that the admiral would release him to take up a new appointment now his work was done. After all, the navy now knew that Hitler's new secret weapon was a magnetic mine and had recovered one. Monty had written his report on the probable causes of all the ship losses around the coast in the last few months and he could see it lying on the admiral's desk. He was of no further use to the admiral, therefore.

'You don't fancy sticking with mines then, Montcalm?' Wake-Walker picked up Monty's report. Monty wondered if the admiral had in mind an appointment to a minelayer or even a sweeping squadron. It wasn't what he wanted. He'd be happy never to see a mine again in his life, but he definitely didn't want an appointment as a flunky on an admiral's staff.

'This is an excellent piece of staff work, Montcalm,' the admiral continued. 'Concise and to the point. I can see your lawyer's mind at work.' Wake-Walker opened the report. 'I like the way you've tabulated the positions of both every sinking and every unexplained explosion. The latter is especially interesting. By correlating the distance of the explosions from every ship, their type, their speed, the depth of water etcetera, you've made a very convincing case that we're not up against pressure or acoustic influence mines. It's good work. Well done.' Wake-Walker closed the report and put it to one side.

Monty straightened with pride in his chair. It seemed that the admiral agreed his work was done and he waited for the news of his new appointment.

'Now we know that, we're well placed to come up with some counter measures and we've made good progress over the past few weeks. Lieutenant Commander Goodeve and Professor Haigh at Greenwich have come up with an idea for two minesweepers to tow a floating electrical cable through which we can pass pulses of electric current to form a magnetic field capable of exploding any magnetic mines lying in their path. But the boys at *Vernon* have really clinched the deal. They've come up with a thing they call a *degaussing girdle* to give ships immunity from magnetic mines.'

'*Degaussing*? I'm sorry, sir, but what's that?' Monty asked.

'Apparently it's named after a German scientist, Carl Gauss, hence *de-Gaussing*.' The admiral chuckled. 'One winds a wire coil completely round the ship, pass through an electric current and the ship's protected. *Vernon*'s trialled it on a trawler, a sloop and even a destroyer with complete success. It's up to the factories to take it forward now.'

'Let's hope it doesn't all end up a wild *gauss* chase then, sir.' The captain spoke for the first time and looked slightly warmer than Monty had hitherto thought.

'Montcalm, let me introduce you to Captain Maitland-Dougall. I've brought him out of retirement especially to head up the DTMI. He's your new department head.'

'But, sir!' Monty exclaimed. 'Don't you want me at sea?'

Wake-Walker seemed a little surprised by Monty's outburst, but wasn't to be swayed.

'No, Montcalm. Why would you think that? The magnetic mine isn't going to be the only new underwater weapon the Germans throw at us. We're going to need you and Captain Maitland-Dougall to investigate the others as they come along. You're too valuable to be wasted at sea.'

It wasn't the compliment Monty was pleased to hear.

*****

Ernst waited an awkward hour and a half before Schott returned. Oddly, he seemed in a jubilant mood. 'Coffee and *schnapps*, Wilhelm,' he ordered as he breezed back into his office. 'Ah Ernst. You're still here. Good. I have good news.

'I'm on the move, Ernst. Göring has appointed me as *General der Flieger* and Chief of Staff to General Coeler. He's to set up and take command of a new *Flieger-Division* at Jever from the first of the month and I'm to be promoted to *Generalleutnant*.'

'Congratulations, General. But how so? Two hours ago, you were expecting a roasting from the *Reichsmarschall*. What's changed?'

'Oh, he roasted us all right. He was very eloquent for some time, but then he let us speak. Koller blamed the navy, of course. Bleated on about how they insist the mine is a naval weapon and how it should be under their control. That softened up Göring. I don't think he and Raeder hit it off and the argument appealed to the fat *Reichsmarschall*'s territorial instincts. I then made the point that our bomber crews are amateurs when it comes to naval operations. They seem incapable of reading a chart or understanding tides for a start, but even so, I reminded him of our success to date. We were then told to wait in an ante-room for half an hour. First Koller was called back in and then me. Göring was all smiles over his fat jowls. He told me that he had decided to form a new *Flieger-Division*, designated the Ninth, of about 250 to 300 bombers to specialise in aerial mining.'

'So, will that affect my position at Travemünde, General? Will you want me to move to Lower Saxony with you? I hear the beer is very good.'

'Not at all, Ernst. I need you at Travemünde more than ever now. We'll need to step up production of the magnetic mine and I want you to liaise with industry on the matter. And on that subject, I've informed Koller that you are investigating the feasibility for a weapon we can drop with precision – that is without parachutes.'

'But we must slow the rate of descent, General,' Ernst interrupted. 'Our experiments to date have all shown the arming mechanism to be too delicate for a great shock.'

'Yes, I know that, Ernst, but it has to be done. In any case, the parachutes make the weapons too visible. Our engineers need to find a way. That's all there is to it. And, moreover, you need to come up with some modifications to stop the Royal Navy countering our weapons. Perhaps, we could delay the arming process or make them less sensitive to sweeps. Do you still play chess? You need to be thinking a few moves ahead.'

'As a matter of fact, I do, General... and I have had a few thoughts. Would you mind if I took that newspaper clipping away with me, General?'

'No. You take it. What do you have in mind?'

'With your permission, I will proceed directly to Frankfurt to discuss increasing our stocks of the magnetic mine. I'll then have a word with *Doktor* Hagemann, the Chief Scientist at Kiel. As you say, General, we need to modify the current magnetic mine or else devise a new form of influence mine. When we do so, we need to safeguard its secrets.'

'Safeguard... precisely. What do you have in mind, Ernst?

'I mean, General, firstly we need to prevent any new weapon falling into the hands of the British. Initially, that might involve more navigational training to the aircrews of your new division or forbidding them entirely to overfly land. But we must, also, consider technical means by which the mine can destroy itself if dropped on land by accident or in too shallow water. Finally, General, this newspaper clipping, gives me an idea.' Ernst studied the image of

Ouvry intently and smiled to himself. 'We need to discourage these officers from interfering with our weapons and teach the scientists at this HMS *Vernon* a lesson they'll never forget.'

CHAPTER 5
March 1940

'I think you will be pleased with this demonstration, Colonel. Please… follow me.' Doctor Kröber led Ernst into the tank room of the *Sperrwaffen Versuchs Kommando* or S.V.K, the German Navy's department for testing mines.

Ernst would rather have rearranged this demonstration for another time. He had to visit Frankfurt and would save much time on the journey if he could hitch a lift on an air force flight going there rather than taking the train. He was anxious to return to the Baltic as quickly as possible. Gisela was unwell and he suspected she had been deliberately poisoned by one of his staff. Moreover, he was more interested in developing a means to drop a mine without a parachute than another form of naval mine. However, he knew he would have to hear out Kröber.

'Admiral Müller has explained how the secret of our magnetic mine has been discovered by the British. Naturally, we have not been slow to analyse their counter measures and we are certain we have come up with something to confuse them. May I introduce Doctors Bartzsch and Hagemann?'

'Doctor Hagemann and I have already met.' Ernst shook hands with the scientists. 'We worked together before the war.'

'Good. That is excellent.' Kröber hesitated before continuing. 'With your permission, I will leave Doctor Hagemann's invention until last. It is quite revolutionary, but it still needs some further development.' Kröber and Hagemann exchanged meaningful looks and Ernst wondered if there was some friction between the two.

'However, Doctor Bartzsch's two modifications to the current arming mechanism will create some headaches to the British. I will let him explain.'

Bartzsch stepped forward and Ernst noted for the first time that unlike the two other scientists, he wore a swastika lapel badge on his white coat. 'Colonel, as you are aware, the *Abwehr* has reported that the British are attempting to immunise their ships from our magnetic mine by two forms of *electro-magnification*. The first is to install coils of electric cables in their ships, through which they generate an electric field to offset the effects of the ship's magnetic signature. Naturally, this is labour intensive and expensive so, for their less important ships, they merely pass an electrically induced magnetic field over their ships. They call this *wiping* or *deperming*. It is only temporarily effective, but we think it works.'

'Yes, Doctor, I have read the intelligence reports, too, and am well versed in the principles of magnetism, so please come to the point. I have to leave for Frankfurt shortly.' Ernst checked his watch impatiently.

'Then you will know, Colonel,' Bartzsch continued unabashed, barely breaking stride, 'that ships built in the northern hemisphere have a different polarity from those built in the south. Our first modification is to make our mines capable of responding to both the red and blue polarities.'

'I can see the sense in that,' Ernst replied more patiently. 'It not only puts their warships at risk in the southern hemisphere, but makes the ships importing their goods from the south vulnerable, too. It's a good idea.'

Bartzsch almost bowed with pleasure before drawing Ernst's attention to a brass arming mechanism. Ernst was very familiar with its workings.

'This is our standard mechanism for the magnetic mine, but let me connect up this modified version.'

The scientist connected two leads to the new device and signalled to his assistant at the other end of the leads.

'Observe the light bulb, Colonel. When it lights up, it will simulate the actuation of the mine's explosion. Now I will ask my assistant to simulate a British minesweeper and send a magnetic pulse to the mechanism. Otto…'

The laboratory assistant flicked a switch and Ernst observed the magnetic needle within the arming mechanism flicker, make contact and a brass cog move with a very audible click, but the light remained unlit. Ernst wondered if the experiment had failed due to a faulty mechanism, but Bartzsch just grinned with satisfaction and signalled to his assistant to repeat the operation. The same thing happened and this time Ernst began to suspect what the new device did. Sure enough, on the sixth click the light lit up.

'Wonderful, Doctor. A delayed action fuze. I can see it now.' Ernst rubbed his hands with glee and smiled broadly. 'The British minesweepers will report their channels swept and clear. Then the next convoy will discover their mistake. And you can adjust the settings, Doctor?' Ernst was visibly excited. His visit to the naval mine shed had been worthwhile, after all. He imagined the harassed minesweeper crews never sure whether they had truly cleared their channels. Without certainty, the British would be forced to keep their ports shut and they would once again be at the mercy of Germany.

'Yes, Colonel. As you have just witnessed, we can set the arming mechanism to trigger up to six times before exploding the mine. I suggest a mixture of settings are used in the same channel to keep the enemy guessing.'

'Thank you, gentlemen. I have very much enjoyed the demonstration and cannot wait to report the news to Berlin. I would like you to implement the modification immediately.' Ernst gathered up his cap and briefcase ready to go. The demonstration had taken less time than he had allowed, but he was halted by Kröber.

'Forgive me, Colonel, but you have yet to hear from Doctor Hagemann.'

'Of course, Doctor. I quite forgot in my excitement. I am sure there is better to come? Please go on.' Ernst put down his cap and briefcase, before checking his watch. He still had time in hand.

This time Hagemann stepped forward and ushered Ernst to a mine in pieces. It looked the same as the Type 'G' magnetic mine, but Ernst noted the fusing mechanism resembled a wireless set with a small microphone.

'Ernst, you will recall that the British invented an acoustic influence mine, but did nothing with it. I think I have come up with a way to make it work, but I need more resources to perfect it.' Hagemann cupped his mouth to prevent his words from being overheard. 'You know how slowly the S.V.K, works.'

Kröber joined Ernst and Hagemann. 'We regret, Colonel, that we aren't yet ready to demonstrate Doctor Hagemann's invention, but perhaps he could explain it. It is rather a… speculative project.' Kröber seemed embarrassed to be wasting Ernst's time, but Hagemann didn't seem to notice.

'By all means, Doctor. We all know that water is a good medium for the transmission of sound. By fitting a hydrophone to the mine, it can listen for the noises of approaching ships, usually from the propellers, but it can detect structural sounds from the hull of a passing ship, too. It's something the British were working on, but I think I can improve on the idea. I hope to make the sensitivity of the device adjustable so that it can discriminate between the noise of say minesweepers and heavy ships. Unfortunately, I have no data on the different noise signatures of the British ships'

'I can see the hydrophone, Frank, but what is that diaphragm for?' Ernst pointed inside the arming mechanism,'

'Ah, my dear Ernst, that is the heart of the mechanism. As I was saying, the diaphragm can be actuated when a certain noise reaches a predetermined intensity or duration. We don't want the mine being triggered by environmental noise for example. That's the element I'm having difficulty in refining. However, once the diaphragm is actuated, it closes a switch like this,' Hagemann reached inside the mine. 'That sets up an electrical circuit to the detonators and the mine is triggered.'

'And how long do you think it will take to perfect this new weapon, Frank?'

'I cannot say. Perhaps a year. Perhaps less with the right resources.' Ernst spotted the exchange of glances between Hagemann and Kröber.

'I see. And what counter measures do we have against such a mine, Doctor Kröber? The High Command is adamant that no mines should be deployed that we cannot sweep ourselves. We mustn't give the enemy a chance to copy them and then use them against us in the Baltic.'

'We are looking into that, Colonel. We think we could modify our mine barrage clearance vessels to carry a special noise maker to detonate mines ahead and in their path.'

Ernst was sceptical of the idea, but he had faith in Hagemann. If he could design a new mine, it might enhance Ernst's standing sufficiently to buy him the time he needed to develop the parachute-less air-dropped mine.

'I see,' Ernst replied. 'Thank you. I will inform Berlin and see what I can do about allocating you more resources for your investigations. I can see the value of such a new type of mine. It would confuse the enemy's minesweepers.' He checked his watch anxiously. 'But now I really must depart. I must get to the airfield before my flight leaves without me.'

Ernst gathered his things together and made to leave the laboratory, but stopped and turned back to the scientists. 'One final thing, Doctors Kröber and Bartzch. We must avoid the British discovering the secret of the delayed arming mechanism at all costs. Success could win us the war very quickly. I shall expect you to put forward some ideas. With a fair wind, we may not have need of your acoustic mine, Frank.'

'Colonel,' Bartzch pushed forward earnestly. 'Might I walk with you to your car? I have something to suggest to you.' Ernst could see the look of distaste on the faces of the two other scientists, but acquiesced.

'Certainly, Doctor. I would be glad to hear any further ideas.'

As they walked to Ernst's waiting car, Bartzch proffered a number of ideas for preventing the British from learning the mysteries of the next generation of German mines. They seemed sensible to Ernst and he readily agreed to them. Harsh as they might be, he had no love for the Royal Navy, but Bartzch wasn't content to let the matter lie there. At the car he had an even more audacious proposal.

'Colonel, I fear my suggested modifications will only delay the British from success in learning the secrets of our mines. Malfunctions occur and it will be only a matter of time before their experts get lucky and succeed in bypassing our precautions. In the event, I have a plan that will put back their scientific advances by many months.'

Ernst listened in awe to the proposal. Even he was surprised at Bartzch's obvious ruthless streak, but the pain in his arm served as a useful reminder of the stakes. He looked at his prosthetic hand intently before coming to his grim decision. Bartzch had come up with exactly the kind of lesson he hoped to teach the British.

'Yes, Doctor. Incorporate all those ideas. It's time the British learned to accept the inevitability of defeat.'

*****

It seemed odd, but Marcia struck him as most attractive on this lovely May evening. Monty had had much time to survey the girl carefully as they dined in the Café Royal. It helped when she removed her spectacles. It seemed to him that her blue-grey eyes sparkled in the light of the chandelier above. He had met up with Marcia again quite by chance in the Burlington Arcade earlier in the day and, since they hadn't seen each other since their days at Oxford, he had invited her to dinner. She still wore her blonde hair pinned behind her ears, a single row of pearls and a tweed two-piece suit, giving her the air of a prim school mistress, but the past six years had given her more grace and a certain charm. Earlier, he had noted the absence of any ring on her left hand.

'So, Monty, do you get to take out *Firefly* much these days?'

'Not for months, Marcy. She's still on the Hamble, but I've been too busy to take her out since about September. I'm not sure I'd be allowed to now anyway. Why? Are you offering to crew for me again, old girl? We were a good team, I thought.'

'It was jolly fun, Monty, but less of the "old girl", please, Monty. I'm twenty-seven and will be an old maid soon enough.'

'I don't believe it, Marcy. A girl with your looks and brains is sure to be snapped up soon enough. It's just that Mister Right hasn't found you yet.' Monty reached across the table and squeezed Marcia's hand fondly.

'Aren't you married yet, Monty?' Marcia gently withdrew her hand from his. 'I seem to recall you were planning on marrying… oh, what was her name? A short girl, reading English… Celia something. Didn't you take her to the Christ Church graduation ball?'

Monty coloured slightly before answering. 'Hardly, old… young thing. She had buck teeth.'

'Oh, Monty! What a wicked thing to say. In any case it didn't put you off my friend, Diane. There was a time when you were in love with her, too.'

'Nonsense, Marcy. She was too tall for me.'

'What? At five-feet-six?'

'Hmm. For me anyway. Mother always says that a girl should come up to one's heart and no more.'

'You certainly know how to kill a girl's hopes, Monty.' Marcy sighed theatrically. 'That leaves me out. I'm two inches taller than you. And there was I thinking you'd invited me to dinner to become another of your conquests.'

Monty blushed brightly and didn't know what to say. 'Marcy, dear. You make me out to be some form of lothario. Naturally, I hold you in great esteem…'

This time Marcia took Monty's hand. 'Oh, Monty. You've made me so happy. Of course, I'll be yours.' She burst out laughing as Monty's jaw dropped and she took her hand away again. 'I'm sorry, Monty. Your face is a picture. I'm just teasing. I won't be bringing an action for breach of promise.' She raised her glass of water before adding. 'Just good friends, hey?'

'You had me going there. I thought I was going to claim the best lady crew in London.'

'Not in London, darling. I'm just up for the night. I'm back at Oxford tomorrow. I've started a new job nearby.'

'Oh, really? I thought you'd gone off to some ministry job after graduating.'

'I did, but now I've been transferred to the Foreign Office.'

'In Oxford? And what's a mathematician doing in the Foreign Office anyway?'

'It's not in Oxford. It's in a country house requisitioned in case London is bombed. I'm helping them with statistics and things like that. It's dull, really, but it keeps me near home.

'And what about you? I read you'd been called to the bar a couple of years ago and yet here you are as a dashing young naval officer.'

'There's nothing dashing about me, dear. I just write reports for the Admiralty. They claim they need my legal mind, but I'd rather be at sea. I suppose I'm a sort of detective. I gather up bits of information and put them in a form others will understand. I suppose it's dreary stuff really, but I find it quite interesting.'

'A bit like my job, I suppose… in statistics,' Marcia added quickly and then changed the subject. 'I say, Monty. What do you say to the idea of cutting dinner and going to a nightclub?'

'A nightclub? I wouldn't have had you down as the sort for that, Marcy.'

'Your tact hasn't improved since Oxford, Monty. As it happens, I've changed a bit since then and, in any case, there's a war on. Let's live it up whilst we can. I've always longed to visit a nightclub and somebody told me the Café de Paris is worth a try. How about it, Monty?' Marcy's face lit up in excitement and again Monty reflected that whilst the ugly duckling of his university days couldn't be said to have grown into a swan, she was rather pretty.

'I'm not a great dancer, Marcy, but I'll give it a whirl. Just let me finish my wine first. Are you sure I can't offer you a glass?'

'No thanks. I'll stick to my water. How are your parents? Are they still living in that huge house in Wiltshire?'

'Oh, yes, they're still there. My elder brother now runs the estate as Father spends much of time up in Cheshire seeing my grandfather. Sadly, the earl's not well and may go anytime.'

'I am sorry, Monty. You're close to your grandfather, aren't you?'

Monty found himself welling up at the thought of his grandfather, but his potential embarrassment was spared by the approach of a waiter.

'Lieutenant Montcalm, sir? There's an urgent message from the Admiralty. You're to ring the office immediately, sir. If you'd follow me, sir. I'll show you to a telephone.'

'I'm sorry about this, Marcy. There must be some form of flap on. I'll be as quick as I can.'

Monty made the call to his office and it was answered by Captain Maitland-Dougall.

'Monty, I'm sorry to have interrupted your dinner. I gather you were entertaining a guest.'

'Yes, sir. A friend from my days at Oxford, that's all.'

'Oh. I just hope I'm not disturbing a tryst as I need you to get your backside over to Clacton right away. There's a car on its way for you. A German plane's come down with a full load of bombs. Amongst the wreckage, the local ARP found what they thought to be a cistern from one of the houses the plane hit, but a bright special constable was more suspicious and rang it through to Harwich as a possible UXB. You know what I'm thinking don't you?'

'You mean its cylindrical-shaped, sir? And I bet it's black.'

'Spot on, Monty. A couple of RMS officers are on their way over from Harwich, but I want your report on my desk in the morning. Now cut along.' The telephone went dead before Monty could ask directions, but the driver of his car would probably have these, Monty thought. He returned to his table and was relieved to see Marcia still there.

'I'm sorry, Marcy, but I have to go. The office is sending a car for me any minute.'

'A car at this late hour. How thrilling. It sounds very dramatic, Monty. I thought you said you just wrote reports... but I know not to enquire further.'

'I'm really sorry, Marcy. Look, I'll be back tomorrow. Perhaps, we could meet for tea?'

'Don't worry, Monty darling. It's been a splendid evening and wonderful to meet up with you again. But I told you... I have to return to Oxford tomorrow.' Monty's face must have dropped because Marcy was quick to add, 'I've written down my address for you, should you wish to write. I'm not on the telephone.' She passed Monty a slip of paper and kissed him softly on the cheek. 'Now, perhaps you'd find me a taxicab.'

*****

Two days later and Maitland-Dougall interrupted Monty's reading.

'That mine you found in Clacton, Monty. I've just received the report from the boffins at *Vernon*. You and the RMS officers who stripped it had a lucky escape by all accounts.'

'You do surprise me, sir. It all seemed quite straight forward to me.'

'Ah the joy of ignorance, Monty. The scientists report that the bomb fuze was in a highly dangerous state. It could have gone off at any second.'

'Crikey, sir!' And to think I told Marcy how dull my job is, Monty thought.

'But there's more. The mine's a new magnetic type. It reacts to blue polarity.'

'I don't understand, sir.'

'As ships in the northern hemisphere are built with a red polarity, the Germans build their mines to react to such a field. Somehow, they've twigged to our degaussing wheeze and are banking on the fact that some of our ships will have overcompensated and now be slightly blue in polarity. It's lucky we found out. We can take the necessary precautions. But first, I have a task for you, Monty.'

'Aye, sir. How can I help?'

'Talk to the information boys. I want them to release to the papers that the plane exploded with its entire bomb load. Let's not let the Germans suspect we've discovered their little secret. Indeed, the less publicity there is about mines the better. Let's keep the enemy guessing, what?'

'Certainly, sir. I'll get onto it right away.' Monty moved to the door of the office.

'Oh, Monty. Just one more thing. The admiral's asked me to tell you that your work over the past few months hasn't been lost on him. He's put you up for a Mention-in-Despatches and is fairly sure it'll go through. Well done.'

CHAPTER 6
August 1940

Despite it being a glorious summer's day, Monty felt flat. France had fallen and what the new Prime Minister had called the 'Battle of Britain' was underway with the slow destruction of the RAF by the *Luftwaffe*. Monty was reading the latest intelligence assessments and they made depressing reading. The RAF was hopelessly outnumbered and in danger of losing air superiority to the Germans. That would pave the way for Hitler's threatened invasion of Britain, although Monty was confident that even without air superiority, the Royal Navy would see off an invasion. The problem was British morale. If the *Luftwaffe* was free to attack Britain's inbound shipping, food supplies would run low and the war economy would suffer. How long would Churchill's government hold out then?

The telephone rang and Maitland-Dougall answered it. 'Oh hello, Geoffrey. What's up?'

Monty recognised that it must be Commander Thistleton-Smith on the line, the Commander Mining at HMS *Vernon*. Such calls normally represented a job for DTMI so Monty stopped reading and waited for Maitland-Dougall to finish the call.

'Yes, that seems straight forward enough. I'll send young Monty to accompany him.'

Maitland-Dougall replaced the telephone receiver and turned to Monty. 'That was *Vernon* on the 'phone. It seems they've been asked to show a few United States Navy officers how we do things... and I've just volunteered you to help.' Maitland-Dougall smiled affably and reached for his pipe. 'You've nothing particular on today have you?'

'No, sir. That's fine. But the Americans aren't even in this war. Why are they sending their officers over here, sir?'

'Search me, but I suspect Uncle Sam's navy might be taking a longer-term view of this war than their president. Maybe they think they ought to learn as much as they can from us whilst they can... just in case. I mean, if Hitler skittles us out of the war, he might see the US as his next juicy prize. On the other hand, perhaps

Roosevelt's thinking that if he can win this election, he might persuade the American public to take a stand against Hitler now. Who knows? Bloody tobacco. I just can't get this stuff to light.' The captain was silent for a minute whilst he had another attempt at lighting his pipe, but gave it up.

'Anyway, returning to the matter in hand. There's a magnetic mine been reported in Kent. *Vernon*'s sending a couple of RMS officers up to deal with it and a USN lieutenant commander to witness the action. As its on our patch, I agreed to send you along to meet and host him. You can demonstrate the principles of the observing officer to him and check at the same time if Jerry's come up with any innovations on his latest mines.'

*****

Later in the morning down in Kent, Monty met the *Vernon* RMS team, comprising a Lieutenant Hodges and Chief Petty Officer Wheeler, and the USN officer. Lieutenant Commander Eastham must have been six-feet-six in height as he almost bent double to shake Monty's hand. In charge of the mine was a party from the Chatham torpedo school. They had been working on it since the previous day and had already dug it out ready for Hodges and Wheeler to render it safe.

'You sure you don't want to help, Monty?' Hodges asked. 'I'm going to use the new safety horn.'

Monty felt tempted, but remembered his task was to guide the American officer in the role of the observing officer. 'No, not this time, but I'll just take a look at her first.'

Monty inspected the mine. It seemed to be a normal Type 'C' mine with no unusual features. He noted that the tear-off safety strip had been removed by the bomber crew and that meant the mine was armed. Satisfied that there was little more to see, he withdrew with Eastham to the shelter 250 yards distant.

'If you don't mind me saying, Lieutenant, that Hodges fella seems a mite old for his rank. That's surely unusual.' Monty had never met an American before and was pleased to hear that Eastham spoke with the same, slow drawl of the cowboys in the films he had seen, although the way the American addressed him as '*lootenant*' grated on the ear.

'I suppose it's the beard, sir, but like me, he's RNVR.' Monty pointed to the wavy rings on his uniform sleeve. 'We've all had other careers before signing up. Hodges was a master at Winchester College before joining last year.'

'Winchester, hey. Gee, that's like our Exeter isn't it?'

'I couldn't say, sir. I suppose it's not a bad school. It turns out some clever types, although not terribly practical. Hodges is a rare exception, though. He seems sound enough.'

'Oh,' said Eastham non-committedly. 'Say, what's this safety horn?'

'It's a new safety device we've been trialling for the last two months, sir. You're probably aware that these mines have a hydrostatic switch. If it comes shallow, the pressure is released on the bomb fuze and it's liable to fire. By screwing this horn onto the fuze, we maintain a steady ten pounds of pressure on it.'

'Neat.'

In the absence of more than a few words of conversation on the part of Eastham, Monty decided on a new tack.

'Excuse me for asking, sir, but why is the United States Navy interested in mine disposal?'

'Because it'll come in mighty handy when we're with you in this goddamned war.'

'So, you think your country will come in on our side, then?'

'Sure. It's just a matter of time.'

'I'm awfully pleased to hear it, sir. I just hope it doesn't take three years this time.'

Eastham turned slowly and stared coldly at Monty before replying, 'So what's with this observing officer drill? Ain't two experts on the job better than one?'

'I can assure you, sir, I'm no expert. I've not been trained in mine disposal, although I know the principles right enough. Ah, just excuse me a moment, sir.' Monty pulled out his notebook and scribbled something in it in response to a signal from CPO Wheeler.

through the barrier. He and Eastham were thirty minutes late, but he hoped… Suddenly, the windows of the car shattered and there followed a thunderous noise. Too late, Monty and Eastham dived for the floor of the car, but both were peppered by flying shards of glass. Stunned, Monty raised his head gingerly. He assumed a bomb had gone off in Portsmouth nearby, but saw instead an equally sickening sight. A pall of smoke lay over the shore establishment and Monty quickly saw that the roof of the mining shed had been blown off. He forgot about Eastham and the driver and just ran towards the wreck of the mining shed. He could feel blood running down the side of his head, but no pain. Out of the corner of a blood-occluded eye, he saw Commander Thistleton-Smith running in the same direction. In the distance, he could hear the bell of an ambulance.

On arrival at the remains of the mining shed, he was met with a gruesome sight. Several sailors were dragging men blackened by terrible burns through the south door. Monty followed Commander M to the north door. The shed was in chaos. The mine from Kent lay in a corner, the roof was open to the summer sunshine and glass was everywhere. Worst of all, the stench of TNT, smoke, dust, blood and, potentially vomit-inducing, burnt flesh, pervaded everything. In the corner lay a man barely recognisable as one, but he was alive despite his burns and a severed leg from which blood pumped like a gushing stream. Monty rushed over and, removing his tie, applied a tourniquet to the upper limb before ripping off his shirt and using it to try to stem the flow of blood. The man's eyes stood out brightly against his black, charred face. The mouth trembled and the eyes expressed fear. Monty almost wept with helplessness. He didn't know what else to do, but took hold of one of the man's hands, now just a claw.

'You'll be all right, old chap,' he lied to the dying man. Monty had no experience of death, but he could see the light failing in the man's eyes. He looked around for medical help, but all he could see was a sailor collecting charred human remains and placing them on a trolley. The bell of the ambulance still sounded shrilly in the near distance. Monty's feeling of helplessness gave way to rage.

What could have happened? That mine had been safe when it left Kent. He looked back at the mine. Its rear door lay several yards from the mine, amongst bits of mangled metal. A portion of the rim of the mine was badly buckled and Monty suddenly understood. The Germans had something to hide and had inserted a special charge to destroy the mine if its rear door was removed. But what were they trying to conceal? It was his job to find out.

His attention was drawn back to the man before him. The man tried to withdraw his claw of a hand and made a gurgling sound as he moved the shreds of skin still serving as his lips. Monty felt sure he said 'Mother' before the light in his eyes was finally extinguished and he stared blankly over Monty's shoulder. Monty knew the man was dead, but how could one be sure? Just then, he was unceremoniously pushed to one side by a Sick Berth Attendant feeling for a pulse in the man's neck. After thirty seconds, he turned to Monty and gently prized his hand off the black claw.

'You done what you could for him, sir,' the SBA said, looking at the tie and shirt over the dead man's stump. 'He's gorn. Now let me take a look at you, sir. You're bleedin' like a stuck pig. Just look this way, sir.'

Monty acquiesced meekly as the SBA removed pieces of glass from his head and hands before placing a dressing over his eye. 'Just hold this in place, sir. Fortunately, the glass missed the eye, but you'll need a couple of stitches. Best you head off to sickbay right away, sir. Somebody'll point you the way.'

By now, several SBAs and nurses were on scene and Monty could see a second ambulance arriving as he left the scene of devastation. Only then did he remember Eastham and the driver. Both were standing around the corner and, like Monty, covered in cuts and bruises. The quacks were going to have a long sick parade, Monty thought.

*****

A few days later, Monty made his report to Maitland-Dougall back in London.

'Take a seat, Monty. You look as if you've gone ten rounds with Joe Louis. I dare say you'll have a nice scar once those stitches are out. You can tell the ladies it's a duelling scar. They'll fall for you in droves. Now tell me what the bloody hell went wrong.'

'It was a new form of booby trap, sir… fitted on the rear door. The detonator, gaine and primer had all been removed, so the mine should have been perfectly safe… but Jerry had something to hide, sir.'

'Interesting. Tell me more, Monty.'

'Jerry must have worked out that we're stripping their mines and probably knew that we're taking them to Gunwharf to do so. Whatever, they placed a charge in the rear section. I spoke to John Glenny. He told me that soon after the last nut of the rear door was removed, he heard a whirring noise and saw a flash as he lost consciousness.'

'Is Glenny going to be all right?'

'Yes, sir. He's still in Haslar suffering from burns and shock, though.'

'That's something at least. He's one of our best RMS officers and I've already seen the butcher's bill. Five dead and several injured. I suppose we should be thankful it wasn't more. So, what are our friends the other side of the North Sea trying to hide, Monty?'

'The withdrawal of that last stud on the rear door completed a circuit to activate a small charge of just two pounds. We were lucky, sir. I suppose the Germans thought that would be enough to explode the whole mine, but they made a mistake. Fortunately, it meant there was enough matter for our scientists to discover the secret of the mine. It's what they're calling a "*clicker*", sir. It's a delay mechanism designed to complicate our minesweeping operations. The Germans can pre-set the clicker to prevent an explosion until a sixth ship sets off the magnetic trip device.'

'Christ! No wonder Jerry wanted to protect its secret. God help the poor sods in the minesweeping flotillas. They're going to have to sweep the channels up to six times before they can be confident they're clear. They're already using matchsticks to keep their eyes open as it is. But what about the boys at *Vernon*? How are they taking this?'

'Some of them aren't happy, sir. Up to now, it's been a battle of wits between them and the Jerry scientists. Now somebody's deliberately trying to kill them... and that makes it personal.'

'I don't doubt it. God, I wish this war was over. And I suppose the genie's out of the bottle. Now they've tried this infernal trick, I suppose we can expect other sneakiness. What precautions are the *Vernon* boys taking?'

'I spoke to Commander M and Rear Admiral Egerton, sir. From now on, all mines recovered are being taken to a remote disused quarry in the South Downs for stripping. Officially it's called the Mine Investigation Range, sir, but Jack's already christened it HMS *Mirtle*.'

CHAPTER 7

Monty was already up and shaving when the telephone in his flat rang at 06.00, less than a fortnight after the explosion at HMS *Vernon*. It was Captain Maitland-Dougall.

'Monty. Did I get you out of your pit?'

'No, sir. It's such a lovely morning, I thought I'd go for a walk around the park on the way to the office, sir. I was just about to have breakfast, sir.'

'Well, you can forget about your walk and breakfast, Monty. There's a car on its way to you. Pack up an overnight bag and get yourself down to Pompey, PDQ.'

Monty's spine tingled. There was something akin to a note of alarm in the tone of Maitland-Dougall's voice. 'What's up, sir? Surely not another accident?'

'No. It's not that, thank God. I've just had Commander M ring me. They had a parachute mine dropped near North Boarhunt last night. Commander M himself went to have a look at it and he's not happy. He thinks there's something fishy about it.'

'Fishy, sir? What do you mean?'

'That's for you to find out, Monty. For a start, Boarhunt's a couple of miles inland from the harbour, so it's an odd place to drop a mine.'

'Was it foggy last night, sir?'

'First question I asked, Monty. As it happens it was. The German pilot might have lost his way and maybe the fog looked like water from the air, but even so, Commander M is worried. And when Commander M's worried, I'm worried. He's a good officer... So, get your skates on. You can breakfast at *Vernon*.'

As Maitland-Dougall hung up, Monty ruefully calculated that by the time he arrived in Portsmouth, breakfast would be over.

*****

When Monty arrived at *Vernon*, not only was breakfast long over, but Lieutenant Commander Ouvry had already left to defuze the mine. Monty caught up with him at the farm where the mine had been dropped. Ouvry was busy scouring the farm for debris and the mine was being loaded onto a truck.

'Good morning, sir. Have I missed all the fun?' Monty greeted Ouvry cheerfully.

'Morning, Monty. It was a simple enough job, but I'm glad you're here. Something's not right and I could do with your detective's brains. Take a look at this.'

Ouvry led Monty to the spot where the mine had been found, marked by a small circle of burnt grass. Ouvry explained. 'The Home Guard found it last night. Said they saw a green flash and heard a slight muffled explosion. Take a look and tell me what you deduce, Sherlock.'

Monty noted that there was no crater, so the explosion had, indeed, been slight. A few yards away lay a heavy cylinder. Monty inspected it carefully and spotted the yellow deposits of explosive all over it. 'It looks like the primer to me, sir,' he observed. 'It's certainly been fitted into the main charge, but I'm surprised it didn't go off.'

'Precisely, Monty. And let me tell you that I removed the detonator and primer before we started recovery of the mine. Neither had fired, but something evidently has. I found the tail fin in an adjacent field and the farmer's found several bits of mangled metal all over his farm. What do you deduce, Sherlock?'

'I'd say, sir, that something is rotten in the state of Hampshire. The sooner we strip this mine, the better.'

*****

After a hurried sandwich back at *Vernon*, Monty, Ouvry and the scientists solved the mystery of the mine. Ouvry requested Commander Thistleton-Smith to meet them in the mining shed.

'Good afternoon, sir,' Ouvry said as he saluted Commander M. 'I'm pleased to report that our little team has solved the crime.'

'"*Crime*", you say, John. What do you mean by that?'

'I mean the crime of attempted murder, sir!' Ouvry said it with dramatic effect. 'Mister Walden will explain, sir.' Walden was one of *Vernon*'s civilian scientists. Strangely, in Monty's view, he was dressed in the uniform of the Home Guard.

'Sir, like the previous mine we examined a couple of weeks ago, this weapon was fitted with an electrical booby trap, set to explode when the rear door was removed. This primer thrown clear from it was the charge for the booby trap.' Walden held up the cylindrical object Monty had found earlier. 'It was originally fitted in the rear end of the main charge, but clearly that's not what caused last night's explosion. We've concluded that two other booby traps accidentally exploded on the impact of the weapon when hitting the ground.'

'Strewth. Three booby traps. Jerry's certainly keen we don't discover the secrets of this mine. Have you discovered something new?' Commander M asked. Ouvry responded this time.

'Oh, I think we could say that, sir, but forgive me for correcting you on a small point. Mister Walden deliberately used the term "*weapon*", for this is not a mine. Not only was the bomb fuze missing and the hole filled with the main explosive charge instead, but it hasn't been fitted with an arming clock or magnetic unit. It would never be able to blow up a ship.'

'But if it's not a mine and had no bomb fuze, why was it dropped?' Commander M began to ask, but then the penny dropped. 'But you've just said it. A triple booby trap and you said attempted murder…'

'Exactly, sir,' Monty chipped in. 'This mine was deliberately dropped close to *Vernon* as a kind of gift, but also, as a trap. A Trojan Horse if you like. Jerry's objective was to kill as many RMS officers and *Vernon* scientists as possible and deter others from going anywhere near them again!'

Commander M rolled his eyes and his mouth briefly dropped open before he pursed his lips and said with determination, 'Right, that settles it. I'm not prepared to sacrifice the lives of my men. I'm going to get onto Woolwich straight away and chase up that new device I've ordered.' Thistleton-Smith turned on his heels and marched quickly back to his office.

Confused, Monty turned to Ouvry. 'What's the new device, sir?'

'Something Commander M discussed with Woolwich after our little accident in the mining shed. He's asked for a new cutting machine that can operate remotely so that we can explore the innards of mines. A trepanning machine, he calls it. Woolwich have given the job to the National Physical Laboratory at Teddington to produce. Come on. Let's go up to the wardroom. I'm going to persuade a steward to open the bar for us. I think we've earned ourselves a drink after this morning's work.'

*****

Monty had only just finished debriefing Maitland-Dougall that evening when Commander M rang again. Maitland-Dougall ended the conversation with the words, 'I think that's eminently sensible, Geoffrey. Keep me informed and I'll send one of my staff down at the appropriate point. I'd be interested to see how your surgery works.'

He turned back to Monty. 'You'll have gathered that that was Commander M again. It seems that Jerry may have dropped us another of his *gifts*. This time, near Portland. It's hardly a coincidence that they should be dropped inland near two of the premier naval bases on the south coast. M's going down tomorrow to have a look at it, but he's determined nobody's going to tackle it until his new mechanical device is ready.'

'And when might that be, sir? I'd like to see how it works.'

'Possibly Sunday.' Monty must have let his feelings show as Maitland-Dougall added, 'That doesn't have to disturb your weekend in Oxford, Monty. I know you've been hard at it these past few months and you need a break. Take that young lass of yours out for a punt or something and pop down to Portland on Tuesday. M's determined he's in no rush to tackle the job this time, so you'll miss nothing.'

*****

In the event, it wasn't until the Wednesday afternoon on the twenty-first that Monty travelled down to Dorset. Commander M's trepanning machine had not been ready in the desired timescale so the *Vernon* team had had to content themselves with using the latest X-ray machine to evaluate the contents of the mine. However, an RMS officer had first removed the detonator and primer.

On the road down to Dorset in the large Humber saloon, Monty had plenty of time to reflect on his weekend in Oxford. It had been three months since he had seen Marcy over his curtailed dinner. If anything, she had looked lovelier, he thought. Had she blossomed with age or were his tastes changing, he wondered. During his days at Christ Church, his relationship with Marcy had always been platonic. Their friendship had started through their shared interest in sailing, but he had quickly appreciated her intellect and ability to talk knowledgeably on a wide range of topics beyond her passion for mathematics. Before long, he had come to regard her as a sort of sister and had found her insight into the feminine character fascinating when discussing his relationships with her fellow students at Lady Margaret Hall. He felt guilty at the impropriety of the feelings he had had for her over the weekend. They were not of a brotherly nature. Several times he had wanted to hold her tightly and kiss her madly, but there had been no indication that she reciprocated those feelings. The emotions surprised him. Marcy wasn't really his sort of girl. It wasn't just that she was too tall for him, but if he was frank with himself, pretty as she now seemed to be, she wasn't cut of quite the same cloth as the girls with whom he had dallied at many a ball. Perhaps he put that badly. She just wasn't… dazzling. Moreover, whilst he prided himself on his academic success and prowess at the Bar, he wasn't sure that she might not just be his intellectual superior. That was hard for a chap to take and yet… There was certainly something different about her. He couldn't put his finger on it, but it had been an awful wrench to part from her that Sunday evening. And she had kissed him on the lips as they had said goodbye. That had to mean something, didn't it?

'Oh, for God's sake, Monty. Pull yourself together. You've a job on,' he muttered to himself.

'Beggin' your pardon, sir. I didn't quite catch that,' the seaman driver replied.

'Sorry, Stone. I was just talking to myself. I suppose it's the war getting on my nerves.'

'Can't blame you for that, sir. I 'eard what happened at *Vernon* a couple of weeks back. Jerry's getting right on my wick, too.'

The men were silent again until passing Salisbury when Stone struck up conversation again. 'I was just wonderin', sir. You can probably tell from my accent that I be from Dorset.'

'Really? Of course, I took you as coming from the West Country, but I hadn't worked out it was from Dorset specifically. Anyway, what of it?'

'Well, I know it's probably a liberty, but my family comes from a village near Charminster and I ain't seen them for a good few months, sir. I wondered if, perhaps, you'd mind if instead of me stayin' in barracks tonight, if I took the car to stay with my folks. I promise I'd be back well afore breakfast to collect you again, sir.'

Monty thought about it for a short while. Would Captain Maitland-Dougall object were he to know, Monty wondered. Probably not, he decided. The Boss was quite liberally minded and cared for all his staff. And it would be a pity if Stone couldn't see his family.

'Fair enough, Stone, but I want you outside the wardroom by 06.30. Understood?'

'Don't you worry about that, sir. I'm much obliged. We'll be just about passin' my parents' house tomorrow. I gather we're going to Piddlehinton.'

'You know more than I, Stone. I was only told it was a little inland of Weymouth.'

'More than a little, I'd say, sir. Must be a good ten miles. Seems like Jerry was well off course with that one.'

'Mmm, I wonder. It's a strange name, Piddlehinton.'

'Not round these parts it isn't, sir. Piddles are marshes, sir, and we've the River Piddle, too. We're not short of piddles and puddles in Dorsetshire.'

'Thank you for that, Stone. It still seems an odd place to drop a mine. Unless it was planted,' Monty added quietly to himself.

*****

Monty found the mine in a beautiful valley not far from Piddlehinton. The gentle breeze brushed the tall grasses like the waves on the shore and the air was full of the chattering of skylarks and the buzz of insects. The opposite side of the valley was a patchwork of different greens, brown and yellow. A bright-red tractor was gently running up and down a wheat field cutting the crop, the sound of its diesel engine faint, but nonetheless intrusive on the peaceful landscape. It reminded Monty that he was in Hardy country. It was too beautiful a day to go to war.

A group of soldiers was guarding the mine and had dug a slit-trench shelter in the neighbouring field. Monty was met by Mister Walden and a Chief Petty Officer Thorns. On this second meeting, Walden was unshaven, but still wearing his khaki battledress.

'Hello again, Leonard.' Monty proffered his hand to Walden.

'We meet again, Lieutenant. Sorry about my dishevelled appearance. I've been working on this contraption most of the night.'

Monty inspected the cutting machine. It was made of non-magnetic metal with a huge cutter, currently clamped onto the outside of the mine. As far as Monty could see, the rest of the machine seemed to comprise just an air compressor and a series of cogs from which a twin flex extended towards the slit-trench.

'It seems a standard type 'D' to me. Anything odd about it, Leonard?' Monty asked.

'Definitely. For a start there was no clock or bomb fuze. And then our X-ray machine has shown up a booby trap linked to an electrically fired auxiliary charge. It's Boarhunt all over again, I'm afraid.'

'So, what's your plan then?'

'Sidney Anderson's the RMSO dealing with this. He's gone to find me more compressed air. Then I'm set up to cut a four-inch hole at one end of the battery. Sid's then going to cut the power to the auxiliary charge. We might as well join the soldiers whilst we wait. They usually have a fanny of tea on the go.'

Soon afterwards, they were joined by an Australian reserve lieutenant who introduced himself as Sid Anderson.

'I hadn't appreciated we had any Australian officers over here,' Monty remarked.

'Strewth, yes, but just a few for now. There's a whole shed-load of others on the way, too, so you'd best get used to it, mate. Right, Len. Let's get going.'

Everyone took shelter in the slit-trench and, when comfortable, Walden made the switch to start the cutting machine. Suddenly, the languid summer air of Dorset was rent by the high-pitched screaming noise of the cutter in operation. There seemed little to do but wait and take advantage of a mug of tea offered by one of the soldiers. At frequent intervals Walden would stop the machine and they would all wait for five minutes before Anderson hopped over the stile to check on progress. Repeatedly he returned with the report, 'Still a long way to go.'

Monty had taken the precaution of asking the staff at Portland to make him up a packed lunch, as had the chief, but the thought hadn't occurred to Anderson and Walden had been working all night. As a result, Monty felt obliged to give his lunch to them. His afternoon hunger only made him more impatient for the infernal, wailing machine to finish its work. On the upside, Stone had returned about tea time with a massive basket laden with produce from his parents' village. Either the villagers had been extremely generous or rationing didn't seem to apply to the people of Dorsetshire. Monty was enjoying a slug of cider with a slice of cheese and onion pie when Commander M arrived. Slightly sheepishly, he stood to greet the commander. The latter had not failed to spot the basket.

'I say, Monty. What have you got there? Eggs? You've not been plundering the countryside, have you?'

'Not at all, sir. My driver's a local and these are the gifts of a grateful nation. Help yourself to anything, sir. The eggs are hard-boiled.'

Commander M helped himself to two eggs and used the bowl of his pipe to crack the shells. As he did so, the whine of the drill changed its note. Everyone's ears pricked up.

'I think we're through, sir,' Walden suggested. 'Or at least part way. We'll give it five minutes and take a look, sir.'

Monty was impatient to take a look, but Commander M seemed unperturbed and began shelling his eggs. After eating the eggs, he lit his pipe and puffed at it contentedly. Once he was satisfied it was drawing properly, he turned to Walden. 'Right. You go, Mister Walden. It's your show.'

Within a few minutes, Walden returned and spoke to Thistleton-Smith. 'It's cut through on one side, sir. I'll finish the job with a hacksaw. Shouldn't take me more than a minute or two.'

The naval officers and CPO Thorns waited another five minutes before following Walden to the mine. On their arrival, he was just finishing off his cutting and Monty took his turn at peering through the neat hole in the mine's casing. Thistleton-Smith and Anderson were pleased with the positioning of the hole. According to them, it was in exactly the right place for Anderson to squeeze his hand inside to cut and insulate the battery leads to the auxiliary charge. As a matter of caution, he and Walden were about to retire to the slit-trench when Thorns spoke out with a note of alarm. 'Wait, sir. Do you smell anything?' Monty noted it, too, and began to fear the cutting operation had ignited a slow fuze to another booby trap.

'It's getting worse,' Anderson added. 'I think we'd better retire ruddy quick.'

'My God, Anderson. You're right. It is getting worse. What do you think it is?' Commander M asked.

Monty was now quite decided in his own mind that it was the right time to dash back to the shelter, but felt he should take his lead from the senior officer present.

'I think it's pitch, sir,' Walden responded after sniffing a little more.

'No, it ain't, sirs,' Thorns interjected. 'Look out, sir! You're on fire!'

Monty swung round to follow Thorns's gaze and was surprised to see Commander M enveloped in clouds of smoke and a pocket of his reefer jacket well ablaze. Together with Walden, he immediately patted down Thistleton-Smith to extinguish the fire which by this time had already destroyed the lining and part of the commander's jacket. Commander M's look of surprise quickly turned to one of understanding and he reached into the ruined pocket and withdrew his pipe, still alight.

'Well bless my soul,' he exclaimed. 'I'd quite forgotten about it in the excitement. Sorry to alarm you chaps. I fear Mister Gieve will have his work cut out to repair this little mess.' Everyone burst out laughing. 'Come on chaps, we'd better retire whilst our Aussie friend deals with his booby trap.'

As the party walked back to the next field, Monty noted how the shadows were lengthening. Commander M had noticed it, too. On their return to the shelter of the slit-trench, he turned to Walden and Thorns to discuss the next phase of the defusing operation.

'I was thinking about the explosive charge in the rear compartment. We know it's mechanically operated and the scientists haven't yet worked out how best to tackle it. You're just about out of compressed air for your machine, Mister Walden, and I'm not sure your machine will clamp on the rear end properly either.'

'That's true enough, sir. That ribbed end makes it awkward and it'll take time to modify the cutting apparatus.'

'Exactly. Moreover, it's getting late and we've all been on this job too long already. We know it's a booby-trapped dummy and I doubt we'll learn much new from it anyway. Chief, I think this might be the right time for you to try your plastic explosive. I know you've been dying to use it.'

Thorns beamed in reply. 'Aye aye, sir. I'll be ready in a jiffy.'

Meanwhile, Anderson had dealt with his booby trap. Commander M strode off to brief him on the next steps. Monty waited with Walden for Thorns to return with his kit.

'You ever seen this stuff before, sir?' Thorns asked him. 'All I need to do is place a two-inch ring of the stuff on the rear door, insert a detonator to fire it and attach a fuze to light it. I reckon two minutes should be about right.'

The chief showed Monty the plastic explosive. As far as Monty could see, it was just like the Plasticine from his days in the nursery. It sounded very simple.

'I say, Chief. Do you think I could see the bang? I'm interested.'

'Don't see why not, sir. We just need to find some cover nearby, that's all. You up for it, too, Len?'

Commander M and Anderson had already selected a fold in the field about 250 yards from the mine as a safe place of observation, so Monty and Walden joined them whilst Thorns set his charge. The birds were singing and all around it was peaceful as they watched Thorns light his fuze and sprint to their place of shelter. Even the tractor driver had gone home. Twenty seconds later, the charge fired, the noise causing the roosting birds to take flight. Monty shivered as the sun disappeared over the rise behind him. He turned on his back and watched a Spitfire, or was it a Hurricane, he wondered, fly overhead. Apart from the drone of the far-off aircraft, the only sound was that of the rustling of the branches above in the gentle breeze.

'Come on then. It should be all right now,' Commander M announced. 'Let's go and take a look.' He set out briskly about twenty yards ahead of Monty and the others, all struggling to keep up with him.

Suddenly, when he was only fifty yards short of the mine, a great flash of blue seemed to envelop the commander, like a great halo, and simultaneously a sharp crack sounded. Everyone hit the ground instantly. Monty buried his head in the long grass and wished it would offer more protection as he heard pieces of the mine, stones or clods of earth landing around him. He raised his head tentatively to see Commander M equally prone and the heavy battery of the mine land just a yard from him. The mine was ablaze and pieces of its metal casing were still raining down around him and the other men.

    Slowly, the men stood up and checked each other was all right. Mercifully, none had been injured, but Commander M was nursing a bad headache. It had been a close call and Monty decided that working with mines might be just a bit too interesting. Perhaps I'd be better volunteering for submarines, he thought. It might be safer.

*****

On the Saturday night, back in London, Monty wrote up his report of the incident. Initial investigations by the boffins at *Vernon* of the mine's debris had confirmed that it had not contained a magnetic unit, but had contained at least three booby traps. Without a doubt, the mine had been dropped and designed to kill those attempting to take it apart. Monty wondered if this was evidence that his department and the men at HMS *Vernon* were beating the Jerry scientists in this first round of the war. He decided to include in his report the comments of Commander M as Monty had made his farewells. 'This gives you a queer feeling, Monty. Up until now, everything's been impersonal, but this was aimed at us individually. Almost a personal present from the Führer.'

PART 2

The End of the Beginning
September – December 1940

CHAPTER 8
September 1940

It was impossible to sleep. It wasn't just the noise of the German aircraft above, the sound of the anti-aircraft guns, the whistling of the bombs, the explosions, the shattering of glass, or the screaming of the women and children sharing the shelter in Caryl Street with Stephen. It was the fear. When the bombing of Liverpool had started a few weeks ago, he had only felt a tightness of the chest and a slight trembling, but as the air raids had continued and the bombs had come closer, the pain had moved to the stomach. It was held in a vice and now it felt as if rats were gnawing at him from inside. How could that old man opposite be sleeping through this, he wondered. He just wanted to scream or run out into the dust-filled air.

Stephen had remembered to bring a coat and a pillow this time and he adjusted them to afford a more comfortable position. From his sports jacket he withdrew his pocket-sized copy of Trollope's *Framley Parsonage*, long dog-eared by frequent use, along with several other novels by the same author. As he replaced his round spectacles to pick up the plot where he had left it earlier in the evening, he noted a small girl staring at him with wide, white eyes. She was wringing her hands on her rag doll and staring unblinkingly. He smiled at her reassuringly, but it was a false show of confidence. He was terrified, too. He found an old envelope in his coat pocket and quickly drew an amusing cartoon for the child, but she didn't react.

Disappointed, he placed the drawing in front of her and breathed deeply to calm his own anxiety. That wasn't a good idea. The air stank of human bodies confined in a stuffy, dark and dusty space. And there was another smell. The smell of fear. This must be why Dad hated war so much, he thought.

John Cunningham had served as a mechanic with the Friends' Ambulance Unit at Ypres. Dad didn't speak much of it, but Stephen suspected he must have been shelled at some point, either in the town or the trenches. All Stephen did know was that Dad had been gassed with chlorine in April 1915, and then shipped home as unfit to continue his service on the front. Poor Dad still suffered from a bad lung today.

The little girl's mother drew the child towards her and cuddled her tightly. 'C'mon, princess. Leave the man alone, will yerr.' She turned to Stephen. 'Sorry about that, luv. She's not been right ferr a week now.'

'It's all right. She w-wasn't b-b-bothering me. This must be t-t-terrifying for her.' Stephen smiled again at the little girl, but she turned away and buried her face in her mother's breast.

'Ain't you scared then, luv? I know I am. Sounds like the docks at Birkenhead are getting a right battering tonight. It'll be our turn next.' The mother picked up the envelope and drawing. 'My, that's good. You've real talent.'

Stephen merely shrugged in reply. He didn't like making small talk as his stutter made him feel awkward. Ever since his time at Lancaster Royal Grammar School, he had noticed how often people lost interest in what he had to say and looked at him in pity or embarrassment, as he fought to utter his staccato sentences. It had improved at university, but even today, most members of the school staff room tried hard to avoid engaging him in conversation. It was worse in the class room. Who said there was a fairer sex? The girls were merciless in their teasing of him. He hated teaching, but what else could a physics graduate do if one had a moral objection to war?

He listened to the sound of the bombs and feared the woman might be right. They did seem to be coming closer. He tried hard to ignore the cacophony around him and focus on God, as he had been taught. It was important to look for the inner light and he quietly intoned a prayer to himself.

'Lord God, I pray for your protection as I end this day…' He froze. It was impossible to think in this noise. The ground shook and with each blast, dust covered everyone in the shelter. There was no doubt. The droning of the enemy engines above was coming closer. This wave was attacking the docks and the accompanying noise was becoming ever more terrible. The deafening thunder of the explosions was too much to allow Stephen to hear himself think.

Some of the women began to scream and many prayers were said aloud, but barely audible above the shriek of the dropping bombs and the reverberations of the explosions. Now the blasts couldn't get any nearer. It was just a question of time. Suddenly, Stephen knew he was about to die – in this dirty, cramped, dark and stinking cellar – like a rat.

Sure enough, the end came. The doors of the shelter were blown off and Stephen was thrust against the wall behind him by the powerful shock waves. He couldn't hear anything and he knew he was dead.

Stephen's welcome to Heaven was a wet feeling in his lap. He felt his ears ringing and the vibrations of the barrage around him. Everything was black and he was coughing from dust. A strong smell of urine offended his olfactory gland. Then, he remembered to open his eyes. It was dark as there was no lighting. Oh Lord, he thought. Why have I been condemned to Hell and not to the bright light of Heaven? But there was light. Looking up the steps, Stephen could see the entrance to the shelter where the great double doors had once stood. A flickering light showed the air to be thick with dust and figures nearest it were slumped inert. Now it dawned on him that he wasn't dead, but still in Hell – and he had wet himself.

*****

A few days later, Stephen picked his way round the bomb craters as he headed for Lime Street Station to seek a train that might eventually take him to Preston, or even Lancaster. He had no luggage as he owned nothing other than a pillow. Even his trousers had been a gift from a kind ARP warden a few days earlier. Thank the Lord he had taken his coat to the shelter. Even so, he had been one of the lucky ones from that shelter. Five soldiers near the doors had died in it. Stephen recalled how one hadn't had a mark on him. His face merely registered surprise. When Stephen and the others had emerged from the shelter, they had found the city destroyed or ablaze. Everywhere there had been, and still remained, masses of rubble, broken glass and furniture and, for some reason, several pianos, now piles of matchwood. Oddly, the most vivid sensation he had experienced was the smell of beans in the air. One of the scousers had remarked that a cargo ship in the docks must have been carrying them. He had returned to his lodgings to find little left of the street in which he had previously lived. His landlady's house had been completely destroyed and he had been directed to a communal rest centre for the remainder of the night. Subsequent nights had been spent living in the crypt of St Michael's. His coat, the pillow and the clothes in which he stood were now his only possessions.

He passed a group of workmen shovelling rubble into some of the craters the bombs had left behind. Three days after the last raid, women still wandered the streets in a daze. Half the houses were no more than empty shells or piles of rubble. Stephen had to climb over one such pile to make his way up the street, scuffing his once-shiny, now well-worn brown brogues in the process. Everywhere was covered in thick layers of dust, adding to the gloom of the city and casting a surreal aspect to the streets. To his right he saw a grey Salvation Army van dispensing tea and he decided he might obtain a sandwich for his journey. He took his place in the queue behind a man in khaki, wearing the flashes of the Royal Engineers on his shoulders. The soldier ordered a mug of tea and a sticky bun, but the Salvation Army lady volunteer refused payment.

'You 'ang on to yerr money, luv. You fellas a' doin' a grand job. Ta very much.'

Stephen paid his four-pence for a hot mug of tea and a stale corned-beef sandwich and stood near the soldier. The man wore three stripes on his arm and Stephen recognised that this denoted the rank of sergeant. The soldier in turn surveyed Stephen.

'You look on your uppers, mate. Been bombed out by any chance?'

'Y-y-yes, s-s-sergeant. F-f-five nights ago. I'm heading home n-n-now.'

'That's a crying shame, mate. I feel sorry for you. Bloody 'itler. What's he bombing civilians for? Where's home then, chum? Not far, I hope.'

'N-n-no, b-b-but far enough. D-Dolphinholme. It's a s-s-small village n-near Lancaster.'

'Can't say I've ever been there. I'm from Northamptonshire myself.'

Stephen was surprised that the sergeant didn't seem to mind his stammer, so he ventured a little conversation.

'W-w-what are you d-doing in Liverpool then?'

'Me? Bomb disposal, me.' The sergeant pointed to the badge on the lower left sleeve of his battledress. It was an image of an inverted bomb of dirty, red felt. 'Designed by Queen Mary herself, this,' he added proudly. 'There's a UXB up Hope Street and my lads are digging down to it so that our officer can defuze it.'

'A UXB, s-s-sergeant? W-w-wh…'

The sergeant cut him off. 'Sorry, chum. An unexploded bomb. On every raid, Jerry sends down a few. Some don't go off through a problem with the fuze. Others… well let's just say Jerry's a mischievous and devious bastard. He's taken to sending down a few with delayed action fuzes. It creates more chaos, see?'

Stephen said nothing in reply, but the sergeant noted his puzzled expression. 'Every time we have a UXB, you see, we have to cordon it off for 400 yards. That's when we can find them. That means closing down roads and nearby factories. Evacuating factories. Stopping trains. Even stops the Ack-ack boys firing their bleedin' pop guns. It's a bigger nuisance than a bomb that does its proper job and explodes on impact.' The sergeant poured away the dregs of his tea and made to leave.

'Right, I'd better be off now. Can't keep you from getting your train and I'd better check my idle conchies are still working on that pit.'

'W-w-wait.' Stephen laid his hand gently on the sleeve of the engineer. 'W-w-what do you mean by c-c-conchies and how d-d-do you d-d-defuze the b-b-bomb?'

'Conscientious objectors, mate. They're pacifists. They don't believe in fighting, but don't think them cowards, now. It takes cool courage to dig near a UXB. Those bombs are evil buggers. One minute they're just a piece of metal, but hit them with a pick or shovel - or even out of mere cussedness - and up she goes. You don't stand a chance. Bomb disposal teams don't have no graves. There ain't nothing to bury.'

With that the sergeant picked up his gas mask and walked away. Stephen finished his tea and carried on his trudge to the station. The last words of the sergeant played over and over in his mind. Conscientious objectors – pacifists like him – were risking their lives to defuze these bombs for the benefit of the civilian population. Might this be something for which he should volunteer? Of course, he didn't have a clue how to defuze a bomb, but there had to be a science to it. Moreover, working in Dad's garage as a boy had taught him some mechanical skills. Ah, but Dad. He couldn't see Dad approving of his only son joining the army. Whilst Dad had been happy to leave his wife and child to join the Friends' Ambulance Corps in the last war, he had done so to help the Belgian civilian population and had refused to join the medical corps. He and his Quaker friends believed that even the treatment of wounded soldiers was aiding the war effort by giving them the chance to fight again. It wasn't something on which he and Stephen agreed.

Lime Street Station was bursting with people, many of them carrying suitcases with the obvious intention of evacuating the city. Stephen felt guilty to be among them. It seemed to be a form of giving in, but what else was he to do? He had to go home. He had nowhere else to go. Not only had his lodgings been destroyed – and new accommodation was likely to be almost impossible to find – but he had lost his livelihood. The girls' high school where he had taught was now just a pile of astringent, smoking embers after being struck by incendiary bombs. It had taken him nearly a hundred applications to find this job as a physics and general science master. The now former headmaster hadn't offered much hope of him finding a new post. Teaching was becoming the preserve of men over the age of forty, not liable for conscription.

Whilst he queued to buy his third-class single ticket to Lancaster, Stephen surveyed his surroundings. Mercifully, the huge, smoke-stained, glass and iron curved roofs of the station seemed to have survived the recent bombing without damage. As on the streets of Liverpool, gusts of wind produced flurries of dust to cover every surface possible, but this dust was black – a mixture of acrid soot and brick dust. The platforms were thronged with people, including several children, some with pillow cases slung over a shoulder containing their belongings. They looked so pathetic, many dressed in their school uniforms, holding each other's hands. Clearly, some parents had now reconsidered their decision of the year before to keep their children at home. Who could blame them, Stephen thought.

At long last, he arrived at the front of the queue. The man behind the window of the ticket office took his money and informed him that a train for Preston would be leaving at about two-thirty. He would just have to take his chances for a connection to Lancaster. There were plenty of trains going up to Carlisle. He couldn't be more specific. It was chaos on the network on account of Jerry and all this bombing. Stephen checked his watch. It was only a little after one o'clock. There was nothing for it but to wait it out. He joined another long queue at the station buffet.

Stephen didn't have much of an appetite. He never ate much as he was anxious to avoid putting on too much weight. As a result, his tall frame of five-feet-eleven-inches in height had a gangly look and his clothes hung on him loosely. Since his school days, he had always been a keen athlete and at university he had been awarded not just his blue, but the *Victor Ludorum* trophy for his performances in the 100 metres, 200 metres and long jump events. When it was his turn to place his order, he merely ordered a cup of tea. He had planned to buy a Wet Nelly, but the sight of the thin layer of dust over them had put him off. Now he looked for a table at which he could sit to while away the next hour. It didn't look as if he would be in luck. Like the rest of the station, the buffet was crowded with fellow passengers.

As he gave up the attempt and resigned himself to wedging himself into a corner, standing to drink his tea, he heard somebody calling 'Stephen'. It was a common enough name so he paid it no attention, but then he heard the same person calling out, 'Cunningham you clot. Over here. Look over here.'

He turned and peered in the direction of the person calling. 'Stephen, come over this way.' To his surprise, the man calling him was his former professor from university, James Chadwick. The sight of a friendly face cheered him greatly. Taking great care to avoid spilling his tea, Stephen barged his way through the crowd across to the opposite side of the buffet. Chadwick, meanwhile, was persuading an old lady to move along one space at the end of her table so that he and Stephen might sit together.

'Stephen, how nice. I thought it was you. Didn't you see me waving? No. Clearly not. I forgot your eyesight is a little on the dim side. Come take a seat. This lady has kindly made room for you.'

Stephen hadn't seen Chadwick since June 1936. Chadwick had joined the University of Liverpool the year before from the Cavendish Laboratory at Cambridge after being awarded the Nobel Prize for Physics for his work in discovering the neutron in 1932. On his arrival at Liverpool, he had immediately set about upgrading the university's antiquated laboratory facilities and, by persuading the university's great and the good to install a cyclotron machine for accelerating charged atomic particles, he had transformed the place into one of the world's foremost centres for the study of nuclear physics. His work on the use of neutrons as a possible weapon in the fight against cancer had attracted Stephen to spend the last year of his degree specialising in the study of nuclear physics.

'So, what brings you to this crowded hole, Stephen? I see no luggage.'

Stephen felt embarrassed as Chadwick's searching gaze fell on his ill-matching trousers. He felt shabby by comparison with his former professor, dressed in a made-to-measure, grey, double-breasted suit with a silk tie.

'I'm g-g-going home. I've b-b-been b-b-bombed out, sir.'

'My! That is bad news.' Chadwick seemed unsure what to say and began to polish his handsome, gold-framed spectacles. Stephen thought of the unfavourable comparison with his celluloid-framed spectacles. It was another reminder of his present circumstances. He sipped his tea in silence and briefly wondered what might have been had he accepted Chadwick's invitation to study under him for a doctorate, but quickly dismissed the thought. Although he was not as committed a Quaker as his father, he was still a pacifist.

'I seem to recall your home is in the sticks somewhere, isn't it?' Chadwick examined the lenses of his spectacles and, apparently satisfied, replaced them. 'Have you a job to go to? You're still teaching, I assume?'

'Y-y-yes, sir. And n-n-no. I mean, I d-d-do live in the c-c-countryside and I was t-t-teaching in Aigburth, b-b-but the s-s-s-school's b-b-been bombed out, too.' Stephen finished his sentence with relief and saw the look of patient pity in Chadwick's eyes. For some reason his stutter seemed more pronounced in Chadwick's presence today. It hadn't always been thus.

'Gosh, that is hard luck. Aigburth, hey. You know what they say of that round here?' Stephen nodded silently, but Chadwick carried on nonetheless. 'Egg, buth no bacon. Er, yes, it is a tired joke,' he added in response to Stephen's pained expression. 'And you've nothing lined up, I suppose?' Stephen didn't bother to reply, but shook his head instead. Chadwick checked his watch. Stephen knew the signs. Chadwick would look for an excuse to cut the conversation short. It often happened this way.

'Tell me. When's your train? Mine's not for half an hour yet. I'm off up to London. Have you time for a short walk? We can't talk freely here. Walls have ears.' Chadwick gestured with his eyes to the people crammed in the table around them. Stephen noted how Chadwick had retained his habit of firing off questions in succession. That suited Stephen as it meant he didn't have to respond at length. He nodded and rose from the table, gathered his coat over his arm and stood back to allow the professor a path to the exit of the buffet.

Without discussion, Chadwick led him past Saint George's Hall to Saint John's Gardens. It was only once they had found a park bench on which to sit that Chadwick resumed their earlier conversation. It was a warm day and he removed his hat. Stephen didn't have one to remove.

'Look, I've been thinking, Stephen. There's no reason why a bright fellow like you should be without a job. The country needs such minds at present and frankly, you're wasted teaching kids.'

Stephen knew what was coming. It was why he had turned down the offer of study for a doctorate, but he didn't interrupt his former mentor.

'To win this infernal war we're going to need brains as well as the courage of our fighting men. I know of plenty of people who would give their eye-teeth to have you working on their teams. What d'you say?'

'You mean to research w-w-weapons, sir? You know my f-f-feelings on the s-subject.'

'I do, indeed, Stephen,' Chadwick replied wistfully. 'I still regret your decision to turn down a doctorate. You have a brilliant scientific mind, Stephen.'

'B-b-but you wanted me to w-w-work on an idea for a n-n-neutron bomb, sir! Something that c-c-could k-k-kill thousands of p-p-people.'

'I'm sorry. I shouldn't have raised the matter, but let's not debate that now. There are plenty of other fields of research not related to munitions where we could harness your talents. In the field of detection systems, for example. You could work on radio range finding. That might help put an end to this dreadful bombing. Would that fit in with your pacifist scruples?'

Stephen thought about it for a while before replying. 'It w-w-would still be a w-w-weapon of war, sir. Helping m-men to k-k-kill other men.'

'I see.' From the expression on Chadwick's face, Stephen could see that the professor didn't really understand his point of view, but he didn't feel obliged to justify his beliefs. 'Look, I'll tell you what. I have to catch my train now, but write down the address and telephone number where you'll be staying for me.' Chadwick passed Stephen an elegant notebook with a gold-coloured pencil. 'I'm going to be in London for a fortnight attending various meetings with the scientific community, but I'll ask around and see whether we might find you gainful employment in a way that doesn't contradict your moral principles. Will you return with me to the station?' Chadwick took back his notebook.

'N-n-no thank you, sir. M-m-my train's not due for a w-w-while yet.'

'Well, I'll say goodbye then.' Both men rose and shook hands. 'Look after yourself, Stephen. I'll be in touch as soon as I can, but remember – your country needs you.'

Chadwick walked off at a brisk pace in the direction of the station and Stephen sat down again. As he did so, he felt a plop on his hatless head and his vision in one lens of his glasses was obliterated by the splatter of seagull excrement. According to Mother, that's a lucky sign, he thought. But in actual fact it's just crowned my day.

CHAPTER 9

Stephen read his father's copy of the *Daily Mirror* over a late breakfast at the table of his mother's small kitchen. The clock in the hall chimed nine times. He should have been helping Dad in the garage, but trade was slack. Dad only had Doctor Arkwright's car to service today and reckoned he could handle the pumps on his own. As he had said, since the introduction of petrol - or *motor spirit* as they had to call it now - rationing the year before, he was unlikely to be rushed off his feet and had managed well enough whilst Stephen had been away.

'Could you manage another egg, love?' Stephen's mother asked solicitously. 'I'm sorry I couldn't offer you any bacon, but it's on the ration and you've no book yet. We've plenty of eggs, though. The hens are laying right well just now.'

'N-n-no thanks, Mum. I've had quite enough, but I w-wouldn't mind another m-mug of tea. I'll get it.' Stephen rose from the table, but his mother put her hand on his shoulder.

'No, you just bide where you are and read the paper. You deserve a good rest after what you've been through. I don't know. No home, no job. What are we to do with you?'

Stephen returned to the newspaper. 'Have you read this, Mum? The Germans have s-started bombing London n-now.'

'I heard it on the wireless early this morning, love. That Hitler. He deserves a right good punch on the nose. Don't you tell your Dad I said that. It'd offend his pacifist scruples.' She and Stephen laughed at the thought.

'You f-forget that I'm a p-pacifist, too, Mum.'

'I know, but you know what I mean. You don't go on about it quite the same. Look at the to-do we had over your idea of enlisting in the Home Guard. Your Dad would rather we were all raped and murdered in our beds by those horrible Nazis than raise a hand to defend us. Is there anything else in the paper, love?'

'Not much. It's all about the w-w-war, of course. They say the RAF shot d-down 68 enemy b-b-bombers, but the d-docks fared badly.'

'Anything on Liverpool, love?'

Stephen scanned the rest of the newspaper whilst chewing his dry toast. 'N-n-no, it seems to have been spared since I left.'

'That might be good news, then. Couldn't you find another teaching post, Stephen? The kids have still to be educated, war or no war.'

'Of course, I'll try, b-b-but look how long it took to find my last p-p-post. Only the f-factories and the army seem to be taking on anybody n-now.'

'Oh, Stephen! I didn't take on two jobs to get you through the grammar school and university for you to work in a factory now.'

'W-w-well the army's n-n-not an acceptable option to D-D-Dad either, is it? Anything that m-m-might support the w-w-war effort is a n-n-no-go area. I s-s-suppose…'

'Calm yourself, Stephen. You're getting' yourself all of a lather. Now there's a fresh pot of tea. Just let it brew awhile and relax.' Jane Cunningham kissed her son on the forehead. 'Now, let me take your plate and I'll finish the washing up.'

Stephen blew on his tea to cool it and looked around the kitchen whilst his mother worked at the sink. He had always liked this room. It's solid-oak furniture somehow seemed to represent the family. Although he and Dad didn't agree on politics or the war, Stephen and his younger sister felt they belonged to a solid family and Mum was at its heart. Whenever he was away from home, he always pictured Mum in the kitchen, baking, cooking or helping them with their homework when he and Lucy were children.

'I c-could work on the land. I don't m-mind manual labour and we need to feed the nation. Even D-D-Dad couldn't object to that.' Stephen felt better that his stammer was back under control.

'It's still not what I want for you, lad. In any case, they're takin' on lasses for the job now. This new Land Army. Mind you, you might find a bonny lass there.'

'None bonnier than you, M-Mum.' His remark caused his mother to smile and, despite her greying hair and tired face, the effect made her look younger. Stephen loved that smile and it was rarely replaced by a frown, despite a life of bringing up two children on little money.

'I'm off to peg out the washing.' Jane lowered the drying rack from above the range and began to transfer the garments into a basket.

'Mum, just before you g-go. I've had an idea, but I'm not sure how D-D-Dad would take it. I'd like your advice.'

'On you go, then, but make it quick. It's another sunny day and I don't want to waste it.'

'I was g-g-given the idea in Liverpool and I've been thinking about it these past couple of days. I met this s-s-sergeant in the army. He was in bomb disposal and he told me…'

'You're not thinking of bomb disposal, love? Surely not.'

'Hear me out, Mum. He said that there were quite a few C-Conscientious Objectors serving alongside him and they were d-doing a good job. It struck me that I might do that. I'd be s-saving lives and not taking them. What do you think?'

'Well, I can see that right enough. But wouldn't it be dangerous?'

'I'd say no more dangerous than serving on the f-front line… or living in London or Liverpool during this b-bombing.' Stephen shuddered at the memory of his last night in the air raid shelter. 'In any case, surely we've all to d-do our bit in this w-war? After all, D-D-Dad served in the last war.'

'Yes, and we all know how that panned out. Gassed at Wipers and a dodgy lung ever since.' Jane folded the washing whilst Stephen sipped his tea, but as she gathered up her basket, Jane asked, 'Do you think they'd make you an officer, Stephen… with your degree and the like?' Stephen was surprised that she sounded quite excited.

'I very much doubt it, Mum. I've no m-military experience. I expect I'd just be d-digging to make room for the experts to work. In any case, I'm no born leader and I s-stutter in the p-presence of people I don't know. I'd be a laughing stock in a p-position of authority.'

'You can't say that, Stephen. When you're not frettin' your stutter's not too bad. You don't know what you can do until you've tried it, but I don't like the idea of you crawling about in holes. You're worth more than that.'

Stephen finished his tea. 'Perhaps you're right, Mum, but I can't hang around here all d-day doing nothing. When were the hives last inspected?'

'Last Tuesday. The bees are still active in this fine weather and there's the heather to feed on.'

'Good. I m-might check them later in the m-morning.'

'You do that, love. I'm sure they'd be pleased to see you again. I tell you what. If you put in the clearer boards, you could take the honey off them tomorrow for me. You know I hate that job.'

'Fine, Mum, but I'll f-first go f-for a walk around the village.'

*****

'So, Ernst, I finally get to see you in an air force uniform. Congratulations on your promotion.'

'Thank you, Max. And my congratulations to you on your Knight's Cross.'

His younger brother fingered the Knight's Cross with Oak Leaves at his throat in response. He had been awarded it in June following the success of *Case Red*, the campaign to subjugate France. 'Ach, I didn't deserve it. It was like shooting fish in a barrel. The Dutch and the French folded like a card pyramid. All my *Junkers* 87s had to do was turn up on demand to break up any mounting counter attacks. Then General Guderian's tanks had all the fun. They smashed through the enemy lines like a knife through butter to cut them off from the coast. The Chief of Staff reckoned it was like calling a taxi. In as little as ten, and no more than forty-five, minutes after receiving a request from the army, we were blasting a path for the tanks. It was… exhilarating. Certainly, our finest hour.'

Max's bright-blue eyes shone with pride. Whilst his elder brother had taken their father's looks with his dark hair and brown eyes, Max had his mother's eyes and fair hair. People rarely believed them to be brothers. Ernst smiled outwardly at his brother's pride in his success, but inwardly he resented his sibling's glory. Was it not all thanks to him, the dull older brother, after all? It was Ernst who had scrimped and saved to keep his younger brother for five years after the war. It was he who had found him the job with Aero Lloyd and financed his lessons to become a glider pilot. That had led to Max's job as a pilot with Deutsche Luft Hansa and recruitment into the *Luftwaffe* in 1933. None of Max's success could have been achieved without the support of the cripple now sitting before him.

'I can imagine the experience was… enthralling, dear brother. My work seems dull by comparison, Max, but I think it may prove no less important.'

Ernst looked disapprovingly at Little Maxi's attire. Arrogantly, in Ernst's opinion, Max was wearing his aviator's leather jacket in the restaurant of one of Lübeck's finer hotels when, like most other diners, Ernst was wearing his service dress. He glanced around the room. It was full and the wine was flowing in proportion to the volume of gay chatter. He sipped his own wine before changing the subject from the fall of France.

'And is your room comfortable, Max?'

'Not bad. Better than the barracks in Jagel anyway. I'm sorry I could only be spared the one night, Ernst, so we will have to make the most of it. Cheers.'

'Cheers.' The two brothers clinked their glasses together. 'Your telegram didn't mention why you are in Schleswig-Holstein. It's a long way from France.'

Max lowered his voice and leaned across the table closer to his brother. 'Not for long, Ernst. We've just a week of anti-shipping practice in the Baltic and then we're back to France. From now on our targets are British shipping. For once, dear brother, we have common targets. Let's drink to success.'

Max drained his glass and discovered with obvious disappointment that the nearby wine bottle was empty. Ernst noted this with disapproval. He had still to finish his first glass of wine. However, he signalled to a waiter to bring another bottle. Little Maxi's face had already begun to flush a little to a shade of pink sharply contrasting with the blonde of his closely-cropped hair and the blue of his slowly-dulling eyes. Again, it struck Ernst that his little brother resembled the true Aryan warrior. What must people think of me by comparison with my thinning hair and missing hand, he wondered.

The waiter uncorked another bottle of wine and poured each of the brothers a fresh glass. 'Heil Hitler.' Ernst raised his glass in a toast. However, Max paused his glass in mid-air and his face betrayed a look of puzzlement.

'Cheers,' he replied before taking a large sip of his wine. 'I'd forgotten you're still a member of the Nazi Party, Ernst. You should have been one of Dönitz's U-boat men.'

'Hush, Maxi. It wouldn't do to be overheard. The Party has been good to us. Just remember how far we've come since the *Führer* came to power. Ten years ago, you had no job nor any prospect of getting one. Then came a good job, a career in the air force and now… you're a war hero.'

'All right, all right, Ernst. I'm not ungrateful. Just don't expect me to be a fanatic, that's all. You know I'm not happy with some of the Nazi policies. Take the way the Nuremburg Laws are being interpreted.'

'You mean on the protection of German blood? But we've no cause to be worried, Max. We're both of pure German blood.'

'Maybe. Look at this.' Max reached into his jacket and extracted his wallet. He pulled out a photograph of a girl and passed it to Ernst. 'What d'you think of her, Ernst?'

Ernst thought the woman's looks very striking. She had dark, collar-length hair, bright eyes and a beautifully curved mouth with evenly-spaced teeth. 'My Little Maxi! She's beautiful. Who is she?'

'She's called Else.' Max took the photograph back and gazed at it lovingly. 'She's my girlfriend and I think I love her.'

'I admire your taste. But what's worrying you?'

'She's an eighth Jewish.'

'Never! Let me see again.' Ernst snatched the photograph back and scrutinised it carefully. 'She doesn't look Jewish.'

'I know, but nonetheless, her great-grandmother was.'

Ernst returned the photograph. 'I can't see you've anything to worry about. By the race laws, she's still considered German-blooded and entitled to citizenship of the *Reich*.'

'But for how long, Ernst? How much longer?' Max didn't wait for an answer before drinking more wine. 'Let's change the subject.' Max put away the photograph and his wallet. 'Let's drink to the invasion of Britain,' he said quietly.

'Do you think it'll be soon, Max?' Ernst, too, spoke softly.

'I suppose it has to be. I cannot see the British people taking much more of our bombing. Personally, I think we should still be pummelling the British air force rather than the cities. Our troops will need air superiority if they are to cross the Channel in safety, but I suppose the fat *Reichsmarschall* knows what he's doing. How's your *Labskaus*?'

Much as Ernst liked the Lübeck version of the traditional seaman's dish of corned beef, mashed potato and pickled herring, he wished he had opted for Max's choice of roast suckling pig. 'It's very good. You know I always enjoy it. And your pork?'

'Excellent.' He took a large gulp of wine. 'Where was I? What were we talking about?'

'The invasion of Britain, Max, but keep your thoughts on Göring to yourself. You know walls have ears.'

Max leaned forward and put an index finger to the side of his nose. 'Quite right, big brother. I was saying that we should be knocking out the enemy air force. They can't have many pilots left. My *Stukas* can take care of the British navy, but we don't want enemy fighters around. We should be flattening their airfields, not killing civilians.'

'But I'm told the raids were ordered by the *Führer* himself, Max. In retaliation for the terror-flyers' raid on Berlin.'

'Yes, I heard that, Ernst, but do you know what one of my engineers thinks? A clever man that. Not a pilot, of course, but still a clever man. Hans thinks we should change the fuzes on our bombs. Instead of having them explode on impact, we should fit our bombs with some form of delayed action fuze. You're the expert on these things. What do you think?'

'I don't follow, Max. Everything I've read and heard suggests that our bombing campaign is having a devastating impact on Britain's war machine and civilian morale. The incendiary bombs are most effective.'

'Maybe, Ernst, but Hans is a scheming bastard. He thinks that a delayed action bomb would create more disruption. Imagine. The area would have to be cleared. That means factories closed down more effectively than by a couple of bombs. Transport systems shut down. People evacuated from their homes. How long do you think a civilian population would put up with that, Ernst? It's a cunning plan, but I'm just a simple pilot. I leave it to you chaps on the General Staff to do the clever thinking. Now drink up. I can't drink this bottle on my own. I'm flying tomorrow afternoon.'

Ernst allowed his glass to be refilled and as he took a deep draught of the wine, he thought about what his brother had just said. This engineer might, indeed, be a clever man. The British thought their terror-flyers could create fear in German cities and Ernst assumed the German air force must already be using delayed action fuzes on its bombs, but he knew of a weapon that would be far more effective at spreading terror in the enemy's civilian population.

CHAPTER 10

Stephen returned from his walk to find his mother in a state of excitement.

'There's a telegram for you, Stephen love.' She held out the envelope with a trembling hand. 'I hope it isn't bad news.' She continued to watch over Stephen as he ripped open the envelope and read the piece of paper within.

Stephen read the message over again and then placed the paper in his pocket. He looked into his mother's anxious face and smiled. 'It's nothing bad, Mum. It's from P-Professor Chadwick. You remember him. M-my tutor at university.'

Jane relaxed at the news. 'Yes. I remember him. You and he had some form of disagreement by my reckoning, so you gave up on your doctorate.'

'S-something like that, Mum, but we p-parted on good terms. Indeed, I saw him only a c-couple of days ago. He says he's f-found me a job… in London.'

'In London? But it's not safe with this bombing, love.'

'Maybe, b-but I can't s-stay here and Liverpool's just as d-dangerous.'

'I see.' Jane slumped onto a chair at the kitchen table. 'And what is this job and when are you to start?'

'I don't know, M-Mum. It's secret. I'm to report f-for interview right away. You read it.' Stephen withdrew the telegram from his pocket and passed it to his mother.

Jane fetched her reading spectacles from her sewing table in the living room and returned to the kitchen table. 'It says here you're to report to a Captain Currey at the Admiralty. What would the navy want with you, Stephen? You know nothing about the sea or boats. And you're to show this telegram to the local police station and ask them for a railway warrant. What's one of them?'

'I d-don't know, Mum, but I'd b-better pack a case.'

'Well, you're not leaving this afternoon. You wouldn't get to London afore the middle of the night and you've nowhere to stay.

We'll go and see PC Ryding and find out what this warrant thing is. Then we'll tell your Dad.'

*****

Stephen arrived in London in the middle of the following afternoon, having exchanged the rail warrant issued him by PC Ryding for a return ticket to London. He proceeded from Euston Station to The Aldwych by bus. It was only a half-hour walk, but the upper deck of the bus gave him a good view of the many changes that had taken place in London since his last visit as a student. Sadly, many of the changes had been brought about by Göring's bombers. Even the station and its hotel had suffered. However, he was surprised to see that the Londoners seemed to be going about their business much as normal. The pedestrians below didn't seem to have the dazed look he had witnessed in Liverpool. The bus was delayed briefly by a contra-flow system set up to allow traffic to pass by another bus on its end, leaning into a row of terraced houses. Debris from the houses lay all about, but soldiers and ARP workers were busy working to clear it and had already cordoned off the bomb site with wooden barriers. As the bus passed Holborn underground station, Stephen noted that the underground appeared to be operating normally, but nearby firemen were tackling a fire in some offices still ablaze from the previous night's bombing. To the east, on his left, Saint Paul's Cathedral still stood proud of the surrounding buildings, like a beacon and seemingly undamaged.

He alighted on Kingsway and walked the short distance to Fanum House, the headquarters of the Automobile Association. An AA motorcycle with sidecar was parked across the road and although in the circumstances Stephen saw nothing unusual in the patrolman wearing a tin hat, he was surprised to see his vehicle painted in khaki. It wasn't something he had seen in the north. Like most office entrances, the entrance to Fanum House was surrounded by a wall of sandbags. Stephen showed his telegram to the security guard and was directed into the main entrance hall. There, he reported to a second guard and was instructed to sit down and wait.

Stephen rubbed the toecaps of his shoes against the back of his trouser legs, polished his spectacles and smoothed his dark hair to lie flat over to his right side. He wished he had possessed a suit, but it had been lost in the bombing of his digs in Liverpool. Although still smartly dressed in his tweed jacket and flannel trousers, he was conscious that the addition of his battered leather suitcase gave him the appearance of a travelling salesman.

After a wait of five minutes, he heard his name called. Looking up, he saw a naval officer approaching with two thick gold rings on his sleeves and a thinner one in between. Stephen didn't know the officer's rank, but recognised the naval uniform from his days in Liverpool. Now it struck him how the navy and gold combination with the double row of buttons on the jacket looked much smarter than the khaki of army uniforms.

'Follow me,' he was instructed.

Stephen picked up his suitcase and duly followed the naval officer through a doorway marked, *'No Entry Except on Authorised Business'*. The door led to a larger, but darkened room. From the light of the far-off open doorway, he could see half a dozen coffin-like objects, covered in white sheets. The hairs stood up on the back of his neck. Stephen had never been in a chapel of rest, but this is how he imagined one would look. He shuddered at the thought and quickened his step in the trail of the officer ahead. He was led into an office in which stood another naval officer, this one with four stripes on his sleeves.

'Cunningham, sir,' the first officer announced and withdrew, shutting the office door behind him.

'Well done, Cunningham. I'm very glad you made it here. Take a pew.' The second officer gestured for Stephen to take a seat. He had a deep voice that seemed to bounce off the walls and spoke directly. 'My name's Captain Norman Currey and I want you to become one of my élite officers in my Bomb and Mine Disposal Department.'

Stephen was too stunned to reply. His brain focused on the words *'élite officers'* and *'bomb disposal'*.

'You've come highly recommended to me by Professor Chadwick,' Currey continued and picked up a document from his desk. 'A keen mind, or so he says. First in Physics from Liverpool University and should have gone on to gain a good PhD, but opted for teaching instead. A waste of talent according to Chadwick. So, what do you think? Not any relationship to ABC by any chance?'

'ABC, sir?' Stephen spoke at last.

'Admiral A B Cunningham, C-in-C Med.'

'N-n-no, sir. I've no c-c-connection with the n-n-navy.'

'Relax, old chap. I'm not here to eat you. We need you too much for that. Just catch your breath and come with me.' Currey opened the door and indicated for Stephen to precede him.

Stephen walked back into the darkened room and heard some clicks behind him. Slowly, the room was bathed in light from a huge gantry hanging from the ceiling. Currey overtook him and went up to one of the coffin-like objects draped in a sheet. 'Now what I'm going to tell you is secret, Cunningham. You are not to discuss it with anyone else for now. Understood?'

Without waiting for an answer, like a magician, Currey pulled a sheet completely away from the object beneath. To Stephen's relief, he saw that it was not a coffin, but, nonetheless, it looked very sinister. It was black, long and cylindrical with a bulbous end on which somebody had painted a caricature of Winston Churchill smoking a cigar.

'This is Hitler's latest terror weapon, Cunningham. The *Luftwaffe*'s been dropping them all over London and a few other cities.'

'W-w-what is it, s-sir? It seems too large and the wrong shape to b-b-be a b-b-bomb.'

'Well spotted, Cunningham. It's not a bomb. It's something more terrifying. A mine.' Currey paused to allow Stephen to interrupt, but Stephen remained silent. 'You probably think a mine's an underwater weapon and are wondering why they're being dropped on cities. Well, water's where they belong, sure enough, but some bugger's worked out that these monsters can cause more destruction than your ordinary bomb. For a start, they carry a ton of explosive. That's twice as much as a conventional bomb. But whereas a bomb sinks into the ground before exploding, these buggers come down by parachute and get caught up in buildings, trees or anything. That means they don't go off immediately and when they do, the blast is above ground and kills more people.'

'You say they d-d-don't explode immediately, sir.' Stephen remembered his conversation with the sergeant in Liverpool a life time previously. 'So, you have to c-c-cordon off the area and that c-c-creates d-disruption?'

'Bang on, Cunningham. You are sharp. You're going to fit in well on my team.'

'B-b-but why me, sir? I d-don't know anything about m-mines, sir. I thought you w-w-wanted me to work on research.'

'Because of your background in physics, Cunningham. I haven't mentioned it yet, but these aren't any ordinary mines and there may be worse to come. They're what we call an influence mine, fired by proximity to magnetism. We have a team in Portsmouth who've worked out the secret for dealing with them for themselves, but Jerry's upping the ante all the time. Now he's started throwing them all over the place, the *Vernon* boys are too busy to deal with them all. I'm setting up a team to deal with these monsters wherever they land in the country and to work out what Jerry's up to next. I can't be sure - and this is most secret, Cunningham - but we think they've moved onto an acoustically-triggered device. Imagine what chaos that would inflict on a noisy city.'

'B-b-but I know nothing of the n-n-navy, sir – or m-m-mine disposal.'

'Don't worry about that. It doesn't take as long to train a naval officer as it does a physicist. Six weeks at *King Alfred* and two weeks at *Vernon* and we'll have you at your first mine.'

'K-K-King Alfred, sir?'

'It's near Hove. We've taken over Lancing College and a girl's school to train all RNVR officers and you'll become an RNVR Special Duties officer. I've booked you to start on Monday.' Currey waved and the other naval officer appeared, as if by magic. Stephen hadn't seen him approach. 'Lieutenant Commander Foster will sort out all the admin *bumph* with you and fix you accommodation for the night. You can travel home tomorrow, but we'll expect you in Hove on Sunday. Welcome to the team, Cunningham.' Currey shook Stephen's hand and disappeared back into his office.

*****

That evening, as Stephen lay in bed in the hostel at which he was staying, he recalled the day's events. Nobody had asked him to volunteer. It had just been assumed that he would agree – to make his contribution to the war effort. He quite liked that approach. Similarly, he wasn't being asked to become a scientist to research these new weapons. He would be required to disarm them. He shivered at the thought and the memory of the line of the shrouded mines, but for some reason, the thought appealed to him. To think - next week he would be a Special Duties Temporary Acting Sub Lieutenant in the RNVR. He imagined himself wearing the smart uniform of a naval officer. Mum would be proud, but breaking the news to Dad would be a challenge.

CHAPTER 11
October 1940

Seven weeks later, resplendent in his new uniform, Stephen stepped off the train from London. He had never visited Portsmouth before and it had a different atmosphere to that of London and Liverpool. Liverpool was very much a maritime city, with its long and not always proud history of shipping. Portsmouth's harbour was far smaller than the port of Liverpool and everything about the city reeked in some way of the Royal Navy. Disembarking at Portsmouth Harbour station, he had seen the tall masts of the grey warships berthed alongside the jetties. The train had been full of sailors, several of whom were now queuing to take a ferry across the harbour. Naval trucks and cars scurried about the streets like ants. His ears were assailed by the throbbing of diesel engines from the many boats crossing the harbour, shrill high-pitched notes of some form of whistle, muffled announcements over loudspeakers, and the *whoop, whoop, whoop* noises of the grey ships moored in the waterway, one of which was manoeuvring now. It was complete chaos.

   He approached what he now knew to be a petty officer. The rating was armed with a clipboard and was directing many of the young sailors alighting from the train in different directions. In response to his request for directions to HMS *Vernon*, the petty officer eyed the single, wavy, gold stripe on each of Stephen's sleeves with disdain before peremptorily pointing him towards a truck nearby in which several sailors were hoisting their kitbags. Stephen noted how the petty officer had not saluted him, but he lacked the confidence to upbraid the man. Instead, he trudged over to the truck indicated and joined the queue to board the truck for what proved to be a very short journey to the Royal Navy's centre for mine warfare, HMS *Vernon*.

*****

'Right gentlemen. This is the beast. The magnetic mine. Horrible thing ain't it?'

Stephen thought their instructor, Petty Officer Dawlish, rather young to be such a senior rating. He guessed he was of the same age as him or possibly even younger since Dawlish's beard might make him appear older than his true age. The lecture was being given in the mining shed of HMS *Vernon* and Stephen was accompanied by three other students. One, an American officer, he had met at *King Alfred*. The other two were both lieutenants in the RNVR and closer to thirty years of age.

'Now for the time being, we're going to concentrate on the magnetic mine. Next week, there'll be time for bombs, ack-ack shells and the like, but this week we're focused on mines… and I mean we're really focused on them, sir.' Dawlish gave a pointed look at the tall, bearded lieutenant on the course who had just passed a remark to his fellow lieutenant, an extraordinary-looking officer with a bright-red, pointed beard and a moustache whose ends were curled.

'Now look at this contraption in the cradle.' Stephen and the other students peered at the object only the size of a tea caddy. 'That's the heart and secret of the mine, sirs, and it's a beautiful piece of engineering. If the thing wasn't so ruddy dangerous, I'd say it was a work of art. Anything magnetic comes near it, that little needle flickers. Watch.' The petty officer fetched a coin from the bench near him and passed it over the magnetic unit.

'See how the needle moves, but the magnetic pull's not quite enough to close the electrical circuit to fire the detonator. Then we'd have three-quarters of ton of TNT lobbing us up to collect our wings and harps from the angel Gabriel. But don't worry, gentlemen. We've steamed out the explosive. Can't do us no harm now.' The red-bearded lieutenant had taken a pace backwards.

'So, as I was saying, if the magnetic pull is powerful enough - take a ship for example – the detonator fires the primer and the primer fires the charge. The explosion cracks the hull of the ship like a cold dish on a hot stove, the ship goes down and that's that.'

'Ah, but I thought we were degaussing our ships now, PO,' the dark-bearded lieutenant, Charles Lawson, asked. Stephen hadn't taken to Lawson when they'd met the night before in the bar of the wardroom. Lawson had been serving at sea in a minelayer since the beginning of the war.

'Quite right, sir. What Lieutenant Lawson means is that we change the magnetic field of our ships to cloak them from setting off these here mines. But don't you worry your privileged little heads about sea mines as you ain't going to be concerned with them. You chaps are going to be concerned with them on land.

'Now remember what I just showed you about coins. Watch what happens when I pass this spanner over the magnetic unit.' Stephen watched the magnetic needle inside flicker once more, but this time it made an electrical circuit that lit an electric lamp to one side of it.

'What that light means, sirs, is that you're dead. Don't worry about the cost of a funeral, though. There won't be enough left to bury. RMS officers don't have no graves. Over the next fortnight, I'm going to let you pull this mine to bits as often as you like. Do it blindfold if you can, but remember what I told you just now. Ferrous metal will kill you, sure as eggs is eggs. Before you go anywhere near one of these bastards or what you think might be one of these bastards, mind you empty your pockets. You leave behind your fancy cigarette cases, jewelled tie-pins and silver hip flasks - even your watch. The buttons of your jacket are all right. They're brass, but watch what anybody else in the vicinity is wearing, too. You take off your belt buckle and your braces. Invest in non-magnetic braces or accept your trousers will fall down. You don't bring pocket knives, old screws, coins or anything metal anywhere near these bastards and you only use non-magnetic tools. That's Lesson Number One. You got that, gentlemen?'

Stephen nodded with his colleagues. Like him, they seemed subdued by the instructor's words.

'Now in a moment I'm going to take you all for some exercise and fresh air. But before I do, I'd like you to look at this.' He held aloft a small cylindrical, metal object. 'Not much of a thing is it, but it's your first job on land and your first danger. It's the bomb fuze. There's two problems with it. Firstly, even when you've removed it from the mine, it contains enough explosive to blow your hand off, so always put it in one of these shock-proofed cases. The second, is that it contains a time clock and that's what we're going to learn about now. Follow me gentlemen. We're off to the rugby pitches.'

*****

A short while later, the four officer students assembled with Dawlish at the nearby United Services rugby ground. The on-shore wind from the sea blew across the pitches, scattering several recently fallen leaves from the nearby trees. None of the officers were wearing their great coats and the wind cut through their serge reefer jackets. The red-bearded officer beat his sides and jumped up and down on the spot.

'Don't you gentlemen worry about the cold. I'll have that sorted very soon. Each of you muster over there.' Dawlish pointed to the furthest of five horizontal lines the physical training staff had marked out, spaced about one hundred yards apart.

'Time for Lesson Number Two.' Dawlish held up the bomb fuze again. 'This clock will run for seventeen seconds. If you hear that clock tick, you run like Hell. You see a ten-foot wall in your way, you leap over it. You spot a beautiful women, starkers, on the way, you don't stop to tickle her fancy. Your aim is to be 400 yards from your mine when that clock stops running. That's the farthest marker over there.'

'Run 400 yards in seventeen seconds, PO? You must be joking?' Lawson commented.

'It ain't no joke, sir. It's a matter of life or death. And just to make life more interesting, sometimes the clock stops. Something sets it going and a speck of debris stops it or such like. You come against it and you've no idea whether it's got ten seconds left to run, five or even none. It's a bummer right enough. What we call life in a blue suit. So, if you're ready, gentlemen, I'm going to start the clock on this fuze and let's see how far you can get before it runs down. No sports kit or gym shoes, mind. You're dressed just as you'd be dealing with a mine. So, take your marks.' The officers spread apart with one foot on the white line in the grass. 'Get set. Go!'

Everyone sprinted as if their lives depended on it and Stephen, as a former winner of the Victor Ludorum trophy for athletics at university, quickly took the lead. Within no time at all, they heard the crack of a starting pistol and stopped running. Only Stephen had made it beyond the 100-yard marker with the American just short of it. The two lieutenants had barely covered 80 yards. Both were doubled up gasping for breath. Dawlish gave them time to recover and drew them closer to him again.

'So, gentlemen, you're all dead. Accept it now, sirs. As RMS officers, you're dead already. Now every day you live is a bonus. That's Lesson Number Two. But I've got a couple of tips that might just see you through to draw your next tobacco ration. First, get yourselves fit. Your life might depend on it. Secondly, think about your escape route. Now you've proved you can't run 400 yards in the time, but you'd be amazed how far you might get with the adrenaline glands pumping furiously. In the open, you might just make 250 yards, so dig some form of hole or trench in which you can dive head first. More often than not, you'll be in a city, so look out for walls behind which you can take shelter. If you're working in the docks, jump in the water. And if neither option is available, just keep your hand in with God and pray.'

*****

'So, what does one make of our Petty Officer Dawlish then, darlings?' the red-bearded student asked over dinner in the wardroom that evening. Stephen didn't like the way that Reginald Bacon spoke. It seemed so affected and reminded him of his undergraduate days when such students had often been given a ducking in one of the nearby docks. However, Bacon had introduced himself as a former actor before the war, so perhaps all actors behaved that way, he thought.

'He s-s-seems quite young and c-c-competent,' Stephen replied.

'Probably licked a few arses to get the rate,' Charles Lawson offered. 'He can't have been in the mob more than ten years.'

'Ah, but boys, didn't you notice the medal ribbon on his chest? Navy with two vertical white stripes,' the American, Dwight Johnson the Third replied.

'Hardly, darling. It was such a dull colour on an already blue background. If I win any medals, I shall demand they have a bright-coloured ribbon… say orange or yellow.'

'What of it then, Yank?' Lawson asked.

'It's the DSM, the Distinguished Service Medal. He must have done something truly courageous and earned himself accelerated promotion.'

'Foolhardy more like,' Bacon suggested.

Stephen decided it would be best to change the subject. He turned to the American. 'W-w-what brings you to these shores, D-D-Dwight?'

'Same as the rest of you, I suppose. Action, adventure or maybe I just hate the Nazis. When war was declared between your country and Germany, I was already in Europe. I'd seen the effect of the Nazis on Germany, so I joined the American Ambulance Corps, but that didn't work out…' Johnson's voice trailed off.

'W-w-what happened?' Stephen pressed him.

'Oh, I was just captured by the Germans, made a prisoner-of-war and escaped. I made my way to England and volunteered to join up. Before I cut college, I studied mining engineering. I suppose it was somebody in the navy's idea of a joke that I should work with mines.' The remark caused an outbreak of laughter from the three listeners. It brought a steward over to clear their cheese plates.

'But what's with this fancy handle of "*Dwight the Third*"? It makes you sound like a king or something,' Lawson remarked.

'That's down to the sins of the father. My Pa's called Dwight and my Grandpa was, too. Pa's a senator in my home state of Virginia, and Grandpa fought with Jackson at Bull Run, so I figure they wanted Grandpa's name to live on.'

'It's a bit of a mouthful, though, luvvie. Dwight Johnson the Third. I don't think we can keep calling you that,' Bacon said.

'Just call me Dwight.'

'I know what we'll call you,' Lawson interjected excitedly. 'We'll call you Johnny.'

'W-w-why?' Stephen asked.

'You know. After Johnny Reb, the nickname for the Confederate soldiers,' Lawson replied with a look of scorn on his face.

'Whatever suits you guys,' Johnson responded, 'But just don't call me Billy.'

'B-Billy?' Stephen was just as confused.

'After Billy Yank. That's what our troops called those of the north,' Johnson replied. 'I'm no Yankee.' Stephen could see that this was new information to Lawson, too. Johnson pushed back his chair and placed his napkin on the dining table. 'Now what do you folks say to christening my new name with a proper drink? I'll treat you all to one of those pink gin things.'

'N-n-no thanks, Dwight. I'll just have c-coffee, thanks.' Stephen, also, rose from the table.

'I'll join you, Johnny,' Lawson said. 'But I'll have a whisky and buy my own. You know the mess rules. No treating.'

The four student RMS officers moved into the ante room of *Vernon*'s wardroom. Stephen fetched himself a coffee and sat alone in a corner of the mess doodling on a scrap piece of paper, a habit he often had when alone, but was soon joined by Johnson.

'Say, I couldn't leave you to drink alone. It's a bad sign you know.' Johnson sat down opposite Stephen and examined his tumbler of whisky. 'There are two things I miss about my country – cold beer and ice in my bourbon.'

Stephen said nothing in response and concentrated instead on his coffee. He would have preferred to have been left alone, but Johnson seemed keen to strike up a conversation.

'You don't say much, do you? If it's the stammer that's bothering you, don't worry about me, pardner. I've a little sister with a stammer far worse than yours and I just love her to bits.'

The last remark endeared Johnson to Stephen and he decided to make an effort at conversation. 'I'm s-sorry. I didn't mean to b-b-be anti-s-social.'

'No need to apologise, friend. I just thought we should get to know each other better. The two lieutenants over there seem to be keen to stick together.' Johnson indicated Lawson and Bacon, sitting on the other side of the ante room deep in conversation. It was only then as Stephen saw the glint of the wardroom lights being reflected off Johnson's face that he realised he was wearing spectacles, too. In Johnson's case, they comprised thin metal frames, barely noticeable.

'I d-didn't realise you wore s-spectacles.'

'Sure I do, but only when my eyes are tired. During the day I can see well enough, but it still cost me my career in the US Navy.'

'You applied f-for the US Navy, then?'

'Sure did. I even graduated from the academy, but they wouldn't give me a regular commission. That's why I went to a mining college.'

'So w-what brought you to B-Britain, D-Dwight?'

'Oh, call me Johnny like the rest of 'em have decided to. It kinda fits well enough, my surname being Johnson an' all. What brought me to England? I hankered for more of an outdoor sorta life than sticking my head down a mine. Figured I'd join a steamship company. That brought me to Europe and like I said earlier, I ended up in England. Say, what did you think of our PO's little fun this afternoon? Gee, you ran well.'

'I enjoy running. I've always d-done so.'

'I guess we'll just have to hope we never have to do it for real. It's kind of daunting, huh? What d'you think goes through a fella's mind if one has to do that? I mean, literally run for your life?'

Stephen thought about the question for a moment. 'I s-s-suppose you d-don't have time to think. You're t-too busy running and have to t-trust G-God to take c-care of you.'

some reason. Possibly, the vibration from their footsteps had started it running again. Or maybe the mine just had their names on it. Moore heard the explosion and was the first to see the two corpses. Thankfully, there's something left to bury and according to Moore, Ryan had a smile on his face. Typical Ryan.' Maitland-Dougall's voice broke and Monty could see his eyes water. He had never seen his captain show such emotion.

'He was probably thinking of his wife, sir. She's due to give birth any day.'

'Oh, Lord. I'd forgotten.' Maitland-Dougall groaned and slumped in his chair. 'This damned, damned war. Why must the innocent suffer? I'd better go and see her.'

Both officers were silent for a while, reflecting on their own memories of Ryan and Ellingworth. Monty thought he had never seen Maitland-Dougall look so old. He seemed robbed of his usual vigour. Eventually it was Monty that broke the silence.

'Would you like me to break the news to Mrs Ryan, sir? I knew Dick Ryan and Margaret quite well. Dick and I were the first two officers to work for your predecessor, sir.' Monty regretted adding the last remark. It didn't seem necessary and seemed designed to distance Maitland-Dougall from Ryan.

'I could leave first thing in the morning, sir. She's at a nursing home in Surrey. I didn't know Chief Ellingworth as well, sir.'

'Yes, Monty. I think that would be a good idea. I never knew Mrs Ryan. I'll telephone Commander M at *Vernon* and ask him to have someone break the news to Mrs Ellingworth. He was married, I take it?'

'I believe so, sir. Certainly, he had a son.'

The following morning, Monty had driven down to Surrey. He sobbed again at the memory of Margaret's calm courage on his visit. She had just said, 'Don't worry, Monty. I know. I've already heard the news. Joyce Thistleton-Smith came round to tell me after breakfast.' A few days later, she had lost the baby.

*****

Monty followed Commander M into the mining shed to address the throng of men assembled there. These included scientists, *Vernon*'s already experienced RMS officers and the latest batch of trainees. The large number of parachute mines being dropped on British cities during what was styled the *Blitz* had necessitated a call for dozens of volunteers to train to deal with them. DTMI hoped to form several teams comprising an officer and senior rate to be permanently stationed across the British Isles. Everyone came to attention on the entry of Commander M.

'Stand easy, gentlemen. Now I know that many of you already know Lieutenant Commander Montcalm from the Admiralty,' Commander M announced. Monty acknowledged the nods and smiles of several officers and scientists with whom he had already worked.

'And on your behalf, I congratulate him on his well-deserved promotion.'

'Hear, hear,' many in the shed responded, but Monty heard a familiar voice call, 'Bloody Hell! If it ain't Titch.' Half way back in the hall he recognised Charles Lawson amongst a group of other RNVR officers. Monty had been bullied by Lawson at Eton.

'Lieutenant Commander Montcalm has kindly agreed to give of his time to brief us all on Jerry's latest rather chilling development. Monty – over to you.' Thistleton-Smith stepped off the make-shift podium of crates to give way to Monty.

'Gentlemen, I'm here to warn you of a potentially new influence mine that we think the Germans have been using over the past six or so weeks,' Monty started. He scanned the audience and noted he had their rapt attention, but he deliberately avoided the eye of Lawson.

'Our suspicions were aroused at the end of August when a Dutch coaster was mined off the Humber. The explosion didn't occur directly under the ship as we would expect from a magnetic mine and the channel had already been swept for contact mines. A few days later, still off the Humber, the *Galatea* reported an explosion forty yards off her bows. A week later, the cruiser reported the same thing, but this time in the Thames estuary. Since then, we've had daily reports of odd explosions.' The news evoked some murmuring from the assembled men, but Monty continued.

'Our experts have come up with three potential theories. Firstly, they could be a ruse by the *Luftwaffe* to keep our shipping lanes closed. We know that until recently, they've been short of mines, so they might have been dropping conventional bombs with a delayed action fuze. It would keep our minesweepers busy looking for mines they couldn't possibly detonate.' Monty let that theory sink in and noted a few nods, but also, much scepticism on the faces of the experienced *Vernon* staff.

'Another option is that Jerry is deploying new and especially sensitive mines that have accidentally detonated due to changes in the earth's magnetic field. The RAF met. experts point to the fact that some of these mystery explosions have occurred during magnetic storms.' Monty was pleased to see the response to that theory from the audience was blank incredulity.

'However, Captain Maitland-Dougall and I subscribe to the theory that Germany has manufactured a mine that is activated by noise – an acoustic mine, in fact.' This latest theory was greeted by gasps and some muttering.

'As yet, we have recovered no such mine, but that doesn't mean it doesn't exist. Several MTBs have reported similar explosions twenty to thirty yards from their vessels when operating at high speeds. My own analysis shows that the majority of the merchant ships involved in these mystery explosions were noisy, diesel-engined coasters. If we are right…' Monty paused for effect. 'If we are right, that Jerry has produced an acoustic mine, those of you dealing with the bally things in cities are going to need to take extra care. The slightest noise of vibration could be enough to set the things off. We all know what happened to Dick Ryan and Reg Ellingworth,' Monty added sombrely.

*****

In the mess at lunchtime, following the talk by Lieutenant Commander Montcalm, Stephen sat with his course colleagues enjoying half a pint of bitter. Montcalm was at the bar with Commander M and a number of other officers.

'So, you know this Montcalm guy then, Charles?' Johnson asked.

'I do, Johnny. He was a couple of years my junior at Eton. Hark at him now, swanning around with his half stripe. The way some of the chaps spoke, you'd think he was some sort of expert on mines. Bet he's never seen one in his life.'

'Must have gotten that oak leaf on his breast for something, though,' Johnson retorted.

'Probably for shuffling paper. He went up to Oxford to study law after Eton.'

'And I suppose you have seen many mines in your illustrious career, dearhart?' Bacon twirled the ends of his moustaches.

'Dashed right I have. Laid plenty of them when I was in my minelayer.'

'So, what brings you to this dreary backwater to honour us with your presence, dear boy?' Bacon retrieved a red-spotted, silk handkerchief from his left sleeve and mopped his brow in an exaggerated fashion.'

'Action. That's what. True, I had a few hairy moments laying mines off the Friesians and running from E-boats, but speaking frankly,' Lawson lowered his voice and leaned forward. 'It's not going to win any DSOs is it?'

'W-w-what about MTBs?' Stephen asked. 'P-p-plenty of action there and b-b-back in time for tea and m-medals.'

'Hah! Some idiot thought me too old for MTBs.'

'And so, whilst the flotillas of MTBs mourn their loss of what might have been, luvvie, we are the one's blessed with your erudition, wit and charm. Oh, hark. The God is descending Olympus to speak with us mere mortals.' Stephen followed Bacon's gaze to see Montcalm approaching their table.

'Hello, Lawson. I thought I saw you in the hall. So, you've volunteered for Special Duties, too, then?'

'Indeed, Titch.' Stephen saw Montcalm wince at the nickname. 'I thought with my experience in a minelayer, I might be of some use. And what is it that brings you to our little circle? Are you preparing a case for the prosecution against Jerry for dropping mines in international waters… Titch?' Lawson added provocatively.

'We're not at Eton now, Lawson,' Montcalm responded.

'Ah, Eton on whose playing fields were won the Battle of Waterloo. But I seem to recall you weren't one to frequent those playing fields, were you, Titch?'

'No.' Montcalm coloured and tugged at his collar. 'Sailing was more my line, a pastime, perhaps more suited to a career in the navy than rugby.'

'Except you've not been to sea, have you, Titch? You've a nice, cushy job in London instead.'

Stephen noted that Bacon and Johnson seemed equally embarrassed by this exchange and Montcalm was now quite flushed.

'Indeed, Lawson, but might I remind you that I still carry a half stripe more than you and in future you will conform with the custom of calling me "sir".' Without another word, Montcalm returned to the bar.

Stephen decided he didn't like this Montcalm. Officers insisting upon being called "sir" before earning the respect of their subordinates didn't fit in with his Quaker upbringing, but then he didn't like Lawson either.

CHAPTER 13

Immediately following the explosives course at *Vernon*, Stephen and his fellow newly-qualified RMS officers were sent for two days to HMS *Excellent* on Whale Island, the Royal Navy's gunnery school. Stephen immediately hated the place. Everyone, even officers, was expected to run or 'double' about the place and, so it seemed to Stephen, drill sergeants – the navy called them gunnery instructors or GIs – littered the establishment, hiding behind bushes, fences, walls, anything in fact, ready to bawl at one for some failure to observe King's Regulations in one's dress, deportment or drill. No wonder, Stephen thought, that the place was described as 'all guts and gaiters'. It was a mad house. However, *Excellent* was, also, home to the RN's diving school. It had been decided that it may be necessary to render mines safe underwater and so a trial was underway to select suitable RMS officers for specialist diving training.

It was a grey day, with a leaden sky and a sharp, easterly wind that not only pierced Stephen's clothing, but raised a choppy sea in the harbour. He and the other three new RMS officers were taken three hundred yards across the water to an old tug that had been converted into a diver training unit. Even that short crossing had been rough enough to persuade Stephen that a life at sea was not one for him. Bacon seemed to be of the same mind, but Lawson just looked at them with scorn and Johnson took it in his stride. A red flag flew from a halyard on the tug to warn the myriad of small boats on the water to keep clear and reduce speed as the tug was conducting diving operations, but everyone seemed to ignore it.

There was no accommodation on the tug, so the four officers huddled by the wheelhouse to keep warm whilst a Scottish chief petty officer diver, 'Bunny' Warren, briefed them on their forthcoming dive. Anything less like a cuddly rabbit, Stephen couldn't imagine. Warren appeared to be only about five-foot tall and almost as broad, with a misshapen nose and a scar down one cheek. Apart from the frequent expletives, Stephen found it hard to decipher his words, but a leading diver was on hand to translate.

'Nah who's ganging doon fust?' Warren asked. Johnson looked at the others and half raised his arm.

'Well done. Now strip doon to yer fookin' underwear and these two fuckers'll dress you.'

Reluctantly, Johnson removed his outer clothing and stood in his diver's one-piece woollen underwear, shivering in the easterly wind. Warren spotted him shivering. 'Doon't you worry about the cold, sonny. Get yersel' into the suit and you'll be all cosy. The rest o' you watch fookin' carefully as you'll be acting as dressers next time.'

Johnson climbed into the Admiralty Pattern diving suit and was told to sit on a box whilst his dresser tucked in the neck ring to protect his shoulders from the heavy, brass corselet about to be fitted.

'Nah this suit weighs a hundred and sixty fookin' punds in all, includin' twenty punds of lead in each boot, twenty on yer chest and another twenty on yer back. If yer not fit, you'll find out soon enough. An' if you were on the pop last night, you'll fookin' suffer, too. Any o' you gen'l'men know what the bends is?'

'You mean decompression sickness, Chief?' Lawson replied. 'It's caused by the nitrogen you exhale being absorbed into your bloodstream. Come up too quickly and the nitrogen bubbles grow too large and cause blockages in the bloodstream.'

Warren eyed Lawson in a queer way, Stephen thought. 'Right enuff then. But that's not the only fookin' problem underwater. You need to tak things slowly and control yer fookin' breathin'. Work too hard and yer breathes out too much fookin' carbon dioxide. You ken what happens then?' It seemed to Stephen that Warren was daring Lawson to answer.

'No, Chief,' Lawson replied and Warren seemed satisfied with the answer.

'It can make you feel sick an' it can make yer feel offa sleepy. Now the seabed isn't the best place for a wee nap. If yer not fookin' careful, it becomes the sort of nap yer never wake from. So, tak it easy. Are yer comfy there, sonny?' Johnson gave the chief a thumbs-up signal.

'Guid. Now put yer boots on and youse better tie them on. If yer need to release them in an emergency, they're yurr knots and nobody else's. You get my meaning? Guid. Now pay attention to these lines all o' youse. The first is yer lifeline. I'll be givin' it a wee tug from time to time. You tug me back. If yer don', I'll think yer in fookin' trouble or havin' a wee nap. The other's your airline. It's connected to that wheel oer there. Each o' youse'll tak a turn at the fookin' wheel. That way, you'll know what it's like when it's yurr turn to be doon there. Like as not you'll be feelin gye lonely and thinkin' yer mates don't gi'a fuck aboot ye. It'll keep you warum, too, as I can see snow comin'.

Stephen looked out to the land and could see the approach of several snow showers. It made him shiver even more. He had noted that Warren didn't address either officer as 'sir', but he decided he would not be the one to raise it with him.

'Right, when yer ready, son. Over the side onto the ladder and we'll fit the helmet. Then you follow the fookin' shot rope to the bottom. It'll be warmer doon there. When on the bottom, jest relax and adjust yer air intake 'til yer feel comfy wi'yit. Yer stay doon fer twenty minutes and come back up when I gi'ye four sharp tugs. Clear?'

'Yes, Chief,' Johnson replied as he struggled to lift his legs over the side of the boat. Once he was on the ladder, a diver placed the heavy brass helmet over his head and locked it onto the corselet with a twist. Stephen was detailed to take the first turn at the air pump under the supervision of the leading diver. As Johnson's face piece was being fitted, the leading diver instructed Stephen to start pumping. Stephen was surprised by how stiff the handle was to turn, even with both hands. It suddenly struck him that Johnny now depended on him for his air supply. Johnson disappeared beneath the waves and Stephen immediately discovered that the deeper Johnny went, the stiffer the resistance of the pump handle. After just a few minutes, he was sweating and panting. After ten minutes, Lawson relieved him.

It was now Stephen's turn to dress. He noted that there only seemed to be large suits available, but this suited his tall frame, although he felt sorry for Bacon who was three inches shorter. Warmed up by his recent exertions, he didn't feel the cold as he stood in his woollens waiting to step into the suit. The diver assistant showed him how to tie quick release knots for his boots and he was ready just as Johnson emerged from the dark water below. Warren removed his helmet and helped him inboard.

'How did that go then?' he asked.

'Not bad, Chief, but I couldn't see much. It's very muddy.'

'Aye, well that's aw there is to see in this heathen country. It's different, mind, on the west coast of Scotland. That's real divin'. Now time for the next one.'

Stephen stood and quickly discovered how heavy each of his feet were in the lead boots. With a huge effort, he managed to swing one leg over the side of the boat and onto the rung of the ladder, but he felt almost too exhausted to bring the other leg over. Then he saw Lawson gazing across at him scornfully and it fired him to get onto the ladder if it killed him. With a grunt, he managed it and hung onto the ladder as if his life depended on it.

'Don't worry about it, sir,' the diver attendant said quietly. 'If you use this valve here, sir, you can inflate a little air into your suit. Then you'll feel free enough to dance down there if it takes your fancy. Mind, though, sir. Don't over inflate it or you'll pop to the surface like a balloon. Many's the time we've had a laugh at that, sir.'

The diver fitted the helmet and when it was locked home, signalled the leading diver at the air pump and Lawson began working the wheel like an organ grinder. Stephen felt the puffs of air from the vent over his right ear. His attendant fitted the face piece and screwed it into the helmet. The action made Stephen want to panic as the noise of the air being forced into his helmet was deafening. He felt the diver attendant push his head down and he started his slow descent into the grey water below. It surprised him how rusty the side of the tug was for a naval vessel, but soon his head slipped below the water and there were no more rungs on the ladder. Remembering the briefing ashore, he felt for the shot rope to his right - the thick line attached to a heavy weight on the bottom that would act as his guide rope to return to the surface.

Hand over hand, Stephen descended. He was shocked by how dark it was already, just a few feet beneath the surface, but the noise of the air pumping into his helmet lessened. Again, he almost panicked at the thought of how thin the air hose was compared with the volume of oxygen he imagined he must need. He hoped Lawson was up to the job of turning that blasted wheel. Of course, he was. He was a strapping rugby player, after all.

As Stephen progressed a little deeper, he felt the pressure of the seawater on his suit. Would his suit leak, he worried. He looked down for the bottom, but could only make out the tops of his boots. That meant the visibility was less than six feet yet he could see the vague outline of the hull of the tug above where the light penetrated this gloom. He was relieved to see a line of bubbles floating to the surface from his escape valve. Time seemed to stand still and he forgot how deep he was meant to be going. When would he find the bottom? The weight of his boots helped him make his way slowly deeper.

After an age that he couldn't estimate, he finally hit the bottom in a splash of oily mud around him. It suddenly occurred to him that he had no ladder on which to climb to the surface. Again, a flash of panic overcame him and he caught himself breathing hard. This suit with its brass helmet and stiff canvas could easily serve as his coffin. What was it the chief had said? Breathe slowly or else he would feel sleepy. He forced himself to be calm, but he felt sorry for himself and very alone. Now what, though? If he volunteered to be trained as a diver, he would have to perform a variety of underwater tasks, but for now all he had to do was wait until recalled to the surface. The leading diver had mentioned that a distance line was attached to the shot rope if he fancied a stroll on the bottom, but had warned them all not to venture too far.

He groped at the bottom of the shot line and found it strewn across the mud. Johnny must have had the same thought as the leading diver had said it would be neatly knotted. Holding the line for dear life, Stephen attempted to walk, but he couldn't. Something was wrong. The water was like treacle and he couldn't make any progress. His suit must be leaking and full of water. Oh Lord, I'm going to drown he shouted, but there was nobody to hear. He checked his panic. He could still breathe and his air bubbles were rising steadily to the surface outside his helmet. He made more effort and found the visibility only six inches. He wasn't walking, he was crawling on the bottom. He raised his head and could see a few feet ahead, but still he couldn't stand upright. Then he remembered his attendant's words and he adjusted his air intake to allow a few extra puffs of air into his suit. The action created an odd sensation as the seawater pressure was eased off his body. It was as if he had wet himself. Now he recalled why divers were required to wash their own underwear and suits. However, just that little extra buoyancy enabled him to stand upright and take some hesitant, leaden steps forward. Gently, he circled clockwise, using the distance line to keep a fixed distance from the shot rope.

All too soon, he received the four tugs on his safety line telling him his time was up. He had completely lost track of how long he had been underwater. Now he had to find a way to return to the surface without the aid of a ladder. He remembered the air intake valve and adjusted it to allow him more buoyancy. Immediately, he was propelled to the surface like a cork. Stephen tried to shut off the valve, but his suit was too inflated to allow his arm to reach his helmet and he kept going. In seconds, he shot out of the water and lay helpless, floating on the surface. He felt the pressure of the lifeline going taut and was aware that he was being towed to the tug. He blushed with embarrassment. He was as helpless as a baby. As he approached the tug's side like a whale caught on a harpoon, he could see the smiling face above of the diver attendant holding a broom. He reached down, released a spit cock in the helmet to allow air to spurt out of the helmet and used the broom to push Stephen's legs down so that he floated upright in the sea. Feeling wretched, Stephen climbed up onto the tug and gave in to being unceremoniously dragged into the boat. The whole experience determined Stephen that he would not be volunteering for diving duties.

Only twenty minutes later, Stephen's shame was allayed a little when Bacon, too, shot to the surface, ten minutes before he was due. Stephen was manning the air pump and noticed that the leading diver wasn't laughing. 'No wonder. He should've worn a smaller suit. Too much buoyancy for him in that one.'

Lawson was still getting dressed and he, too, overheard the leading diver's remarks. He turned to the chief and said aggressively, 'Just you make sure that nothing like that happens to me. You got that, Chief?'

Stephen heard Warren reply grudgingly, 'Aye, son. I'll fix it.' Johnson took over the pumping duties and Stephen went across to help Lawson finish dressing. Lawson seemed to have less of a problem in climbing over the side of the tug to stand on the ladder. Like Stephen and the others, he waited to have his helmet fitted, but first Warren came over with a three-inch wide leather strap. He passed it between Lawson's legs and secured each end on the horns of the front and back of the brass corselet. He bent over towards Lawson's face and murmured in a menacing tone, 'There you are, sir. As ordered, I've fookin' fixed it.' After his face piece was fitted, Lawson disappeared beneath the waves for his first experience of diving.

Twenty minutes later, Warren gave the recall signal on Lawson's lifeline. Nothing seemed amiss at first, but after a few minutes, Stephen saw a bubbling of water and Lawson, too, bobbed out of the water like an underwater rocket. Stephen rushed over to help pull him back to the tug, but Lawson didn't move. The leading diver took charge of the air pump and all three diving students had to help heave Lawson's prone body out of the water. On removing his helmet, they discovered him unconscious, but he came to as the officers were undressing him. He howled with pain and when his underwear was removed, Stephen noted the red and spreading weals in Lawson's groin area.

'No wonder he was in a rush to return to the surface,' the leading diver remarked. 'As his suit inflated, he'd have been in agony, the poor sod. The chief can be a right bastard when…' He was interrupted by Warren's approach.

Warren looked at the injury first with a look of malevolence, then with great satisfaction and said to the semi-conscious Lawson, 'There you are, *sir*. I said I'd fookin' fix it.'

CHAPTER 14

Following completion of their course, Stephen and Johnson spent the Sunday night at the Green Park Hotel in Half Moon Street prior to taking up their new appointments in the Admiralty. Bacon and the half-crippled Lawson remained in Portsmouth for the time being. The Germans, too, decided to visit London that night and the city took a pasting. To Stephen it seemed that the whole night was interrupted by the pounding of anti-aircraft guns, the drone of wave after wave of German bombers, the clanging of emergency vehicle bells and, worst of all, the thud and rumbling of explosions. On one occasion he heard the whistling of bombs near the hotel, immediately before his bed was shaken by the blast of nearby explosions. Stephen knew he should have joined Johnson in the air raid shelter, but he couldn't rid himself of the thought of that night in a Liverpool shelter. What if the bomb had not just blown off the doors, but buried them all alive? He shuddered at the thought, put his head under the pillow and tried hard to sleep. However, sleep seemed to elude him until he was woken by the knocking on the door of his room. He ignored it. He was too tired.

Johnson burst into the room. 'You're kidding me, Stephen. Get up.' Johnson shook Stephen hard.

'Leave me b-b-be. I'm tired.' Stephen pulled the bedclothes over his head.

'Jeez, Stephen. It's eight-thirty. We're due at the Admiralty at nine. Christ, Stephen, we're going to be late. Get up.' Stephen again felt Johnson's rough shaking of his right shoulder.

Slowly, his sleep-deprived brain registered the information. It was his first day of duty and this was bad. He jumped out of bed in a flash. 'W-w-why didn't you c-c-call me before, Johnny?' He headed for the basin to wash his face.

'Heck, I just assumed you'd already had breakfast. I didn't figure you'd still be in bed.' Johnson rummaged in Stephen's suitcase. 'Here's a clean shirt. I'll try to find us a cab.' Johnson headed for the door, but called over his shoulder as he passed through it. 'And don't forget to shave.'

Ten minutes later, Stephen found Johnson at the entrance to the hotel. 'Any luck, Johnny?'

'None. We're too far off the beaten track. Let's head down to Piccadilly. If we can't find one there, we'll have to cut across the park, but we'll be late either way. Jeez, it's started to rain, too.'

Stephen thought about returning to his room for a coat, but realised this would make them even more late. Poor Johnny. He'd be in the soup, too, and it wasn't his fault.

It was only a short walk to Piccadilly, but they first had to negotiate a pile of rubble caused by the collapse of a nearby building in the bombing. Stephen was shocked by its proximity to the hotel and rued his decision not to visit the air raid shelter during the night. He looked up at the sky. Above him and all along the sky line he could see barrage balloons, smoke and the black rain clouds, but the rain refreshed him. He and Johnson stood on the kerb of the busy thoroughfare seeking a vacant taxi, but the few that passed were always taken.

'We'll never find a cab in this rain, Stephen. We'll have to cut through the park. You up for a run?'

'B-b-but there's a taxi approaching. Look, it's s-s-slowing down.'

'No, Stephen. It's not for hire. There's someone in it.'

The taxi stopped right in front of the two worried officers, but it was, indeed, occupied. Its occupant wound down the window and he, too, wore the dark cap of a Royal Navy officer.

'You chaps going my way?' he asked cheerily. He was an RNVR lieutenant commander. The two sub lieutenants saluted him.

'Yes siree, we sure hope so,' Johnson replied enthusiastically. 'Would you be heading for the Admiralty?'

'Sure. Hop in.'

Stephen and Johnson stepped into the taxi much relieved. The original occupant was a fair-haired officer with a cheerful smile.

'My name's Montcalm. Did I meet you at *Vernon* a fortnight ago?'

Now Stephen recognised the Old Etonian friend of Lawson. 'Y-y-yes, s-sir.'

'Oh, don't worry about the *sir*. Call me Monty. Everyone else does. Besides, we're a close-knit team in RMS. To a large extent, we're our own masters and don't bother too much about rules and regulations. You'll be working for Captain Currey, then?'

'That's right, sir, I mean, Monty,' Johnson replied. 'What's he like?'

'A truly delightful man. You'll like him immediately. He'll give you his unstinting support, but there is one thing he can't abide. A lack of punctuality. Shouldn't you be reporting by 09.00?'

'It was m-m-my fault. S-s-sorry. I overslept.'

Monty smiled at Stephen pleasantly. 'Don't be alarmed. I'll come up with some excuse for you. I'm surprised you were able to sleep at all last night. It was quite a show, wasn't it? But I think I ought to explain a few ground rules. Just to set you fair for the future. From now on, your time's not your own. We're pretty stretched and need every pair of hands available. When on duty, you report in every hour to your officer-in-charge. When you're not on duty, you still report in when you move from place to place with your whereabouts, a telephone number or both. Air raids don't run to a timetable. In return, we're treated like kings. We have a driver and a fast, posh saloon car to take us from A to B. No public transport for you from now on when on duty. And when you're dealing with a mine, you're in charge of everyone and I mean everyone. That includes the PM!'

'S-s-sorry, Monty, I d-don't understand.'

'No, you wouldn't. It's a funny story. I'm not actually an RMS officer, but work very closely with Captain Currey's team and that at *Vernon*. One of the RMSOs had a mine in Saint James' Park the other day. You know… just behind Whitehall. He told the police to clear the area out to 400 yards as per usual, but that included Downing Street. The constable wasn't too happy with that news, but our friend said, "*Constable, even if Winnie himself arrives, you keep him the other side of the barrier. Is that understood?*"

'Of course, about an hour later the PM himself fronted up. "*What's this nonsense?*" he snorted. "*I'm sorry, sir,*" said the poor policeman, "*There's a naval officer dealing with a mine and he says not even you can cross this barricade.*"'

'He surely didn't?' Johnson interjected. 'Not the great Winston Churchill?'

'Dusty Miller swears he did. Anyhow…'

'Why *Dusty* Miller? Why do you call him "*Dusty*"?' Johnson interrupted.

Monty considered the question for a moment and shrugged. 'I don't know. All Millers are called *Dusty* in the navy. It's just the way it is. I don't know why. Probably something to do with flour.'

'It's a p-p-plant – Dusty M-Miller,' Stephen explained.

'Is it by Jove? How did you know that?' Monty asked.

'I k-k-keep bees… or rather I used to.'

'Really? How fascinating. You'll have to tell me about it some time, but rather you than me. I'd far rather face a Jerry mine than a hive full of bees.'

'You were telling us a story, sir,' Johnson reminded Monty.

'So I was, but I've forgotten where I was up to. It was about Dusty Miller wasn't it. A good chap, Dusty. For a Wykehamist, I mean.'

'A W-W-W…?'

'After Bishop Wykeham who founded the school… Winchester College. It's not as good as Eton, of course, but it still turns out some bright chaps. But you must stop interrupting me or I'll lose my thread and we're almost there.'

'S-s-sorry.'

'No matter. So Dusty was working on all fours, digging beneath his mine when the constable comes over to him. "*The Prime Minister wants to know why he can't return to his office, sir,*" said the plod. "*He's demanding you explain it in person, sir.*" Poor Dusty, covered in mud and a mere lieutenant, he was quaking in his boots as he approached the barrier. "*What's this nonsense, boy?*" the great statesman asked. "*Do you know that you're interfering with affairs of State?*"

'Poor Dusty didn't know where to put himself. He reckons at that moment the PM was about forty-feet tall, but he summoned up his courage and replied, "*I'm sorry, sir, but there's an unexploded bomb over there and I simply can't let you in. It could kill you and His Majesty would not like that one bit.*" He thought he might have pushed his luck a bit with the last remark as the PM quivered like jelly, briefly went red in the forehead and boomed back, "*Could it? And how long are you going to be?*"

Both Stephen and Johnson wriggled with laughter at the image of a giant prime minister towering over a tiny, mud-spattered junior officer. 'S-s-so what did he d-do?'

'He says he raised himself to his full height and replied, "*I don't know, sir. It could take an hour, but it could take all day... anything in fact.*" Winnie just glared at him and replied, "*Just make sure it's an hour, my boy,*" then turned on his heels and trudged off.'

'And how long did it take, Monty?' Johnson asked.

'Do you know what? Dusty said he'd never worked so fast and had the mine safe inside forty minutes. Hark, we're here. Better step lively and report to Captain Currey. His office is almost next door to mine.'

The two new RMS officers followed Monty into one of the Admiralty buildings and through the maze of corridors to *RMS Admiralty*, the only operational command of the Admiralty. They were met by the Officer of the Day, the very same Lieutenant Miller. Monty introduced them.

'Hello, Dusty. We were just talking about you. Here's two waifs and strays I picked up on the way here. Reinforcements, but I forgot to ask your names. How silly of me.'

'Dwight Johnson, sir.'

'S-S-Stephen C-C-Cunningham, sir.' Both sub lieutenants saluted Miller.

'Oh, for God's sake, chaps,' Miller replied. 'You're not in *King Alfred* now. Firstly, subs don't salute lieutenants and you don't salute *any* officer without his cap on. He can't return the salute, you see. In any case, we don't go in for that bull here. Call me Dusty. It's self-discipline that counts... and on that subject, you're adrift. You should have reported to the Old Man ten minutes ago.'

'Not their fault, Dusty. The end of their street was blocked by a bombed-out house and they were lending the ARP a hand to check for survivors. That's how I came to give them a lift.'

'Oh. Fair enough. In any case, the Old Man's not in yet. Nobody's in. Everybody's either in bed or on the job. Busy night last night. We can't all work in Intelligence like you, Monty. The Old Man went out with one of the teams at oh-crack-sparrow and won't be in for a bit.'

'Fine. Then I'll just clear off to my desk and leave you to show these chaps round. Cheerio for now.'

Stephen joined Johnson in saying farewell to Monty and thanking him for the taxi ride. He decided that this Montcalm wasn't such a bad person, after all. He looked around him. It was an uninspiring place for the headquarters of the RMS command. It comprised just the one long narrow office in which there stood a couple of tables and chairs, the occasional bomb-fuze and several charts on the wall. Two doors other than the entrance led off from each end of the office. It all seemed very stark and cold.

'Welcome to the madhouse,' Miller greeted them. 'Not much to see really. That's the Old Man's cabin and office over there and at this end is the ratings' mess. You'll each be allotted a rating to join you and a driver. Your rating carries your tools and the driver takes you wherever you want. First-class all the way. You'll see quite a bit of the country in this job. It's not a bad show.'

Just then a captain and a lieutenant walked through the office door. 'Good morning, sir,' Miller piped. 'Two new recruits fresh out of *Vernon* just arrived, sir. Sub Lieutenants Johnson and Cunningham, sir. I've just been showing them around.'

Stephen snapped to attention and surveyed the Old Man. Despite his early start, he was clean-shaven and his slightly angular nose gave him the appearance of a bird. However, his eyes were the dominant feature of his face. Grey and deep-set, they flickered in a very alert fashion and seemed to pierce through to Stephen's soul. Having taken in the measure of his newest officers he turned to Miller.

'Ask someone to fix me a mug of black coffee will you, Dusty. You, gentlemen, follow me.'

Stephen and Johnson followed Currey into his cabin and were invited to take a chair on the other side of Currey's desk. Currey threw his cap onto his bunk, removed his greatcoat and hung it on the back of the door.

'We meet again, Cunningham,' Currey began. Only then did Stephen recognise Currey as the captain he had met just a few months earlier. The change in building had thrown him and it had been dark, too. 'I'm delighted to have you onboard. Jerry's been a little more inventive since we last spoke, so we'll need your brains.

'And, Johnson, you're an American, I see.' Currey flicked through a couple of sheets of paper. 'Dwight Johnson the Third, I see. I presume the Second is your father?'

'Sure is, sir. He's a senator for the state of Virginia,' Johnson replied proudly.

'The Senator Johnson who's making speeches urging your countrymen to come in with us in the war?'

'That's him, sir. According to Pa, we were late into the last war and soon enough we'll be dragged into this one, so we ought to be a bit snappier this time.'

Currey seemed to dredge his mind for something. 'Wasn't he a colonel in the last show?'

Johnson seemed impressed. 'Sure was, sir. Came over to France with General Pershing.'

'But, of course. I briefly met him at a reception after the war. That's all it was, though. I can't say I know him.' Currey placed the papers back on his desk and leaned forward.

'Now, there's something on which I need to impress you. This job comes with an element of personal risk. You'll have heard that at *Vernon* and I don't want to frighten you, but I don't want any of my men to come into the job with his eyes shut. If you're ever in any doubt about the job, you pull out. I won't think you a coward. There are plenty of other jobs you can do that will require courage, but this job's different and here's why. I served at sea in the last lot, but when I faced the enemy, it was with my shipmates. Men I trusted and men who all shared the same danger. When you go to work on a mine, you're on your own. Sometimes, you'll have a crew, but they retire to safety before you begin work on the mine. Every time you go out to a mine, you have to gird your loins for a fresh danger. At sea, danger's a constant. You don't wake up each day having to think about it. And we've lost some good men. Dead men tell no tales and we don't know why. For that reason, if you come across something out of the ordinary, you stop and report it. Is that clear?'

Both junior officers nodded in silence. Stephen found Currey's words chilling, but he wouldn't pull out now. The die was cast.

'If that's clear, one last thing,' Currey continued. 'I'm privileged to command a very special breed of officer. You're all brave men and selected to think independently. You'll get little leave and will rarely be truly off duty. As a result, I allow my team a certain latitude. If you want to go to the pub after rendering a mine safe, that's fine by me and the drivers know that. Use the car and driver as your own. But the duty officer is to know your whereabouts at all time. Sleep with who you like, but you pass on an address and telephone number every time. Follow these simple rules and we'll rub along together very well. Any questions?'

'Y-y-yes, sir.' Stephen mustered the courage to speak.

'W-w-will someone show us how to d-d-defuze our first m-m-mine, sir?'

'No, Cunningham. You've done the course and you can practise on a few dead mines here. I'll be sending an experienced officer with you on the first jobs, but we're all learning on the job. Learn from each other. Pass on your experience. But I am never going to risk more than one officer on a job at a time.'

Chapter 15
November 1940

Stephen and Johnson were billeted together in a flat in Jermyn Street. It had the benefit of having its own telephone, except it rang at 06.00 on a cold and dark November morning. Stephen, a lighter sleeper than Johnson, answered it sleepily.

'Stephen, is that you? Dusty here. As you answered the call, it's your mine. Be here in half an hour.'

The telephone call roused Johnson. 'What's up, bud?' he asked drowsily.

'It's a m-m-mine. My f-f-first job.' Stephen trembled as he spoke.

'Gee, that's swell. I'll get dressed.'

'No!' Stephen replied forcefully. 'It's m-m-mine. All m-mine.'

'But come on, old fella. You're shaking like a leaf. At least let me help you. We'll tackle it together. We're buddies.' Johnson turned to return to his room, but Stephen called him back.

'Johnny, you c-can't.' Actually, Stephen thought he would welcome some moral support in tackling his first mine, but he wasn't just afraid of the mine. He worried that if Johnny was with him, he might chicken out of tackling the mine. He would rather die than do that.

'Remember w-what the Old M-Man said, Johnny. N-never two officers on a job. I have to s-s-start sometime.' He stared part defiantly, part pleadingly at Johnson. Johnson met his eyes, hesitated and then his face softened into a broad smile.

'Sure thing, pardner. I remember. Now you just get yourself ready whilst I fix you a sandwich for breakfast. But for the Lord's sake, Stephen, you take it easy. No unnecessary risks and make sure you goddamned ring me when it's over.'

*****

Twenty-five minutes later, Stephen had washed, shaved, dressed and walked the half-mile to the RMS office. Miller met him at the entrance.

'Bravo, Stephen. Come along. The car's just over at The Mall.'

A couple of minutes later, they found the car. A junior naval rating, Miller's usual assistant, was sitting in the passenger seat next to an army driver. The rating had already loaded the precious non-magnetic tools into the boot of the Humber, painted khaki, but with its distinctive red front denoting it was a bomb-disposal vehicle. As soon as the two officers had settled themselves into the rear, the driver started the powerful engine of the car and headed onto The Mall.

'I bet you're raring to go,' Miller suggested. Nothing was further from Stephen's mind. He was too busy trying to remember all the extra training he had had the previous week. Currey had come up with a new tool he and the other officers called a gag. It was like an old motor horn connected to a bicycle pump that was screwed to the top of the bomb-fuze. The aim was for the increased air pressure to trick the mine into thinking it had landed in the sea. The increased pressure depressed a rubber diaphragm to release a safety pin and render the self-destruct mechanism harmless. The rest he had learned at *Vernon*.

'W-w-where is this m-mine?' Stephen asked.

'Down near Rochester way. Somewhere in the country. How long do you reckon it'll take us, Brooks?'

'This time o' the morning, sah, I'd say an hour and half. I'll put my clog down.'

'Just get us there in one piece, Brooks. My friend here will value every one of those ninety minutes. So, Stephen, plenty of time to catch up on some shuteye.'

Stephen pretended to sleep whilst Miller chatted to the seaman and driver. He didn't hear what they said. He was too busy rehearsing in his mind what he had to do and thinking of his family. Suddenly, he felt cold and trembled slightly. It was a movement that attracted Miller's attention.

'I say, Brooks. It's a bit parky back here. Any chance of a bit more heating?'

'Sorry, sah. It's already full on.'

Stephen wondered if Miller had taken the trembling as a sign of fear and had acted to cover Stephen's potential embarrassment. He pulled his cap down tight over his forehead and thrust his hands out of sight and into the warmth of his greatcoat pockets. He wondered if, despite what Currey had said, Miller would help him with the mine. After all, he had come along. His thoughts returned to the lectures he had received at *Vernon* as the car speeded down Watling Street.

By nine o'clock they were in deepest Kent. It was light, but nevertheless gloomy. The hedgerows were bare and the sky dark and forbidding. Stephen wondered whether it might snow.

The driver stopped a policeman at Meopham and asked for directions to the unexploded mine. The mine wasn't in Meopham as reported, but somewhere on the road to the nearby village of Sole Street. A mile down the road, they enquired of a passing farm labourer and were directed down a farm track. There they found another policeman. His face was raw with the cold of the easterly wind and he was relieved to see them.

'Your mine's just over there, sirs. In that field.'

The rating unloaded a bag of tools and a bucket whilst Miller opened the farm gate to the field. To Stephen's surprise, the driver reversed back up the track, followed by the policeman. 'W-w-where are they g-g-going?' he asked of the rating.

'Out of range, sir. To a place of safety. Cars are valuable. Officers aren't.'

Stephen was relieved to see Miller going towards the mine. Did that mean he would deal with it and show him the ropes, he wondered. He followed Miller across the wet and newly-ploughed field. The mud stuck to his shoes and soon he found the going hard. At times he sank ankle deep in the soft earth and felt his socks becoming wet. Then he realised that Miller and his assistant were both wearing seaboots. He resolved to obtain a pair and to keep them with his kit in future, but it was too late now. Behind him he could hear the clanging of the tools in the rating's bag and the quiet purr of the Humber reversing up the track. In the nearby trees several rooks *cawed* and a few fluttered onto the ground to his right. It was a miserable day and a desolate place to die, he thought.

Miller had stopped about 150 yards short of a tree stump ahead, but as Stephen closed him, he saw a splash of darker green to one side, billowing slightly in the wind. It was a parachute from which stretched a tangle of cords to the tree stump, only it wasn't made of wood. It was a large metal object lying at a slight angle, partly buried in the mud. That's my mine, he thought.

'This is close enough. Pass us the shovels, Nixon.' The rating withdrew a couple of shovels from his kit bag. 'Right, let's get digging, Stephen. This is the procedure. If there's no other cover, you dig a hole and you dig it deep enough to save you from the blast. Before you go near any mine, Stephen, you plan your escape. Out in the open, a haystack or a hedge or a ditch would be first class. In a warehouse on the banks of the Thames, you don't have time to run down its stairs. You might be five floors up, but you jump through a window or loading door and take your chances on the mud or water below. Who cares if you break your legs? If you're working at height, say on the first floor of a house, have a ladder ready. Same thing if you're down a sewer. Whatever you do, don't forget your escape route or change your mind part way through.'

Stephen removed his coat and joined Miller in digging. The rating merely watched with wry amusement. Stephen was surprised that the work was being left to the officers. It didn't seem very hierarchical, but the physical labour quickly warmed him and he felt calmer for it. Perhaps, that was the routine. Hard physical labour helped clear the mind prior to tackling the mine. Stephen didn't notice the rating disappear with the bucket, until he returned with it full of water and continued to look on sardonically, but once the hole was deep and wide enough to provide cover for two men beneath ground level, he just nodded and trudged back in the direction of the track.

'Dusty, w-w-where's he g-g-going?'

'Safety, old chap. Mustn't kill a rating you know.'

Stephen looked down at his sodden shoes and trousers caked in wet mud and thought about the task before him. It seemed a high price to pay for the supposed prestige of being an officer. He would tell his mother that when he next saw her. If he ever saw her again.

'Right, Stephen,' Miller said as he dressed again in his jacket and coat. 'I'm getting into this hole whilst you deal with the mine.'

'B-b-but aren't you…?'

'You didn't imagine I was going to do it, did you? It's your mine and we all have to face our first one. We've all done it. Call it a rite of passage, but you've got to do it on your own, Stephen. If you can't, find yourself a job censoring mail or something.'

'B-b-but s-s-supposing I can't run 150 yards in this m-m-mud?'

'You'll have to, Stephen. It's not my mine and it's not my risk. Look, if you get stuck, come back here and ask me. Make sure you identify it first. But don't shout. Don't talk to yourself whilst working on it. Just be as quiet as you can. Chin up, old chap. You'll be fine.'

Stephen picked up his jacket, but left his coat behind. He wanted as much freedom of movement in his arms as possible – and less encumbrance if he had to run. After donning his jacket, he picked up the tools and bucket and squelched through the mud to the dark cylinder ahead. This was what his colleagues were starting to call '*the long walk*'.

'Good luck,' Miller called after him softly.

As Stephen approached the mine, he began to tiptoe to reduce the noise of his footsteps, taking care not to lose any of the precious water in the bucket. The tools in the bag jangled alarmingly in a discordant symphony of sound. He placed them and the bucket on the ground. Looking back, he could see only Miller's head. Suddenly, the birds were no longer *cawing*. There was only silence. The world had stopped whilst he faced his fear.

He crept around the mine, six feet of which leaned out of the ground. He could see the fuze and detonator a little above the ground. It meant they were accessible without the need to dig. The mine's serial numbers were clearly visible, too. It was a Type 'C'. It seemed to have no unusual features. For the first time, Stephen caught himself breathing. How long had he held his breath? He tried to imagine the ton of TNT before him as one of Dad's cars in need of an engine service. It was a routine job. He'd done it many times before. It was important to be organised and have his tools in the right order. To have them to hand. He laid out his tools on a piece of hessian the way a surgeon lays out his knives. First, he would need the gag, but before that he had to check it was working. He connected the bicycle pump to the long, straight length of brass tubing clipped to the motor horn, opened the tap and began pumping until the rubber bulb was fully inflated. Then he placed the bulb in the water of the bucket to check for leaks. He prayed he would see no bubbles. Any loss of air pressure would raise the diaphragm of the mine's hydrostatic unit and release the safety pin of the bomb-fuze again. Then it would only be a matter of time before the clockwork fuze started its deathly run.

There were no bubbles. It was time to begin work. He went down on his knees and, taking a deep breath, screwed the gag's adaptor onto the threaded top of the bomb-fuze. The threads mated and Stephen exhaled quietly. Gently and quietly, he turned the adaptor of the gag through one revolution and listened carefully for the deadly buzzing of clockwork. All was silent. He risked another turn of the adaptor… and another. His hands trembled. Nothing else in the world now existed beyond this fuze. His knees were wet, but he didn't care. Still there was no buzzing. He tightened the gag's adaptor all the way home and wiped away beads of perspiration with the back of his other hand. Now for the moment of truth. He turned the tap of the brass tube and held his breath again, placed his ear to the top of the bomb-fuze and listened carefully. He heard a loud click.

Stephen breathed out quietly. The increased air pressure had caused the safety pin to click home. The mine was still not safe, but he had passed the first hurdle. Now he took the heavy two-pronged brass spanner to begin work on the keep ring, the ring that locked the fuze into the mine. The gag was in his way and pressed up against his armpit. It made turning the spanner extremely difficult, but he didn't dare remove the gag. Clumsily, he loosened the keep ring and it hissed slightly as the ring turned in its aluminium thread. Stephen worried that the pressure of his body on the bulb of the gag might cause it to leak through the adaptor and the keep ring. He promised himself a break from the mine if he could first remove the keep ring. He couldn't stop now. Another quarter turn of the spanner… listen… another quarter turn. He lost sense of time. The keep ring came free. Now he had to ease it up the brass tube to give him room to remove the fuze. If only his hands weren't trembling so much. Was it the cold or fear? It didn't matter.

Brain said, you promised yourself a rest from the mine once you reached this stage, Stephen. I can't just yet, Voice replied silently. I must remove the fuze first. It's in too delicate a state to leave it now. Just give me another minute and then we'll take a break.

With his left hand holding the keep ring on the gag, Stephen used his right to remove the two-inch-long silver fuze from its housing in the mine. Now he needed to unscrew it from the gag. With his free hand, he placed the gag on the ground. In the other, he now held a bomb in its own right. Attached to the fuze was the gaine, a vicious black cylinder containing the high-explosive designed to trigger the main charge. With care bordering on tenderness, he unscrewed the gaine from the fuze. He shook it and the tiny lumps of black explosive fell onto his hessian sheet, but he was still not safe. Mines were built like Russian dolls. Within the shiny cylinder of the bomb-fuze, now separated from the gaine, lay a small detonator with enough explosive to blow off a man's arm. It fired the gaine and that fired the main charge.

He picked up a small screwdriver and with infinite care, unscrewed one of the two tiny screws in the side of the bomb-fuze. He placed it in his pocket alongside the gaine. Now for the tricky bit. He turned the bomb-fuze over and caught the tiny detonator, no bigger than the head of a match, in his hand as it dropped out. This he placed in its own box. Now he could relax for a short while.

He eased himself from his knees to stand at the side of the mine. His joints and muscles were stiff and he took long and deep breaths. The mine wasn't yet safe, but he had promised his brain a short rest. He took a circuit of the mine to restore his circulation. It seemed to wake up the world and now, as well as the rooks, he could hear cattle lowing in a far-off field. 150 yards off, he could see Miller waving encouragingly. Stephen waved back. How he longed to join Miller in that hole, but he still had a job to do. All he had done so far was disarm the self-destruct mechanism of the mine. He still had to deal with the main detonator.

This time, Stephen approached the mine with less fear. No longer did it seem to have a will of its own. It was an inert object built by Man. He was capable of beating the engineering ingenuity and science of its German makers. He knelt by the mine again and reached for a larger screwdriver. Patiently, he removed four screws from the plate giving access to the main detonator. Now he had to think about possible booby traps. The four-inch plate had to come off for him to access the mine's interior, but might there be a pressure switch to trigger the charge? There was no way of telling until he tried and it was his job to try. He was an RMS officer and this was his mine. Gently, with the end of the screwdriver, he eased out one corner of the plate. He couldn't feel any easing of the pressure of a spring behind, so he eased out another corner of the plate. So far, so good. Now he went for broke and carefully removed the plate, screwing his eyes tightly shut in expectation of the inevitable explosion that would send him to meet his God.

Nothing happened. Inside, he saw a huge, black bakelite bung, just as he had seen on all the mines on which he had practiced. Behind this lay the main detonator. Stephen could feel sweat dripping down his spine, despite the intense cold of the day. It was time to go to work with the huge, bronze handled, four-pin bung spanner. It was heavy and Stephen took his time in placing its pins in line with the slots of the bung. It was a straight forward enough operation to turn the spanner. There was no gag in the way this time. He applied force to the spanner to turn the bung. Except the bung didn't turn. It just squeaked in anguish.

Come on, Stephen, Brain said. You've got more than that. Stephen tried again with more force and this time the bung moved. After a couple of turns, Stephen laid the bung spanner to one side and spun the bung with his fingers. He removed it and peered into the mine with some trepidation. He was now looking at the main detonator. This bakelite unit was connected to a nine-volt battery and the magnetic unit of the mine by two electrical wires running to the tail. He knew he had to cut the wires, but he hesitated. His knowledge of physics warned him another circuit might be attached so that as the wires shorted on being cut, they sent an electrical impulse by another route to detonate the mine.

Stephen felt blindly inside the mine, but could find no trace of other wires. With his heart in his mouth, he cut the wires. Nothing happened. He looked for the time, but his watch wasn't on his wrist. He remembered that Miller had it along with the contents of his pockets. He wondered how long he had been working on his mine. Hours probably, he thought, but he still had much to do. First, he had to remove the detonator. He picked up another long-handled spanner and reached deep into the mine to engage the two slots of the detonator. It came free easily enough and as Stephen pulled it out by its two cut wires, he thought how it would be easy enough to booby trap the unit. However, there it was. A solid base of black bakelite into which was slotted a two-inch-long pencil tube of copper, the main detonator. Reverently, he placed it with its colleague in the box provided. Two down, two to go he thought and wished he smoked. He desperately needed something to calm him. His every nerve seemed to be on edge. He thought he might burst.

Best to get on with finishing the job then, he thought, but I might take up smoking afterwards – if I survive! He went back to the side of the mine to the void from which he had removed the bomb-fuze. Deep in its recess, lay the primer charge, but he was on the final straight now. The job was routine from here on. Unconsciously, he used his collection of spanners and rods with claws to remove first the primer keep ring, the plug and finally the primer itself. It was the size of a cocoa tin. It contained a large quantity of picric-acid pellets, a powerful explosive capable of destroying a building. Stephen uncapped the unit and poured the pellets over the lumps of explosive from the bomb-fuze gaine and set fire to them.

As he did so, Stephen suddenly felt exhausted and he could barely move his leaden legs. He still had one job to do before he was done, but he was already spent. He was hungry, too. If only he'd thought to bring Johnny's sandwich, but it was lying with his coat in Dusty's dugout. He sat on the bare earth and leaned back onto the mine casing. Somewhere in a pocket he found part of a partially-melted bar of chocolate. He placed two squares in his mouth and savoured the creamy texture of the chocolate. It helped him think. Technically, the mine was now safe on land and he could leave it to others to remove the hydrostatic unit. But it was his mine and he wanted to see the job through. He had four of the mine's prizes – the bomb-fuze, gaine, detonator and primer – but there were five to be had. All the clock did was to set in operation the magnetic unit, so it could be left in place. But what if that had been booby trapped? Somebody else would pay the price for his laziness. No, it was his mine and he would see the job through. He ate the final two squares of chocolate and set to work.

This was the most physically demanding task of them all as the spanner was not just the heaviest, but the clock weighed six pounds. Nevertheless, despite his tiredness, Stephen tackled the job swiftly. The mine might still be booby trapped, but it held no fears for him anymore. He found the clock and with his eyes shut, pulled it out of the casing. Nothing happened. There was no booby trap. With much satisfaction, Stephen cut the six wires and placed the clock on the hessian sheet with his other prizes. He had a full set and he looked at them proudly. Quickly, with renewed energy, he packed up his tools and trophies, before walking back to re-join Miller. He felt good about himself and about two inches taller.

'All done, Dusty,' he said proudly.

'Well done, Stephen. Let's see what you've got.'

Stephen laid out his trophies and was now extremely glad he'd bothered to collect the hydrostatic clock.

'Good work. How do you feel?' Miller shook Stephen's hand warmly.

'Quite wonderful.' Stephen beamed at Miller and smiled broadly. 'But I do feel very hungry.'

'I'm not surprised. It's lunchtime and you didn't have your breakfast. You were on that mine nearly two hours.'

'So, what now, Dusty? Back to London?'

'First we'll return to the police station at Meopham. Tell them everything's safe and sound. Then we'll ring London and arrange disposal of the remains of the mine. They might have another job for us, too. These mines are always dropped in pairs. But first, we'll find ourselves a spot of lunch. I say, I've just noticed something.'

'What's that, Dusty?'

'You've lost your stammer, old boy.'

CHAPTER 16

Bitter and resentful, Monty wrapped himself in a blanket in a vain attempt to make himself warm in the back of the army Humber on the morning of his grandfather's funeral. He had only arrived in Cheshire the night before and now, not only had he been dragged out of his bed in the middle of the night, but he would miss the funeral. He hadn't been very close to Grandfather, but he had wanted to support Father. Father would now inherit the title, of course, and his elder brother James would become a viscount. Through the ATS driver's windscreen it wasn't difficult to spot the area of Liverpool's docks. The fires from the previous night's bombing were still ablaze. Monty wondered what he would encounter on his arrival at the Garston gasworks.

Captain Maitland-Dougall had been very apologetic about recalling Monty to duty.

'I know you're up there to attend a funeral, Monty, but this is top priority. There's something damned fishy about that mine and I want my own man on hand to report on it.'

'I see, sir. What's special about it?' Monty wondered if there really was cause for concern, but he would have to attend nonetheless.

'Jerry dropped a packet of parachute mines on Liverpool last night, one of which has already taken 600 houses with it. Your mine landed on the gasworks and is concerning our local land incident section. It's penetrated the top of a gasometer, full of gas, and should by rights have exploded. It's definitely a mine as it has a parachute, but clearly, I've no idea whether it's magnetic or acoustic. Let's just say that an old seaman's feeling in the bones says it contains a new delayed-action fuze. So, get your skates on, Monty. One of our RMS officers will meet you there.'

The driver took the car across the bridge at Runcorn and turned left into Speke. There seemed to be no other traffic on the road. Even a few miles from their destination, Monty could smell the effects of the air raid. He had come across them often enough in London. Firstly, there was the smoke and the smell of charred wood.

Then there would be the smell of cordite from the anti-aircraft guns, explosive from the bombs and the foam of the firefighters' hoses. In residential areas there would be the smell of escaping gas, charred paper from walls, blood, disinfectant and the rotting bodies of pets buried in the rubble. It was depressing and he wondered how long the British people could take this new form of warfare. Right now, he wished he could be at sea, smelling the tang of salt air.

The driver sought directions and was told to follow the railway. It was Monty's first visit to Liverpool and as his driver threaded her way through the abandoned streets of Halewood, he was reminded of London's East End. The southern end of the city seemed to be full of factories, railway goods yards and other industrial sites, between which were packed street after street of tiny terraced houses. As someone who had had the privilege of growing up in the Wiltshire countryside, he couldn't imagine the lifestyles of the people who must live in such conditions.

The driver pulled up at a barricade near a railway station and explained her business to the police constable manning the barrier. He beckoned to a colleague to move the barrier and allow the car to pass, but first addressed Monty in the rear of the car. 'Mind how you go, sir. One of the beggars has already gone off, taking a railway bridge and half the line with it. There's another in Whithedge Road. I'll just jump up and show you the way to the gasworks. One of your colleagues is already there, sir.' The policeman mounted the running board and directed the ATS driver.

Monty soon found the RMS officer in charge and was surprised to see it was Cunningham. He was talking to a civilian whose striped pyjama jacket showed through under his coat. A policeman and a couple of Auxiliary Fire Service personnel were listening to their conversation.

'Hallo, Cunningham, I'm surprised to see you here. I thought you were in London.'

'I was until yesterday, s-sir, b-but …'

'Monty, please. Call me Monty.'

'Fair enough, M-Monty. I forgot, but you must c-call me S-Stephen then. As I was s-saying, I w-was in London until yesterday afternoon, but Liverpool's taking a b-bit of a p-pasting and Captain C-C-Currey thought I might lend a hand to the local unit.'

'I'm glad he did, Stephen. What's the situation here?'

'Let me introduce you to S-Section Officer B-Banks. He's in charge of the local fire station. This is Chief Inspector C-Caton. His men have c-cleared the area and secured the p-perimeter.'

'Yes, Chief Inspector. One of your men kindly showed us the way here.'

'We're glad to see you, Commander. We've not just had to stop the railway and the factories working, but evacuate 6,000 souls from their homes.'

'And let's not forget the disruption to the gas supply,' the pyjama-clad civilian interjected. 'There'll be no gas to the whole of the south and east of Liverpool until you sort this mess out.'

'This is M-Mister K-K-Kermode, Monty,' Stephen introduced Monty to Kermode. 'He's the manager of the g-gas works.'

'I'd say that's the least of our worries, *lar*,' the fire officer addressed Kermode. 'If that gasometer goes up, it'll obliterate the whole of bleedin' Garston.'

'Would you mind if I had a private word with my colleague, gentlemen?' Monty ushered Stephen away from the group. 'Have you seen the mine yet, Stephen?'

'N-not yet, M-Monty. I've been up an AFS ladder to the top of the g-gasometer and the m-mine's inside. There's a hole in the top through w-which I could see the p-parachute and its c-cords. I'd say the m-mine's still s-suspended by the cords, b-but who's to say how long that'll last.'

'Tricky. Very tricky. Forgive me for asking, Stephen, but you're barely out of *King Alfred*. Are you up for a job like this?'

'I d-don't honestly know 'till I've tried, but it's a c-c-category A mine and I've done t-two, so I'd say I've little choice. There's a d-dye factory on one side and a m-munitions f-factory on the other, as well as thousands of houses, a railway and the d-docks in the vicinity.'

'Good man, Stephen. That's the spirit. Look, it's your mine, but I'll help out where I can. Pull a bit of rank, if necessary, to get you what you need. I'm keen to have a look at that mine, but I need to warn you of the risk, Stephen. My captain fears that mine might have been fitted with a delayed-action fuze. That's why he sent me. If he's right and the clock starts ticking, you'll have no escape. It'll be curtains.'

'I know that M-Monty, b-but what else is there to be done? I'm a k-k-king's officer and this is what I've been trained to d-do.'

Monty patted Stephen on the back. 'Stout fellow. Let's see what Mister Kermode and the fire officer have to say.'

'Tea, sirs?' A policeman thrust two mugs of tea into the hands of the naval officers.

'Mister Kermode,' Monty asked. 'Is there any other way my colleague can enter the gasometer, other than through the top?' Kermode shook his head. 'So, it looks like he'll have to be lowered down in a harness. Can you arrange that Mister Banks?'

The fireman looked up at the gasometer, from which Monty could now see the mine's parachute billowing slightly, even though there was no wind. 'Yeah. I think we could manage that.'

'Good. Mister Kermode, what hazards? Other than the mine, of course?' Monty tried to force a laugh, but failed. 'What's my friend, Stephen, going to find inside that tank?'

'There's the gas. It's not just explosive, but poisonous. You'll need to wear an oxygen mask.'

'Could you not shut off the gas to the tank and purge it somehow?' Monty asked.

'Oh no!' Kermode answered nervously. 'The tank floats on the pressure of the gas. Expel the gas and the whole structure could collapse on top of the mine. There's another consideration, too.'

'Is this job interesting enough for you yet, Stephen? There's more?' Monty addressed the last question to Kermode. Kermode replied directly to Stephen.

'You need to be aware that this is coal gas we're talking of. It means that there'll be a layer of tar and oil at the base of the tank.'

'Yuck. What a charming site you run,' Monty replied before turning to Stephen. 'I could send for a diving suit. If you wore that, you'd have your own air supply.'

'Is there n-nothing else f-for it? What about one of those s-s-submarine escape k-kits? I wore one of those d-d-diving suits at *Excellent* and hated it. They d-don't just m-make one feel c-claustrophobic, b-but they don't offer any f-freedom of movement.'

'I suppose that's a fair point,' Monty conceded.

'There is another option,' Banks spoke. 'You could borrow one of our breathing sets. The only trouble is that each cylinder only lasts about thirty minutes, so you'd have to keep coming up to change them. The diving suit might make better sense.'

'N-no, I'm not wearing a d-diving suit. Show me how to use one of your b-breathing sets, Mister B-Banks.'

'No problem, sir. We'll rig you up with some lighting, too. It'll be pitch black in there.'

'Absolutely n-n-not!' Stephen surprised Monty with the vehemence of his reply. 'What I m-mean to s-say is that any electric c-current might induce an explosion of the g-gas. We c-can't risk it.'

'I suppose you're the scientist, Stephen, but you can hardly light a match down there either, can you? What else do you have in mind?' Monty had no ideas himself.

'I'll have to w-work by touch alone. After all, I've p-practiced it b-blindfolded before now.'

*****

Two hours later, Stephen was hauled out of the gasometer after his preliminary inspection. Monty met him on the ground. Despite the winter air, Stephen was wringing with sweat as well as being completely filthy. He smiled wanly at the warmth of Monty's greeting.

'I m-might be lucky with this one, Monty. The m-mine's upright, leaning against a b-brick pillar, but it's under about s-seven feet of oily w-water. Your idea of a d-diving suit might have been the right one, but I'll s-stick with these oxygen cylinders for n-now.'

'Did you note anything unusual about it, Stephen?'

'N-no. It seems t-typical of a Type 'C'. I can reach the hydrostatic clock k-keep ring, but I'll have to turn the mine f-first, to reach the b-bomb-fuze. It's g-going to be a long job. I'll get out of this g-gear and we can come up with a p-plan over breakfast.'

Chief Inspector Caton escorted the officers to the nearby police station and arranged for them both to wash. He even found them both some shaving equipment. Feeling distinctly refreshed, Monty and Stephen sat down to an extremely hearty breakfast of bacon, sausages, eggs, mushrooms and black pudding. Monty ate his breakfast with relish, but a sense of guilt, too. Somebody must have given up a week's rations to serve them such a wonderful breakfast. He wiped away a tear at the thought of the generosity of people in such adversity.

'You're going to need a hand to turn that mine, Stephen. I'll go down with you next time.'

'N-n-no, Monty. It's kind of you to offer, b-but it's not p-practical. With t-two sets of harnesses and ropes along with the c-cords from the parachute, we w-would risk becoming entangled. It's b-b-bad enough as it is. The last thing I w-want is to shift or chafe those c-cords.'

'All right. Draw me a sketch of the mine's position and let's work out a way of you turning it.'

Monty examined the rough sketch. 'Stephen, I've an idea. Supposing you laid some sandbags around the nose of the bomb and attached a hook to the shackle at the rear. We could winch up the mine by a few inches, just enough to take its weight, and you could turn the mine by yourself.'

'That s-seems reasonable, b-but it'll take time. I'm g-going to need rest, too.'

'I'll see you have it, Stephen. I've seen several mines deloused in the past few months and I'd say this is the most difficult yet. You finish your breakfast and rest. I'll telephone London and let them know what we're up to.'

*****

That evening, Stephen and Monty were guests of Garston Police Station, each allocated a cell for the night. The policemen served them up a plate of 'scouse', Monty's introduction to Liverpool's famous dish of mutton, potatoes, carrots and onions. Whilst Stephen tucked into the side dish of pickled cabbage, Monty opted for the more familiar chunk of bread to accompany it. They each washed it down with a bottle of beer from the nearby Cains brewery.

'This makes a change from the Café Royal, Stephen, but is no less good.'

'I've never been to the C-Café Royal, Monty. Dinner at the Adelphi would be a treat for me. I was s-sorry to hear about your g-grandfather, Monty. Your driver told me. It was the f-funeral today, I understand.'

Monty stared at the label of his beer bottle for a moment. 'It can't be helped, old man. War seems to be so terribly inconvenient at times. I heard something about you, too, today. I gather you're a bit of a local. Went to the university here. A boffin some say.'

Stephen blushed modestly. 'Hardly a b-boffin. I taught at a school here and wasn't very g-good at it. The g-girls teased me for my s-stammer.'

'They'd think you a hero now, Stephen. And the stammer's barely noticeable now. Did you grow up here?'

'No, a bit further n-north of here, near Lancaster. My d-d-dad runs a g-garage there in a tiny village.'

'I bet the countryside's beautiful there. I was raised in Wiltshire and loved it. Are you keen on walking? A great place for dogs, I would imagine.'

'Possibly, b-but I've always preferred cats to dogs… and running.'

Monty laughed. 'Useful in this business. It won't help you tomorrow if all goes wrong.'

'Nor you, Monty. If I b-blow myself up, you'll be joining me at the P-Pearly G-Gates.'

'Let's hope not for both our sakes. You've at least managed to make the mine secure with your sandbags and the block and tackle.

Now you've turned the mine, it should be straight forward enough to take out the fuze in the morning.'

'I hope s-so, Monty. You forget I'm w-working under water, though. It took m-me three trips just to get this f-far.'

'I know. It's time consuming and tiring to have to come back up after thirty minutes to change your oxygen cylinder. But it should only take you… say two more trips tomorrow. We'll be through about lunchtime and then somebody can have a crack at that mine in… I've forgotten the name of the street.'

'Whithedge Road, M-Monty. Now, if you don't mind, I m-might try to get some s-sleep. I'm very tired.'

'I'm not surprised. Up and down those ladders all day. Go ahead. I might go for a walk in the blackout, though. Stretch my legs and tire my brain a bit. See you in the morning.'

*****

The morning of the thirtieth was a brighter day and the light pierced through the splintered hole at the top of the gasometer to offer some assistance to Stephen working twenty feet below. With his oxygen mask steamed up by the condensation of his own breath and inked out by the tarry, black water in which he was working, he was still more or less working blind, but the light was still welcome. Gingerly, he secured the detonator of the bomb-fuze in its box and pocketed the cylindrical fuze unit. Events had been relatively straight forward this morning. He had rigged a ladder inside the tank the previous day, so no longer needed to be suspended in mid-air by the harness he was wearing. This gave him more freedom to manoeuvre. He had plenty of time to remove the primer and main detonator before he had to return to the surface to exchange his oxygen cylinder. Notwithstanding the difficulties his present location were causing, the actual rendering safe of his third mine now seemed quite mechanical. It was very like car mechanics. Except, get it wrong and I'll set off a ton of TNT, he reminded himself.

Stephen had rung his father's garage the night before to speak to both his parents. It had been the first time he had done so since leaving to join the RNVR. To his surprise, this time Dad had spoken to him very warmly. He had no idea why the navy was involved with bomb disposal, but had read plenty of reports of the work of the army teams in defuzing the many unexploded bombs that had fallen on London. He even referred to them familiarly as UXBs, not that any bombs had yet landed near Lancaster. Hitler seemed more intent on hitting the docks, to stop food coming in and starving the British people. Dad hadn't actually said it – he wouldn't would he – but Stephen suspected that Dad was proud of him.

He cut the wires to the main detonator. It was impossible to tell whether the unit might have been booby trapped in this light and these conditions, so he just did it without hesitation. Now all he had to do was withdraw the detonator block and climb back to the top of the tank. He would need to turn the mine back again to access the hydrostatic clock, but that could be done on a fresh cylinder. With the block spanner, he turned the detonator until it was loose. No problems so far. He felt a tug on his safety rope. It was the warning from his breathing apparatus controller above that he had five minutes left before he must return to the surface. Ample time, Stephen thought. I'll just withdraw the detonator block... and there she is. Carefully, he withdrew the copper tube comprising the detonator. Then disaster struck.

The oily water had made his fingers slippery and he dropped the detonator. At any second Stephen expected the detonator to explode as it hit the floor of the tank. It would be enough to ignite the gas and that would be the end of him and the suburb of Garston. He froze. There was no point in running. He couldn't go anywhere. He intoned a prayer to God and... nothing happened. Stupid me, he thought. The water will have cushioned the fall of the detonator. But that didn't mean all was well. He had to find that detonator. Were he to tread on it, it would still explode and the site wouldn't be safe until he removed it.

With infinite care, he reached down to the bottom of the tank. He felt the sludge of tar, lying about two feet thick at the tank bottom. Surely, he had no hope of finding a two-inch-long tube by feel alone in this mess, but he had to. Many lives now depended on him. He gently trailed his fingers through the surface of the tar, hoping not to dislodge the detonator deeper into the sludge. How far might it have fallen from where he dropped it, he wondered. The resistance of the water would have stopped it falling vertically. After two minutes of searching, he began to despair of finding his quarry. Had he been complacent, he wondered. What's the point of wondering, he asked himself. You must find that detonator. He extended his search area by a foot and as he did so, he felt a triple-tug on his safety line. It was his signal to clear out. Should he do so and return with fresh oxygen or stay to find the detonator? No, he had to stay. He would have no chance of finding it next time.

Again, Stephen extended his search area, trying hard not to move his feet for fear of disturbing the surface tension of the tarry layer of sludge. He knew there must be a safety margin for his air supply, so he didn't worry unduly about it, but he willed himself to breathe calmly and shallowly.

Now he had searched to the extent of his reach, it was necessary to take a tentative step forward. He made it, hoping he had not disturbed the sludge too much and began to feel the ground beneath him again. It was becoming more difficult to draw air from the cylinder into his lungs and he knew he had very little time left. He forced himself to keep moving his hands gently. He moved his right hand in an arc from beside him to finish ahead of his chest and repeated the movement with his left. It was becoming yet more difficult. He felt tired. It was harder and harder to take a breath and each one never left his aching lungs unsatisfied… but what was that? His left hand thought it had touched something. He moved his hand back an inch and felt something thin and hard. He grasped it with his hand and knew by its shape that it was the detonator. Somebody was tugging frantically on his lifeline. He felt like a puppet on a string. Just leave me alone. I must find the box for the detonator. It was in his tool bag, secured to a support pillar. No longer caring about disturbing the sludge beneath, he stumbled to his kit and placed the pencil tube into its box securely. Now he needed to get out before he passed out. His head was throbbing and he was sure he could hear his blood pumping even above the din of his own breathing. It seemed to have gone darker than when he had entered the gasometer and he had to feel for his ladder, but it wasn't far away.

Already exhausted, his chest heaving, he began to climb the ladder, the detonator box safely tucked into the front of his borrowed overalls. He managed two steps, but had to rest. How many were there, he wondered. He couldn't remember. One step this time and rest. What was I doing? He clung to the sides of the ladder whilst he tried to work out where he was and what he was meant to be doing. Who's that treading on my head? This is my ladder. Go away.

*****

Stephen didn't know how long he had been unconscious, but realised he must have been as he lay on the top of the gasometer. He couldn't remember climbing out of the tank, but peering at him through their own oxygen masks, two firemen were securing a different mask to his face. He didn't move. He was too tired to move. He just sucked in that sweet, slightly metallically-tasting air and let his brain absorb the fact he was alive.

The two firemen lifted him and one of them took him over his shoulder. From this position, Stephen, could see a church opposite, with a crowded cemetery. Then his view was of the ladder of a fire engine being wound in towards the earth. A crowd of firemen waited on the ground below, except they weren't all firemen. He could see two women in tin hats, too. One had curly hair spilling out from beneath her helmet and she looked very pretty. He smiled at her before he realised she wouldn't be able to see his smile behind the mask, but as he reached ground level, the man carrying him removed the mask and then his own.

'You all right, *lar*?' the fireman asked. 'You had us right worried, you know?'

'I'm fine, thanks.' Stephen's brain engaged and he reached for the box in the front of his overalls. He was relieved to find it was still there. Out of the corner of his eye he saw Monty rushing towards him.

'Stephen, you idiot. What were you playing at?' he called angrily.

'S-sorry, Monty. I dropped the main d-detonator and had to find it.'

'Well, you're bloody lucky to be alive is all I say.' Monty's face softened. 'And that pleases me. So how far did you get?'

'The p-primer's out, but I left it down there. Here's the b-bomb-fuze.' Stephen reached into one pocket for the cylinder and pulled a paper bag from the other. 'That's the g-gaine powder. There's just the p-primer to collect and the clock to come out, but I'll have to turn the mine b-back again.' Stephen made to stand up.

'No, Stephen. You've done quite enough. I'll deal with the rest. You're all in.'

'Sorry, Monty. It's my job. It's m-my m-mine.'

'Bother to all that. You stay here.' Monty pointed to the rings on his left sleeve. 'That's an order, all right?'

This time Stephen did manage to stand up. 'Sorry, s-sir, but it's not down to you to g-give me orders. I was g-given the instruction to render that m-mine s-safe and I'm jolly well going to do just that.' Stephen swayed drunkenly and stared grimly at Monty, his eyes like coals against the fair skin where his mask had protected his face from the filth of the gasometer. Satisfied he had made his point, he smiled and squatted. 'But let's have a spot of lunch first. I'm famished.'

'Sub Lieutenant Cunningham, you are the most stubborn man I've ever met, but one of the bravest, too, and I'm delighted to call you my friend.' Monty held out his right hand and Stephen shook it gladly.

CHAPTER 17

With no further raids on Liverpool, Captain Currey summoned Stephen back to London, but was gracious enough first to give him the Saturday night off to recover from his ordeal in the gasometer.

'We could travel down together should you wish, Stephen.' Monty offered. 'I've still got the car and driver. I could give you a lift home and put up for the night in a local pub. What do you say?'

'Thanks. That would be g-great. I've not been home for nearly three months. I'm sure my m-mother would be p-pleased to meet you and there's a pub not f-far away.'

*****

The journey home proved simple by car and only took two hours. Stephen had telephoned his father's garage first to warn of his arrival, but he hesitated as he stepped out of the car on the opposite side of the street, unsure of the welcome he would receive from his father after such a long absence. He could see a chink of light peeping through a corner of the blackout curtain in the parlour. Suddenly, the front door opened in a blaze of light, all blackout precautions forgotten and his mother, Jane rushed up to him and folded him in a tight embrace.

'Oh, Stephen, it's so good to see you again.' Eventually, she stood back and Stephen saw the tears of joy in her eyes. 'My! Don't you look smart in your uniform. Who'd have thought it? Our Stephen an officer.'

Stephen didn't feel smart. He had washed a little at the police station before setting off from Liverpool, but he was conscious of his dirty collar, the lack of creases in the right place in his trousers and his scuffed shoes. His mother didn't seem to mind though and she squinted through the open door of the back of the car. 'Aren't you going to introduce me to your friend, lad?' she asked.

'Of c-course,' Stephen replied, 'but shouldn't you first shut the d-door, Mum. You'll have the ARP w-warden on your back any m-minute.'

'I doubt it, love, seeing as how the ARP warden's your father. Now who have we here?' Monty had alighted from the car and compared with his own appearance, Stephen thought Monty looked the very image of the dashing naval officer.

'This is Lieutenant C-Commander Montcalm. We s-sort of w-work together, Mum.'

'Call me Monty, ma'am.' Monty shook Jane's hand warmly.

'I'm right pleased to meet you, sir. Come in out of the cold.' Jane ushered Monty through the front door of the sandstone-built house, attached to the side of the garage.

Jane directed Monty into the parlour and Stephen followed her. He could smell the scent of polish. Clearly, Mum had been to a little effort to welcome Stephen. It was a rare event to use the parlour. A log fire blazed in the hearth. Despite the smell of the wood smoke and polish, Stephen's keen nostrils detected, too, the pleasant waft from the kitchen of something good roasting in the oven. Under the circumstances, it was hardly likely to be a fatted calf, but he knew he was in for a treat. Normally, Mum cooked a roast on a Sunday, but obviously today was a special event.

Monty glanced round the room, politely complimenting various ornaments and pictures, but Stephen felt embarrassed by the room's modesty. However, he knew Monty to be a good-natured and tactful man, and felt sure Monty wouldn't say anything to upset his mother's feelings. Jane had noticed that Monty had remained standing.

'Won't you take a seat, sir?' she asked.

'Do call me, Monty, Mrs Cunningham. Everybody else does.'

'Very well, Monty. But take a seat.'

'Thank you, but I'm not staying. My driver and I need to find accommodation for the night, but I'll be back in the morning. Is there somewhere you could recommend, Stephen?'

'You could try The Fleece. It's not far from here by car. Mum used to work there, didn't you, Mum?'

'But you'd be welcome to stay here and you could stay for your supper. I've a brace of pheasants in the oven and they'd easily stretch to another plate.'

Stephen knew that the house had only three bedrooms and one was occupied by his sister, Lucy, so he cut in. 'I think Lieutenant Commander Montcalm would be m-much more c-comfortable in The Fleece, Mum. In any c-case there's the d-driver to consider.'

'Oh, Stephen! Where are our manners? You said nowt about a driver and in all the excitement, I clean forgot. You've left him outside on a night such as this. Invite him in for a brew at least.'

'It's a she, actually,' Stephen replied. 'We have a f-female driver.'

'Stephen Cunningham, I'm ashamed of you and your late fancy ways. Go and invite the poor lass into the warm.' Jane slapped Stephen on his shoulder with the back of her hand, but before Stephen could move, he heard his father calling from the hall.

'Hey, Mother. You'll never guess what I've just found outside.' He popped his head around the door of the parlour and Stephen wasn't sure who was the more surprised – his father at seeing Monty or him at seeing his father wearing the black uniform of an ARP warden. John Cunningham shifted his gaze from Monty to Stephen before continuing to say to Jane, 'I found this lass outside, alone in that big army car. I've put her in the kitchen. Could you make her a brew?'

'That's just what I was going to do, love. Stephen, what must your guests think of our northern hospitality? Now, Monty, you just park yourself there until I get back with a pot o' tea and then we'll discuss where you're going to stay.'

Five minutes later, Jane returned to the parlour. 'Right. That's all fixed. Your driver's going to stay with Mrs Roper up at Sickens Farm. Her boy's away in the RAF, so she'll be glad of the company for supper. Stephen, your Dad's just gone over t'road to borrow a mattress from old Mister Burns afore he starts his shift with the ARP. You can kip on the floor and Mister Montcalm can sleep in your bed. You don't mind sharing, do you, Monty?'

'Not at all, Mrs Cunningham. I would be delighted, but I hope I'm not putting you to too much trouble,' Monty replied.

'Call me Jane. And it's no trouble. No point being a squanderbug and wasting government money on accommodation when we can make do here, is there? It's just a shame your Dad's on duty tonight, Stephen, but he'll join you for breakfast in morning. Now get yourself upstairs, lad. You look like you could do with a good bath and the water's hot. And mind to give me that uniform and dirty shirt. I'll give the suit a good pressing and wash the shirt by hand. You can forego your fancy uniform for one night, surely?'

Half an hour later, bathed, much refreshed and wearing an old pair of flannels and a cardigan, Stephen joined Monty in the parlour. He was enjoying a bottle of beer whilst Jane talked about Stephen.

'Is there another b-beer g-going, Mum?' Stephen asked to stem the embarrassing flow of conversation. 'And where's Lucy?'

'Hold your horses, lad. I'll fetch you a beer in a moment. Lucy'll be back soon, too. She's been helping Mrs Bottomley lay out old Joe Higgs. He passed away this afternoon. Doctor thinks 'twere pneumonia. Talk of t' devil, I think that's her.'

Stephen heard with a thrill the front door open. He liked Lucy and couldn't wait to see her. Jane met her in the hall and she must have given her the news of Stephen's surprise visit because Stephen heard Lucy shriek with delight before she burst into the parlour.

'Stephen!' She threw her arms around him and kissed him on both cheeks.

'S-steady, siss. We have a g-guest.' Stephen pulled his head back from Lucy's. She spun round to see Monty for the first time.

'Oh, do forgive me. Stephen, you'd better introduce us.' Lucy blushed slightly and patted both sides of her dark, curly hair. Stephen was amused to see her sneaking a glance at the mirror over the fire. Vanity, he thought.

'This is my friend, M-Monty. Monty, my daft s-sister, Lucy.'

'How do you do, Miss Cunningham. I'm charmed to meet you.' Monty shook hands with Lucy gently and offered a slight bow. 'Your mother was just telling us that you have been on an errand of mercy.'

'Forgive me. I must change out of these awful clothes.' Lucy suddenly left the room leaving Monty looking shocked.

'Was it something I said?' Monty asked.

'D-don't worry about it, Monty. I told you my s-sister's daft.'

Forty-five minutes later, Stephen was finally able to sit down at the head of the kitchen table to eat. In the absence of his father, Jane had asked him to carve the pheasants.

'You might have left me some hot water, Stephen. I had to do a strip wash,' Lucy chided her brother.

'Sorry, s-siss, but I w-was awfully f-filthy today,' Stephen replied in slight discomfort.'

Monty came to Stephen's defence. 'And that's not the least of it, Miss Cunningham! Over the last two days I witnessed your brother perform the bravest act I could ever imagine. The state he was in afterwards, you'd not deny him a month of hot water.'

Stephen suddenly felt embarrassed by the looks of shock on both his mother's and sister's face. 'It was n-n-nothing. Honestly. M-M-Monty…' He focused on carving the birds instead of finishing the sentence. He could feel himself blushing,

'Nothing my foot, Stephen. I'm going to see to it you're given a gong for your efforts, old chap. Miss Cunningham, your brother's a hero.' Monty gave a brief summary of Stephen's actions in Liverpool, but Stephen noted he called the mine a bomb. The navy didn't want the Germans to read in the newspapers that RMS officers were being successful in defuzing magnetic mines. Stephen squirmed inwardly, quietly serving the pheasant and helping himself to vegetables. His mother and Lucy sat transfixed by Monty's tale.

After an absolute age, Lucy finally interrupted the story. 'So, what would have happened if the bomb had started ticking? How long would my brother have had to escape?'

'Seventeen to twenty seconds at the maximum. Not enough, I'm afraid. But don't worry, he wouldn't have heard it ticking in his breathing apparatus, so would have known nothing about it.'

'Oh, Stephen.' Jane burst into tears. 'I had no idea…'

As Stephen rose to comfort his mother, he noticed a flash in his sister's dark, brown eyes and a colouring in her neck. Her blood was up. 'You seem very casual about the risk, Mister Montcalm. And what were you doing whilst my brother was risking his life? Merely watching?'

'Please call me, Monty. I'm afraid you're right. I was just observing the operation. That's my job.'

'I see,' Lucy said icily. 'The privileges of rank… and your class, I suppose?'

Stephen knew his sister's moods and realised it was time he intervened. 'That's n-n-not true, Lucy. S-see that oak leaf on M-Monty's uniform? That's a d-decoration.'

'An oak leaf, I see. Yes, I think I have a similar brooch. I wear that for decoration, too, Mister Montcalm.'

'N-no, no, n-no, Lucy. It means M-Monty's been m-mentioned in d-despatches' Stephen replied in a pleading tone.

'There is an irony there, Miss Cunningham,' Monty laughed. 'You could say it was for writing despatches.'

Monty's false modesty began to annoy Stephen. Monty didn't know Lucy and Stephen could tell that Lucy's hackles were up. 'B-but Monty. You d-defuzed the other m-m-b-bomb, didn't you?' He turned to Lucy looking for her reaction. She seemed intrigued.

'I had to do something whilst you were performing your heroics. I was bored. Besides, the local team were short-handed… and it's not as if my bomb was anywhere near as difficult as yours. It was just lying in the street,' Monty said modestly.

Jane had recovered her composure during the exchange. 'Well, I think you're both awfully brave, but there's good food going cold on the table. Help yourselves to vegetables and tuck in.'

Stephen was relieved at the temporary silence as everyone served themselves a huge plateful of vegetables and gravy before eating. The food was as delicious as he remembered it to be. Nobody could make roast potatoes, mashed potatoes and gravy like Mum. However, his relief was short-lived as Monty struck up conversation with Lucy.

'So, are you a nurse, Miss Cunningham?' he asked.

'Goodness, no.' Lucy laughed and flicked her hair away from her face. 'Why ever would you think that?'

'It was just your mother mentioned that you were helping with the laying out of a neighbour. I'm sorry. I jumped to a false conclusion.'

'You certainly did, Mister Montcalm. No, I'm a teacher. I was only helping with the laying out of a neighbour because he's a member of our church and nobody else would do it.'

'No, Lucy,' Jane interjected. Lucy ignored the warning.

'Is it surprising, Mother? He was a randy old goat.'

'Now really, Lucy!' Jane exclaimed. 'Not before our guest.'

'I'm sure you don't mind a bit of plain speaking, do you, Mister Montcalm? The fact is that old Joe was like an octopus. Hands everywhere and you can't deny it, Mum. You had your bottom pinched often enough, too.'

Jane's neck flushed bright pink. 'You shouldn't speak ill of the dead, Lucy. It's as well your father's not here,' she chided.

'Do you teach at a secondary school or a primary school, Miss Cunningham?' Monty switched the conversation.

'A primary school. Some of us didn't have the benefits of Stephen's university education.' Lucy stared at her mother meaningfully.

'Not that again, Lucy. And in front of a guest, too. You know we would have sent you if we'd had the money.' Lucy broke her stare and turned to Monty.

'What were you doing before you joined the navy, Mister Montcalm?' Stephen noted Monty's crestfallen look at continuing to be addressed so formally by Lucy.

'I was a barrister in London,' Monty replied matter-of-factly.

'Golly! We are honoured to be in such distinguished company.'

'Lucy!' Jane shot Lucy a warning look. Stephen was relieved to note his mother had spotted the danger signs, too. Lucy could be quite wearing company, he thought.

'And which university did you attend, Mister Montcalm? I mean, you must have studied law at a university before being called to the Bar. Is that the correct term?'

'Indeed, it is. You're very well informed, Miss Cunningham.' Stephen winced inwardly. From his sister's reaction, he knew that that remark was going to cost Monty dear. 'I was fortunate to study at Oxford.'

'My! How grand. I suppose you went to Eton first? Or might it have been Harrow?' Lucy asked sarcastically.

'Eton, naturally. It produces more prime ministers,' Monty replied immodestly.

'But the present prime minister is an old Harrovian, is he not?' Lucy shot back.

'True. Harrow gets a turn from time to time.'

Stephen remained quiet and concentrated on his pheasant. Whilst he knew that Monty was merely being his usual light-hearted self, he was acutely conscious, too, of his sister's firm socialist beliefs. It might have been better had Monty stayed at The Fleece, after all.

'So, you are an advocate of the privileged retaining the levers of power, then?'

'Lucy, don't talk politics at the table. It's not fitting, dear,' Jane interrupted.

'I agree, Mrs Cunningham, that politics has no place for the drawing room… or the dining table for that matter, but do let me reply to that last point. And then, perhaps, we could focus on this delicious meal. I don't think I have ever tasted finer roast pheasant.' Jane smiled modestly at Monty's compliment.

'It ain't nothing special. His grace's gamekeeper slips us a few from time to time. You know, the estate at Abbeystead?'

'Oh yes. Bend'Or's place. My late grandfather knew him well. My father and brother have shot there, but I've never been fond of the sport. Now, Miss Cunningham…'

'Sorry, Monty. What do you mean, "Bendor"? I was referring to the Duke of Westminster,' Jane asked.

Monty laughed apologetically. 'I'm sorry Mrs Cunningham. I was speaking of the duke. Bend'Or is his nickname, but I can see that may have come across as rather pretentious. Forgive me. But to return to our sparring, Miss Cunningham. Where were we?'

'I think you were about to justify why the upper classes should continue to be the ruling classes,' Lucy responded archly.

'Oh, yes. We were discussing privilege. I admit to having been blessed with a very privileged background. For that reason, I tend not to delve into politics. But, if pressed, I would argue that all men – and women, of course – should have unfettered access to the highest levels of education, irrespective of their means. I just wouldn't want to see girls at Eton. They would be too much of a distraction… and too clever for the boys.'

To Stephen's relief, Lucy suddenly smiled and said, 'Mister Montcalm, I think you're pulling my leg.'

'Perhaps just a little, Miss Montcalm. But seriously. I may be privileged, but I wash behind my ears at night, I keep a civil tongue and I give up my seat on the Underground and raise my hat to ladies. I don't think I'm a monster.'

'That is something you have still to prove if you are to avoid the tumbrils and Madame Guillotine, Mister Montcalm.'

Jane began to clear the plates and Stephen helped her. He hoped it might divert Lucy's attention and spare further embarrassment. Jane let out a small cry. 'Oh dear. Dad's left his Thermos flask behind with his cocoa. He'll need it on a chilly night as this. Lucy, you couldn't drop it down to him, could you? It'll only take a few minutes.'

'Very well, Mum,' Lucy replied without hesitation and rose to leave. Monty rose, , and pulled her chair away for her.

'It's a dark night. Perhaps I might escort you there and back,' Monty offered. 'That is if my privileged presence would not offend you.'

'Why, Monty. That would suit me well.' Monty smiled broadly as Lucy fluttered her eyelashes in response before fetching her coat and scarf.

After they left, Stephen turned to his mother. 'Do you think it was a g-good idea to let them g-go together, Mum? They might now b-be fighting like cat and d-d-dog.'

Jane smiled in return. 'You've much to learn about women, Stephen. I tell you, she's taken with him. Poor Monty. He's got his hands full there – privileged or otherwise.'

CHAPTER 18

Despite his relatively short absence in the north, Monty found a mountain of signals and messages on his desk in the Admiralty, all requiring his urgent attention. However, one of his first priorities had been to see Captain Currey to brief him on Stephen's extraordinary courage in Liverpool. He had suggested to Currey that a DSO might be appropriate, but Currey had responded that he thought the new George Cross might be more fitting and he would discuss it with the higher echelons. He had been grateful for Monty's written report.

It was already lunchtime, but having cleared the priority stuff, he could turn his attention to the routine intelligence and technical reports. It gave him time, too, to cast his mind back to the weekend events after the visit to Liverpool. He had felt most comfortable and welcome at the home of the Cunninghams. In particular, he had enjoyed meeting Lucy. She was quite unlike any girl he had ever met. Naturally, he had met several bright young women at Oxford. Marcy was a good example, but Lucy had a passion and intensity he had not come across within his usual social circle. It was clear that they would never see eye to eye on politics, but he had found the conversation stimulating. He had never given much thought to politics and when he had bothered to vote at all, had voted for the Conservative Party out of habit. Although Lucy would never give him credit for it, despite his class and privilege, he had already begun to soften his ideas since the outbreak of the war. Nobody who had seen the bombing and consequent suffering of the civilian populations in London and Liverpool could do otherwise. Some of the sailors he had witnessed working on the unexploded mines came from those same overcrowded and impoverished streets. He hoped that once the war was over, the government might endeavour to spread the prosperity of the nation more evenly. But the end of the war seems such a long way off, he thought and stifled an audible sigh for fear of distracting Captain Maitland-Dougall on the other side of the office.

Amongst the intelligence reports, there was some good news to counter the gloomy thought that had just passed through his mind. When he had attended the defuzing of the magnetic mine at Shoeburyness, he had taken away some lengths of the mine's parachute cords with the idea that they would make excellent dressing gown cords. He had later thought better of it and sent them off for analysis. The report of the analysis gave him an idea. He turned to Maitland-Dougall.

'Sir, have you a minute?'

Maitland-Dougall put down the paper he was reading and smiled at Monty. 'Absolutely. Shoot.'

'I have the analysis of the parachute cord being used on the magnetic mines and it's very interesting, sir. According to the scientists, they're made of a form of hemp only grown in Yugoslavia.'

'All right. What's your point, Monty?'

'I wondered whether we might find a way to shut down the production of the cord, sir. Cut off the supplies of the hemp or cord and we slow down the production of the magnetic mines.'

Monty looked expectantly at his commanding officer, but Maitland-Dougall said nothing. It was one of his habits not to give an immediate answer to a problem. Instead, he churned over the facts in silence, weighing up all the possible solutions, their pros and their cons. The silence lasted two to three minutes, but whereas at first Monty might have wondered if he had been heard, he was now used to these prolonged silences and had learned not to disturb the captain's concentration. At last, Maitland-Dougall's normally cold, blue-grey eyes sparkled and he laughed.

'By Jove, Monty! I think you're on to something there. I'll contact the Ministry of Economic Warfare and ask them to pay whatever price necessary to buy up the entire crop. That'll spike the Germans' game. Well done, Monty.' Maitland-Dougall reached for the telephone, but it buzzed before he had time to touch the handset.

Monty basked silently in the praise and picked up the signal pad, but his attention was diverted by Maitland-Dougall's exclamation.

'Absolutely not. Signal Cardiff and tell the admiral that under no circumstances is anyone to touch that mine. I'm sending Monty down there right away. Thanks for the heads-up.' Maitland-Dougall replaced the receiver and walked over to one of the maps on the wall of the office.

'Monty, pack your bags and get yourself down to Porthcawl in Wales. A mine's been found in the mouth of a river near there. Here it is.' He pointed to the map. 'The River Ogmore.' The captain immediately pulled out a folio of charts for the area. Monty was now at his side. 'There we are. The Ogmore. Depth five fathoms at high water, but high and dry at low tide. Either the German pilots are piss-poor at navigation or they still don't get how far the tides recede around our coasts. Leastways, it gives us a chance.'

'Are you thinking this could be an acoustic mine, sir?'

'Exactly and that's why I want the mine recovered intact. Flag Officer-in-Charge Cardiff proposed exploding it.'

'But what makes you think it could be the new mine, sir?'

'It was dropped last night and sighted this forenoon. By chance, an RMS officer was on leave in Cardiff at the time and he had a look at it. According to Chapple, there's something a little different about this mine. All the *Vernon* personnel are still hard pushed with a plethora of mines in Cardiff, but I'll ask RMS to have someone meet you.' Maitland-Dougall checked the clock on the wall of the office. 'If you get your skates on, you should make it there in time for the next low tide. Good luck.'

*****

It was evening and consequently dark when Monty arrived in Porthcawl. Added to the darkness of the hour, a fine drizzle was coming across the beach. It was what his Scottish aunt called a *dreich* night. He was glad he was wearing his white, high-necked, Coastal Forces' sweater. He was met by an RNVR sub lieutenant. He seemed familiar, but Monty couldn't place him in the dark until he heard the unmistakable accent of an American when he introduced himself.

'Dwight Johnson, sir, but everyone calls me Johnny.'

'Of course. You're Stephen Cunninghams's friend. So, what have we here?'

'I think it might be an acoustic, sir.' Johnson pointed a couple of hundred yards out to sea.

'That's why I'm here, but it's Monty, remember? How much experience have you had in dealing with mines, Johnny?'

'Jeez, plenty. Too many, but I grant I've never been on my own. Somehow or other, we've broken the rules and I've always kind o' been the assistant. I take it you'll be wanting me to assist you on this one, too, Monty?'

'Not at all, dear chap. It's your mine. I'm merely here to observe matters, but I'll give you a hand where I can. If this is an acoustic mine, we need to recover it intact.'

'I need to warn you that there's no saying it is an acoustic mine, Monty. It's just Lieutenant Commander Chapple had a funny feeling about it. I guess we'll have to take extra care anyway.'

'That might be a sensible course, Johnny. With that in mind, we might wait until daylight until you tackle the job, but let's see the beast first, shall we?'

The two men withdrew their non-magnetic torches and headed down the sandbank towards the mine. The beach was sandy and after about a hundred yards, it was fairly firm underneath to make walking easier. Johnson carried his non-magnetic tools and Monty a stake and length of rope to tether the mine until the next low tide. In the drizzle the coast seemed featureless and Monty felt as if he and Johnson were cut off from the rest of the world. He wondered at the motivation of the young American to risk his life for another country. Was the bond to the old country still that strong?

As Monty and Johnson walked further, Monty could see the white caps of the breakers reflecting in the light of his torch beam. If they walked much further, they would be getting their feet wet, he thought. They should have come across the mine by now.

'Are you sure about the position of the mine, Johnny?'

'Not entirely, sir, I mean, Monty. A sergeant in the local ack-ack battery offered to illuminate it for me, but that would have involved a generator... and if this baby's acoustic, I didn't think that a good idea. I was told it was about a hundred yards above the low-water mark.'

'So that would mean we've walked about fifty yards too far. Let's retrace our steps and search in opposite directions.'

It was easy enough for the men to retrace their steps. Their footsteps were clearly marked in the soft, wet sand. It was barely a minute after splitting up that Monty heard his name called in a low voice. He turned about and headed in the direction of the torch beam. On joining Johnson, Monty noted five yards ahead the outline of a dark, bulbous shape lying on its side in a shallow depression in the sand. Johnson spoke quietly.

'There's our baby, Monty. No sign of the parachute. It must have been taken out to sea in this offshore breeze. Be my guest.' Johnson stepped to one side and gestured for Monty to precede him in inspecting the mine.

As always when Monty inspected a mine, his skin crawled with fear. The mine before him looked to be a standard Type 'C', containing over 1,500 pounds of explosive. Having landed in at least seven feet of water, the hydrostatic pressure switch would have stopped the clockwork bomb fuze from operating, but the mine's magnetic mechanism would now be armed. He and Johnson had already taken the precaution of removing any magnetic material from their persons, but if this was one of the new acoustic mines, the slightest noise of any frequency might be enough to vapourise them instantly. To think he might have had a cushy number on an admiral's staff, but here he was in the cold and wet and liable to be blown to smithereens at any minute. Monty shuddered. Such thoughts were for back in London and not on a desolate beach.

He examined the mine carefully by torchlight and made a note of its serial number. It began with the letters 'Ld' and the hairs rose on the back of Monty's neck. Only a month ago he had been examining some bomb craters in another part of Wales. He had been there as there were suspicions that acoustic mines had been dropped in the Bristol Channel. Two mines had been dropped on some waste ground near a railway embankment and he had approached to examine them. However, just as he began his wary approach, both mines had exploded without warning when he was still two hundred yards distant. Had he set off a few seconds earlier, he would not have been on this beach here today. He had recalled that a shunting engine had been operating on the embankment and he suspected that the vibration of the engine had triggered the bomb fuzes. Amongst the debris of the mines, he had found a tail cone bearing the letters 'Ld'.

He gestured to Johnson to retire and held a finger to his lips to warn him to be silent. Carefully, the two officers retraced their steps fifty paces. 'Johnny, I think Chapple was right. There is something odd about this mine, but it's too difficult to explain my suspicions.' Monty spoke in a whisper. 'Don't take offence, Johnny, but you need help with this mine and somebody more experienced than I. I'm going back to tether that mine and then I'll summon help from Cardiff. We must recover this mine intact.'

'I'm glad you didn't say that I was the inexperienced one on this job, Monty. I appreciate that.'

Monty returned to the mine and took one last look. He couldn't see underneath the mine, but in all respects it seemed standard. He admired Chapple's instinct that there was something odd about it. He spotted that the safety ring of the primer release was still in place even though the forked pin holding it in place was missing. By rights this mine should have exploded. To ensure it didn't, he pushed his stub of a pencil through the ring to stop it popping when the tide returned. He then drove his stake into the sand and tethered the mine with his rope through the parachute shackle. The last thing anyone wanted was this menace floating free.

*****

It was nearly two weeks later that Monty read the report on the mine recovered at Porthcawl. It had been safely dismantled and then recovered for analysis at the chalk quarry near Buriton in the South

Downs, the navy's new investigation range for recovered mines. It had taken a team of three RMS officers to defuze the mine and Monty was pleased to learn that Johnson and one other had been recommended for the new George Medal. However, the technical analysis of the mine's parts had made him tingle with excitement. The mine had contained two special features. Firstly, the clock had proved to be a new form of 'clicker' unit, that could be set to be activated up to six days ahead. The earlier versions were already making the work of the minesweeping flotillas even more difficult and Monty thanked his luck that he was in his nice *safe* billet ashore. However, it was the second technical development that really excited him and he couldn't wait to brief Maitland-Dougall. Mounted on a bar welded across the dome of the rear door of the mine was a small microphone attached to a new form of firing mechanism. The *Vernon* men had recovered their first German acoustic mine and now knew the exact frequency on which the unit within operated. The scientists were even now designing a modification to various minesweepers comprising a Kango hammer tuned to the appropriate frequency and housed in a water-tight compartment beneath the ships' keels. It was another victory for the *Vernon* team.

CHAPTER 19
December 1940

Stephen didn't know how long the telephone had been ringing. He had been in a deep sleep after an exhausting few days of clearing mines in London's docks, but in his dreams, he kept hearing the sound of the ambulances time and time again. His focus had been on clearing the parachute mines, but the Germans were now making widespread use of incendiary bombs and, according to the RMS scuttlebutt, so-called 'Satan' bombs of up to two tonnes in weight. These powerful bombs could devastate an entire street in the same way as the mines. Either the *Luftwaffe*'s navigational prowess had dropped markedly or the Germans were now increasingly conducting a terror campaign against the civilian population. There was a rumour that the RAF had won the Battle of Britain and to cause Hitler's invasion plans to be postponed, but perhaps now they intended terrorising the civilian population into suing for peace.

Slowly, it dawned on his weary mind that the ringing noise in his dreams was the telephone. He groped for it just to shut it up so that he might continue his well-earned sleep, but a metallic voice squawked at him from the earpiece. Gradually regaining consciousness against his will, he placed the receiver to his ear.

'Cunningham, you cloth-ears. Answer damn you. Cunningham…'

'S-speaking. W-what is it?' Stephen switched on his bedside light and picked up his watch. It was two in the morning.

'At last… and about ruddy time. I've been ringing you for five minutes now.'

'Who is it?' Stephen was confused that the voice on the other end had an Australian accent. He didn't know any Australians.

'It's the duty officer at RMS. Who the hell else would be ringing you at this stupid hour? Now unstick your back from your pit, mate, and pack yourself a suitcase. There'll be a car along inside the next half hour. And Cunningham…'

Stephen swung his legs out of his bed and prepared to stand up. He regretted the decision immediately. The linoleum flooring of his room was ice-cold. He held the telephone with his left hand whilst reaching out for his dressing gown. 'Where am I g-going?'

'Crikey, mate. Don't be a drongo. You know better than to ask that over the blower, mate. I just wanted to warn you that you might be away for a few days.' The duty officer hung up.

Stephen registered the information and looked at yesterday's calendar date, the eleventh of December. He hoped he would be back for Christmas, wherever he was going. He had won the ballot to have a forty-eight-hour pass for Christmas with his family in Lancashire. But first, he needed to get dressed and packed.

It was bitterly cold outside with slush from the previous day's snow lying in the scuppers of the streets. He was glad he hadn't shaved – not through laziness, he was most particular about being clean-shaven – but due to an absence of hot water. The cold always dried up his freshly-shaved skin to cause him an itch and rash.

He didn't have long to wait in the cold as within three minutes he spotted the thin slashes of a car's headlights approaching. It was unlikely to be a civilian car at this time of day and sure enough, a khaki Humber drew alongside the kerb. Stephen placed his suitcase in the boot of the car and as he stepped into the back, he was surprised to see another occupant on the other end of the seat.

'That you, Stephen?' There was no mistaking the slow, warm drawl as that of Johnson.

'Here. Take the other end of this, buddy.' Johnson passed Stephen the end of a rug to wrap round his lap. 'I don't suppose you prepared yourself a Thermos flask either, did you?'

'N-no, Johnny. There wasn't time.'

'Don't worry. I was just going off duty when the shout came in, so I've brought us some coffee. Sorry, it's black mind.'

Stephen gladly accepted the proffered beaker of the scalding coffee. After just one sip, his brain seemed awake again. 'Do you know where we're going?'

'Birmingham. And unlike Alabama, it's going to be goddamned cold. There's a nasty frost out there and the roads are bad, so tuck in tight. You ever been to Birmingham before, Stephen?'

'No. I c-can't say I have.'

'Me neither, but Jerry has. The city's taken one hell of a beating. I've heard it may be as bad as Coventry. In all, there's seven cars on the way – nearly half the team. Unexploded mines scattered all over the city like confetti by all accounts. Sure hope you've brought a change of underwear.'

As the car left London, the roads became more slippery and on more than one occasion the driver temporarily lost control of the Humber's rear end. Stephen peered through the windscreen, but all he could see was blackness and he worried how the driver could see at all. Johnson had already fallen asleep and Stephen thought it might be a good idea to follow his example, but the coffee had had its effect and he could only doze, coming to with a start every time the car lurched on the black ice.

At about 06.30, exactly when Stephen thought he must have only just nodded off, the car slowed and came to a stop. 'Here you are, gentlemen. You hungry?' the driver asked.

Stephen rubbed the frosted window pane and peered into the darkness outside. They were in the car park of a public house and there seemed to be much activity outside. 'W-where are we? And w-why have we s-stopped?'

'The White Hart at Saint Albans, sirs. The kind Admiralty's booked all you gentlemen in for a hearty breakfast at seven. We're a bit early, but I put that down to my superior skills as a driver.'

Stephen and Johnson alighted from the army car and Stephen had to catch Johnson as he skidded on the ice. It was still very dark and clearly cloudy as not even the stars were visible. Although the pub was supposedly open, it was bathed in darkness such that Johnson had to use his torch to guide them to its main entrance. Snow on the edge of the path reflected in the torchlight. Johnson headed into the pub, but Stephen spotted a sign for the toilets or *heads,* the term he had learned at *King Alfred* that the navy used for toilets. There he met Lawson. He hadn't seen him since the diving course at *Excellent.*

'M-morning, Lawson. How are you?'

Lawson looked at Stephen as if he was having difficulty remembering him. 'Oh! It's you. I heard you were still in the outfit.' Lawson then left the lavatories without another word – or washing his hands. Stephen tutted in admonishment behind Lawson's back.

He first went to the main bar, but it was crowded with sailors, some of whom even at this early hour were nursing pints of beer and who directed him to the next-door saloon bar. There, he discovered that Johnson had already poured him a hot drink.

'There you are, buddy. Tea with milk this time, but there's no sugar. I'm afraid there's no breakfast for another fifteen minutes or so either. We're early. Sure is good of the Admiralty to fix this up for us, though. I bet we can thank Captain Currey for that.'

Stephen looked around the other officers as he sipped his tea. He recognised Dusty Miller, but Lawson was talking to him so he gave them a wide berth. Also at the bar was a lieutenant he recognised, but whose name he had forgotten, talking to an Australian sub lieutenant. Stephen approached them to introduce himself.

'G-good m-morning. I'm S-Stephen C-Cunningham. We've met b-before,' he said to the lieutenant.

'That's right. I remember. Gilbert Stubbs.' Stubbs shook Stephen's hand and turned to Johnson. 'Johnny Johnson isn't it?'

'That's right, Gilbert. We met at *Mirtle* a couple of weeks back.'

'So we did. Have either of you met Hughie Syme? He and a few of his colleagues have come all the way from Australia to help us out. Hughie, Johnny here's a fellow colonial, but from America.'

The four officers found a table away from the bar to await their breakfast. Gilbert seemed to be the one who knew what was going on. 'Dusty over there's in charge. As soon as we've eaten, we're to scoot up to Birmingham. It's the worst raid they've had and things are quite bad by all accounts. I say, Stephen, I've just noticed you've shipped your second stripe. Congratulations. When did that happen?'

'Oh that.' Stephen reddened with embarrassment. 'Just a c-couple of w-weeks ago. I haven't become used to it myself.' Before Stephen could say more or face any scrutiny over his early promotion to lieutenant, there was a roar of laughter from the bar. Stephen looked up to see Reggie Bacon make an entrance. Bacon responded by bending one knee, half bowing, stretching out his arms beside him and pirouetting on the spot. Then Stephen saw the reason for the laughter. Bacon had parted his bright-red beard into two equal and pointed halves at the chin.

'Greetings, gentlemen,' he announced in a stage voice. 'I thought that on such a devilish day, I would act the part. If I am to meet Saint Peter today, I hope he will take the hint and send me downstairs where I am sure far more *de-lic-ious* pleasures await.' Bacon finished by performing a short jig before approaching the bar. Stephen hoped Bacon wouldn't encounter too many old ladies. He felt sure Bacon's bizarre appearance would send them to an early grave.

The proprietor and a woman appeared suddenly, bearing trays of food that were immediately seized upon with hungry relish by those at the bar. Stephen's party joined them and queued for their chance to help themselves. Dusty Miller came over to them holding a large bacon sandwich in one hand and his cap in the other.

'Good to see you chaps. I'm O-I-C, so I'm going on ahead to set up a command post. I'll be aiming for the town hall, but if it's not there now, just ask a policeman and you'll find me. Take your time. The roads are deuced tricky and some of the chaps have already had minor encounters with lamp posts, so warn your drivers to take it easy. Cheerio.'

After helping themselves to some welcome breakfast of bacon and plenty of eggs, Stephen and the others returned to their table. Halfway through the meal, Syme asked of Stephen and Johnson, 'I suppose you chaps have plenty of experience in dealing with these mines?'

Johnson replied first. 'I've dealt with a few. We both have. You?'

Syme shook his head. 'First time, mate.'

Stubbs cut in. 'Don't worry, old chap. You'll do just great.'

Refreshed and replete, Stephen and Johnson prepared to leave for the journey north, but were waylaid by Lawson. 'Do you have your stopwatches with you?'

Stephen and Johnson looked at each other puzzled. Stephen just nodded, but Johnson replied. 'Sure we have them. What of it?'

'I just thought we might make things more interesting. I'm having a little sweepstake with the others as to who can strip a mine the quickest. Five bob in and winner takes all. What do you say?'

'Are you m-mad?' Stephen was appalled by the idea. 'I've n-never heard anything s-so s-s-stupid.'

'Steady on, Cunningham. Don't take on so. You're not afraid, are you?'

Stephen's blood boiled and Johnson must have noticed as he lay a hand on his arm. 'Of c-course I'm afraid, b-but I'm no c-coward. B-b-but a race! That's sheer s-stupidity. Oh, w-what's the point?' Stephen shook off Johnson and headed outside, quickly followed by Johnson.

'Just wait here, Stephen. I'll tell the driver we're ready to go.' Johnson disappeared back into the pub. Stephen noted that the sky was still grey, but the dawn was coming. He wondered why he had reacted so badly to Lawson's wager. There was just something about Lawson that seemed to rile him. No, he wouldn't take part in the bet. He didn't care about losing five shillings, but if he was afraid each time he tackled a mine, it was his job to overcome that fear and to live to tackle the next job. He wasn't going to take unnecessary risks for the sake of kudos.

*****

It was testament to their driver's skill that they arrived in Birmingham in one piece. They had passed one of the other cars being towed out of a hedge by a tractor and Stephen later learned that theirs was the only car not to have suffered some damage. Birmingham was a shambles. Stephen had heard about the raids on Coventry and prayed that Birmingham would not be as bad, but it looked as if his prayers had been ignored. Their driver became lost as street after street was blocked by rubble or barricades. Fire hoses snaked everywhere and damaged hydrants plumed fountains of gushing water high into the air, the water turning into steam as it hit the smoking and burning remnants of what had once been homes. People stood in groups, silent and pale… just watching and waiting. They needed courage and above all, hope.

The driver enlisted the help of a policeman who took the passenger seat to guide them through the ruins and misery of a proud city to the vicinity of the town hall. He had to stop short on account of the wreckage, but the town hall was still standing and Stephen walked there with Johnson. Outside the town hall a mass of people congregated. Many were maimed, the blood seeping through makeshift bandages of sheets, towels and anything else that had been to hand after the horror of the bombing. Doctors and nurses made rapid and cursory examinations of the wounded, summoning stretcher bearers to take the worst inside the town hall for urgent treatment and away from the cold and awful stench of death, blood and gore. Stephen welled up on seeing that the misery included children and young babies. Neither he nor Johnson spoke for fear of croaking and betraying their emotions.

Somewhere amidst the chaos of the dead and dying, the medical staff, the council officials and the clusters of air-raid wardens and policemen, Stephen and Johnson found Miller at a trestle table alongside an easel holding a large map of Birmingham marked with the sites of the unexploded mines. Miller was talking to the regional officer, but smiled at their arrival and indicated for them to help themselves to tea from the large urn on another table. The hot liquid and caffeine helped revive Stephen from the shock of what he had seen so far this morning. Despite having witnessed the aftermath of the bombing in Liverpool and London, the suffering in Birmingham seemed more pronounced. Miller finished talking to the regional officer and beckoned to them to come over to the map.

"'fraid we're all going to have a busy few days, chaps. We're short of manpower so it's one after the other. Johnny, you take this one and Stephen you this one. When you've finished the job, report back here and I'll give you another.' Stephen noted that Dusty looked pale and tired. The responsibility for the operation was clearly weighing on him.

The regional officer turned to them. 'I'll have one of my men guide you to your targets.' He beckoned two elderly wardens. Stephen and Johnson followed them out of the town hall and down its steps.

The wardens forced a passage for them through the sullen and despondent crowd and as they did so, Stephen heard soft voices whispering, *'They're the blokes who delouse the mines'*, *'They're bloody heroes'* and *'God bless 'em'*. He found it odd. He didn't think of himself as a hero. He was just doing his job even though each time he approached a mine it frightened the living daylights out of him.

At the cars Stephen and Johnson parted, wishing each other luck. Stephen was glad to gain the relative warmth of the car. He was shivering from the cold, even in his greatcoat. The roads and pavements were still rimed with thick ice or frozen snow. Stephen felt melancholy and dazed by the scenes all around him.

Perhaps a quarter of an hour later, the car stopped and the rating accompanying the driver hauled Stephen's tools from the boot. The policeman at the barrier across the street moved it to let Stephen and the rating pass. Crowds of people stood either side of the car. Seeing Stephen's glance, the policeman volunteered the information that the area had been cleared for a radius of 400 hundred yards and wished him luck. The policeman's words were echoed by the crowd calling, *'God bless you, sir. Good luck.'* Stephen found the crowd's faith in him humbling.

The escort remained at the barrier so the streets echoed only with the steps of two lonely men as they followed the directions given through deserted streets, past silent factories and empty homes. To Stephen's left on the corner of the street, he spotted a sandbagged dugout. With a pang of nervousness, he realised that his quarry was just thirty yards around the corner. It was the second time he had been impressed by the preparations of Birmingham's ARP organisation. First, the welcoming urn of tea and now this.

He rounded the corner and saw the mine. It lay on its side, on a heap of coke and snow. It seemed straight forward enough for once. His assistant laid down the bag of tools and bucket of water. Stephen turned to him, 'Thanks. You can withdraw to the dugout now. I'll call if I need anything.' With a look of relief, the rating thanked him and headed back down the street. Stephen examined the mine carefully. The fuze was covered in ice and that would make life complicated. He didn't fancy chipping away at the ice in case the vibrations should set off the fuze, but there was an alternative. He had been a science teacher after all, he thought.

He tried a few front doors and found one unlocked. On the ground floor to the rear of the house he found the kitchen and its larder. There he collected some salt. The salt would lower the freezing temperature and defrost the ice around the fuze. It gave him an idea. He wondered whether dry ice could be used to freeze the clockwork mechanism of a mine, but his thoughts were interrupted. He heard a noise upstairs and a stifled voice. He was puzzled. The area had been cordoned off and evacuated. Could it be looters? Would they offer violence? Stephen swapped his salt for a poker from the range and quietly ascended the stairs. The threadbare carpet muffled his tread, but near the landing the stair creaked under his weight. He heard a muffled giggle from the room to his right overlooking the street. Wielding the poker above his head he opened the door slowly and was shocked by the sight within the bedroom.

Chapter 20

Two young boys were trying to hide behind the bed, but Stephen quickly spotted them and stood over them, lowering the poker as he did so. The boys responded with cheeky grins. Something snapped inside Stephen. 'W-w-what are you d-doing?' he shouted. That wiped the grins off the boys' faces and frightened them.

'Please, sir...' one of them cried as the other said, 'We weren't doin' nothin'. Just watchin'.'

Stephen dropped the poker onto the bed and lunged at the boys. He planned to bang their heads together. It was bad enough he had to risk his life to delouse these beastly weapons, but stupid that two kids should treat it as a matter of fun. The kids evaded his grasp and fled downstairs. By the time Stephen reached the street, they were well out of sight. Still angry, he retrieved the salt and returned to his deadly trade.

Two hours later, he carried his trophies and bucket back to the barricade, his assistant following with the tools. He informed the policeman at the barrier that it was now safe to let people back into the area and was surprised by the almost instant response from the crowd. Suddenly and as one, the people started cheering and several took his hand to shake it. Others slapped him on the back. Some laughed and some cried. Stephen was completely flummoxed by the reaction. 'W-what is it?' he asked the policeman.

The policeman, too, slapped him on the back. 'Congratulations, sir. You've just saved their ruddy homes, that what's up.'

Stephen tried to make his way through the crowd back to his car, but the people had other ideas. As a mob, they pushed him down the street and through the doors of a pub. Behind the bar the landlord began lining up glasses and without any words, pushed a pint of bitter across the bar towards Stephen. The other guests began to sing *For He's a Jolly Good Fellow* and urged him to take the beer. Despite his usual modesty, Stephen's heart filled with pride and he struggled to hold back a tear as he basked in the admiration of the crowd. Then, to his acute discomfort, somebody passed around a hat and presented it to him, stuffed with notes and coins.

'N-n-no!' Stephen cried out and felt the tears begin to well again. 'I c-can't take it. I w-was just d-doing my job.' He couldn't believe that these people who had suffered so much recently could be so generous of spirit. He was truly humbled and drank his pint gratefully.

*****

Stephen had lost count of the number of mines he had stripped since his arrival in Birmingham the morning before. He hadn't minded the work, but he felt dog-tired. Now he and Bacon, with his ridiculous beard, were being dropped on the outskirts of the city to attend to another pair of mines. Stephen, the more experienced RMS officer these days, took the nearest mine as it would be the more difficult. It was embedded in a pavement, about two feet deep and at an awkward angle. Stephen and Bacon examined it together.

'Rather you than me, dear boy,' Bacon observed. 'You'll have the devil of a job withdrawing the hydrostatic clock at this angle and it wouldn't surprise me if those fiendish Visigoths haven't furnished it with one of their Zus 40 booby traps. Give me a shout if you need a hand.'

'Thanks, B-Bacon, but you know the Old M-Man's rules. Only one officer p-per mine.'

'Of course, so I will bid you adieu and exit stage left.' Bacon bowed and retreated to deal with his own mine.

Stephen reflected on Bacon's words. He was probably right. There might well be a booby trap beneath the hydrostatic clock or the bomb fuze or even both. Were he to remove either by more than half an inch from its housing, it could release a spring-loaded firing pin underneath that would strike a percussion cap and detonate the mine. The evil device had only been discovered at the expense of the lives of RMS officers whose every move had been recorded by observing officers. Stephen decided it would be wiser not to undertake unnecessary risks. He would use cords to remove the units remotely from the safety of a nearby dugout. With the help of his rating assistant, he ran out the cords, but was interrupted by the return of Bacon.

'Cunningham, dearhart. I must crave a favour.'

'Yes. W-what do you n-need?'

'It would please me greatly if you would swap mines with me.'

Stephen was hugely surprised at the request. 'B-but why? You said yourself you d-didn't envy me?'

'It's difficult to explain, old boy. My mine's an absolute sitter and I fear it has my number on it. Today's the thirteenth and I've just remembered this is my thirteenth mine. Call it the superstition of the stage, old boy, if you like, but I have a strange feeling that this isn't my lucky day. That mine may have my number on it, so I want to swap mines. Give me something more challenging.'

Stephen didn't understand Bacon's reasoning, but didn't want Bacon to attempt to strip a mine if he wasn't in the right frame of mind. 'D-do you really w-want to take my m-mine, Reggie?'

'Indubitably. Absolutely. You're a very fine fellow, Stephen. A real brick.' He gestured to the cords Stephen was rigging. 'And I see you've taken my advice to treat this object with especial care. It'll be all right for me.'

'W-well, if you're sure.' Stephen shrugged his shoulders and collected his wellington boots from the car before heading off to the middle of the field where lay the other mine of the pair. Nothing about it seemed out of the ordinary, but that didn't stop him feeling nervous. Bacon's words of caution over the Zus 40 echoed in his head, but he didn't feel the need to tackle this mine remotely. He could take the weight of the fuze in his fingertips and by moving it from side to side, he would soon feel if something more sinister lay beneath it.

Slowly and methodically, he went about his normal routine. He applied the gag and began to turn the keeper ring, but a sixth sense stopped him going further. He knew something was wrong and nervously listened for any sound of ticking. Mercifully, there was none, but he then spotted that the gag was lying limp. The gag was losing pressure and that meant the mine was still live and the merest touch could set it off. The thought crossed his mind that Bacon's instinct had been right. This might not be a lucky day for the poor RMS officer stripping the mine. He thought about just blowing up the mine. It was in a field and would not harm the neighbourhood, but pride cut in. This was his mine and he would beat it or die in the process.

Carefully, he unscrewed the gag, conscious that any false movement could set the fuze running. He crouched as he worked so that if he had to run, he would already be on his feet. Earlier, he had spotted a deep ditch just 150 yards away. Can I run that distance in seventeen seconds, he wondered. What if the fuze has already run down and stopped? He might have as little as one or two seconds. If so, there was nothing he could do about it and what was the point in worrying about something he couldn't do anything about?

The gag came away in his hand and the clock hadn't started to run. Stephen pumped the horn again and tested it in the bucket of water. There were no bubbles. Hardly daring to breathe, he screwed the gag back onto the mine and opened the tap. The only sound was that of the safety pin dropping home. Relieved, Stephen began to unscrew the keeper ring and checked the motor horn's bulb for tautness. It was slack and that meant it was still leaking.

Stephen's confidence took a knock. He had to be able to rely on his equipment and his gag was clearly faulty. Again, he considered blowing up the mine, but decided to make a third attempt. The gag had to come off again.

For the third time he refitted the gag and loosened the keeper ring. This time he worked quickly and less cautiously. His fingers were already numb from the cold, his legs were cramping beneath him and he would just have to trust the gag's air pressure to last. Should that safety pin move back, he would be dead. He used one hand to force the horn onto the fuze to prevent air escaping, but this meant he needed an extra hand to feel for a booby trap whilst he teased out the gaine. Somehow, he managed it by tucking the gag underneath his arm.

As he sat on top of the mine to rest before tackling the hydrostatic unit, Stephen reflected on how reckless he had behaved. He should have blown up the mine. He probably would have had he not been angered by Lawson's reckless race to strip a mine? It meant that he had behaved as badly and for what purpose? He vowed to be more careful in future.

He walked around his mine to stretch his tired limbs and restore the circulation to them. As he did so, he felt a huge pressure wave bowl him over and immediately afterwards, he heard a tremendous crack. In the direction of Bacon's mine he saw a huge plume of dust rise about 200 feet skywards and he had to shield his face from the falling shower of brick and stone chippings. He instantly made to spring to Bacon's aid, but realised there would be no point. He couldn't help Bacon and nor would anybody else be able to. His best course of action would be to finish stripping his own mine.

Sickened and shocked, he finished the job. As he had known he would, on returning to where he had last seen Bacon, all he could see was a huge crater in the street, rubble and dust. Of Bacon there was nothing left to see. One of this country's actors had shuffled off this mortal coil. There wouldn't be anything left to merit a grave. As the car took him back to the town hall for his next task, Stephen couldn't help wondering if Bacon might still be alive if they hadn't agreed to swap mines. Or might he be the dead one? Whether through relief, guilt or tiredness, he couldn't help himself. He began sobbing quietly and he didn't care that the driver and rating in the front knew it.

*****

Despite the outside temperature, Ernst stood in his undershorts as he smoked a cigarette and looked up at the sky through the windows of the hotel room's balcony. Whether through the fire still burning in the grate, his exertions a couple of hours earlier with the whore sleeping in his bed or his recurring nightmare about the last war, rivulets of sweat streamed down the centre of his back. He was tempted to open the windows, but didn't want to wake his sleeping partner. He heard her snore softly and looked back to the bed. She had thrown off the covers and he could see she had moved over to his side of the bed. He smiled as he took another drag of his cigarette. As she lay on her back, her small breasts resembled fried eggs, but she knew how to pleasure a man. A stirring in the loins at the memory tempted him to wake her. After all, he had hired her for the night as he had felt in need of some solace after the disappointment of the latest trials. He remembered now. Helga was her name and he looked forward to renewing his acquaintance with her before long.

Again, Ernst heard the low rumbling like thunder and this time he could see the bombers in the light of the quarter moon. He thought they might be Heinkel 111s, but couldn't be sure. Although a colonel in the air force, he knew little about aircraft. He presumed they were off on a raid over Britain. Ernst wondered what Little Maxi would be doing now. His wing had been taken off operations over the Channel now that the *Führer* had suspended the planned invasion of Britain. Despite thinking the plan futile, Max had enjoyed his time in France, but now he was destined for the Balkans. Where, he couldn't say, nor why. Ernst hoped they might meet again soon. He wanted to congratulate him on his engagement to Else, his little Jew girl. He chastised himself for thinking it. She was only an eighth Jewish and that made her German under the current race laws.

So, the British had managed to stave off defeat after all, Ernst thought ruefully. He felt certain that if only the *Luftwaffe* had been more careful with where they had dropped the new magnetic mines, his master plan for victory would have been successful. The navy were blaming the air force and he had lost the friendship of his former naval colleagues for turning his coat. He had won few friends in the air force either. The pilots were blaming their mistakes on the parachutes needed to slow the descent of the mines and indirectly, him for not yet coming up with a mine that could be guided more accurately. He had tried, of course, but the early trials of the *bombenmine* had been a failure. The metallurgy just hadn't been up to the requirements, but the latest developments had been more promising. He would prove his critics wrong. Until then, he still had a few surprises up his sleeve. The acoustic mines were a great success and should the British scientists devise a counter measure, they would be sure to struggle with the next variant, an acoustic and magnetic mine combined.

    The thought made him feel better. 1941 would be a new year and he had plans to ensure the secrets of the new *bombenmine* would be impregnable. This time his mines would make the difference to win the war for Germany. He flicked his cigarette stub into the dying embers of the fire. Lisa turned away from him to expose her naked buttocks. The sight restored his lust for her and he decided he would wake her, after all.

PART 3
The Ebbing Tide
January – June 1941

Chapter 21
January 1941

To his relief, Stephen had managed to take his forty-eight hours of leave at home before being sent to Manchester to help with the aftermath of the air raids. His friend and flat mate, Johnson, had spent Christmas in Cardiff. The two were enjoying a quiet beer together in The New Yorker on Park Lane. It was a smart watering hole that had the virtue of opening at 15.00 when the pubs shut. This suited the twenty-four-hour lifestyle of the RMS officers. Stephen found the place too smart for his tastes, but Johnny had discovered it and insisted he wouldn't drink alone. Johnson had his left arm in a sling and clearly had not enjoyed his visit to Wales.

'But I rather like the W-Welsh, Johnny. We used to s-spend some jolly fine holidays at B-Betws-y-Coed and Llandudno.'

'Give me the English every time, Stephen. I've never met a more stubborn race.'

'You've not m-met the Irish.'

'Mebbe, but I can't help but think they'd be no worse.'

'So, w-what went wrong?'

'Just about everything. Where do I start? Dusty was in charge and I'd been sent there with a couple of those new Australians. Good guys by the way. My first mine was in a railway yard. The local police wouldn't clear the area and set up a cordon… until I threatened to arrest them.'

'You w-what? You threatened to arrest the p-policemen?' Stephen dabbed the front of his jacket with a paper napkin where he had spilt his beer in surprise.

'Sure. I told them I wouldn't deal with the mine whilst I had a crowd. They were obstructing me in my sacred duty and I answered to nobody but Captain Currey.'

'And that w-worked?'

'Yeah, to a limited extent. Once I'd arrested the sergeant in charge, he suddenly became more amenable. But just as I was getting started on the mine, I could hear vibrations. Turned out there was a truck headed my way despite my instructions of no movements within 400 yards of the mine. I tried to stop the driver, but he kept coming on... so I shot his front tyre out.'

'Cripes, Johnny, this isn't the W-Wild West.'

'You're kiddin' me. It's west of the West Country and those Welshmen are pretty damned wild.'

'S-so, what happened next?'

'What d'you think? The driver had no choice. The driver cut his engine and slinked off to make a complaint to the police and I deloused the goddamned mine. But my next job was even worse.'

Stephen couldn't reply. He was convulsed with laughter at the thought of an American brandishing his revolver in Wales, shooting out tyres.

'It wasn't funny, Stephen. I coulda been killed. My next job was in a school yard next to the local telephone exchange and it sure was icy. Sheets of the stuff, frozen puddles, the whole shebang. The fuze was covered in a thick layer of it. I didn't dare chip at it so I used a screwdriver to scrape it away.'

'Did you use salt?' Stephen began doodling on a dry napkin.

'Gee, no. I didn't think of that at the time. It might have saved me a whole heap of trouble if I had, as I'll explain. But I thought I had a better idea. I drained some hot water from the radiator of the car. The trouble was it worked too darned quickly. The ice snapped with the noise of a firecracker and then I heard the fuze run!'

'Lord, Johnny. The f-fact you're here to tell the tale m-means it worked out, but w-what happened?'

'I ran, that's what happened. I was like a skater on that ice, but I made it round the corner of the telephone exchange and waited. Nothing happened, so I had to return to the mine. Boy did I hate that thing. The fuze was still covered in ice, so I had no choice but to pour more hot water over it. Bar tender, may I have a whisky, please?' Johnson was trembling at the memory and Stephen could see the experience had shaken him considerably.

'I think I w-would have burnt it, Johnny.'

'Yeah, I thought of that. That great ugly thing sat there as if nothing had happened, but I knew the fuze had run... and I didn't know for how long, but there was the street to consider, the school and the telephone exchange. I thought I'd give it just one more go and so this time I was dead careful as I poured the water over it. Jesus, Stephen, the fuze started running instantly! I ran like Hell, but slipped on the ice and broke my collar bone. I was winded and couldn't get up. I just said goodbye to my folks and waited for the end. It was a strange feeling, Stephen, just lying there knowing you're going to die. I wasn't afraid, just mad that the brute had beaten me. But you know what? I survived. That lousy mine didn't blow, but I'd lost my nerve. I rang Dusty and told him the mine had me by the short and curlies. He didn't hesitate. He told me to burn the darned thing and to Hell with the consequences if she blasted.'

'G-good old Dusty.'

'Yeah. It sounded good advice, so I dug out the aluminium powder and magnesium ribbon, lit my crucible and got out of the goddamned way real quick. After ten minutes it had blown so I started to relax and enjoy a couple of smokes. Would you believe, the darned brute blasted after forty minutes? It took out the school, telephone exchange and half the street. Had my shoulder not hurt so much, I'da felt sick with shame.'

'But it w-wasn't your fault, Johnny.' Stephen made to put his arm on Johnson's shoulder, but stopped himself just in time. 'What did D-Dusty say?'

'He was real sweet about it, but he advised me to get out of town hellish quick. He warned me there was a posse of angry Welshmen on their way to whomp me and the police had no intention of stopping them. Seems I'd made myself unpopular and whilst the Welsh will accept Adolf destroying their homes, when it happens it by accident, it's our fault. It sure don't make one feel valued does it?'

Stephen agreed that it was unfair, but was interrupted by the barman. 'Are you Lieutenant Cunningham, sir?' Stephen nodded. 'I've just taken a message, sir. You're to proceed to Regent's Park immediately.'

'Thanks.' Stephen turned to Johnson. 'I'll s-see you later. Here. This is f-for you.' He handed Johnson the napkin on which he had drawn a cartoon of a cowboy in boots and Stetson, toting two revolvers and shooting a lorry's tyres. As he left the bar to the sounds of Johnson cackling in delight, he spotted a striking redhead seated near the exit drinking tea with another young woman. He thought her stunningly good-looking. She caught his gaze and smiled at him. Embarrassed, Stephen hurried through the door.

*****

Stephen's driver found the barricade north of Regent's Park, at Primrose Hill, and Stephen questioned the duty policeman.

'Have you s-seen the mine, c-constable?'

'I have, sir. It's in the retaining wall of the dam. Look up there, sir, and see it for yourself.'

Stephen followed the direction of the policeman's outstretched arm and saw the tell-tale parachute. 'Did you s-say dam?'

'Yes, sir. Well, more like a storage reservoir, sir. If it blows up, it'll flood the park and all the 'ouses round here. Course, we've evacuated 'em, but we've 'ad to evacuate the ack-ack battery, too. Didn't think you'd take kindly to a load of gunfire when you're dealing with that bastard. Dare say Jerry'll be payin' us a visit tonight.'

How true, Stephen thought, but nor did he fancy dealing with a mine in the middle of an air raid. He and his rating slipped under the barrier and walked the two hundred yards up the slope to the reservoir. He couldn't see the mine – just the parachute. He hoped the parachute was hiding it, but his luck was not in. On removal of the parachute, he still couldn't see the mine, but he could see a short set of cords leading into the ground. His worst fears had been realised. The mine must be buried to its full depth and he could only access it by digging.

On his hands and knees, he approached the spot where the cords led. The impact of the mine had created a vertical shaft and he saw the top of the mine nine feet down.

'Lord!' he exclaimed.

'Is it that bad, sir,' the sailor behind him asked.

'Take a look f-for yourself.' Stephen made way for the rating to peer into the dark shaft.

'Bloody hell, sir! The fuze must be a good eleven feet down.'

'More likely twelve.' Stephen walked about ten yards away and sat on the slope overlooking Regent's Park. The rating joined him.

'Fag, sir?' The rating proffered a packet of 'blue liners', the Royal Navy issue cigarettes. Stephen drew one and accepted a light from his assistant. 'I suppose we could dig a shaft, sir?'

Stephen considered the idea for a moment as he surveyed all the housing to the south and west. He had to do something. Were the mine to explode, it would flood all the housing down the hill. He tried to guess at the number, but gave up on the job. 'I suppose we have to d-dig, but any c-clay we dislodged could f-fall on the mine and s-set it off,' he muttered aloud to himself. He stood up and walked back to the mine. No, he didn't like the idea of digging. He pondered erecting a scaffold and winching out the mine. He could secure a cable to the parachute shackle. Vibration might be an issue, but that could be managed. But the back pressure? He realised that the suction of the upward movement of the mine when lifted would create enough pressure to set off the mine. It couldn't be done. He stubbed out his cigarette. Somehow, he would have to dig a shaft adjacent to the mine and take his chances that the vibrations or movement of the soil and clay didn't disturb it. He didn't fancy his chances. Not only would he never hear the clock tick, but there would be nowhere to go anyway. He thought of Bacon and wondered how long he had before joining him. It was only a matter of time before his luck gave out. Then he had another idea.

He shone his torch down onto the mine. He spotted a ridge on the tailpiece. They were always in line with the fuze and that meant the fuze was facing downhill. He lowered a line down to the top of the mine and noted its depth. He drew one side of a triangle in his notebook and wrote the depth beside it. He paced out 10 yards down the slope and estimated the angle of it. Yes, that could work, he thought, as he made a simple calculation of trigonometry. His decision made, he dug his heel into the soft grass and called across to his assistant.

'Scout around for any digging tools you can find, but make sure they're non-magnetic. I'm g-going to s-sap a trench from here underneath the m-mine. If I g-go in at an angle, I c-can come up underneath the m-mine. It'll be d-dark soon, so we'll s-start in the m-morning.'

*****

The following morning, Stephen returned to Primrose Hill dressed in overalls and wellington boots. His assistant rather shame-facedly handed him a toy bucket and spade. 'It's all I could find, sir – non-magnetic, I mean.'

Stephen took the wooden tools and smiled. 'They're ideal. Thank you.' Leaving his assistant at the car, Stephen headed up the hill to his mine. Within an hour, he had dug out a hole about two feet wide at an angle of about thirty degrees down. The clay was yellow and sticky. It was slow work as although it didn't take long to fill his little bucket, he had to keep wriggling backwards to empty it, but even so, by the afternoon he had managed a length of six feet. He made a mental note to bring a miner's headlamp the following day. By dusk he estimated he was ten feet into the earth and called it a day. He was tired. His muscles ached and he was absolutely filthy. On his return to the car and despite the cold, he stripped off his overalls to his underwear and wrapped himself in the car rug to prevent making a mess of the interior. That was another lesson for tomorrow, he thought.

*****

That evening, washed and refreshed, he met Johnson in the New Yorker. Johnson had news.

'No more cantankerous Welshmen for me, Stephen. You're welcome to them.'

'W-what do you mean, Johnny?' Stephen worried that Johnson was about to announce his return to the United States.

'Captain Currey called for me and asked me to volunteer. I'm going to learn to dive. I'm to specialise in dealing with underwater mines as soon as I've done my course.'

'But w-why?' Stephen had vowed he would never dive again after his sole experience at HMS *Excellent.*'

'You want to know the truth, bud? When I was told the Old Man wanted to see me, I thought it was to be carpeted after my time in Cardiff. I was so relieved I wasn't in trouble, I just said yes when he asked me. Besides, why not? It's something new.'

'S-so when do you do the c-course? I mean w-what about your shoulder?'

'Yeah, that's the little fly in the ointment. Turns out *Vernon* have put up their own candidate and we were to train together, but I guess I'll have to wait another couple of weeks. A pity, though. I'da liked to have been the first. How did your day go?'

'N-not great. I've been like a dog hunting for a b-bone.' Stephen explained his problem and how he was tackling it, but Johnson cut him off with a hand gesture.

'Looks like we've got company and very pretty company at that.'

The red-haired young woman Stephen had spotted two days before approached them. Although slightly plump, she had beautiful shoulder-length hair and brilliant white teeth showing where her mouth parted into a permanent part smile. She addressed Stephen in a Scottish accent.

'Are you the officer dealin' with the mine up at Primrose Hill?'

'I'm s-s-sorry, m-m-miss?' Stephen replied shyly, avoiding full eye contact.

'I saw you this mornin' and asked the polis man. He said ye're digging a tunnel.' The young woman fixed him in the eye confidently and smiled slightly coyly. Stephen found the action a little too familiar and regarded his beer with fascination.

'I d-d-don't know w-w-what you m-mean.'

'Now don't be modest. It's wonderful what ye're doin'. My house is in Saint Edmund's Terrace. Now, can ye make the mine safe?'

Stephen looked at Johnson for support, but Johnson only had admiring eyes for the women. She didn't wait for a reply.

'Look, whenever ye've finished for the day, you find my house.' She took out a notebook, wrote something and tore out the sheet. 'There's my address. My bathroom's at yer disposal. Make sure ye use it. Ye'll find hot watter and clean bath towels ready for ye.'

'B-b-but the area's c-cordoned off. How w-will the w-water be hot? How can you have everything ready?'

'That's my problem, my *braw* laddie. Just make sure ye use it.' She kissed her fingers and placed them tenderly on Stephen's cheek before walking back to her friend with a wiggle of her fine hips.

'Best close your mouth, buddy. You'll catch flies that way. Gee, if it wasn't for this darned shoulder, I'd finish the job for you.'

Stephen still gazed at the woman. She was now sitting with her friend. She saw him watching and smiling broadly, waved at him. Stephen felt he had just been struck by Cupid's arrow.

*****

Stephen dug deeper all morning, but the task was becoming ever more difficult. The downward angle of his tunnel was causing the blood pressure in his head to rise. Wriggling uphill, feet first from the tunnel to empty his small bucket was becoming more difficult on account of the sticky clay. Moreover, he was suffering from claustrophobia. With little room to manoeuvre, he was conscious that the tunnel might cave in and he would have no means of escape. Nonetheless, he forced himself on, setting himself targets of the number of bucketloads before resting.

Unsure of the time, but estimating it to be close to lunchtime, he sat on the grass for a decent rest. He wondered if it was time for a Plan B. He knew the tunnel was becoming too deep and steep for him to wriggle out at some point and that risked him being buried alive. This was no longer a one-man job and he needed help. Too tired to walk down the hill and back up, he waved to the car below. Eventually, and after some hollering, he managed to attract the attention of his assistant, deep in conversation with the driver. The sailor trotted up the slope, out of breath by the time he reached Stephen.

'I need s-some help. D-do you have a long length of rope in the c-car?'

'Aye, sir. Probably about 300 yards in all. You want me to fetch it?'

Stephen nodded tiredly. 'And bring some d-digging tools. N-normal ones will s-suffice. I want you to d-dig a safety trench for yourself.'

A short while later, Stephen and the rating dug a shallow trench a little short of 200 yards from the mine. Stephen explained his plan.

'I'll f-fasten one end of the rope round my ankle. You s-stay here and when I tug, you p-pull me out. You think you c-could m-manage that? The rope's heavy enough.'

'Aye. No problem, sir. I've a good strong arm.'

With the rope knotted round his ankle and the sailor to pull him out, Stephen made faster progress. He estimated that it took about three to four minutes to crawl down the tunnel, scrape away the clay at the face until his bucket was full, give the rope a sharp tug and then to be hauled out of the tunnel to empty the bucket. Each time he was glad of the fresh air as the air inside the tunnel was fetid. His lungs were fit to burst from the effort to breathe and his elbows and knees were badly chafed. He thought sympathetically of his father's lungs after the gassing at Ypres.

He took a break to eat a tablet of chocolate. He felt exhausted and wondered how much longer he could carry on. Glancing down the hill, he picked out Saint Edmund's Terrace and he wondered which was the house where the hot water might be waiting. He couldn't imagine the pleasure a hot bath would bring to his aching and chafed body. The thought rejuvenated him and he checked again his calculations. The sun was beginning to fall and unless he found the mine soon, he would run out of time to deal with it. He must be close now, he thought.

A couple of trips down the tunnel later, Stephen felt his tiny spade hit metal. The relief was enormous. He hadn't dug too deep or wide of the mine. However, if the mine was acoustic, he was now in an extremely perilous position. He rested a few seconds, contemplating his next move, but instead his thoughts turned to the woman he had met the night before. The barman had told him that she was called Carol Templeton and worked as a nurse at a nearby hospital, but he couldn't say where. She just came in regularly, sometimes after a shift at the hospital.

He forced himself to concentrate on the present and very carefully and quietly, he scraped at the clay. A couple of bucketloads later, he felt sure he had exposed the fuze. Only he hadn't. Instead, he had uncovered a disc of dark-grey metal. It was the cover to the detonator, the other side of the mine from the bomb fuze.

Chapter 22

The telephone on Monty's desk rang and he answered it within his customary three rings.

'Montcalm,' he answered curtly.

'Hallo, Monty. Benson here.' Monty knew this to be Squadron Leader Benson of Air Intelligence.

'Good morning, Alan. What can I do for you?' Monty replied breezily.

'It's more a matter of what I can do for you, old chap. I have some intriguing information that I think will interest you. Can't give you the details over the 'phone. Any chance you might pop up to Cockfosters?'

'Certainly. Is it urgent?'

'Well… probably not, but it might be worth seeing you ASAP.'

That was a signal to Monty that the information probably was urgent. He had made it his business to cultivate various officers in RAF Intelligence in order to be kept informed on the enemy's air activities. He had learned that Benson wasn't somebody to exaggerate a problem. Monty checked his watch. He had to go down to Norfolk, but he would just have to be later than planned and call in at Cockfosters on the way.

'How about 15.00?'

'If you mean 15.00 hours, then that would be lovely, Monty. I look forward to seeing you.' Benson hung up having made the point that the navy's method of stating the time was out of synchrony with the custom of both the RAF and army.

*****

A good fifteen minutes before three o'clock, Monty's ATS driver drove through the gates to Trent Park. The present-day security arrangements were much tighter than when the house had been used to entertain half the British aristocracy. King Edward VIII himself had played golf on the park's course. Now the country house was heavily guarded and festooned with barbed wire. The Middlesex country house had been the home of Sir Philip Sassoon, cousin of the poet Siegfried Sassoon, but on Sir Philip's death in 1939, the government had requisitioned the house and it was now used as a prisoner-of-war camp for *Luftwaffe* aircrew. Within the rooms MI19 had planted microphones to listen in to the private conversations of the inmates – or guests as they were regarded.

Monty had visited Trent Park before and had been impressed by the relaxed atmosphere, quite unlike that he imagined of a prisoner-of-war camp. The guards, or hosts, were sympathetic and patient to their guests. However, unbeknown to the Germans, their captors were skilled interrogators and excellent psychologists. Their warm attitude led the Germans to drop their guard and speak more freely than they planned. A few innocent questions could carefully guide the prisoners into revealing interesting information that they had not realised held true value. Benson was in charge of one of the interrogation teams.

Monty was shown into a beautifully panelled and lined small library, and given a tray of tea and biscuits whilst he awaited Benson. It had all the trappings of arrival in a discreet hotel. Benson didn't leave him waiting long and brought with him a portable gramophone. He gave Monty a translated transcript and put a record on the gramophone. It was a recording of a recent interrogation of a *Luftwaffe* pilot. Monty listened to the record's conversation and followed the interrogation in German with the aid of the translation.

'*Stand to attention when you are addressed by a senior officer... Stand up and stand to attention when I order you.*'

'*You are not my senior officer. You are a representative of a spineless nation. I have no intention of obeying you and your kind.*'

'*Really? And what makes you say that?*'

'*Because you're finished. We have conquered Europe and only you stand alone, but soon you, too, will know defeat.*'

'*You do surprise me. And I thought we were doing rather well on our own.*'

'*Ach. You British are so naïve. You are entirely dependent on your Merchant Fleet. Göring has promised us delivery of a new weapon that will wipe your fleet off the seas within six weeks and then you will face the choice of starvation or surrender.'*

Benson lifted the needle from the record. 'Hereafter, the interrogator thought it best to steer the conversation away from the new weapon so as to feign a lack of interest in it, but it sounds to me as if that conceited fool was referring to some new form of mine. That's why I called you.'

'It sounds like that and I'm grateful for you involving me. What will you do now?'

Benson helped himself to one of Monty's biscuits and stroked his moustache before replying. 'My men are briefed to be listening out for any talk of a new mine. We're always getting fresh batches of Jerries in here, so the chances are that if Göring's been addressing the *Luftwaffe* about it, we'll soon hear some corroboration and more detail. It could be mere propaganda, of course, but we'll treat it seriously until we know better. That all right with you, Monty?'

'Thanks, Alan. If that chap's telling the truth, we could be in for something out of the ordinary. I look forward to you keeping me informed. Now, if you'll excuse me, I've a car waiting to take me to Norfolk.'

'I presume this isn't a short seaside holiday, Monty. It's on the Firm is it?'

'Sadly, that's true. I need to see the RMSO in Yarmouth. He keeps a macabre museum of bits and pieces he's stripped from mines recovered on the east coast. He wants me to take a look at them for anything new.'

'Enjoy the sea air then, Monty… and haste ye back.'

*****

Stephen tugged on the rope and was dragged back to the surface of his tunnel. Despondently, he sat down on the hillside and thought about the implications of his recent find. Perhaps the Germans had changed the design of their mines and were mounting the parachute coaming a different way. More likely, he deduced, the coaming had come away from the mine and twisted a full 180 degrees after penetrating the earth. Either way, he would have to spend another day digging. It would mean digging round the mine and coming back up to it on the opposite side. There was no point starting now, but that wouldn't deny him the promised bath.

Stephen retrieved his bucket and spade, met up with his assistant in the nearby trench and together they paced down the hill to the waiting car. The driver and naval rating were surprised when he told them of his plan to have a bath and for them to wait for him. However, the rating was kind enough to carry his clean uniform to the address of Miss Templeton.

Stephen was surprised at the grandeur of the house. It was beyond the affordability of an ordinary nurse. As he stood at the gate of the front garden, he examined the thick yellow mud on his boots and overalls, and had second thoughts about defiling this lovely house with his filth. Then he reflected that unless he deloused that mine, this home and hundreds of its neighbours would be destroyed by the explosion or inundation of the reservoir water. A bit of mud was a small price to pay for his efforts.

He opened the front door and it was not locked. Down the hall he saw a trail of newspapers across the carpet leading to the rear of the house. He smiled at the sight. Miss Templeton was no fool. He followed the newspapers, treading as lightly as he could, but was still dismayed to see the trail of mud he left behind. The newspapers ended at a downstairs bathroom. Arrayed over the side of the cast-iron bath were plenty of large, clean towels. A table was stood next to the bath on which had been laid a tablet of fresh soap, a decanter of sherry and a plate of biscuits. Clearly, Miss Templeton was a lady of refined tastes. Stephen longed to know her better.

He turned the tap and, as promised, the water was hot. He ran the bath and stripped off. As he relaxed in the deliciously hot water, he decided that he wouldn't mind crawling back into his filthy and stinking tunnel tomorrow if this was the reward that would await him.

*****

Stephen returned to Saint Edmund's Terrace in the morning to collect his overalls and boots. They had been so filthy he had not wanted to put them in the back of the car. Now he realised the folly of his decision. Had he taken them back to his billet, he might have had a chance to dry them. As a result, he would have to change out of clean uniform into wet and filthy clothing. To his amazement, however, the overalls were draped over the side of the bath in place of the wet towels he had left there the night before. They had been washed, dried and pressed. His boots sat proudly on a nearby sheet of newspaper, gleaming in the reflection of the light above. Stephen's heart swelled with affection for the wonderful Miss Templeton. Somehow, she had not only evaded the barricades to re-enter her house, but in doing so had risked her life. She must have worked though half the night, he recognised.

His morale high, he returned to the hill and briefed his assistant on his new plan, but the rating had an objection.

'Sir, if you dig round the mine, the tunnel will curve. How will I pull you back round a curve? You'll get stuck.'

'Yes. You're right. I hadn't thought of that. B-but I c-can't think what else to do. I'll just take my chances.' Stephen had meant to sound confident, but he was worried that his assistant's warning might prove true.

Even so, he wriggled his way into the tunnel and began work. He set himself a target of fifty buckets and achieved this by lunchtime, by which time he had dug much of the curved path around the mine. Working in the curve was draining. As the rating had prophesied, it was difficult for him to pull Stephen around the bend and Stephen had to wriggle and squirm to avoid becoming stuck. Moreover, he had to do so without knocking or disturbing the mine. He did the work gladly, though. He was determined to protect the beautiful house in Saint Edmund's Terrace.

Finally, late in the afternoon, Stephen reached his goal, the white disc of the bomb fuze. Lying on his side, barely able to move his elbows, he removed the fuze to the surface and rendered it safe. After the toils of the previous three days, he thought it would now be a relatively simple operation to erect a winch to withdraw the mine from its shaft and to strip it, but it would have to wait another day. A wave of exhaustion overcame him and he felt desperate for a bath.

*****

Stephen woke to find Johnson sitting at the end of his bed reading a book – except it wasn't his bed. He was lying propped up on several pillows edged with lace and the bed was covered in a peacock-blue embroidered quilt. Plainly, this was not his room, but Stephen couldn't account for his present whereabouts. Suddenly, he was wracked by a hacking cough at the end of which he brought up yellowish-grey mucus. He desperately searched the bedside table for a suitable repository of the phlegm. He found a small porcelain spittoon.

'Jesus, Stephen, you worried us. It's sure as Hell good to see you back in the world of the living.'

Stephen gasped for breath and lay back against the pillows, exhausted by the bout of coughing. 'W-where am I and how?' he wheezed.

'Hell, Stephen. Have you no idea?' Stephen just looked back blankly, too tired to speak for the moment.

'You hit the jackpot, Stephen. You're in the bed of that beautiful redhead we met the other night in the New Yorker. Just hang on a second. I'll holler to tell her you're awake.' Johnson stepped over to the door and called out, 'Nurse. He's come to.'

'But how?' Stephen whispered. He feared too much exertion would set him off coughing again.

Before Johnson could answer, Miss Templeton walked in wearing the starched white cap and apron of a nurse. Stephen noted that the belt highlighted the plumpness of her hips, but she was nonetheless beautiful and the belt highlighted her ample bosom, too. Above all, her broad smile seemed radiant.

'Nurse, Stephen was just asking how he came to be here. I figure you can tell him the story. I'll just leave you two to catch up awhile.' Johnson discreetly left the room.

'Hello, Lieutenant. I'm glad to see ye awake at last. Just stay still whilst I check yer temperature.'

Stephen made to speak, but found his mouth full of a thermometer. Miss Templeton took his wrist to check his pulse and as she did so, he recognised the smell of freesias in her soap or perfume. When she had finished counting, she plumped his pillows and checked the spittoon. Stephen again tried to speak, but his chest hurt and the thermometer impeded him.

'Just lie still, *braw* laddie and I'll tell ye everythin'.' Miss Templeton spoke gently to him, as if he were a child. 'Ye're a real hero, Lieutenant, and there are plenty of my neighbours keen to thank ye in person for saving our homes when ye're well enough, but it's come at a price.' She reached across to remove the thermometer and examined it disapprovingly. 'Still high,' she announced as she cleaned the thermometer with a sterile swap and packed it away, 'but ye'll live – if ye rest.

'I came home two nights ago to clean up after you and was shocked to find you unconscious in the bath.' The news alarmed and embarrassed Stephen, and he tried to reply.

'You m-m-mean…' His words broke off as he went into another spasm of coughing.

'Hush, you wee *laoch*. Save yer strength and I'll do the blethering. Aye, ye were in yer birthday suit, but I've seen it all afore. I'm a nurse, mind.' Stephen blushed even more deeply than a moment previous.

'I don't ken how long you'd been lying there, but the water was awfu' cold when I came back. I had to get a polis man to help me lift ye and put ye to bed. The doctor's been round and reckons ye've got bronchial flu… and if ye don't mind his instructions, it'll be pneumonia, so ye're to keep to yer bed.'

'B-but I c-c-can't stay here. You c-can't look after me. You've your w-work to g-go to.' At last Stephen had managed to get in a word.

'Oh, Lieutenant, ye don't just realise what a hero ye are round these parts. I've seen that lovely Captain Currey and he told me so himself. Says ye deserve a medal fer what ye did, but he didna need to tell me that.' Miss Templeton took Stephen's hand fondly. 'So, it suits me jes fine to look after ye fer a few days… until ye get yer strength back. As fer the hospital, they're jes fine with it all. The sister thought it was the least we could do for one of Britain's heroes.'

Stephen lay back taking it all in. Him a hero? Hardly. He was just a simple physics master who had somehow found himself caught up in this war. But something grated about Miss Templeton. 'W-would you s-stop c-calling me "Lieutenant"? My n-name's S-Stephen.'

Miss Templeton patted his hand before releasing it. 'That's jes fine wi' me. My name's Carol.'

Chapter 23
February 1941

'How're you feeling now, Cunningham?' Captain Currey asked seated in his office.

'Fine now, thank you, s-sir. I'm ready to g-go back to w-work.'

'I'm glad to hear it. Mind you, you had the best of care. That nurse of yours is a real smasher.'

'I gather you've m-met her, sir.'

'I'd say so. I went round as soon as I heard about your collapse, but you were out of it. I'm sorry, but I've not had the time since. Bexley Heath and the Thames Estuary had a bit of hammering whilst you were away. Oh yes, I met Nurse Templeton and I can tell you, Cunningham, had I not embargoed it, you'd have had the whole RMS team visiting you. Boy, you're a lucky chap.'

Stephen thought that, too. He had been in heaven over the last week and was now totally smitten with Carol. However, something was worrying him. He delved into the pockets of his reefer jacket and pulled out a gold cigarette case and lighter.

'S-sir, I was left these b-by the residents of Primrose Hill. They w-wanted to thank me.' Stephen's voice croaked with emotion.

Currey picked up both pieces and tried the lighter. 'Nice pieces and real gold by the weight of them. But I'm not surprised. They're a well-heeled lot round Saint John's Wood.'

'B-b-but I c-can't accept them, sir!' Stephen rose from before the captain's desk. 'It w-wouldn't be right.'

Currey was silent for a minute before replying. 'I don't see why not. You did well and but for your dedication, the residents of Primrose Hill would have lost far more than a few quid in a bowl to pay for these trinkets. If your Quaker principles are bothering you, Cunningham...' Currey paused and Stephen's face clearly transmitted that that was just what was bothering him. 'I won't condone any of my team taking money as a reward for risking their lives, but I don't mind them accepting the odd pint from grateful locals. Think of it in those terms and in any case... you can't really give them back now, can you? Take my advice, Cunningham, take them as a reminder of a very nasty job well executed.' Currey pushed the lighter and cigarette case back across his desk.

'And talking of which, Cunningham, you're proving a bit of an embarrassment.'

Stephen flushed immediately and couldn't imagine how he might have failed in his duty, but held his tongue.

'I shall be putting you up for a gong for your brave conduct and devotion to duty and I have no doubt my recommendation will be accepted. The trouble is that I've just received this from their Lordships.' Currey picked up a slim file from his desk and opened it.

'Ah yes, here we are. It concerns your little escapade at Garston Gas Works last year and I quote the words written here. *"The King has been graciously pleased to approve the Award of the George Cross, for great gallantry and undaunted devotion to duty to: Temporary Lieutenant Stephen Arthur Cunningham, RNVR."* Congratulations, Cunningham. It'll be gazetted at the end of the month.' Currey leapt to his feet and smiling broadly, shook Stephen's hand warmly. Stephen was dumbfounded with amazement.

'You see my problem now, Cunningham? When I put you up for another award, it's going to look like favouritism.' Currey returned to his desk and picked up the same file.

'Thank… thank you, s-sir. I'm… I'm honoured.' Stephen couldn't believe what he had just heard and sat back down in his chair.

'I've some other news for you, Cunningham. Hitler seems to have changed tack and is hitting our ports and dockyards hard. Poor old Guz has taken a pasting and the local team need reinforcements. I'm appointing you to Plymouth as the local Bomb Safety Officer with immediate effect. I'm afraid it will mean saying goodbye to the delectable Nurse Templeton for a while, but it can't be helped.'

Stephen's mood changed immediately from amazement and pride to one of desolation.

*****

It was the first time Stephen had been a member of a mess since his training at *Vernon* all those months ago and he delighted in the pleasure of the company of other officers at mealtimes. The night before, the officers of the wardroom in the Devonport barracks had held a guest night and Stephen had marvelled at the richness of the table decorations, several of which were of solid silver. Coming from his humble background, it had been a real treat to be served so efficiently and solicitously by the naval stewards. He had heard that the mess was to hold a ladies' night in the spring and he wondered whether he might persuade Carol to come down for it.

Stephen had been kept very busy with mines and bombs in the dockyard and city, but his patch extended all the way down to the tip of Cornwall, too, so in many ways his itinerant lifestyle had not changed from his days in London. However, whereas he had always had a car and driver in London, now he was often reduced to a motor cycle.

So far, he had only had one letter since taking up his new appointment and that was from Johnson. Stephen had still to inform his parents of his new address and he had hoped that Carol might have written. Then again, why had he raised his hopes so, he asked himself. He had given her his new address and asked that she might write to him, but she would be busy at the hospital. Moreover, she had given no indication that she felt the same attraction for him as he did for her. Why would she? She was stunningly attractive and came from a wealthy family. He was no Adonis in looks and before the war had been a humble science master – and not very good at that either. He had dared too much to hope. She had just felt sorry for him and caring for him had only been another of her contributions to the war effort. And she was showing her gratitude for saving her house, of course. However, she might appreciate a change of scene and be interested in attending a ladies' night, so he would still invite her.

Johnson's letter had been full of news about his first week's experiences on his diving course. He fully intended to recommend the United States Navy to set up a similar course. Moreover,

Johnson had learned that he, too, was to be decorated. He was to be awarded the George Medal for his part in recovering the acoustic mine at Porthcawl and he hoped his investiture at Buckingham Palace might coincide with Stephen's.

There was a knock on the door. It was a Saturday afternoon and Stephen was enjoying a rare afternoon off in his cabin. A young RNVR sub lieutenant had a message for him.

'Sorry, Bombs. A dredger's brought up a large mine and according to our boys, it may be magnetic, so that's above our pay grade. I've alerted your team.'

Stephen hastened to his motor bicycle and within ten minutes was at the scene in the dockyard. He was met by Chief Petty Officer Dawlish, his former instructor from *Vernon*. It had come as a most unexpected and pleasant surprise to discover that Dawlish would be working for him in Plymouth. Dawlish was a good hand.

'Good afternoon, sir. Shame to disturb you. It was your afternoon off, but I think you'll agree it was best you were called.'

Stephen noted that the dredger had been hastily berthed alongside the jetty before the crew had abandoned ship. The dockyard police had cleared and sealed off the area to all bar members of the Naval Land Incident Section. Dawlish had already detailed off men to rig a hose pipe to clean off the mine as for the present it was covered in a layer of filthy grey mud. Even so, it wasn't hard to deduce that it was probably a magnetic mine as the green parachute was still attached. Stephen and Dawlish clambered on board the dredger to take a closer look.

'Mmm, I don't like the look of that, sir.' Dawlish pointed to the fuze. It had been badly dented, presumably by the dredger's bucket during its capture on the sea bed. 'Perhaps a hose won't be the best option for cleaning it down.'

Stephen agreed. In its present condition the mine was likely to be highly unstable and he didn't fancy stripping it. He thought about his options for a few minutes. He would have dearly liked to have burnt the mine, but he couldn't afford for it to explode within the dockyard. Even if he was willing to strip it, like as not it would explode anyway. He could think of only one option.

'I'll c-clean this m-mud off by hand, just to g-get a better look at it, b-but I think we need to take it out onto the m-moors for disposal.'

'Fair enough, sir. I'll ask the bomb disposal blokes to fix us a truck and then I'll give you a hand to clean this muck off.'

'N-no, Chief. It's a one p-person job. N-no unnecessary risks.'

'Aye aye, sir. You're the officer. Quicker to train an officer that a chief petty officer in my experience.' Dawlish smiled and winked.

Stephen cleaned the mine carefully with a broom and scrubbing brush. As he had feared, the mine had taken quite a bashing in its descent into or ascent from thirty feet of water. It was a wonder it hadn't gone off in the dredger's bucket and it clearly wasn't one of the new acoustic types. He would feel much happier when it was out on Dartmoor. To further dampen Stephen's mood, it began to rain cats and dogs.

The bomb disposal team took charge of lifting the mine and packing it into the back of one of their trucks so Stephen was superfluous to requirements for a couple of hours. Even so, he stayed to watch. It was now his mine. Eventually, the truck started on its journey from the dockyard to the moors with an army and police escort. Stephen and Dawlish followed in one of the section's cars. The streets of Devonport and Plymouth along the way had been evacuated and Stephen recognised that his was not the only quiet Saturday afternoon to have been interrupted. He thought it quite an impressive operation. Fortunately, the rain had stopped and the late afternoon sun was drying the roads.

As the convoy proceeded up Crown Hill, a built-up area, the driver of the section car remarked, 'Hey, Chief. That lawry's awn fire.'

Stephen joined Dawlish in looking through the windscreen. He expected that the driver had merely seen a thick puff of smoke as the lorry changed gears to ascend the hill, but he quickly changed his mind when he spotted flames. Dawlish, too, had spotted the flames.

'Alf, put your clog down and stop that truck.'

'N-no, Chief,' Stephen countermanded Dawlish. 'G-get the lorry d-driver to follow us to an open area. There's too m-many houses here.'

'Good point, sir. Right, Alf. You heard the officer. Get alongside and tell him to turn off and follow you over Bircham way.'

A short while later, the truck was stopped in a clearing. Stephen and Dawlish rushed to the back and lowered the tailgate. Alarmingly, they could both smell burning explosive. It was very evident that some sacks used to stabilise the mine were ablaze. Dawlish pulled out the sacks whilst Stephen retrieved the section's wooden spades. One of the spade handles promptly caught fire and Stephen used a wet sack to douse the flames.

'What the bleeding hell's happening, sir?' Dawlish scratched his beard.

With the smoke clearing and all the flames doused, Stephen entered the lorry to conduct a thorough investigation. He picked up some of the unburnt sacks and sniffed them. It was a familiar smell, but he couldn't place it immediately. Then he smiled and passed it to Dawlish.

'S-smell that, Chief. Recognise it?' Stephen held out the sacks.

Dawlish was flummoxed for a moment and then it dawned on him, too. 'Phosphorous, boss?'

'P-precisely.' Stephen started to chuckle. 'There's n-no m-mystery here. The b-bomb d-disposal truck must have b-been on another job.'

'And it was raining.'

'Yes. The team using this truck must have b-been clearing incendiaries and the sacks are c-covered in c-clay from the mine. It acted as an insulator.'

'So, what you're saying, Boss, is that once it stopped raining and the sun came out, it dried the sacks, exposing the remains of the phosphorous to the air and pow! We have a fire. I taught you well, sir.' Dawlish bowed and he and Stephen burst out laughing. Dawlish wiped away a tear from an eye. 'I tell you one thing, Boss. Those lazy bastards in bomb disposal are in for a rocket.'

'I think that an unfortunate term, Chief. And remember, they w-were c-called off the job in a hurry.'

'You're far too understanding by my reckoning, sir. Right, we need to get these tools cleaned down and then I've a good mind to put one of those bomb disposal clowns in the back of the truck with a fire bucket for good measure. Hey! Have you noticed something, boss? We seem to have lost our escort when we turned off. I wonder if they've noticed they're missing something to escort yet.'

An hour later, Stephen had the satisfaction of seeing his mine blown to pieces in the safety of the designated quarry on the moor.

Chapter 24
March 1941

A week earlier, the Germans had dropped a parachute mine in Falmouth's Inner Harbour. The fall of the mine had been observed by the Home Guard, but its exact location on the sea bed was not known. Although within Stephen's geographical area of responsibility, the *Vernon* experts had been summoned to assess whether it might be feasible to recover the mine for investigation. Dealing with a potential magnetic mine underwater was still an unknown craft. The necessity of wearing a diving suit meant it was more difficult to manoeuvre and handle tools and, moreover, there were issues with the movement of the currents.

Stephen was impressed by the extent of the equipment that had already been designed for such a task. A launch and diving boat were requisitioned locally, but a small craft, *The Mouse*, had been sent overland from Portsmouth. The craft was fitted with echo-sounding gear for the location of objects on the sea bed. This gear had initially been invented by the commander of *The Mouse*, Lieutenant Nicholson RNVR, but since perfected by the scientists at *Vernon*. Furthermore, in order for it to operate noiselessly in the vicinity of suspect acoustic mines, it had been fitted with a silent propulsion system.

Nicholson and his coxswain arrive in Falmouth on Monday the second and it only took them and *The Mouse*'s gear half an hour to fix the mine in a narrow section of the harbour's channel at a depth of fifteen feet. They dropped a marker with a lead sinker to mark the position of the mine. Lead was used as it was not magnetic. Commander M was briefed by telephone and the decision was made that it should be feasible to recover the mine and ship it back to Portsmouth for investigation of any new firing circuit.

Sub Lieutenant Reggie Sutherland and two diving ratings were selected for the task of diving on the mine. Stephen was relieved that it was not Johnson for such an experimental operation. Even so, he insisted that an acoustic sweeper fitted with Kango hammers should first sweep the channel. He argued successfully that it would be too hazardous to work on an acoustic mine, but if the mine was not fired, it would be safe to assume that it was a magnetic version.

It was a fine day as Sutherland and Stephen observed from ashore the minesweeper going about its business in the channel to Falmouth's inner harbour. The sun was shining and the Atlantic breeze blew softly into their faces as they scanned the harbour.

'W-what do you think, Reggie?' Stephen asked Sutherland. Although he and Nicholson were senior to Sutherland, it was Sutherland's call as to whether to make the dive or not. He and his men were the ones taking the risks.

'Without any reaction to the noise-makers, it looks to be magnetic to me, so I think we should go ahead. How about this afternoon?'

Nicholson agreed and offered Stephen a place in his strange command. 'Naturally, I'll have to retire to a safe distance in case of accidents, but you should get a better view of proceedings from *The Mouse* than on shore.' Stephen readily accepted the offer.

In the afternoon, Nicholson towed the diving boat to the site of the mine and left Sutherland and his team to prepare for the dive. Sutherland planned on doing the dive with his men in charge of the guide rope and telephone on the surface. After wishing the divers luck, Nicholson took the boat to a place of safety about 200 yards off the Customs House Quay. He and Stephen watched nervously as Sutherland slipped into the water.

About half an hour later, they saw Sutherland surface again. Gently, Nicholson manoeuvred *The Mouse* alongside the diving boat. 'How'd it go?' he asked.

'Not bad. I found it easily enough and have had a good look around. Mind you, that wasn't easy. There's a deuced amount of mud down there and visibility's pretty thick. The trouble is that the clock and fuze are lying on the underside in thick mud. I can't work on it and nor can I shift it. Do you think you could lend a hand by towing it?'

'Tow? That sounds dodgy. I can't say I'm keen, but I'll give it a go.' Nicholson turned to Stephen for his opinion, but Stephen merely shrugged. It wasn't his operation and he was merely there to observe proceedings.

'It shouldn't be that risky. You can use a long line and I'll attach it to the parachute shackle.'

'Jolly good, Reggie. If you say so, it's your funeral.'

Nicholson decided to engage the help of the motor launch and together they put strain on the tow rope for about ten minutes. They were hoping only to turn the mine and not drag it as Sutherland had explained that the mine was resting on a ledge of mud. He declared himself happy with their efforts and prepared for a second dive.

Soon after withdrawing again, Stephen and Nicholson observed the signal from the diving boat that Sutherland was back on the bottom. Stephen tried to picture Sutherland's next moves. If he came straight back to the surface, it would mean that they had not been successful in turning the mine. If not, Sutherland would be applying his non-magnetic spanner to the keep ring of the bomb fuze. He would have to be careful, thought Stephen. Although the channel had been swept acoustically, nobody could be certain that the mine wasn't acoustic. Then again the density of the water should prevent any...

He never finished his thought. Abruptly, the sea rose in a column 200 feet high as the mine exploded. Stephen and the other personnel on board *The Mouse* were immersed by spray and instantly flung headlong into the water. It all happened so quickly, Stephen struggled to work out what had happened as he fought for his life. The salt water stung his eyes and he could see little in the dark-green water. He didn't know which way was up nor down, but instinctively realised he needed to kick off his heavy sea boots. The effort caused him to exhale involuntarily and lose some of his precious reserve of air, but he spotted the bubbles rising above him. Logic dictated that bubbles would rise to the surface and he kicked upwards and clawed at the water with his arms. His lungs started to feel as if they would burst for lack of air and his eyes bulged. It seemed to take eons, but he finally burst through the surface of the water and gasped for deep lungsful of the tangy air above.

Coughing and spluttering, he trod water and observed that the other three occupants of *The Mouse* were doing the same. *The Mouse* itself seemed unscathed, but there was no sign of the diving boat. Stephen's attention was attracted by a cry of alarm from the other swimmers in the water. The rescue motor launch was heading straight towards them at high speed and there didn't appear to be anybody at the helm. The four survivors of *The Mouse* scattered in panic and Stephen tried to make for the boat, but he knew he wasn't a strong swimmer. He didn't dare turn to look at the approaching launch, but could hear it coming ever closer and fast. Just when he thought he must die, he heard the noise of the throttles being cut to a steady throb.

Soon after being hauled into the rescue launch by the solitary coxswain, he heard that the force of the explosion had bowled over the coxswain and, as he had fallen to the deck, he had knocked the idling engine into gear and opened the throttle. Had the coxswain not recovered control of the launch, there might have been further fatalities.

Twenty minutes later, Stephen and the others were in Falmouth Hospital being treated for shock and some for fractures. There he learned that not only had Sutherland and his divers perished in the explosion, but also, the three crew of the nearby motor launch that had helped Nicholson with the tow. It appeared that despite the sweep by Kango hammers, the mine must have been an acoustic version, after all. Heads would roll if the suspicions proved true that the Kango hammers had been set on the wrong frequency. As Stephen drifted off to sleep, he thanked God that Johnny hadn't been a more experienced diving officer.

*****

It was Ernst's first visit to Jever in Lower Saxony, although during the first war with Britain he had served at the nearby naval base of Wilhelmshaven. Jever was now the headquarters of the Ninth Air Corps where his mentor, Lieutenant General Schott, served as the Chief of Staff. As Schott was still the air force's leading authority on mine warfare, he and Ernst were still in frequent contact. However, this was the first time they had met for months. Ernst tried to remember when that was. He recollected with surprise that it must have been in January the year before. So much seemed to have happened since then.

Ernst felt tired. He had hoped the air force might lay on an aeroplane for his journey from Travemünde, but instead he had been forced to cross northern Germany by train, changing at Hamburg and Bremen. Then he had been made to wait two hours before seeing Schott and forty-five minutes ago the general had been summoned to General Coeler's office. Ernst felt slighted. He couldn't imagine that happening eighteen months ago. Then he had been a rising star with his plan to knock Britain out of the war early. Now even *Luftwaffe* majors seemed keen to avert eye contact. It was understandable that Schott had abandoned him in favour of Coeler, but to make him wait for two hours! Was this a sign that he was losing Schott's favour?

Thankfully, Schott returned to his office at that moment. Ernst had already noticed that Schott had changed in appearance since their last meeting. He was bulkier around the chest and midriff and he looked very tired with bags forming beneath his eyes. Schott flung his cap across the office and invited Ernst to return to the table where they had been sitting earlier.

'I'm very sorry about that, Ernst. The *Führer* wanted an urgent update on our preparations for Operation Otto and Coeler needed some facts and figures.'

'Operation Otto, General?'

'Top Secret, I'm afraid Ernst. I can't even share the plans with an old friend. I'd be shot. Let's just say that the *Führer* has a plan to offer German citizens more *Lebensraum*.'

Ernst took the hint. If Hitler was looking to expand, then he could only be looking east to the territory of their Russian ally.

'But where were we before I so rudely abandoned you? I see you have been given a coffee. I only keep the proper stuff, you know?'

'Yes, thank you, General. I have been most well looked after in your absence. I was about to brief you on some of the different firing mechanisms for the new BM1000.'

'Quite right, Ernst. I remember now. You were saying that the new casing has passed its trials and is now robust enough to be dropped without a parachute and fragmenting on impact.'

'Exactly, General. Indeed, it has been designed to act as a bomb or a mine and, hence, its designation. Dropped on hard ground, it will explode instantly like a conventional bomb. But its real sophistication shows when it is dropped in water. Then the fuze operates a switch to arm the weapon as a mine.'

'That is well and good, Ernst, but you know yourself that we have been caught out by mines being recovered from the many mudflats around Britain. Can we not programme the fuze to be less sensitive so that it still explodes on impact on soft ground?'

'We have thought of that, General, and if you will forgive me, we think we have come up with a better solution. If the mine fails to explode on impact, a delayed action arming device will trigger the main detonator circuit after any pre-set time from 90 seconds to two minutes.'

'Good. That stops the mines being recovered, but how do you make it work as a proper mine, assuming our knuckle-headed navigators succeed in dropping the mine in the correct depth of water? You must have some form of hydrostatic switch.'

'Indeed, we do, General. If the mine is dropped in water deeper than twenty-four feet, the hydrostatic switch will stop the fuze from arming. But we have added a subtle modification, General, to prevent the British scientists from recovering the mine and discovering its secrets. Should the mine be brought shallow, for example in a falling tide, or be heaved out of the water, the hydrostatic switch will automatically operate to detonate the explosive.'

'That all sounds very satisfactory, Ernst. I suppose there is no prospect of the British defuzing the bomb underwater, is there? After all, dear Ernst, it is not the first time your fool-proof plans have been proven not quite so fool-proof, hey?'

Ernst blanched at the reminder. 'I doubt it, General. Our own divers have yet to devise a method of doing so. However, this time I am absolutely determined our plans will not fail. I have asked our scientists to devise a few more anti-handling devices and I feel sure we really do have the answer this time. These diagrams explain the principle. We will be ready to go into production next month.'

Schott took the small docket Ernst had slid across the table and examined its contents with acute interest. He looked up and beamed with pleasure at his protegé. 'God in Heaven, Ernst. This is ingenious. The man that came up with this idea must have a medal. It really is fool-proof. Make a success of this, Ernst, and I promise you Göring himself will be hanging a Knight's Cross around your neck!'

Chapter 25
April 1941

'Hallo, Monty? Benson here.'

'Oh, hello, Alan. To what do I owe the pleasure of your call?' Monty cradled the telephone handset between his shoulder and chin as he continued to browse the latest intelligence digests concerning the loss of shipping to enemy submarines.

'Remember your visit to Cockfosters? I promised to stay in touch and I have a bit more information for you.'

Monty immediately abandoned his reading and held the telephone receiver closer to his ear. 'Really? I'm most interested.'

'We've had the original story corroborated by several other talkative pilots. There's definitely a new weapon on the stocks and the Germans have designated it as the BM1000. We presume that means *bombenminen* and refers to a dual-purpose bomb and mine.'

'That would make sense and it probably means it's 1000 kilogrammes in weight. Do you have any other details?'

'We don't know, but we're guessing it's the same dimensions as their other mines, ie six-feet-two-inches long and twenty-four inches in diameter. That would allow it to be fitted to the existing aircraft mine racks. But the interesting point is that it definitely doesn't need a parachute for dropping.'

'So, it can be dropped with the same accuracy as a bomb, then Alan?'

'I fear so and I've one other piece of information. The *Luftwaffe* are certain that their new weapon can't be recovered. It might create a few headaches, or worse, for your mine disposal boys.'

'You mean it contains a new form of booby trap or traps?'

'None of the prisoners could say. All they know is that their High Command is briefing them that the new weapon and the U-boat campaign is going to cripple our shipping. We'll keep probing, of course.'

'Thanks, Alan, for the information. I'm not looking forward to passing it on, though.'

A shiver passed down Monty's spine as he hung up. Although unwelcome, the news was to be expected. Since the outbreak of the war, the Germans had responded to each of the British counter measures with ingenuity and technical excellence. This latest development was yet another move in the cat and mouse game that had become Monty's life. Now it befell him to lay plans to recover at the earliest opportunity this new BM1000.

*****

Captain Currey had been right. Plymouth was taking a pasting. As the Battle of the Atlantic had increased in ferocity, so had the intensity of air attacks on the naval dockyards desperately turning round ships to provide the ever-so-needed escorts for the convoys. Like Coventry the year before, Plymouth had been virtually flattened and Stephen's team had worked around the clock to render safe not just the mines, but all the other assorted ordnance the *Luftwaffe* had dropped on the city. The ever-increasing piles of rubble were hampering his team's efforts to move around the city. He thought it pitiful on the nights air raids were expected to see the thousands of civilians transported by lorry to Dartmoor to evade the bombing. Worse had been to see the horror on the faces of the men returning from fearsome convoys, firstly, as they saw the utter devastation and then, as it dawned on them that they had probably lost loved ones or at best their homes. It was no satisfaction to Stephen to learn that even his father, the most ardent pacifist he had ever known, had come round to thinking that any means now justified the defeat of Hitler.

Notwithstanding the workload and chaos, Stephen, nonetheless, felt euphoric. It was nothing to do with the navy-blue ribbon adorned with a silver cross on his breast nor the certificate he had received recently with the King's Commendation for Brave Conduct. Currey had written to apologise that the award had not been a George Medal to recognise his courage at Primrose Hill, but it didn't bother Stephen. Somehow, despite the carnage being wrought by the *Luftwaffe*, the barracks' wardroom had managed to host their ladies' night and Carol had come down for it.

At first, Stephen had told himself that Carol had only come down to Plymouth for a change of scene, but that had all changed. All evening Carol had dazzled Stephen's fellow officers with her looks and wit. His heart had burst with both pride and love to be her escort. Afterwards, he had escorted her to the home of a fellow officer where she was to spend the night. On the steps, he had fought to overcome his shyness to tell her how he felt.

'I w-wish you d-didn't have to leave tomorrow.' Carol had smiled back at him so fondly his heart had melted further.

'I wish I could stay, too, Stephen. I've had a lovely time and ye were the perfect escort.' She had leaned forward to kiss him on the cheek and again Stephen had caught that scent of freesias. All of a sudden, he had thought he couldn't bear to let her go and had embraced her tightly.

'I love you,' he caught himself saying to his surprise. He had pulled away in embarrassment that he had gone too far, but Carol had held him close.

'I know that,' she had replied and kissed him fully on the lips before pulling away. 'Good night, my lovely *laoch*. I'll be sure to write,' she had said before she let herself in through the front door.

'Say, Stephen. Are you paying any attention to what I'm saying?'

Stephen came out of his reverie and turned his attention back to Johnson. They were having tea in Torquay where they had been working together to clear a number of moored mines washed ashore in the recent gale onto a nearby beach.

'S-sorry, Johnny. My m-mind was elsewhere.'

'You don't need to tell me that, bud. I bet you were thinking of that gal of yours.' Stephen blushed to confirm Johnson's suspicion. 'Gee, Stephen, aren't you the lucky one? I just don't figure what the heck she sees in you.' Stephen blinked in embarrassment. 'Here's me with my movie star looks and the other night, in the New Yorker, I couldn't stop her asking after you.'

'Did she?' Stephen looked pleadingly into Johnson's eyes.

'Sure. She told me expressly to take her *laoch* her very best love. I guess you're the *laoch*, but what the Hell is it?'

'I think it's Scots f-for "hero" or s-something like that,' Stephen muttered sheepishly.

'That figures. I suppose it's what's within that counts, hey?'

'W-what do you m-mean?'

'I mean, don't judge a book by its cover. That's what Carol seemed to suggest.'

'I d-don't understand.'

'I asked her straight out. I said, "Stephen's a great chap and all that, but what's he got that I haven't?" You know what she said?'

'N-no.' Stephen was intrigued by the answer himself. After all, Carol was not only beautiful and charming, but rich. She could have had her pick of men at the ladies' night, but what did she see in him? An impoverished school master from a working-class background who couldn't string a sentence together without stuttering. Moreover, his life expectancy was minimal. He was no catch.

'As for looks, she said you weren't bad without your spectacles and clothes. Jeez, Stephen, I'm no prude, but...'

'N-n-no, Johnny. It's not like that. She's joshing you. She found me in her b-bath, remember?' Stephen's cheeks were the colour of beetroot at what Johnny might be thinking.

'Well, I suppose that could explain the remark,' Johnson said doubtfully. 'But it don't figure anyway. It seems she doesn't go for guys like me... you know, sophisticated with rugged looks and charm. Says she's constantly pestered by them on the wards. She prefers the quiet type and that lets me out. She showed me one of your drawings, too. Keeps it on her all the time. Shows her as a princess or something.'

Stephen's heart glowed at the news and he didn't know what to say, but thankfully, Johnson seemed to sense it and turned the subject.

'You're a lucky guy, Stephen and I wish you two well... Say, did you hear about Lawson? Damned lucky to be alive.'

'N-no. What happened?'

'He and a petty officer were working on a mine in a warehouse on the Thames the other night. The mine had gone through the roof and lodged on the fifth floor. They'd just started examining it when the clock started ticking. Knowing they'd never make it down again, Lawson kicked open the loading doors and jumped into the Thames. Only trouble was, the tide was out and he landed on the mud. Broke both legs. The PO wasn't quite so decisive and never made it out before the mine went off, taking half the warehouse with it. I guess it'll be a while before Lawson's back to duty.'

'I'm s-sorry to hear it. I don't like the m-man, but wish him no harm.'

'Yeah, that's probably about right. There's no doubting his courage, though.' Johnson contemplated his tea for a while whilst Stephen looked out at the few tourists walking outside. There were a few glimpses of sunshine, but it was a blustery day so the front was still quite empty.

'I guess I didn't tell you about my own little escape from death, Stephen.'

'No. Are you all right?'

'Hell, yes. It was on the east coast a couple of weeks back. A mine on the beach. I can't tell you why, but I just had a bad feeling about it. It was lying flat on the sand, fuze side up, ripe for the picking. Call it a sixth sense, but I just sat there looking at it from a safe distance for a while. Then I saw a crab climb onto the casing and I lay on my front with my glasses watching it... just to see what might happen. I told you, a sixth sense in me told me something bad might happen. Having climbed up onto the top of the casing, the crab seemed to do a tap dance. It scuttled sideways at a fair pace and up went the mine with a huge roar. Turned out it was an acoustic version.'

'Gosh, Johnny, you w-were lucky.'

'I sure was. I suppose you've heard that Jerry's now using a new form of mine. The acoustic-magnetic mine.'

'I had heard that. The n-noise of an approaching ship trips the f-firing device and then the magnetic unit goes off once the ship p-passes over. It b-breaks the ship's back that way.'

'It sure is clever. The magnetic unit can be less sensitive that way and it don't get fired by our magnetic sweeps. Wonder what Jerry'll figure up next.'

Stephen leaned across the table and whispered quietly, 'You've b-been w-warned about the new B-BM1000, I take it?'

'Yes, but nobody's said how to recognise it. Could be just a rumour. You any idea?'

'S-sorry. I just know it d-doesn't have a p-parachute. We'll just have to rely on our s-sixth senses.'

'Hell, I suppose that's a bridge we have to cross when we come to it. Say, it's great news we're to go to the Palace together.' Johnson wore the crimson ribbon with five vertical blue stripes to denote that he had been awarded the George Medal. Both officers were due to be awarded their medals by the King in June. 'Who are you taking as your guests?'

'M-my Mum and D-D-Dad.'

'Not Carol then?'

'No. I c-can only take two g-guests. What about you?'

'I've nobody to take. My folks are in the States and you're about the closest friend I have. Why don't you take my guest passes? Bring Carol.'

'I c-couldn't, Johnny.'

'Sure you could. And whilst you're about it, invite that sister of yours. It would do my ego no end of good to host two lovely girls, one on each arm, for the reception afterwards. Say no more about it.'

Stephen was humbled by the generosity of his friend. He hated to be greedy, but Johnson's offer would suit him very well. When he had invited his parents, he had guiltily hoped that Dad might not be able to come so that he might invite Carol, but Dad had said he would shut the garage for a few days.

'If you're sure? Thanks, b-but I'm not sure my s-sister will come. She d-disapproves of p-privilege.'

'Just make sure you persuade her, Stephen. We'll have a blast.'

*****

At the end of the month, Stephen was delighted to be invited up to London by Currey. It meant he would be able to see Carol again, but first Currey wanted him to meet the Earl of Suffolk.

To Stephen's surprise, Currey's driver headed for the west of London. 'Are w-we not g-going to S-Suffolk, sir?' he asked.

Currey smiled. 'Not today, Cunningham. We're off to Richmond Park. That's where Suffolk conducts his experiments… in an area of the park we've fenced off for him. In any case, his seat's not in Suffolk, but somewhere in Wiltshire. Near Malmesbury, I think.'

'W-why are we g-going to see him, sir?'

'He's a chemist. I think he might have been a cadet in the Andrew once, but now he's working for the Ministry of Supply on research. He conducts various experiments for us and I thought, as a fellow scientist, you might like to meet and share ideas. He's a most interesting fellow. "Mad Jack" we call him. You'll understand this better than I, but he was one of the chaps that organised the evacuation of the French physicists with their *heavy water* from Bordeaux. Fetched up with a boat-load of machine tools and Belgian diamonds, too. Remember Brock's Folly? Mad Jack was behind that.'

Brock's was a company manufacturing fireworks and Brock's Folly was a technique Stephen and other RMSOs had used to burn mines that were too dangerous to defuze.

'Anyway, he's been working on refining our trepanning technique. He wants to show us a way of removing the bomb fuze and any Zus 40 device as one unit. Imagine the difference that would make to us.'

Stephen could, indeed, imagine the benefits of no longer having to fear the deadly booby trap.

Stephen had never met an earl and imagined the Earl of Suffolk as being akin to something out of a PG Wodehouse novel. It came as a shock when he discovered the earl to be even more eccentric than he had pictured. Like Stephen, he wore black-rimmed spectacles with round lenses. He was tall and lean, and his hair, too, was dark and swept back with macassar oil, but there the resemblance ended. He had a neat moustache, but was otherwise unshaven, and his hair was shaggy and uncombed. His suit was dirty with the muddy brown and yellow stains of explosive, and for a hat he carried something made of fur that might not have been out of place in Hudson Bay. More strangely, however, he was wearing a holster under both armpits each containing a revolver.

Charles Howard, the former Viscount Andover and present twentieth Earl of Suffolk, completely ignored his visitors. He carried on his work with the aid of an elderly man and continually dictated notes to a middle-aged woman standing nearby. Stephen was familiar with the mine over which he stood and the contraption he was rigging over it. It was a trepanning machine, but the other machine was quite different from any he had seen before. He approached the earl to examine the strange machine more closely. It comprised a platform on two wheels with four adjustable legs and an engine of some form connected by an armoured pipe to a large tank of water standing above a paraffin heater.

The Earl of Suffolk secured the trepanning machine in place and stepped back. As he did so, he finally noticed Stephen and Currey.

'Ah, Norman. You've arrived just in time. You recognise the brute?'

'I do. An SC1000 Hermann bomb. I don't recognise this machine, though.' Currey indicated the machine connected to the water tank.'

'Yes. It's a new idea I'm working on. I thought you'd like to be the first to see it in action. But where are our manners? Who is the lieutenant with you? By the medal ribbon, clearly a brave man.'

'Quite right, Charles. This is Cunningham, one of my team and presently working down in Plymouth. He's a physicist. Cunningham, this is the Earl of Suffolk.'

'Just call me Charles.'

'I'm p-pleased to m-meet you, Charles. I'm S-Stephen.'

'A physicist, hey? Brains and courage. I suppose you deal with the basic and beautiful whilst we chemists deal with the interesting and useful.'

'B-both have their uses, but whilst we have to b-be exact in our d-discipline, the chemist is *almost* always right.'

'Well said, Stephen,' the earl laughed. 'Now you must meet my assistants. We call ourselves the "Holy Trinity". This is my secretary, Miss Eileen Morden, and my chauffeur, Hards. Now I am about to carry out a most intriguing experiment. You are aware that the battery powering the fuze can be flattened by use of the Crabtree discharger.'

Stephen felt in his pocket for the brass disc about the size of a crown. The Crabtree discharger had been invented in the previous summer and was very useful for rendering safe the Germans' early bomb fuzes. It was screwed onto the fuze and its two lugs depressed two plungers within the fuze. This caused the battery's charge to short circuit and discharge safely over time. It was then a simple matter of removing the fuze remotely with a pulley. Unfortunately, the fuzes of mines were more sophisticated.

'Of course, that's all well and good for something such as the Type 15 fuze, but will be of little use for say the Type 17 and Zus 40 combination. I believe we can overcome that by the use of steam.' Howard pointed to his strange contraption nearby.

As one, Stephen and Currey recognised the function of the strange machine and water tank. It was a steam generator.

'By cutting into the main body of the bomb, I can access the main explosive. We then introduce high-pressure steam to melt and emulsify the amatol - or TNT - so that it can be extracted safely. Then the disposal officer is free to tackle the fuze.'

'That's all well and good, Charles, but that fuze is still enough to kill or at best maim my men,' Currey interrupted. 'I can't see how you extract a fuze mechanically without setting off the Zus 40 beneath, if fitted.'

'Ah, but my dear Norman, that's the next phase. We inject steam into the fuze to heat the capacitors and it will work as well as the Crabtree on simpler fuzes. Have faith and observe. But first, I suggest we retire to a safe distance. This will take some time.'

'I have a flask of coffee and some sandwiches in my car,' Currey replied. 'We'll be safe enough at that distance.'

'Oh, ye of little faith. But I am hungry so your offer is most agreeable, Norman.'

The two naval officers and the eccentric earl sat in the car whilst the trepanning machine went to work. Stephen found the long wait quite boring. He was keen to see how the steam generator performed. However, after two hours, the machine stopped after cutting a disc in the bomb's casing. Then the earl and his chauffeur removed the chains and bolts of the cutter and connected the steam generator. The generator fired up in a cloud of steam.

'It's important to keep an eye on the steam, gentlemen,' Suffolk explained. 'Should it turn blue, it means the copper coil of the steam generator is overheating and needs more water. That thick vaporous cloud is what we're looking for.'

Stephen and Currey watched with fascination as a thick tube of nasty-looking yellow gunge began to be forced out of the bomb casing like sausage meat. Both were aware that without the gaine, the explosive was relatively harmless. Indeed, amatol was used for the stoves of some military camps. This steaming technique was similar to the burning technique currently employed on difficult bombs and mines. One of Brook's Follies was used to burn through the casing and slowly burn the explosive within. Stephen began to hope that thanks to the likes of the eccentric earl and the *Vernon* scientists, Britain might be about to move ahead of the Germans in the war of mine counter measures.

Chapter 26
May 1941

May 1941 heralded another heavy air raid on Liverpool. Monty travelled north in the hope of discovering a BM1000. The bombing was terrible. The visibility had been good and the Germans bombers achieved success in destroying nearly half the berths for the docks and several industrial sites and storehouses. The civilian population suffered greatly, too. There had been widespread use of incendiary bombs. Several thousand homes had been completely destroyed and even more damaged. The civil authorities told Monty that approximately 70,000 Liverpudlians had been made homeless. Water mains, sewers, gas mains, telephone connections and electricity supplies had all been destroyed or damaged, too, as well as countless roads, railway lines and tram lines. Monty had never seen such devastation. Even the cathedral had been damaged. After a few days of fruitless searching for the mystery BM1000, he attended the funeral in nearby Southport of an RMSO who had not managed to run far enough before the clock on his mine's fuze had run down. The officer's parents lived in Glasgow and had been unable to attend the funeral, so Monty had promised to take the officer's ashes up there the next time he visited the city. He then hitched a lift with the Fleet Air Arm from Burscough to Belfast.

Belfast, too, had been bombed in the Germans' efforts to destroy the shipyard at Harland and Wolff. There, Monty thought he might have some luck. Mines had been reported as having fallen around the reservoir. Together with the local RMS officers, he checked each location, but all seemed to have had parachutes attached. There was a report of a mine as having dropped into the reservoir itself, but Monty was informed by the local authorities that the water was needed to fight fires and, thus, there was no prospect of draining the reservoir to search for his mine. Frustrated and dejected, Monty returned to London.

He rang Benson for any further news on the new *bombenmine*. Benson was unable to help much. All he could say was that the RAF believed the weapon was now operational with the

Luftwaffe. There seemed little else Monty could do until he received news from the regional RMSOs of an unusual find. It was just a matter of time, but he felt guilty that he was almost hoping for a heavy raid to offer a greater prospect of fulfilling his quest.

On his return from Oxford one evening after an afternoon with Marcy, Monty heard that a heavy air raid was in place over Clydeside. He immediately resolved to head north again. It was better than sitting around in London and he had the excuse that he was delivering the ashes of the recently deceased RMS officer to his parents. Clydebank had been selected by the *Luftwaffe* for intensive raids over the past couple of months due to the concentration on the Clyde of several shipyards, munitions factories and oil storage tanks.

This time with the assistance of the RAF, Monty arrived in Glasgow to see for himself the desolation the bombers had left behind down both banks of the Clyde as far as Greenock. In Greenock several unexploded parachute mines had been dropped on buildings already ablaze from incendiary bombs. The RMSOs had to work quickly to defuze the mines before the flames reached them. Monty took his turn in dragging out the mines and dealing with unexploded incendiary bombs. He felt better for doing something active.

The following day, he met Johnson near Port Glasgow. Johnson had just destroyed two mines in the nearby sandbanks as there hadn't been sufficient time to defuze them between the tides. They sat together on a grassy bank overlooking the river to Cardross on the other bank.

'Hello, Johnny. I thought you were working on the south coast these days.'

'Not necessarily. I go where the work is. I was in Scapa Flow last week.'

'Have you done much diving since qualifying?'

'Nope. Ever since the death of Sutherland, the powers-that-be have been kinda jumpy about me working on mines underwater.'

'You know it was an acoustic mine that killed Sutherland?'

'I sure do, Monty. I gather it was the sound of his bubbles that triggered the mine. Of all the rotten luck… bang on 250 hertz.'

'It certainly was bad luck. Have you heard from Stephen lately?'

'Not for a while. I guess we've both been kinda busy... and he's got himself a gal now.'

'What, Stephen? Bless my soul. The sly old devil. Have you met her?'

'I have. She's what you Brits would call a *corker*. I don't know what she sees in him.'

'You know that's nonsense, Johnny. You're his best friend. We both know he's kind and loyal.'

'You make him out to be like a dog... You know, a faithful hound.'

'I suppose he does have that sort of quality, but there's none braver or more selfless... and I include the present company.'

'True. I'll concede that. Anyway, we're meeting next month... at the Palace.'

'Of course, your investiture. Sorry, I forgot. Congratulations on your George Medal. And the promotion, too.'

'No sweat. It's kind of satisfying though to think the King of England's going to pin a medal on me, a citizen of the United States.'

'You deserve it, Johnny.'

The two men sat quietly whilst enjoying the relative peace of the river bank. The river, however, was full of activity with several movements of boats, merchant ships, warships and even submarines. There was such a concentrated mass of shipping on the river, Monty wondered why the *Luftwaffe* hadn't sunk more ships at their anchorage.

'I say, Johnny. You've not come across any mines without parachutes, have you?'

'You mean Hitler's latest secret weapon? The word's out to report it if we do, but sorry, no. This fellow might be able to help, though. We've been working with his men for the last couple of days.'

The two naval officers were joined by a Royal Engineers major. Johnson rose and saluted him. 'Sir, may I introduce you to Lieutenant Commander Montcalm?'

The major returned Johnson's salute and extended a hand to Monty. 'Bramby's the name. I'm in command of the Bomb Disposal Unit here. Will you be joining us for the Lord Provost's Banquet tonight?'

'I'm not aware of it,' Monty replied.

'It's to thank all those who've helped out with the bomb disposal work. The navy's invited, too, and it would be good to have a senior naval officer present.'

'Thanks. Provided Jerry doesn't come back, I'll be there then.'

'Great. I tell you what. Would you like to see a really good blow-up? In the morning, my team are blowing up a Hermann over in Dumbarton. You'd be welcome to attend.'

For some unknown reason, the hairs rose on the back of Monty's neck. 'You're sure it's a Hermann, are you?'

'Absolutely. 1000 kg.' Bramby seemed offended by the question, but Monty pressed him.

'I'm sorry, but have you dealt with many Hermanns before? It's important.'

The major stroked his moustache and his attitude softened. 'Well, now you come to mention it, no. Not since training actually. Do you suspect this might be something else?'

'It's possible, but I can have a look in the morning?'

'Only now you've got me thinking,' Bramby carried on regardless. 'One of your RMSOs said to my adjutant that there might be another bomb in the crater. He found something like the batteries of a wireless set or acoustic unit.'

Monty's heart skipped a beat. 'I'm sorry, Bramby, but there's no time to lose. Do you mind missing your reception? Two bombs close together and one of them more elaborate than the norm is too much of a coincidence. Can you take me there right now?'

'But, of course, old man. I'll instruct my driver to put his foot down.'

'Johnny, I shall want you with me. Come on.'

*****

'How much longer to F-Falmouth, S-Stan?' Stephen asked his driver after waking up with a start. He had been dragged from his bed in Devonport in the early hours of the morning following the previous night's bombing of Falmouth. The job was 'Category A'. That meant he couldn't burn the bomb or destroy it and loss of the life of the poor RMSO dealing with it was deemed acceptable. Stephen had decided that it was not a job to be delegated to one of his team.

'About an hour, I'd say, sir. Meanin' if there be no more diversions.'

'I s-see. In which c-case, I'm going to need a c-comfort break s-soon.'

'Fair enough, sir. I'll pull over at the next suitable spot or else we'll be in Saint Austell afore we know it.'

Five minutes later, Stephen found a suitable tree hidden from the road and relieved his bladder. He hadn't had breakfast and had relied on coffee to keep him going, but it always made him want to urinate. He decided he could stretch his legs for a few minutes and smoke a cigarette. He knew he'd got out of bed the wrong side this morning. He felt tired, grumpy and dispirited. Much of that was down to the strain he and his team had been under for weeks on end, but the news the day before of the Earl of Suffolk's death had hit him particularly hard. He knew few details other than that he had been trying to remove the fuze of a bomb when it had started ticking. He had applied the new clock stopper, a huge magnetic collar, but it couldn't have worked. Several men of the Royal Engineers had died in the explosion, too.

The earl's death had forced him to think of his own mortality. Too many RMSOs and bomb disposal officers of the other services were dying. The Jerry booby traps were becoming ever more sophisticated and beating the newer batches of officers from the training schools. Stephen wondered what he would find in Falmouth, but quickly cast his own immediate future from his mind. There would be time for that when he arrived. Instead, he thought back to Carol's latest letter. Despite her long and frequent shifts at the hospital, she was writing to him at least weekly now and not even waiting for him to reply first. That's as well, he thought, as I never was one for regular correspondence, but I suppose the war gives me a good excuse now.

Since the ladies' night dinner, he had learned more about her and her family life. He now knew that she had been born and raised in the Borders area of Scotland and that her parents owned a home near Kelso as well as that in Primrose Hill. Even so, her father, an industrialist working for the Ministry of Supply - and presumably a wealthy man, too, he thought - now lived in the United States. Carol's mother had accompanied her husband to the US. However, only in this latest letter had Carol revealed that she was Jewish. It mattered little to him. After all, in his opinion, the only difference between her faith and his own was that they chose to worship the same God in a different manner and have a different view of the New Testament. Both his parents were committed Christians even though his father was a Quaker and his mother an Anglican. Nevertheless, Carol seemed to hint his religion might be a problem and was going to write to her parents about it. Although not as committed a Quaker as his father, Stephen did wonder why other faiths seemed less tolerant of each other than his own.

His cigarette now down to the butt, he stubbed it out and resumed the journey to Falmouth.

*****

The army car left the Clydeside town of Dumbarton and ascended a steep hill through farmland. The fields were still bare, brown soil reminding Monty that Nature was a long way behind that of his native Wiltshire. Along the whole bank of the Clyde the sky was thronged with barrage balloons to protect the area's factories from air attack. The driver stopped the car and Monty could see a shallow crater in the next but one field and four personnel from the RAF tending to a nearby barrage balloon. He, Bramby and Johnson stepped out of the car and walked across the muddy fields, soon coming across the Hermann.

Monty was immediately disappointed. The bomb was pale blue, the colour of Germany's conventional bombs and looked just like a Hermann, so called by the Germans as its huge, fat shape reminded them of their portly *Reichsmarschall*, Hermann Göring. Even so, he and Johnny began digging around the bomb with their bare hands, too cautious to use tools for the present. They began by clearing away the soil from the bomb's nose cone. This seemed larger and more bulbous than those in the photographs Monty had seen. He and Johnson moved further up the bomb and came across the metal ring where the nose cone was welded to the main cylinder of the bomb. Now the bomb had a more phallic look about it, like a penis with the foreskin drawn back.

'Johnny, does this look like a Hermann to you?'

'I couldn't say, Monty. I've only ever seen photos of them.'

'Same here. We'll keep going.'

Together, the two naval officers continued their excavation. When they had done so, Monty was persuaded that this was no more than a standard 1,000 kilogramme bomb. The discovery of the Rheinmetall fuze had convinced him. This was a contact fuze only used in bombs so as to explode the bomb on impact with hard ground. Disappointed, he stood up and brushed the mud off his knees.

'I thought you said one of the RMSOs discovered bits of electronics with the bomb, Bramby,' Monty addressed the major.

'So I was told, Montcalm. Perhaps my adjutant got it wrong. After all, this bomb has clearly not detonated and he was on about a partly-detonated bomb.'

A sudden thought struck Monty. 'Might there be two Hermanns?'

Bramby was flustered. 'I suppose so. We've been hard pressed these past few days and things have been a bit confusing. Let's ask those RAF boys.' He waved for one of the barrage balloon crew to come over.

An elderly corporal approached and saluted the major smartly.

'Been takin a wee look at our bomb ha'ye, sor? We'll no' miss it when it's gone, the bloody great beast.'

Monty cut in. 'We were wondering if you might have found any other bombs nearby, corporal.'

'No' tha' ain't already exploded. Tha's one oot there yonder tha's made a reet mess o' tha' sheed, mind.'

Monty stared in the direction of the corporal's outstretched hand. About four hundred yards away, he could see the remains of some form of corrugated metal structure and assumed the bomb must have flattened it. He had a hunch it might be worth a look and headed in its direction with Johnson in tow. Bramby returned to his car.

The bomb had left a crater and bits of its casing lay strewn amongst the metal of the farm building. Of more interest, however, were the remains of a wireless set.

'Why do you think Jerry would include a wireless mechanism in an ordinary bomb, Monty?' Johnson asked as he examined the electronic pieces in puzzlement. 'Do you think it could be some new kind of electronic fuze?' Monty ignored him. He had spotted something green in the soil.

Monty picked up a handful of the soil and picked out the greenish pieces. He held them out to Johnson to examine.

'Jeez, you thinking what I'm thinking, Monty? Hexanite?'

Monty nodded. 'If that was a Hermann, it would have been filled with TNT. Hexanite is only used by the Germans for mines. And note that both supposed Hermanns were dropped as a pair. I think Jerry came in low last night heading for the river and distracted by the barrage balloons, dropped his load half a mile short.'

'So, what do we do now?'

'First, we'll confirm it is hexanite. Do you have a light, Johnny?'

'Sorry, Monty. All my kit's still in the car.'

'No problem. We can check it out later, but I'm very confident. I'm going to leave you here now, Johnny. Whilst I'm away, I want you to collect up as many pieces of this bomb as you can. I'll join you later and I'll leave you your tools. I need to telephone London to brief Captain Maitland-Dougall and arrange collection of your bits and that Hermann.'

Monty returned to the car to find an impatient Bramby. 'I say, Montcalm, we're going to be late for the Lord Provost's reception.'

'Sorry, Bramby, but I won't be coming after all. Moreover, there'll be no blowing up of that Hermann tomorrow. I'm claiming it on behalf of the navy. I believe it's a new type of mine and my assistant and I will try to render it safe in the morning. Look what we found at that second bomb site.' Monty held out a couple of green lumps that he had collected.

'Really? A mine you say? What's that you have there?'

'Hexanite. It's not as powerful as TNT so is only used for underwater weapons.'

'Not come across it myself. Do you chaps need any help?'

'Thank you. Yes, as a matter of fact. Could you and your driver take me to a telephone? I need to ring the Admiralty. Then I'll need transport for my assistant and I. More importantly, however, do you have someone to help us deal with that Rheinmetall fuze? It's not something of which we have much experience.'

'No problem at all, old man. I'll lend you one of my subalterns. And another thought. We've a large collection of fragments from that second bomb at our HQ. Would you like them?'

'Yes, please. I'll collect them in the morning.'

Chapter 27

Stephen couldn't see the bomb from the surface of the dry dock. It had landed in the chamber of the sluice valve connecting two graving docks. In each of the docks a destroyer was parked on its timber cradles to enable essential repairs to be carried out on its hull. Stephen noted with irony that one of the ships had clearly suffered damage from a mine. However, the presence of the two ships badly needed for convoy duty explained why this job had been given the highest category. He climbed down the girders of the chamber and thirty-five feet later, arrived at the water level. Now he ought to have been able to see the bomb, but he realised that his task wasn't going to be an easy one.

  The bomb was under the water and Stephen couldn't see how far down. His first thought was to borrow a diving suit, but it brought back still unhappy memories of his familiarisation dive at HMS *Excellent* two years before. This was just the sort of job for which Johnny was trained, he thought. He wondered if there was a way of telling just how deep the bomb had gone and thought a boat hook might help. After returning to the surface to collect a boat hook, he stripped down to his underwear thinking that he might be able to attach a rope around the bomb and use it to pull the bomb to the surface. Although early summer and warm on the surface in the glorious late-morning sunshine, he didn't relish a long dip in the oily black water.

  Back down the valve chamber, he lowered the boat hook into the water and had some luck. He could feel the bomb lodged in the girders at the extreme length of the hook's shaft, about six feet down. Stephen lowered himself carefully into the water and gasped with the cold. The temperature of the sea water had yet to catch up with that on land. However, there was nothing for it and taking a deep breath he gingerly lowered himself beneath the surface. Even with his eyes open, he could see very little. There was too much oil and filth in the water, so Stephen worked by touch alone. He could feel the lug on the bomb casing where it had been held in place in the bomber's bomb bay and thought he might be able to attach a rope through that, but then he had yet more luck. Near the base of the bomb it had been damaged and Stephen could feel a hole. He thought he might be able to fit his boat hook into the hole and use it and the rope to haul the bomb to the surface. With his lungs now painfully demanding air, he continued his fingertip search carefully and felt for the fuzes. Then his luck ran out.

*****

The following morning, Monty and Johnson returned to their suspicious bomb. Bramby had been as good as his word and sent along a Lieutenant Gerald to assist with removing the Rheinmetall fuze. The night before, Monty had shown the remnants of the electronic parts retrieved from the detonated bombs to other RMSOs gathered in Glasgow and none had recognised them. All had agreed that they resembled a mine mechanism, but not one known to them.

Monty had selected Johnson to strip the mine, but thought it only fair to warn him of the dangers as they gathered round it again. 'Johnny, let's confirm we're dealing with a mine before we start. Pass me that sack, will you?'

Monty arranged some pieces of the green lumps he believed to be hexanite into a neat pile. 'Stand back,' he warned as he set fire to the pile. It immediately fizzed with a greenish and brilliant glow like a firework. It confirmed his suspicions. Hexanite was forty percent aluminium.

'Right, Johnny. It's time to come clean with you. It looks as if that was a mine over there and I'm reasonably confident this is its pair. That means we're dealing with a new type of mine and I believe this to be the BM1000 I've been looking for. For that reason, *Vernon* need to investigate it and so you can't burn it or blow it.'

'What's so special about it then?'

'I don't honestly know. All I can say is that our intelligence suggests the Germans are confident we can't strip this type and you know what that means?'

'I figure it means it contains some new form of booby trap,' Johnny said quietly and gazed across at the river. 'Could we X-ray it and then use the trepanning machine?'

Monty sensed and understood Johnson's reluctance to tackle the unknown. He had had the same thoughts. 'We could, but Maitland-Dougall and I are keen to discover its secrets as soon as we can. You've seen how easy it is to misidentify this weapon as a Hermann and we're concerned every day we delay, the more RAF or army bomb disposal officers we risk losing. But it's your call, Johnny. Nobody will think you a coward if you wait a couple of days.'

Johnson breathed in the warm, summer air deeply and looked up at the cotton wool clouds above before answering. 'Hell! As Lady Macbeth said, *"If 'twere done, 'twere best done quickly."* But I shall want a few precautions taken first. Deal?'

Monty smiled and shook Johnson's hand. 'Deal,' he replied. 'Tell me what you want.'

'Firstly, I don't want any traffic on that road in case of vibration and I want this area cleared of potential sightseers. That includes our boys in blue over there. They'll have to suspend operations of their winches, too.'

'Fair enough, Johnny. It shall be done. Whilst it's being done, I'll have some photographs taken, so perhaps you and Gerald could scrape away some more earth.'

'You mean you want evidence of the crime in case I don't make it, Monty?' Johnson smiled good-naturedly.

'Don't worry, Johnny. I'm going to be with you all the way. I'm going to ask Fenwick to act as observing officer.'

'Come on, Monty. There's no need for that. It's your job to be observing officer. Fenwick's a fully qualified RMSO in any case.'

'No, Johnny. Not on this occasion. This is my mine and I'm not going to ask you to face risks I'm not prepared to take myself. In any case, I bet I've attended more strippings than you and Fenwick together. You'll find me a competent enough assistant. Besides, if you come across something unusual, I might just know something about it… And, of course, I am the senior officer here.'

Johnson laughed. 'You're one hell of a stubborn mule, Lieutenant Commander. But I'm glad to have you on board for all that.' Johnson slapped Monty's back. 'Right, let's get on.'

Once all the safety precautions were in place, the three men comprising Monty, Johnson and Gerald set to work. Gerald began by listening to the mine with a stethoscope.

'It's not ticking, so I doubt it's a clockwork fuze,' he said.

'Or else it's stopped for the moment,' Johnson replied. Gerald blanched at the thought.

'You're right. It's a Rheinmetall fuze. Standard issue for Jerry bombs, but the serial number's odd.'

'In what way?' Monty peered at the fuze intently.

'It's 157/3. The highest number we've come across so far has been in the fifties. Do you think that's significant, sir?'

'I do, Gerald. I think it means this bomb or mine was designed for a special purpose.'

Gerald started to unscrew the cap of the fuze. 'It seems quite loose,' he said happily. It set the hairs on the back of Monty's neck on end.

'Stop!' he called quietly, but insistently. 'You'd better let us take a look. Our experience with mines is that Jerry uses a spring-loaded booby trap on his fuzes.'

Monty and Johnson took over. Johnson unscrewed the keep ring whilst Monty kept pressure on the fuze with two fingers to prevent it rising. Once the keep ring had been removed, Monty gently eased the pressure and didn't discern any upwards movement of the fuze.

'It looks all right, Johnny. You feel.'

Johnny put his hand over the fuze as Monty removed his fingers. 'Jeez, I think I can feel it lifting. Run!'

Neither Monty nor Gerald needed any further encouragement. All three officers took to their heels. As they dashed to the safety of Fenwick's dugout three hundred yards away, Monty wondered how far they would get. He glanced at the second hand on his wrist watch and confirmed they wouldn't make it. After what he thought was seventeen seconds since Johnson had called "run", he flung himself to the ground, buried his head in the soil and prayed.

Nothing happened and Monty dared raise his head to check his watch. A further fifteen seconds elapsed and looking up slightly, he noted that the others had clearly not bothered to check their watches as they were at that moment diving head first into the dugout. By the sound of the oaths, one or both had landed on top of Fenwick. Monty waited another thirty seconds and then he, too, ran for the dugout. It was a tight squeeze with four of them in it. Again, nothing happened.

By now, Monty had lost count of the time since starting to run, so he counted off another minute. Still there was no explosion. Johnson was the first to speak.

'Shall we try this from a distance, Monty? I sure don't think I've the puff to do that again.'

His chest still heaving, Monty merely nodded. Johnson made to return to the mine alone with a long length of line, but Gerald stopped him. 'Wait.' He fumbled in the chest pocket of his khaki battledress. 'Here, take this.' It was a special type of grip the Royal Engineers used. 'Just rig a shackle to it before you tie on your line.'

After tying on the line, Johnson returned to the safety of the dugout and heaved on the line. Johnson felt it pull, but there was no explosion. They all waited a full two minutes before Monty and Johnson ventured out of the safety of the dugout and approached the mine on tip toes. Monty began to sing softly to himself something from Gilbert and Sullivan's *The Pirates of Penzance*.

'*With cat-like tread, upon our prey we steal.*
'*In silence dread, our cautious way we feel.*
'*No sound at all, we never speak a word.*
'*A fly's footfall, would be distinctly heard.*'

Johnson looked strangely at Monty and then recognised the tune and the significance of the words. He remembered watching the operetta at The Savoy Theatre.

'*Tarantara. Tarantara,*' he replied in song and both he and Monty laughed gently.

The fuze hung loosely from the rest of the bomb, connected to the interior by two red wires and black wire. Monty pointed out to Johnson that the red wire led to the tail of the bomb.

'That looks like at least one booby trap, Johnny,' he whispered, remembering the deaths of the men at *Vernon* who had removed the baseplate at the rear of an earlier mine that had been retrieved for investigation.

Johnson put his fingers into the fuze socket. 'I can feel the detonator cap and gaine.' He started to scrape out the picric rings of the primer and was then able to see the detonator and gaine better. 'It's a mercury detonator.'

Monty shivered at the news. It was one of the latest type of detonators, containing highly sensitive fulminate of mercury. Johnson pulled out the penultimate picric ring and suddenly stopped.

'I've found something.' He extracted a small torch from his pocket. 'It's red and I think it's another detonator.'

Monty had a look, too. 'I think you're right. Let's leave it alone for a while, shall we?'

'That suits me, bud.' Johnson moved his attention to the rear of the mine. It had cracked and the tail unit had parted slightly from the main body where the explosive charge lay. He looked carefully for the tell-tale examination plughole on the casing which was a hallmark of the presence of the spring-loaded plunger tight against the rear section of the mine.

'Maybe there's no booby trap this time, Monty,' Johnson suggested. 'You want me to separate it?'

'No, Johnny. We'll leave that to be X-rayed. We could be dealing with a new type of booby trap. I'd like to know where those red wires go, though.'

'Let's take a look then, shall we?' Johnson reached into his tool bag for a brace and bit. Gently and slowly, for fear of creating too much vibration, he bored into the soft metal casing of the mine to create several peep-holes near the junction of the main body and tail section. Using his torch, he peered inside the mine. 'It seems to be full of batteries,' he said at last.

'All right, Johnny. I've changed my mind. We'll just cut those wires and have the mine X-rayed after all. We don't know what we're dealing with, but we've found out enough to warn others to treat this type of bomb or mine differently. You take charge of the X-raying and shipment of the beast to *Vernon*. I'm going back to London on the sleeper to make my report to Captain Maitland-Dougall.'

'Sure, buddy. I'm happy with that. I'll just snip these wires and remove the detonators first.' Johnson cut the wires and stored the detonator and fuze in separate boxes. 'Say, Monty,' he called after him. 'You gonna give me a hand with clearing this crater, ready for the X-ray equipment?'

'It'll not be here before the morning, so you'll have plenty of time to work off that Yankee insouciance of yours.'

'In-soossy what? And don't you call me a Yankee,' Johnson called back.

Chapter 28

By touch alone, Stephen discovered two fuzes in the bomb. That meant trouble. He knew that the rear fuze would be the type 17 fuze, a standard clockwork time fuze. He could deal with that easily enough by using the magnetic clock stopper, but that would set off the other fuze. The forward fuze would be much more troublesome. In his experience, it would be the type 50 fuze. This was a 'trembler' anti-withdrawal device – a booby trap.

Stephen returned to the surface of the graving dock to consider his options. First, he dressed as he didn't think he would need to re-enter the water. He planned to lash a rope to the shaft of the boat hook that he had hooked into the bomb. His men could then haul the bomb to the surface. Then life would become more tricky.

The retrieval of the bomb did, indeed, prove straightforward. The safest option now would be to take the bomb out to sea and dump it in deep water, but as Stephen looked out onto the deep-blue River Fal and the trees beyond, he watched a fishing boat heading out to sea. He realised that dumping a dangerous bomb in fishing grounds would be irresponsible. He would have to disarm the bomb, despite the booby trap. However, if anything went wrong, there were two destroyers at risk. That said, he saw a solution.

'D-Dawlish. I think that b-bomb's b-been powder-filled. W-what do you think?'

'I agree, Boss. I can cut a hole in the casing to check, but I think I know where you're going with this. Leave it with me.'

The dockyard had already been cleared of personnel within 400 yards of the bomb as
Dawlish cut a circular hole in the main body of the bomb where the explosive charge was contained. He turned round to Stephen and gave him a thumbs up sign. That was one problem solved, Stephen thought. He left it to Dawlish and his team to cut another hole in the bomb and then to use a hosepipe to flush out the explosive. The next stage would be for him alone. He still felt out of sorts. The letter from Carol worried him. Had she mentioned her religion merely as

a piece about herself or was there a problem? Was she warning him off?

He shook himself and paced the floor of the dock. He had to stay focused on the bomb. Once the charge had been flushed out it would no longer pose a risk to the nearby ships. It would just be a bomb casing with a couple of fuzes. However, there was enough explosive in one of the fuzes alone to kill him. At best he would be maimed, either losing an arm or being stripped. Several unfortunate RMSOs had suffered from having the skin stripped from their arm right up to the elbow when a detonator had gone off in their hand. What future would he have then as a cripple with a stammer? It would be better to be killed outright.

After a while, Dawlish reported the bomb ready for Stephen and the rest of the team took cover. Now Stephen was on his own. Firstly, he had to deal with the type 50 fuze. When he had met the Earl of Suffolk, they had discussed whether it might be possible to freeze such fuzes by the use of something like liquid oxygen, but the earl was now dead and Stephen had to use the tools he had to hand. He decided to use the standard liquid discharger. With his heart in his mouth and unconsciously biting his tongue, Stephen removed the keep ring and, using a bicycle pump, pumped a solution of methylated spirits and saline water into the fuze assembly. The aim was that the electro-conductive solution would short out the fuze's capacitors and discharge the current to render the fuze inert, but it wasn't a risk-free solution. The slightest vibration could set off the fuze. Stephen could feel his mouth go very dry with fear. He thought any man who said he didn't feal fear when dealing with unexploded ordnance was a liar.

All seemed to be well and he retired to safety for thirty minutes. Nothing happened in whilst Stephen smoked two cigarettes and listened inattentively to the chaff of the sailors of his team. He hoped that his men would not think he had wet himself in fright as he was conscious that the water from his soaked undershorts was seeping through his trousers. He felt sure Dawlish would put them right if they did. He's a good man, Stephen thought. Now he felt hungry and looked forward to the job being done.

The half hour up, he returned to the bomb to deal with the type 17 fuze. Dawlish and the team brought the massive clock-stopper, a brass magnetic coil the size of a horse collar. It weighed 90 kilogrammes and its purpose was to lock the steel components of the fuze into place. When the clock was confirmed as stopped, the bomb could be moved safely with the magnetic collar in place.

Dawlish pushed the switch to supply the clock-stopper with its 140-volt supply of electricity. Stephen used a stethoscope to listen for the sound of the ticking. The fuze was still ticking.

'It's not w-working, Chief,' he called. 'Try reversing the c-c-current.' Still the clock continued ticking. Stephen had no choice. He would have to tackle the fuze the old-fashioned way and remove it before the bomb could be removed to safety. He explained his plan to Dawlish.'

'Right enough, sir. D'you need a hand?' Stephen shook his head. His problem now was that he didn't know how long the clock had been running and the remaining run time. He would have to work quickly. Alone again, he set to work to remove first the fuze and then to dismantle the gaine. It was with great satisfaction that he completed the task within twenty minutes and set fire to the picric rings. He thought of Lawson and his stop watch. The poor chap would still be in hospital, but he had survived another day.

Less than an hour later, after a hasty lunch and on his way back to Plymouth, the driver was alarmed by a bang from the glove compartment. Stephen had put the now harmless fuze there for the journey home and the clock of the type 17 fuze had obviously just run down. Stephen regarded his hand and arm. He uttered a silent prayer of thanks. It had been another close call and he wondered how much longer his luck could hold.

*****

Monty had slept little on the night train back down to London. It seemed to him that he had felt every bump as the train had crossed different points and switches on the line. He decided that the term 'sleeper' was a misnomer. By the time the steward called him to advise of the train's imminent arrival in London, he was already up, washed and dressed. Accordingly, he was back at the Admiralty very early in the morning. He wrote up his report on the discovery of what he felt confident was the BM1000 and made a start on his in-tray whilst he waited for Maitland-Dougall's arrival in the office. It was only two hours later that he learned Maitland-Dougall would be late into the office as he had been out all night with Captain Currey visiting various RMS teams at work around London. Monty decided he could afford the time to return to his flat for a bath and fresh change of uniform.

Amongst the mail awaiting him at his flat was one from Lancashire. Monty recognised the small, neat handwriting. It was the third letter he had had from Lucy Cunningham. He felt another pang of guilt as he read it. Most days he felt sure he was in love with Marcy, although she had not expressed any signs that his feelings for her were reciprocated, and each time he received Lucy's letters he felt uncertain of his feelings.

He had been surprised to receive the first letter following their meeting late last year. He had felt sure that she despised him and his class, but she had, nonetheless, asked him for his address and he had been too polite to refuse. This latest letter followed his last visit to Liverpool. They had met for a cup of tea in Preston. He had known that he shouldn't have made the arrangement if he really was in love Marcy, but something had compelled him to ring her.

As he took a bath, Monty examined his feelings for Lucy and couldn't come to any firm conclusions. Perhaps he was merely flattered that she took an interest in him. Then again, he did find her company refreshing. She was quite unlike any of the girls he had dated at Oxford. She was unconventional and questioned the status quo. Would she be the type to introduce to Mother, though? Did that matter these days? And in any case, he was the spare and not the heir. He was getting too far ahead of himself. Although Lucy's letter was warm, it didn't imply anything more than friendship. Friendship. Should he tell Stephen that he was corresponding with his sister? What would he think?

The telephone rang. Monty stepped out of the bath, draped a towel around his waist despite being alone in the flat, and stepped into his living room, leaving wet footprints behind on the parquet floor.

'Montcalm,' he answered in his usual manner.

'Get your backside in here pronto.' The caller hung up, but Monty recognised the voice. It was Maitland-Dougall and he didn't sound happy.

*****

'You're a bloody fool, Montcalm.' Maitland-Dougall waved Monty's report of his visit to Glasgow and Dumbarton. 'You should have been the observing officer and not Fenwick on that job.'

'I accept that under normal considerations, sir...'

'Don't interrupt. I haven't finished rollocking you yet.' There was something about Maitland-Dougall's demeanour that made Monty feel his superior's anger would, as usual, be short lived. He stood at attention ready to let the storm blow out.

'You are an intelligence officer and not an RMSO. You had a perfectly competent RMSO on hand in Fenwick to assist – what was his name?'

'Johnson, sir. The American.'

'To assist Johnson, so you were well placed to act only as the observing officer.'

'I agree, sir, but there were extenuating circumstances.' This time Maitland-Dougall let Monty speak. 'We didn't know what we were going to find so...'

'Exactly. You didn't know what you were dealing with so there was even more need of a competent observing officer.'

'In the circumstances, I thought I had the best intelligence to make any immediate decisions, sir.'

'I would say you showed a distinct lack of intelligence.' Maitland-Dougall sat down and Monty knew his anger had been spent.

'Quite frankly, Monty, I don't know whether to court-martial you for recklessness and disobedience of standing orders or to recommend you for a medal.' Maitland-Dougall smiled for the first time during the interview. 'I'll grant it was well done to stop the army blowing up this weapon and you might well have found our first complete example of Hitler's new mine, but… I suppose we'll have to see what *Vernon* reports before I decide what to do with you,' Maitland-Dougall spoke resignedly. 'When will they begin stripping it?'

'Tomorrow… at the earliest. There was a delay in sending the X-ray equipment, sir. It had to go up from another job in Nottingham and won't arrive until this morning. I'll ring Glasgow and check on progress, shall I, sir?' Monty reached for the telephone in the hope the interview was over, but Maitland-Dougall had not quite finished.

'Sit down, Monty. If that bomb turns out to be a BM1000, I'll probably recommend Johnson for the George Medal… correction, a bar to his GM as I think he's just had one, hasn't he?'

'It's being presented by the King next month, sir.' Monty was relieved to be of assistance, but had noted that Maitland-Dougall had used his nickname again, so he knew he was back on solid ground.

'I don't doubt your courage, Monty, and it must be hard to see others receive their due recognition for theirs, but you must accept that you are an invaluable intelligence officer. The knowledge you've gained on the mine threat over the past eighteen months is incalculable and, more to the point, irreplaceable. Promise me, Monty… No more heroics.'

'I'll do my best, sir.' Monty rang RMS HQ in Glasgow.

*****

The following morning, he was at *Mirtle* in Hampshire to witness the stripping of the mine. It had now been confirmed as a mine since the underside of it was stencilled with the marking, 'BM1000'. Johnson had come down from Glasgow and he would finish stripping the mine before the main charge was removed. This would ensure the scientists were not exposed to any risk, a precaution that had been in place since the explosion in the mining shed. Even RMSOs were less valuable than the scientists.

'Seems you were right about the tail unit, Monty,' Johnson said cheerily as he set to work. 'The X-ray showed the base plate was booby trapped. I figure I owe you my life, Monty.'

Monty reflected that the news might help justify his decision to assist Johnson. Meanwhile, Johnson painstakingly and methodically took the mine to pieces. 'Well, wouldn't you know?' he called out and whistled softly. 'What do you reckon this is, Monty?'

Johnson had removed the dome of the tail unit and was pointing to two small circular glass windows. Monty had a look and noted a broken wire from some electronic device behind the window leading to the detonator.

'Jesus Christ!' Johnson suddenly exclaimed and reached for his torch. He played the torchlight over the electronics behind the glass windows and watched the units move a fraction. Monty saw the blood drain from Johnson's face and he reached for his stool.

'You know what I think we've just found, Monty? We should be dead meat.'

'No. What is it, Johnny?' Monty asked, but a suspicion was already forming in his mind. The torchlight had given him the idea.

'Those are photo-electric cells. Shine light on them or let light in to them and they trigger something.' He stood up again and took the broken wire in his fingers. The solution to the puzzle dawned on him. 'It's a fucking booby trap! Let in light and these nasty critters send a current to the detonator and that's the end of the poor sod who's inspecting the thing.' Johnson looked at Monty with an ashen face and this time it was Monty's blood's turn to curdle. He looked at the colander effects of Johnson's brace two days before and recalled him directing his torchlight into the unit innocently. Johnny was right. They should both be dead. He trembled at the thought. So, Jerry was that determined we shouldn't discover this mine's secrets. He recalled the *Luftwaffe* prisoners' boasts that this mine would be irrecoverable and now realised why. But what were they hiding?

*****

It was not until lunchtime the following day that Monty was finally able to ring Maitland-Dougall with the news that the mine had been fully stripped to reveal its secrets and was now safe.

'This time Jerry's gone for it, sir? It's pure luck we found the mine intact. After falling on soft ground, it should have self-detonated. And then there were the counter measures to ensure we couldn't strip it.' Monty went on to explain the photo-electric booby trap.

'So, what else were they trying to keep secret then, Monty?'

'The magnetic unit, sir. It's been designed to fool our Double-Ell sweep. Our traditional five-second electric pulses wouldn't trigger it, sir. Our minesweepers would have swept the channels and declared them safe only for some unfortunate warship or merchantman to have later gone to the bottom. We need to reconfigure our sweeps to operate on a pulse of twelve or more seconds, sir.'

'Bloody well done, Monty, and in the nick of time, too. Jerry's just filled the Suez Canal with them!'

Chapter 29
July 1941

Following Hitler's invasion of Russia the month before, life for the RMS teams had become decidedly dull. The *Luftwaffe* had switched its attacks from British cities onto Russia, so fewer mines were being dropped in British waters. That had pleased Lieutenant Stephen Cunningham, RNVR GC GM, fresh from his investiture at the Palace. After a number of close calls, he was beginning to feel vulnerable. It was all very well for Dawlish to say he and his fellow RMSOs were dead already, but he had a reason to continue living.

He had enjoyed his visit to London. The King had been pleased to award him not just the George Cross for his valour in the Garton gasworks, but a George Medal for defuzing the bomb in the Falmouth graving dock, too. The process for the citation for his latter act had been accelerated to allow both investitures to take place together. Stephen had noticed that the King, too, stammered and it had made him feel less conscious of his own speech defects. The King had said he had never before awarded the George Cross and Medal together. It had made Stephen feel special.

It had been wonderful to see his parents, Lucy and, above all, Carol again, although he was concerned about Dad's health. He had looked a strange colour at the investiture and seemed more short of breath and more easily tired than usual. Mum had said he had been this way for a couple of months, but not to worry about it. He probably just needed a rest and some good, fresh air. She planned on them taking a week at Llandudno round the August Bank Holiday. Lucy had mentioned in passing that she had seen Monty recently. That, too, had come out of the blue and he was surprised Monty had not mentioned it. Mind you, they hadn't seen each other for a while. Stephen was not very happy about it all. He had often heard Monty talk very fondly of a friend of his from Oxford. He hadn't shared this with Lucy as she seemed quite keen on Monty. It was something he planned to raise with him when he saw him later.

His mind was brought to the present when a blue staff car rolled up and an RAF group captain stepped out. Stephen had met him earlier at lunch and thought him a decent sort. Despite the *Luftwaffe*'s switch of attention to Russia, somebody had still thought it worth mining the north Devon coastline, but the mine had been dropped short of the river mouth and landed on one of Coastal Command's airfields.

The station commander returned Stephen's salute and surveyed the broadening pit around the mine. 'You chaps seem to be making good progress. When can I have my airfield back?'

'Thank you f-for the working party, s-sir. It's made things easier, b-but I'm afraid I c-can't start work until about midnight, sir.'

'But you've nearly exposed the bomb and it's only 15.30 hours. Look, I need the airfield back in operation as soon as possible. I can't keep diverting the bombers to Folly Gate. It reduces their time on task. Why can't you start earlier? In any case, you'd surely find it easier to work in daylight?'

'N-no, sir. That's the p-point. This is a new type of m-mine. That's why I'm dealing with it and n-not your own B-BDOs, sir. It's a Type George, sir. It has a new b-booby trap that's s-sensitive to light. I can only w-work on it in the dark and it's the height of s-summer, sir. S-somebody from Intelligence is c-coming from London to help me, sir.'

'I see.' The group captain twisted one end of his handle-bar moustache meditatively and looked across to the racks of torpedoes and bombs parked a few hundred yards away. 'Hmm, I might have that ordnance shifted then.' He returned to his car.

Stephen shared the station commander's caution. He had only heard of this Type 'G' mine a few days earlier and with the news had come strict instructions that the mines were only ever to be tackled in pitch darkness. Monty was coming down from London with a new type of light to help him see, but had first to collect it from Portsmouth.

'Chief,' he called to Dawlish knee-deep in the mud, wielding a non-magnetic spade with his men. 'I'm g-going to the mess to g-get my head down. Have me c-called when Lieutenant Commander M-Montcalm arrives.'

*****

The station commander joined Stephen and Monty, despite the late hour of 22.00. It was still light and hot.

'My chaps aren't too keen about all dossing down in the one hut. Some of them have just dumped their mattresses on the ground outside. That's what you sailor chappies used to do wasn't it?'

'Yes, sir,' Monty replied. 'They would take their hammock rolls up onto the upper deck. It was cooler there. I'm sorry for the inconvenience, sir, but the accommodation huts were within the 400-yard cordon.'

'Don't worry about it. I've warned the Station Warrant Officer that if anyone complains, he's to detail them to come along and help you chaps. I don't think there'll be much grumbling.' The group captain and Monty laughed. 'Is there anything else we can do for you chaps? Would a field telephone help?'

'That's not a bad idea, sir. Perhaps two? We could rig one between my safety dugout and Cunningham here. I could use the other to keep you up to date. That is if you plan on staying up for the fun?'

'I wouldn't miss it for the world, old boy, but I'm rather hoping it will all be a damp squib. Oh dear. Squib. I meant no pun.'

The station commander left Monty and Stephen to their work.

'Helpful chap, the group captain,' Monty said to Stephen. 'Mind you, I don't think he relishes the idea of the mess 1,500 pounds of explosive would make to his toys.'

'W-what about this n-new light, Monty?' Stephen replied.

'Ah, yes. Here it is.' Monty showed Stephen a lamp that cast a pale-blue light. 'We've discovered that the photo-electric cells are made of selenium. The *Vernon* boffins have reconstructed them and found that this form of light is safe enough.'

'Thanks. I saw Lucy in London last m-month. She told me that y-you've been seeing each other.'

Monty bit his lower lip before replying. 'Ah. But we've only met once for a tea. I was in Southport and met her briefly in

Preston. That's all... It's hardly a romance. I mean, she despises everything about my privileged life.'

'Yes, it is s-surprising, b-but even so, she seems to have t-taken a shine to you. P-please don't toy with her affections, M-Monty.'

'I promise, Stephen. Now I'd better sort out the field telephones.' Monty quickly scuttled off to leave Stephen feeling frustrated that their conversation had not been satisfactorily concluded.

*****

At five minutes after midnight, Stephen informed Monty he was starting to undo the nuts on the mine's tail unit. In the distance he could hear the rumble of another bombing raid. He wondered if it was the sound carrying over the Bristol Channel far to the north.

Half an hour later, he removed his jacket and rang Monty. 'I've n-nearly taken all the nuts off. Just two m-more to g-go. It s-seems very hot. Or is it just m-me?'

'Don't worry, Stephen. It is hot. It must be 70 degrees. You're doing fine. Another half an hour and we can all be in our pits.'

Stephen returned to work. He reported again when all the nuts were off and started to ease off the mine's rear dome. The rumbling of the raid seemed to be getting nearer, suggesting the raid was on Devon, after all. The pale-blue light gave him just enough light with which to see and he worked without difficulty, although with infinite care not to cause too much vibration. At last, the dome was off. Stephen could feel dampness in his shirt armpits as he gazed at the deadly round panes of glass in the rear of the mine. That was odd, he thought. He didn't normally sweat so profusely on a job. Was this a sign of burn out? He had seen other RMSOs relieved of their duties for their own protection. Was he becoming a danger to himself? He spoke to Monty again.

'The d-dome's off. I'm g-going to tackle the s-s-selenium cells in a minute. I just n-need to m-mop myself down. It's hot w-work. C-can you hear ack-ack? It s-sounds as if the raid's c-coming closer.'

'Don't worry, Stephen. It sounds too far off to bother us. Take your time. You have until sunrise. Makes us sound like a couple of vampires, doesn't it?'

Stephen chuckled at the thought and then focused on the next stage. He had to unscrew the switch gear to break both circuits to the booby trap and then he would be free to tackle the rest of the mine. To his relief, *Vernon*'s special light had worked without any effect on the vicious selenium cells.

Suddenly, the world lit up with bright-white light around him followed almost immediately by an enormous clap of thunder. Stephen froze in shock and then fear. Immediately, there was another flash and he looked up to see the sky light up with the flashes of sheet lightning. Each flash lasted half a second. He heard Monty shouting down the field telephone, 'Run. For Christ's sake, Stephen, run!' but there was no point. Stephen was rooted to the spot. Slowly, his thought processes returned. Running wasn't an option. He had to cover those light cells. A fork of lightning flashed across the sky and a second later, Stephen felt the ground beneath him shudder with the thunder. He reached for his jacket and covered the base of the mine with it, praying he might live.

Another flash in the sky rent the darkness. It was a barrage balloon catching fire. Stephen took to his knees and prayed aloud that God might spare him as several more flashes of light reflected off his white shirt. On this occasion, it seemed to Stephen that God heard his prayers as after a last burst of light, the storm passed through and Stephen was alive.

*****

On his return to Plymouth, Stephen was worried about himself. Like the number of mines and bombs he had rendered safe, he had forgotten the number of times he had faced a narrow escape from death. According to the experts who had investigated the BM1000 he had recently deloused, the only thing that had saved him had been the fact the bursts of lightning had been too short. Stephen, however, still wondered if God had interceded. Even so, from now on, he intended taking no chances. As well as carrying black tape to mask the round windows in the rear of such mines, he would work under some form of tent when working with the BM1000.

His disquiet was that the frequency of such near-death experiences had increased and he had started to drink whisky at the end of each day to help him sleep. He never drank to excess - the last thing he wanted was a befuddled brain when dealing with a *Zus* 40 or whatever other device the Germans were now using. The latest anti-withdrawal devices now included mercury tilt switches in three axes, although a Wing Commander Stevens had invented a method for dealing with them. A domed vacuum pump extracted all the air from the fuze and then a solution of alcohol and sugar was trickled into the fuze. Once the alcohol evaporated, the sugar crystals set solid throughout the mechanism.

What worried Stephen was that he had never before drunk spirits – an occasional half pint of beer had been his line – but this latest habit was clearly a reaction to mental strain. How soon before that mental strain caused him either to make a fatal mistake or to crack up? He had thought of discussing it with Monty after the George incident, but the news of Monty's relationship with Lucy had made him wary of confiding too much to him. He didn't want word getting back to his family. He wondered if he should mention it to one of the medical officers, but immediately dismissed the thought. It wasn't as if he was drinking excessively and the authorities might think he was seeking an excuse to be taken off RMS duties. No, he was due leave at the end of the month. He'd keep going until then and after the rest, everything should be back to normal.

Chapter 30
August 1941

The ferry at Torpoint meant that it was only a short drive from Plymouth to Picklecombe Fort, a Palmerston fort, built south-west of Plymouth to protect the Sound with its guns. Now, in addition to its more modern guns, it provided protection by control over an underwater minefield. It was a vital link in the chain defending the Royal Navy's safe harbour at Devonport. Sunday or no Sunday, the Commander-in-Chief Plymouth was consequently very keen that the German mine dropped overnight just off the fort should be cleared with utmost despatch. Accordingly, Stephen was the guest of the army in their crenelated officers' mess of an unusual design said to be based on that of Warwick Castle. It was a perfect summer's day and in normal circumstances he would have relished a break from the city, but today was not going to be normal.

According to the intelligence report, the mine was a Sammy, a magnetic-acoustic mine. Stephen didn't know how this information had been determined and nor was he able to verify its reliability. The mine lay in deep water, not far off the fort, but close enough to the shore to be inaccessible to the minesweepers. Being underwater, it was beyond his reach and a job for *Vernon*. All Stephen could do was to wait for a specialist to arrive from Portsmouth, so he had had no hesitation in accepting the invitation to breakfast from the fort's commanding officer. The weather and location were so perfect that Stephen looked forward to a walk after breakfast on the headland of the Rame peninsular and a generally lazy morning.

*****

Stephen was not surprised when the *Vernon* specialist proved to be his friend, Johnson. Johnson seemed equally pleased to see him. However, Stephen was surprised by Johnson's news.

'I was going to write, Stephen. I want you to come to my farewell party – if you can make it up to London, that is. I'll be holding it in the New Yorker at the end of the month. You can bring that gal of yours along.'

'Farewell p-party? Have you b-been reappointed?'

'Sort of. I'm going home to the States. My navy's taking me back and offering me a commission as a full lieutenant. Isn't that swell news?'

'I s-suppose so, but how c-come?'

'I was asked to see the ambassador. It seems there's a feeling that following Hitler's invasion of Russia, the US might have to take a greater hand in the war. I gather Roosevelt's still holding out on the idea, but the navy wants to be prepared for any eventuality, one of which is a clandestine German campaign to lay mines outside our ports. Following my experience here, I'm to train a new breed of officer in rendering mines safe. Isn't that great?'

'P-probably. I'll m-miss you, though, Johnny. You know there's only you and I left of our c-class now?'

'Not true, Stephen. I saw Lawson the other day. He still needs sticks, but he's walking and been passed fit for duty any day soon. He's changed, though. Seems a bit more sombre and less arrogant.'

'That s-sounds no b-bad thing. As you know, I d-don't like him. But, shouldn't you b-be looking at this m-mine?'

'All in good time. I'm waiting for the diving boat and my gear. It shouldn't be long now.'

'How do you f-feel about d-diving, Johnny? You w-wouldn't catch me d-doing it.'

'Oh, I quite like it. It makes me out as being a bit special, even if there are others now being trained. Mind you, I had a bit of a fright last week.'

'W-with a mine?'

'No. Much worse. I nearly crapped myself. It was in Portsmouth harbour. I was attaching a line to a couple of UXBs Jerry had left behind after a previous air raid. I was standing there on the bottom in about forty feet of water, master of all I surveyed when I spotted something floating in the water.' Johnson shuddered at the memory.

'It was dressed in brown overalls and coming at me, arms spread out to ensnare me. I thought it was the ghost of a dockyard matey. Jesus, it spooked me. It kept coming for me and I was terrified. It had great, wide-open eyes and a huge gaping mouth. I tell you, Stephen, I thought it was going to do for me. I couldn't move for fright.'

'It s-sounds awful. W-was it a c-corpse?'

'No. In the end, I was so scared I hit out at it to try to prevent its arms wrapping themselves around me forever. I used my hammer and shouted at it to go away. It was only when I had hit it once or twice that I realised it was no ghost. No corpse.'

'B-but what w-was it, Johnny?' Stephen asked with great concern for his friend.

'It was a huge piece of corrugated cardboard and in the poor visibility I had mistaken some printing for facial features.'

Stephen guffawed loudly at his friend's late discomfort and Johnson joined him. It was yet another reminder of why he never wanted to dive again. Their revelry was interrupted by a Royal Artillery captain. He looked at the breast of Johnson and then to Stephen.

'My goodness! A George Cross and three George Medals in one place. That'll be something to tell my grandchildren should I live long enough to have any. I'm sorry to disturb your joke, gentlemen, but Lieutenant Johnson's diving gear has arrived. Your boat's coming round the headland now.

'Thanks, Captain.' Johnson looked to his left to see a lorry on the concrete jetty with all his gear being unloaded from it. With the gear was a coiled wire hawser to help him trawl for the mine and snag it ready for raising. 'Just one thing more, Captain. Would you mind hoisting a red flag from your flag staff?'

'A red flag? What on earth for? You're not leading a Bolshevik insurrection, are you?' the captain replied.

'Gee, don't say that in front of my Pa. He hates commies. No, it means "*I have a diver down. Keep well clear at slow speed.*" I wouldn't fancy visitors to the jetty there whilst I'm in the water. One of the team will give you the flag.'

'Right ho. Leave it to me. Good luck.'

Stephen and Johnson headed down to the jetty. Johnson's men were already preparing his suit and the diving boat came alongside the jetty. Stephen was pleased to see that it was made of wood. It would reduce the chance of tripping the mine's magnetic unit.

'Johnny, if w-we are dealing with a S-Sammy, it shouldn't be c-cocked. There's been n-nothing magnetic near it, s-so you should be safe from the acoustic unit.'

'That's my hope, too, buddy. You know it was the noise of his air bubbles that killed Sutherland? I can't hold my breath underwater for ever.'

Whilst Johnson dressed, the diving boat left the jetty with the wire hawser. The crew laid the wire in a semi-circle around the area the gunners had witnessed the mine drop into the water. When this evolution was complete, they drew the ends of the wire inboard and, as they had hoped, it snagged on an underwater object. It was time for Johnson to enter the water.

Stephen arranged for all extraneous personnel to withdraw to the safety of the fort, but he and Dawlish only withdrew to the fort's outer walls so as to be within hailing distance of the boat's crew. He watched as Johnson set out in the boat towards the marker buoy marking the snagged wire. He felt both excited for Johnny that he was returning to his homeland, but depressed, too. Other than Monty, he had no friends and he couldn't be certain of his future relationship with Monty.

One of the diving boat's crew started the air pump ready to supply Johnson's helmet. The throbbing sound carried easily over the water, disturbing a pair of cormorants resting on a nearby rock. They flew off lazily across the rippled sea and the scene enhanced Stephen's feeling of indolence. It seemed a pity to have to listen to the pump's engine when all around was so peaceful. Johnson disappeared into the water with a splash and huge ripple before the sea swallowed any evidence that he had been there. Stephen lit a cigarette and waited patiently, chatting idly with Dawlish about nothing in particular.

It was Dawlish that heard it first. In the distance came another dull throb, but higher pitched than that of the diving air pump. Coming across the Sound, on a course to leave the breakwater to port, was a lovely-looking high-speed motor launch.

'I hope he don't approach too close, Boss. His wash would cause a mighty disturbance in this little harbour. You don't think the noise'll be a problem do you, sir?' The crew of the diving boat were clearly concerned as one of the sailors was waving madly at the launch and pointing to the red flag hoisted above.

'It shouldn't b-bother the m-mine. It needs a m-magnetic influence f-first.'

'What about the wire out there, sir?' Stephen was surprised to see Dawlish so concerned.

'No. These hawsers have b-been d-demagnetised.' Stephen sounded positive, but the fact his former instructor had mentioned the subject made him feel uneasy. For some reason his life began to flash before him. Like scenes from a film at the cinema, he recalled his experiments as an undergraduate at Liverpool on electromotive force and then he saw the scene when the steel hawser had been unloaded from the lorry earlier. Why was that relevant? Oh my God! The hawser had been on a drum! A coil! On its own the hawser wasn't magnetic, but as a coil it had the potential to become a series of magnets, each with a north and south pole. What if the drum had been hung in the diving store facing north-south? A feeling of panic overwhelmed Stephen and he began to run for the jetty. What if the drum had lain unused for months and the earth's magnetic field had remagnetised it?

By now Dawlish was running alongside Stephen. 'What is it, sir?' he asked frantically, but Stephen had no time for him.

'S-s-stop!' he called across to the dive boat and waved his arms above his head wildly. One of the crew heard him and looked at him questioningly.

'The w-w-wire. It c-could be m-m-magnetic. S-s-stop.' Never before had Stephen regretted his stutter so much. He had thought he was overcoming it, but now events were unfolding too fast for him. Far from keeping clear of the diving site, the motor launch altered course to starboard and headed straight for the jetty.

Dawlish ran ahead and shouted to the crew of the launch to turn away. The dive boat crew shouted, too, but the launch was bearing down on them too quickly. 'Everybody down!' he shouted. 'The mine!'

Stephen hit the ground, angry and frustrated. He prayed silently that he was wrong. The steel hawser might not be magnetic and he was fussing... He had no time to give the matter further thought. He felt a massive shockwave before his ears were split by the sound of the deafening explosion. He covered his head and seconds later felt the searing pain of debris falling on him before Death cast his mantle o'er all.

*****

Ernst was pleased to see that life in Berlin appeared fairly normal despite the war. The earlier food shortages seemed to have eased since the start of the campaign in the east and, unlike some of the industrial cities, it was not subject to allied bombing raids. Ernst liked that feeling of relative normality. Out of a feeling of nostalgia, he had even visited the street in which he had lodged for a couple of years during his time on the Naval Staff. Coincidentally, it had not been far from the home of Little Maxi's fiancée, Else. Fulfilling a promise to his brother, he had called on her.

Ernst hadn't been sure what to expect, but even so, he had been surprised. She had been quite normal, indeed beautiful. Had he not known it, Ernst might have forgotten she was Jewish. Even with the knowledge, he found it difficult to trace any obvious signs of her background, but then the interbreeding with Aryan blood would have filtered out her Jewishness, he thought. Actually, he had liked her. She was shy, but sociable... even companionable. He could see what Max saw in her. Indeed, once again he felt jealous of his little brother. He wished there was a woman out there who would talk so fondly of him as she had of Max. Not for the first time, Ernst longed for the company of a woman who wasn't a whore.

Somebody who would be waiting at home for him. Somebody who would listen sympathetically to his troubles in bringing new mines into service. Above all, somebody to offer him something deeper than the affection he received from his cat, Gisella.

He saw General Schott across the street and rose from his table on the pavement outside the café to greet him. Both wore their uniforms. This time there was nothing clandestine about their meeting.

'Ernst. Good afternoon. I'm sorry to have kept you waiting. Am I very late?'

'Not at all, General. I had to make a social call and was late myself,' Ernst lied.

'That's good then.' Schott summoned a waitress and ordered a coffee and pastry before removing his jacket and returning to Ernst. 'My, it's hot today and I have had a series of interminable meetings all day. I'm sorry I couldn't manage lunch and I have a reception this evening.'

'It is very good of you to have found the time to meet me, General. I am very grateful.'

'Nonsense, Ernst. I hope I will always have the time for my most loyal officers. Now what is it that I can do for you?'

'I'm hoping you might gain me the ear of the High Command, General. I have tried my usual chain of command from Travemünde, but cannot get General Rommel to see the wider picture. In any case, this is an operational problem and not one of design. And, of course, I still report to you on these matters.'

'Of course, dear Ernst. I may be Coeler's chief of staff, but I still have Göring's ear on aerial mining strategy. He is pleased by the way with the design of the new BM1000. Once we have completed Operation Barbarossa, we can expect a sustained campaign with the new weapon. Then I will honour my promise to you, Ernst.'

'What promise, General?' Ernst's heart rate increased. Was this news of a decoration?

'Come now, Ernst.' Schott read Ernst's mind perfectly. 'I mean the Knight's Cross, of course. When we finish England with your mine. At this rate, the war in the east should be over very soon. But we are diverting from the subject you came to discuss.'

'As I have said before, General, I work only for the Fatherland. The defeat of the British will be reward enough for me.' Ernst was discomforted by the way Schott seemed to accept his last statement so casually, but was saved by the arrival of the waitress with Schott's coffee.

'At least it tastes of coffee. I've had worse.' Schott put down his coffee cup and began work on the pastry instead.

'General, it is partly in relation to the BM1000 I asked to see you, but there is something more pressing I must discuss first.' Ernst smiled at his unintentional pun concerning the word 'pressing'. 'I have in mind a new type of mine that will be just as revolutionary as the magnetic mine and BM1000, but I am being blocked by Engineer General Rommel.'

'Really?' Schott replied, spitting flakes of pastry over his chest. 'Do we need another form of mine? I thought we were doing well enough with the combination of the new acoustic mine, the magnetic-acoustic mine and now the BM1000. What more do we need?'

'I like to keep a step ahead of the British, General,' Ernst replied with rancour in his tone.

Schott finished his pastry, dabbed his mouth with his napkin and started to brush away the flakes of pastry from his uniform. 'All right. I'm listening.'

'Do you recall Fett's idea, General?'

'Ach, it wasn't Lieutenant Fett's idea. It was a British invention. He merely offered the idea as his own.'

'He's a lieutenant commander now, General. But the British abandoned the idea and Fett has improved on the original. I have had tests of his new design conducted and am satisfied that with a few modifications, the concept it practicable. But that needs funding and I am being blocked.'

'Have we come up with an effective sweep yet?'

'Er, no, General. And that is why I am being blocked. But our engineers make progress every day and with more time, I am sure we can conquer the mine, General.'

'Mmm, I'm not sure even I could persuade the *OKW* to abandon what seems a sensible policy to me. There must be something behind this, Ernst. Come clean with me.'

You know me too well, Ernst thought with regret. He had hoped to avoid this and saw his hopes of a Knight's Cross fading. He pulled a newspaper clipping from his briefcase and handed it to Schott.

'What's this, Ernst? It's in Russian. You know I don't read Russian… but wait a moment. Surely, the diagram is of the BM1000.' Schott went pale. 'But how…'

Ernst handed Schott another piece of paper. 'General, this is a translation. The newspaper report was published recently in Russia. It boasts of how the Russians have successfully taken apart the BM1000 and learned its secrets.'

'But how can that be, Ernst? As you know, we haven't yet deployed the BM1000 in Russia. Has there been a leak?'

'No, General. I think it is worse than that. I think it is the British who have somehow analysed the contents of the BM1000, perhaps using Doktor Röntgen's machine, and they have helpfully passed the knowledge to their new ally. Now do you see why I wish to develop a new weapon, General?'

Schott took a deep breath and glanced down the street before replying. 'I confess I do not relish passing on this latest piece of news to the *Reichsmarshall*, Ernst. We may both have to lie low for a while, but yes. You will obtain your funding. I guarantee it. You must develop the new mine. This time we must finish off England for good.'

Chapter 31

It took Stephen a while to recognise his surroundings. He was in a hospital bed and not alone. Sunshine beamed through the nearby window to dazzle him, so he turned away and noted that there were other beds in the ward. A naval nurse was talking to a patient at the far end of the ward. She spotted Stephen move and approached his bed side.

'So, you're back in the world of the living then, sir. I'll tell the doctor.' She smiled sweetly and disappeared, leaving Stephen with his pain.

He tried to localise the pain. At first, he thought it was his chest, then his left shoulder, before he decided on his back. He couldn't get comfortable and wriggled some more in his bed, turning over to his other side, but then he was blinded again by the sunshine. It was easier to lie facing the window and to shut his eyes. The windows were open and he could feel a welcome breeze waft through them. He could hear the sound of a petrol-driven lawnmower. The combination of its noise, the warm sunshine on his face, the breeze – it all seemed so gentle and soporific. At any minute I'm going to hear the sound of bat on ball, he thought. Just as he started to dream of an English summer's day, he remembered the mine explosion at the fort and immediately felt anxious. He wasn't one for false optimism. Johnny had to have died in that explosion. Johnny who had shared so many experiences with him. Johnny his friend. Tears welled in his eyes. Johnny who was so looking forward to returning home. Johnny whose farewell party he would not be attending. His emotions overcame him and he started to weep. Johnny and Bacon from his course. Then there was the Australian... what was his name? Red they called him... Oh yes, Kessack. Sutherland, Lavender and Reg Ellingworth. He had known them all. And so many he hadn't known. So many fine men... and yet he had survived. Stephen cried like a baby, shaking uncontrollably despite the pain and he didn't care who saw it. He felt another pain and the tears were somehow helping to expunge it. Washed out, he fell asleep.

*****

When Stephen woke again, he was surprised to find himself in a ward on his own. Somebody in a white coat was hovering nearby.

'Cunningham. Cunningham, can you hear me?' the white-coated figure asked. Stephen nodded in reply. The physical pain had returned and this time there was no doubting it was from his back. He shifted his weight to try to ease the discomfort.

'Cunningham, I'm Surgeon Commander Ross. I'm the surgeon who operated on you when you came in. Can I get you anything?'

Stephen felt he just wanted to be left alone, but didn't wish to be impolite. He tried to speak, but his mouth was too dry at first. Then he felt incredibly thirsty. 'Some... w-water... p-please, sir.'

The surgeon nodded to somebody out of Stephen's sight and then came up to him. 'No need for the *sirs*. Doctor will do. I just want to look into your eyes a minute.' Ross felt Stephen's forehead and then, holding each eyelid open, shone an ophthalmoscope into the backs of each of Stephen's eyes. 'I think you'll do.' Ross stepped further back and a nurse brought a cup of water to Stephen.

Stephen tried to take the cup with his left hand, but he couldn't move his arm. He took it instead with his right hand and swallowed the water gently. 'Thank y-you. M-may I have some m-more?' He held out the cup feeling like Oliver Twist. The nurse had anticipated the request and topped up his cup from a jug. 'Thank you,' he said again, feeling better. He lay back into the pillows.

Ross brought across a chair and sat at his bedside. 'I expect you have all sorts of questions so let me explain a little of your circumstances to anticipate a few. Are you feeling up to it?'

'Yes, p-please, d-doctor.'

'You were brought in two days ago with several shrapnel wounds... amongst other things. I had to removed half a boat from your back and left shoulder. One piece of metal lodged near your spine worried me in particular, but I'm optimistic you'll be able to walk again soon. You can feel your toes, I take it?'

That piece of news startled Stephen and he wiggled his toes in the bed. Like many RMSOs he would prefer to die than be maimed or crippled. After all, they were all dead anyway and just on borrowed time. He suddenly remembered Dawlish.

'Yes, I can feel them. S-sorry, d-doctor. How m-many survived?'

Ross blanched before answering with discomfort in his eyes. 'Everyone from the fort, but from those on the water or jetty… just you, I'm afraid.'

So Chief Petty Officer Dawlish is another name to add to my list, Stephen thought. He should have stayed instructing. Stephen felt himself welling up again, but controlled himself. He would do his mourning in private.

Having let his news sink in, Ross continued. 'In a quirk of fate, the motor launch that set off the mine was taking an army chaplain to the fort to deliver divine service to the gunners. He's now with his god sooner than he planned. You're in Stonehouse, of course. We've moved you in here for some privacy as there's a queue of senior officers and others all wanting to see you. C-in-C Plymouth amongst them. I'm impressed, but not surprised now I've heard something of your record. You're a brave man. And lucky, too.'

'How long w-will I be in here, d-doctor?'

'I can't answer that. It depends on your body's healing powers and whether I removed everything from your back. Your left shoulder only had a splinter, but it took a pounding from about half a ton of rock, too, so you might find it awkward to move. But that should heal in time. I'd say you'll be in bed for another week and then we'll just have to see. I can't say more than that… other than it'll be a while before you're fit to return to the front line… if that's what you chaps call it. Now unless you've any urgent questions, I'll leave you. I'm under strict orders to ring Admiral Forbes's secretary as soon as you recovered consciousness. No doubt we'll have the admiral here again before too long.'

'No, s-sir, I m-mean doctor.'

It was only after Ross had left that he thought about his family. Would the Admiralty have sent them a telegram? Would Mum be worrying?

*****

Despite a myriad of visitors, Stephen found time hanging heavy in hospital. He had asked to be moved back to a main ward, but the authorities had refused. His constant stream of visitors would disrupt the routine of the ward too much. Two days after his initial conversation with Ross, Captain Currey came to see him.

'Good to see you, Cunningham. How are you feeling?'

'Much b-better now, thank you, s-sir,' Stephen answered truthfully. 'I c-can move my shoulder now.'

'That's good. I've brought you a letter from Monty. He's been a regular pest in the HQ seeking news of you. And I spoke to your mother yesterday. She sends her love. Don't worry. I didn't tell her everything.' Currey had spotted the alarm on Stephen's face. 'The sawbones told me it was touch and go to start whether you'd make it. I just told your mother you were healing nicely and no doubt might earn a spot of leave soon.'

'Thank you, s-sir.'

'I meant it, too. You're due some leave, but we need to get you out of here first. The quacks tell me that it's too early to say when that might be. Need to check on your mobility… that sort of thing.' Currey stepped over to the window. 'Damned fine view of the quadrangle from here,' he muttered absent-mindedly before turning back to Stephen.

'We need to plan for your future, Cunningham. Stalin's taking some of the heat off us so we're less pressed and I think it's time you had a break. Recharge the batteries and all that.'

Again, Stephen was alarmed. Was Currey about to take him off RMS duties. Would he find himself censoring mail or something instead?

'You'll need some time to recuperate, take some overdue leave and so on, but then I'm reappointing you to Scapa Flow. The

Flag Officer up there apparently has plenty for you to do up there. You'll be doing training, etcetera.'

The news was not welcome. Stephen thought Orkney too far from London, but he didn't choose to voice this concern. 'I'd rather be d-delousing, s-sir. C-could I not help on the east c-coast or something, sir?'

'I'm sending Lawson to help Edwards… until he finds his feet again, as it were. I don't doubt you'd rather be in the thick of it, but my mind is made up. How long have we been together? Nearly two years. It's too long. There's only so much a man can take and you've seen more than most. Besides the other RMS officers are complaining that you're taking all the medals. They want their turn.' Currey smiled at Stephen. 'But you don't fool me Cunningham, despite your obvious sense of duty. You're thinking of your red-headed filly, aren't you?' Stephen couldn't deny it.

'Well, I have some news for you there, too, Cunningham.' Without another word, Currey walked over to the door of the room and opened it. Three seconds later, in walked Carol. She rushed over to him and smothered him with kisses. Stephen was embarrassed by such a public display of affection and glanced over to see Currey's reaction, but he had gone, shutting the door behind him.

'Och, Stephen, my true *laoch*. What a worry you've been to me.' Carol sat on the bed by Stephen's legs and dabbed her eyes with a handkerchief.

'B-but w-what are you d-doing here?'

'I've come to see you, of course, you eejiut.' Carol crumpled her handkerchief in her fist.

'I m-meant, how did you g-get here?'

'I came down by car with Captain Currey last night. Oh, Stephen, what a perfect gentleman he is. He told me hi'self about you… and poor Johnny, of course. Och, I was awfa sorry to hear about Johnny.' Carol squeezed Stephen's hand and tears returned to her eyes. 'I know he was yer friend.'

Stephen looked at the window to avoid meeting her eyes. He didn't want to give way to his emotions in front of her. His feelings were still too raw. At the thought of Johnny or the mention of his name a vice seemed to clamp his heart and at the same time triggering tears. He composed his emotions and turned back to Carol.

'He's a good b-boss, Captain C-Currey.'

'He's a darling. He's giving me a lift back to London, too, so I can't stay more than an hour or two. I don't know how long the captain will be. He says he has to see the admiral and some BDOs, whatever they are.'

'Bomb Disposal Officers.'

'Aye, well that'd make sense right enough as he said he wanted to see your men. Och, Stephen, you do get yersel' into o'sorts of trouble, don't you? But we're going to get you jes fine again. I've seen the surgeon and he says that if you can walk right enough once you're out of bed, he can discharge you to a cottage hospital for convalescence and mebbe a wee bit of physiotherapy. Captain Currey told me you're going up to Orkney once you're well again.'

'Yes. So I've just heard. I don't w-want to go. It w-will be dull and too f-far from London.'

'Ach, well it can't be helped. It's time ye had a wee break. So, Stephen Cunningham, you just do as you're told once in a while coz between the surgeon, the captain and my ward sister, I've hatched a wee plan. The captain reckoned on sending you to Lancashire, so ye could be near your family, but I've had a better idea.'

The news cheered Stephen. He would enjoy seeing Mum again, but what did Carol mean that she'd had a better idea? Was he going to London again? His heart leapt at the thought.

'I'm going to have our house in the Borders opened up again. Then, once you're fit for discharge, the surgeon and Captain Currey have agreed you can spend your convalescence either in Kelso or under my charge at home. I'm a trained nurse, after all. And I've cared for you once before. And you'll be half way to Orkney and it's not so far from your home, so it all fits, don't you see?'

Not for the first time, Stephen's heart melted with love for Carol. She was amazing and he struggled to think what to say until a doubt clouded his happy thoughts.

'B-but for how long? W-won't you b-be needed at the hospital in London?'

'I told you. I've fixed it with my ward sister. She's a real softy and you're a national hero. She thought it the least I could do for the one I love. I'll work extra shifts until you're fit to leave here and then I can take at least a fortnight... more at a push.'

It took a few seconds for Stephen to take it in. Carol had just said she loved him. A strange sense of euphoria swept over him, blocking out his pain and discomfort. 'Carol. You s-said you loved me.'

Carol stared him in surprise momentarily and then laughed. 'Why, Stephen, of course I do. How could you ever have doubted it?' She kissed him swiftly on the lips. 'Now don't you fret yersel'. It's all fixed. You just get better.'

'B-but, Carol, my d-darling. I'm a p-penniless failed s-school master. W-what can you possibly s-see in me?'

'Och, Stephen. Will you never have confidence in yersel' or are you jes fishing for compliments?' Carol paused a moment to consider her answer.' 'I could say that it's your selflessness, your devotion to duty or your kindness. Or mebbe it's just yer funny drawings. But who cares? I jes love you and that's all there is to it.'

His heart bursting with love, Stephen reached out his right hand and drew Carol's face close to his to kiss her passionately. 'I p-promise you, d-doctor's orders or no doctor's orders, I'll be w-walking again next week.'

ACKNOWLEDGEMENTS

I am indebted to many people for their help in writing this novel. Firstly, Sue Williams, the daughter of Lieutenant Commander John Bridge, GC, GM and Bar, for giving me access to her father's memoirs. I am very grateful to Commander Rob Hoole, Secretary of the Royal Navy's Mine Clearance Diving Officers' Association. Rob not only put me in touch with Sue, but provided research material on German mine warfare and offered some corrections on the diving sequences in the story. He, also, put me in touch with Rear Admiral Paddy McAlpine, the Royal Navy's most senior mine clearance and diving officer to date, who kindly agreed to provide the Foreword to this book.

As if he had not done enough already, Rob recommended me to Steve Venus, an expert in German explosives and fuzes. Steve, an historian who advised on the technical content of the TV documentary *Danger UXB* and TV drama series *Foyle's War*, gladly gave of his time to check the accuracy of the mine disposal scenes in my tale. Rob put me in touch, too, with Tony Boyle who re-enacts the WW2 operations to render mines safe and who stars in the cover photograph of him giving one of his presentations. I owe thanks to Kath Robson, too, for her work as an unpaid literary consultant, suggesting weaknesses in my original story and character development. Thank you, Sue, Rob, Paddy, Steve, Tony and Kath. I am grateful, too, to a small team of volunteers who kindly read the book in advance of publication and pointed out a few typing errors in the manuscript. They know who they are.

This book could not have been written without the material offered in several books I used for my research either. These include those of Ivan Southall, John Frayn Turner, Ashe Lincoln, Maurice Griffiths and Noel Cashford. I wish to thank my wife, Hilary, for her patience and forbearance when I bored her to death about my book or locked myself away to write instead of helping with the household chores. The spouses of authors all have to be long-suffering and patient. Finally, I owe a huge debt of thanks to all those who have been kind enough to leave reviews on-line on my earlier books. Such reviews are the oxygen of publicity to feed the visibility of authors. All too often after finishing a book, it is too easy to forget about it. Please do take the time to keep the reviews coming. Thank you to everyone above.

AUTHOR'S NOTE

The events portrayed in this book are not far-fetched, but based on actual history and accurately told. It was the mine threat that nearly brought Britain to its knees and not that of the U-boat. However, I have used fictional characters to tell the story. Whilst the actions of these characters are based on those carried out by a number of real people, my descriptions of their frailties, personalities and conversations are entirely fictitious.

This story was inspired a few years ago when I heard a lecture about the wartime exploits of Lieutenant Commander John Bridge RNVR. Bridge ended the war as the most highly decorated man in the British Empire with a George Cross, two George Medals and the King's Commendation for Brave Conduct. His gallantry awards were almost matched by those of the Australians, Lieutenant Hugh Syme, GC, GM and Bar, and Commander John Mould GC and GM. The exploits of my hero, Stephen Cunningham, incorporate some of those conducted by all three of the above officers and that of Lieutenant Commander Harold Newgass, GC, in defuzing the mine at Garston Gasworks. Unlike Stephen, however, Bridge was a very successful physics master who had a successful career in education after the war. I am planning a sequel to feature yet more of his extraordinarily brave actions.

Monty is fictitious, too, and his fictional role as an observing officer is to describe diverse extraordinary events that occurred across the breadth of the United Kingdom. His investigative activities, however, are more factual and loosely based on those of Commander Ashe Lincoln, QC, RNVR.

My aim in writing this story was to bring to life the courageous actions of several extraordinary RMS officers who quietly went about the country risking life and limb to make this country safe during WW2. This is an activity that continues today with members of all three Armed Forces contending with not just unexploded ordnance left over from WW2, but with the explosive devices of terrorists. However, we should not forget the work of the British scientists who risked their lives, too, to discover the secrets of the German mines and the poor unrecognised souls of the minesweeping flotillas working round the clock to clear the sea lanes. Many suffered death or severe injury when tripping mines too close for comfort.

Website: www.shaunlewis-theauthor.com,
Facebook: shaunlewistheauthor
Twitter: @shaunlewis1805
Email: shaunlewisauthor@gmail.com

Made in the USA
Columbia, SC
27 November 2021